A BETTER PROPOSAL

You have found an early, unedited edition of A Better Proposal. While there are a few errors, I hope you will still enjoy this love story.

BY ELLORY DOUGLAS

♡ Ellory

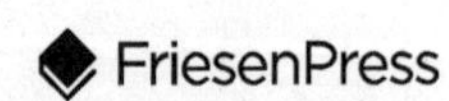

One Printers Way
Altona, MB R0G 0B0
Canada

www.friesenpress.com

First Edition — 202

ISBN
978-1-03-918747-4 (Hardcover)
978-1-03-918746-7 (Paperback)
978-1-03-918748-1 (eBook)

1. FICTION, ROMANCE, CONTEMPORARY

Distributed to the trade by The Ingram Book Company

PROLOGUE

Jill Northrop had no clue what she was supposed to do now.

She stared at the identical glass bottles, their clear contents waiting to be solved, but the samples lined up in front of her refused to reveal their secrets. None of the labs had covered this, and it hadn't been in any of the lectures.

She would know. She hadn't missed a single class.

Pushing her safety glasses up her nose with her shoulder, she bent to the beakers and a trickle of sweat beaded between her shoulder blades.

Stirring, stirring.

Nothing.

Shit.

This was bad. Really bad.

For the first time, she was about to fail.

Her classmates shifted and sighed at the stations beside her, pipettes clinking against flasks the only sound in the otherwise silent lab. Her hands shook as she transferred the solution to the graduated cylinder, struggling to focus on the measurement lines. The pipette knocked against the sides and a few drops of solution spilled on the table.

Don't panic. She forced herself to take a deep breath through her nose. The spill was probably fine. This was a first-year chemistry lab. They wouldn't be working with anything dangerous.

"Fifteen minutes!" the teacher's assistant barked from the front of the room, and the students in the first two rows flinched.

Actually, he might have given them a toxic substance to handle.

Focus, Northrop.

Time dilated, turning each minute into a second, the pounding in her chest making her eyes jump off the problems in front of her. She wasn't even halfway through. She hadn't checked her answers. She was—

"Time's up! Thirty seconds to record your results and five minutes to clean up and get out."

Jill's mind froze as she stared at the blank page in front of her. That was it. Her entire first year out the window. All because of one lab. Her GPA would tank for a class that wasn't even her major.

Her mother was going to be furious.

With exaggerated care, she disposed of her materials and cleaned her station as if a land mine hid among the beakers. She kept her eyes glued to the floor as she walked up and placed her paper on the TA's desk, swiping at the tears she refused to let fall. Even out of the corner of her eye, she felt his scowl on her back as she hurried to her station, and she snatched up her bag to rush out of the room.

You're going on academic probation. They're going to make you leave university. You're going home a failure.

The trip to her dorm passed in a blur. She sat statue-like on her bed, staring at the collage of vintage posters her roommate had put up. The prescription of Ativan sat in her night table drawer, and it would stay there. The first—and only—time she took one, she'd stumbled through a fog for hours. The thought of dealing with the murky side effects again made her recoil.

She could do this.

Inhale slowly, exhale deeply. Hand on heart. Recite the mantra.

I am worthy. I am capable. I will get through this.

Lather, rinse, repeat.

Steady oxygen and nurturing words weren't magic, but they helped her stop her thoughts from spiralling. It usually worked. Usually.

Like now. The anxiety ebbed, letting her chest unclench and ears stop buzzing. Her heartbeat was almost steady when her door burst open.

"Beer pong in the common area!" Sophie blew in, her radiant expression falling as she saw Jill's tense form. She whipped out her phone, tapped a quick text, and crawled in beside Jill. Minutes later, the door opened without a knock. Kyle scooted Jill over enough for all three of them to fit on the single bed.

"Okay, Jillybean," said Sophie. "What happened?"

Jill stared at the lights she had strung above their beds. She'd have to take them down when they kicked her out of university. She released a shaky breath. "The final chem lab," she paused to refocus, "it was killer. It didn't cover a quarter of the material we studied in lectures. I was completely unprepared."

"Aw, Jilly. I won't say that it's not that bad," she gave an encouraging smile, "but do you think it might not be that bad? Remember how you felt after the mid-term? And your first paper?"

Like this. Frozen and wrapped in her blanket and sure this was the end of her post-secondary education. "I know, but this was different! I barely recognized a single instruction. I failed. I know it." Jill tucked her feet under the covers. What on earth had made her think doing a chemistry minor was a good idea?

Oh, right. It hadn't been her idea.

Kyle turned on his taking-care-of-Jill voice. "What do you need, Northrop? Do you need time? Or do you need to do something?"

She needed exactly this. For Sophie to hug her and Kyle to talk sense into her. She pursed her lips. "I need to do something."

"Okay," said Sophie, smiling as she squeezed Jill's arm. "That's great. Do you want to talk to the prof?" When Jill nodded, she continued, "She doesn't take shit, but she's super reasonable if you can explain the situation. When are her office hours?"

The syllabus claimed her professor would be available the next day. If she didn't change her schedule. Again.

Better than nothing.

Make a list, Northrop.

"Alright. First, I'm going to email the prof and tell her I need to see her tomorrow. No wait. She doesn't read email. I'll go by during her office hours. Second, I'm going to list the topics from the lab that weren't covered in the lecture. Third, I'm going to ask that she reconsider the weighting of the lab."

How were they supposed to be tested on things they hadn't learned yet? Completely unfair. Her remaining panic slowly morphed into frustration.

"I heard the TA wrote the course work this year." Kyle scowled. His grade was worse than Jill's. "Bet he wrote the lab."

That would explain a lot. Jill had heard a few people muttering this year's class average was significantly lower than prior semesters. From the limited interactions she'd had with him so far, he'd been a short-tempered, unapproachable dick. Two weeks ago, she emailed him with a question he didn't reply to until after the assignment was due. Even then, he just said to check the syllabus. Which she had already done. She bristled at the seventy-one percent he gave her on the assignment she would've aced if he'd responded on time.

She added inability to do his job to the list of his sparkling personality traits.

At least fifty other students were having the same meltdown as her right now. Well, not the same meltdown, but definitely not having a great afternoon, and fifty more would have a terrible day tomorrow, including …

"You guys have the lab tomorrow!" Jill said, bolting upright. "I need to help you study!"

Sophie snorted. "If a quarter of what you say is true, there's no way we can study enough in the next sixteen hours to scrape a pass. There's nothing else for you to fix right now." She bounced off the bed and linked arms with Jill, pulling up Kyle to join them. "Now, we have beer to drink and second years to embarrass."

At eight a.m. the next morning, her professor's office was empty. So was the lecture hall. Jill hesitated before knocking on the lab door, where her professor huddled with a grad student over a series of slides, washed in the neon glow of fluorescent lights.

Her professor looked up at the knock without a flicker of recognition. "Can I help you?"

Jill stepped into the bright lab, the scent of disinfectant and latex gloves filling her nostrils. Her speech was brief but convincing. She hoped. "There were several sections of yesterday's lab that had not been covered in lecture and aren't on the syllabus. I would like to know if this is a standard lab, or if this is unusual. I don't think we were set up for success."

Stop talking. She should stop talking.

"And this is for…"

Jill swallowed. "General Chemistry. First year," she squeaked out.

Her professor pinched the bridge of her nose with a sigh. "Of course, it is. I'll talk to your TA." She turned back to the samples in front of her. "Thank you for bringing this to my attention."

"Our grades—"

"It has been less than twenty-four hours since you completed the lab," she huffed, looking somewhere between amused and exasperated. "They are not marked and won't be this week."

"Yes, of course. Thank you, Professor," Jill said while bobbing her head and retreating into the hall.

Well, that went better than expected, she thought, trotting through the maze of the chemistry wing. If she hustled, she could make it on time to her favourite class and sink her brain into the calculus lecture ahead of her. Sweet, predictable math, with a TA that answered Jill's questions. Bliss.

She hadn't wanted to sign up for this stupid course. Sure, it had made her parents happy when she followed in their intellectual footsteps: majoring in commerce as her father had and minoring in chemistry after her mother's field of choice. But if she dropped chemistry now, she could transfer into the joint honours commerce and accounting she had wanted in the first place. With a twist in her gut, she braced herself for that delightful conversation with her mother. Points and rebuttals already forming in her mind, she rounded the corner to a main hall at full speed and ran smack into a brick wall.

A warm, flannel-covered brick wall. With pectoral muscles.

"Sorry!" Jill flustered out, her hands flush on the broad chest in front of her. She snatched her hands away, tucked her fingers into her armpits, and looked up.

Her TA loomed over her with his brow furrowed. Like he knew exactly why she'd been speaking to the professor. Which he couldn't have known. Not yet. Unless her prof had already sent him a text.

She swallowed her guilt. "Sorry," she said again, and faked a smile.

A flash of recognition crossed his face. "Given your grade, I assume you're coming to beg for extra credit."

"No! I just ..." Jill stammered. "I'm not—"

"Good," he said. "Then mind getting out of my way?"

Her jaw nearly dropped. No "are you okay?" or even a "no problem, my fault, too."

So, he was a complete asshole all the time, not just in the lab. She sidestepped him without a backward glance, settling her indecision on whether to drop her minor and losing any guilt she may have had going to the professor.

I hope she tears a strip off him, preferably from somewhere painful, she thought and dashed off to a class she cared about.

Jill made a plan. First, study her ass off and scrape a pass. Second, help Kyle and Sophie pass as well. Third, switch her minor and never, ever have to deal with chemistry again.

ONE

Eight years later

"You have arrived at your destination!" the tinny voice of her phone's GPS announced cheerfully. "Are you satisfied with your trip?"

That is yet to be determined, Jill thought, peering up at her new apartment building and performing a parallel park job she was rather proud of.

Early March was just as messy as back home, and while a season of dirty snow greyed the city streets, the thin winter sun gleamed from the bluebird sky. The most efficient route from Toronto to Calgary took three days through four states and three provinces. Jill followed every turn. She had left Saskatchewan at eight that morning, and after a brief lunch stop for a sandwich of suspect quality, she reached Calgary city limits with the sun still in the sky. Jill juggled her phone and keys in one hand, suitcase rolling behind her as she crossed the lobby to the elevator.

Blackburn Inc., her firm, had taken care of the entire relocation. Jill's list of conditions to her transfer advisor had been short but non-negotiable. Apartments must be (1) less than sixty minutes' drive to head office; (2) close to running paths; and (3) cost less than a small used car in rent. The advisor had laughed at her list and assured her there would be no issues meeting her criteria. Sure enough, he sent her enough listings that, after a few hours of research, she signed a year-long lease on a one-bedroom apartment that could charitably be called cozy, with a sliver view of the river and the decadence of in-suite laundry. No more creepy basement trips for gross shared washing machines and rickety dryers for her.

Jill turned the key to her front door, satisfied with the deadbolt's assertive thunk sliding back. She dropped her keys on the counter and sent a few texts in quick succession.

Hey Mom & Dad. Just got in.
Love you.

Hi Angela - no issues on the trip out. I'll settle in this weekend and see you first thing Monday! Call me if you need anything before then.

She wavered on including the exclamation mark, but went with it. *So glad to be here!*

Salut ma poulette

I regret everything

I ate a gas station sandwich and am going to die. If you don't hear from me tmr, send help

PS I'm here. Love you!

Check-ins complete, she looked around the space that would be hers for the next year.

Well, she thought, tucking her fingers into her armpits, *here goes nothing.*

Jill Northrop had a plan.

That plan consisted mostly of putting half a country between her and her problems and using said distance to get her shit together. The timing of her boss offering a promotion and a year-long transfer to Calgary the month before couldn't have been scripted better, and she had leapt at the chance for a fresh start. Her mind had been made up before the plane's wheels had touched down for the weekend-long wooing session to convince her. Even the frigid temperatures in the middle of February weren't enough to deter her. She could always wear more clothes.

"There's a big difference between running away and taking yourself out of a toxic situation," her therapist had said. "Only you can figure out which is which."

Jill had never lived alone in her entire life. She had gone from her childhood bedroom, to sharing a university dorm, to living with her ex, before landing back at her parents' home.

Unpacking her suitcase in her tiny new apartment, in her strange new city, getting ready for her exciting new role. Through her nerves, another new something sprung up in her core for the first time since she could remember.

Hope.

—

The rooster ringtone crowing from her floor bounced off the bare walls. Jill gave up trying to fall back asleep and squinted through the darkness, fumbling for her phone and answering without checking the caller. In third year, she, Sophie, Kyle, and a half of their International Marketing class had an infamous night involving an unknown number of karaoke bars, an ambitious volume of beer, and an inadvisable amount of chicken wings. Sophie's ringtone had been a rooster call ever since. When Jill called Sophie, an 8-bit version of a Québécois classic folk song played, of which Jill had attempted a heartfelt but ultimately off-pitch rendition. Kyle's ringtone had been a clip from the old Sister Sledge song "We Are Family" they'd sang duet that night. She hadn't heard that ringtone in a year and a half.

Jill rolled onto her side and smiled into her phone. "Do you have any idea what time it is?"

"Good morning, sunshine!" Sophie's effervescence bubbled into the morning. "Just making sure you weren't dead."

"It's five a.m. We have time zones now, remember? Two of them."

"Like you weren't up. Want to call me back?"

"No, I'm awake." Jill slipped the elastic off her braided ashy blonde hair and shook out the soft waves. Might as well get on schedule for tomorrow.

She padded from her bedroom into the kitchen, bare feet silent on the pale laminate floors. The empty apartment had the plain white walls and bland features of a thousand other rentals like it. Everything that mattered had come with her in her hatchback: clothes, a few books, her favourite mug, and stovetop espresso maker … and not much else. Furniture, plates, linens. All of it left behind. Jill wasn't a sentimental person—it was just stuff—but she still felt a pang when she thought of starting from nothing. The larger, pragmatic side of her groaned inwardly at the hassle of having to go on a mega-box-store shopping trip.

Okay, I get one pout, she thought, and she scrunched her face and fists in a fit of pique.

Sophie turned on her magic and recounted every detail in the last seventy-two hours Jill had missed while on the road. She listened while making coffee, nodding to the updates on the new guy Sophie was seeing (hot but dumb), her job (a new client wanted her to make his company's denture cleaner to go viral), and her newest shoes (red chunky ankle boots and, yes, they were practical).

After Jill had consumed enough coffee that her replies turned cheerful, Sophie asked, "Okay, how are you *doing?*"

Jill looked around her barren apartment, empty takeout containers from last night's dinner stacked neatly on the counter, her few boxes already unpacked and broken down. The starkness of her current reality hit her again.

"I'm okay. Tired. I didn't sleep great again. Could be sleeping on the air mattress. Could be, you know—" she gestured vaguely around her "—everything."

Sophie hummed sympathetically. "What's on your list?"

"Get a bed so I'm not sleeping on a crappy air mattress, some towels so I'm not drying myself off with a tee shirt." She squinched her nose. "And some kitchen stuff."

"Why? Like you're going to cook?"

"Shut up. I'm going to learn. Then I have a meeting at the Humane Society to sign over a year of Saturday mornings, so you don't need to worry. It's a big change, but I really am okay."

She would keep herself busy enough she wouldn't have time to wonder if she wasn't okay.

"You know I'm always going to worry about you," Sophie said, but sounded placated. "It's good to hear your voice. Love you, Jillybean."

"Love you, too, *ma poulette.*"

The city wouldn't be up for hours. Outside her window, the city lights twinkled against the inky sky, not even a hint of daybreak on the horizon. Jill sat on her bare floor, cross-legged, and made a list.

Ikea, here I come.

—

Blackburn Inc. occupied a small office on the twenty-seventh floor of a tower at the edge of downtown, providing sweeping northwest views and an inadequate cafeteria. While the firm was well-established in Toronto, its Calgary office had opened the previous year, providing consulting services for whatever clients needed. It had made a name for itself in three diverse but simpatico areas: branding, proposal writing, and financial consulting. While Jill's limited brand experience was keeping up her reputation for being fully self-possessed, and her success with proposals was zero, she was an exceptionally talented financial consultant.

Angela Blackburn had recruited Jill before she had graduated from her MBA program. In her short tenure with the firm, she'd taken on an incredible breadth of clientele and moved from a junior role to a senior analyst faster than anyone in the organization's thirty years. She loved digging into a problem and finding solutions, the rules that created her profession's integrity, and advising clients on how to make their business more profitable. Heaven for a control-obsessed numbers nerd like herself.

By the end of the first day, Jill had learned names, shaken hands, watched orientation videos, forgotten half the names, learned where the best bathrooms were, and made fast friends with Omar, her onboarding buddy. By the end of the first week, she was ready to dive in, and the Friday meeting to discuss her portfolio assignments left her buzzing with anticipation.

Jill peeked into the boardroom ten minutes early.

Empty. Excellent. Now she could set herself up in peace. Not worry about tripping into the room first and dump an oat milk latte all over a client. Or position herself to hide the spectacular period zit that sprouted on her chin overnight. Or find out she had forgotten to pull up reference documents as she presented and stumble as a deafening silence stretched out into a room full of impatient people …

Oh, hi, intrusive thoughts. None of those things have ever happened. Ever. Let it go.

Inhale slowly, exhale deeply. She put her hand on her heart to feel her pulse steady.

I am worthy. I am capable. I've got this.

Her mantra had changed slightly over the years, but it helped give her a sense of control over her anxiety. A few things helped. Like planning. Lists. And building in ten-minute cushions before meetings to manage the rare spikes that appeared out of nowhere. For her, anxiety was like running into wildlife in the woods. Know it's out there, and she probably wouldn't run into one, but if she did, back away slowly, don't make any sudden movements, and speak calmly and softly.

Or at least that's what she had heard you should do. She'd never run into anything more terrifying than a deer at her family's cottage.

Her breathing had returned to a normal rhythm by the time Angela entered the boardroom, her silver pixie cut making it look like she electrified the space around her.

If she wasn't so kind, Jill would have been terrified.

"So good to see you here in Calgary," Angela said, greeting Jill with her legendary warmth. "I spoke with the president of Braeside yesterday. Their new Peterborough location is online. He says hi and thanks. Again."

"I'll have to send him an email." Jill stood to greet her mentor and boss, smoothing her navy pencil skirt as she sat back down. "How was the flight this morning?"

"No lines, for once." Angela ignored her laptop and focused her laser attention on Jill. "Omar says you're settling in well."

"He's been great. I feel like I know this place as well as the Toronto office already."

"And how are things at home?" Angela asked carefully.

"Good. Fine. I let my parents know I got here in one piece." Jill kept her expression neutral. "That's it."

"Excellent." Angela smiled her famous warm smile again and shifted gears briskly. "Your last files closed strong. Your analysis on the TRG Foundation's cash flow and forecasting resulted in their board green-lighting a twelve percent increase to base funding."

Jill nodded. It had been her first file with a board of directors. Her knees had shaken for the first ten minutes she'd presented her recommendations to the suits around the table, but her voice had been clear.

Angela continued, "Your work on the Elgern Logistics audit found significant efficiencies in their warehousing operations and saved two sites from shutting down."

The eighteen people who had their jobs saved had sent her a thank-you card after. Jill posted it beside her whiteboard.

At least some parts of last year had been a success.

"So, with that in mind," Angela said, "I want to talk about next steps."

Next steps weren't on their meeting notice. She hadn't prepared for next steps. Jill clasped her hands under the table. "Okay."

"I don't usually spring these conversations on people, but I want to put you on track for divisional management in the next few years."

Manager? By thirty? Jill opened her mouth, closed it, and tried again. "I'm excited to hear that."

"Good. We've been impressed with your work, and you've displayed an aptitude for leadership. We'll need to build in development opportunities to round out your skill set. With that in mind, I have your next assignments ready."

Angela clicked through the slides on the screen beside them and Jill locked her bouncing foot around her chair leg.

"McGregor Fine Foods. You'll supervise a new team on the analysis."

Jill nodded serenely, tapping her pen against her lips, insides exploding in fireworks. She was going to have direct reports! Sort of. Temporarily.

"Palliser Industrial. They are going up for IPO and need their financials audited. Not a complex file, but their CFO is an excellent contact. When they go public, I want Blackburn at the top of their list for future work."

Butterflies swarmed her stomach. The financials would be a snap; networking would be a push. Still, it came with the territory, and that was literally how she'd gotten this job. She swallowed her nerves and nodded again.

"Finally, you need experience with proposals. You'll take the funding file for CMR Environmental. They're a remediation start-up looking to coordinate a federal grant with a venture capital proposal."

Grant writing? VC proposals? She'd never done anything like that before. Jill blinked. "That's … different."

"That's the point. In a divisional manager position, you'll need to have experience with the proposal writing arm of our work. It might never be part of your main portfolio, but you'll need to understand the business when you have a team working on this."

Anxiety percolated through her chest. Or excitement. Or both. Her foot freed itself from the chair leg and bounced under the table as she continued to hold up her calm facade.

"One more thing. Blackburn is looking to recover our reputation in environmental consultation. This will be our first environmental client since the Crestwell file fell through last year. There isn't any room for mistakes." Angela levelled a serious look at Jill. "I would have put one of our seasoned analysts on this file, but everyone else is at capacity. Still, I trust you can handle this."

So, no pressure. Metaphors of swimming and deep ends circled her brain.

"This will be a fantastic experience," Jill said, hoping her terror read as earnestness.

"Excellent," Angela declared, signalling the end of their discussion. "Eileen will set up your initial client meetings for next week and send you the files."

Jill stopped at the admin assistant's desk to coordinate schedules and rolled the new accounts over in her mind. Palliser would be a slam dunk. She understood the needs of what the McGregor file entailed, and it would be interesting—fun, even—to lead a team through it. CMR gave her pause. Even so, grants and funding were numbers. That was her jam, bread, and butter, and Jill had written loads of papers in university.

She could do this.

—

She couldn't do this. Not one more night.

Situation Sleeping-on-the-Floor needed to end, and Operation Sleep-in-a-Bed needed to start before she irreversibly aged her back. The air mattress had developed a slow leak, and she gave a little internal prayer of gratitude this would be the last week she woke up on it. If the bed and couch delivery arrived next Saturday as planned.

Note to self: reconfirm the delivery time.

As she waited for her alarm to announce the start of her week, she gingerly stretched her tired legs. Yesterday's run had given her an unpleasant surprise. Despite the crisscross of fabulous pathways she only got a little lost on, it had never occurred to her to account for the elevation change from her old home. The thin air of the Rocky Mountain foothills had left her sucking wind as soon as she left her front door, and she tried to convince herself it was extended altitude training for the Toronto marathon next year. It didn't work.

But despite the unpleasant realization, the run did what it was supposed to and had reset her mood and the rest of her day had been tranquil. Really, her first truly restful day in … had it been months? Longer? The last several weeks had been hectic as she prepared for her cross-country move. Nothing was ever restorative under her parents' roof. And her time with her ex, Connor … well, walking on eggshells and guarding her thoughts had consumed a shocking amount of energy. Jill felt the old scars tug in her heart. Parallel thoughts of *I'm so glad to be out* and *I can't believe it took me so long to leave* swirled in her mind.

Nope. Only positive thoughts this morning, like *I'm almost sleeping on a complete bed!* Buoyed by the mini celebration, Jill stretched out the stiffness in her legs and reviewed her morning routine.

Today was Meet New Clients Day. She scrutinized her closet for something that said, *sure I'm a young-looking woman, but I mean Business and You Will Take Me Seriously.* Her lucky stilettos, always. She was a perfectly respectable five-foot-five, but the extra height made her feel powerful, and she'd take any edge she could. She added a pair of slim black pants and a white buttoned shirt so crisp it crackled along the ironed creases. Another night of fitful sleep left her looking pale, so she added a swipe of lip tint and fringed her clear grey eyes with a touch of mascara to make up for her drawn complexion. One quick twist of her hair, and she was done.

Simple, professional, modest. Perfect.

Thirty minutes later, she sailed across the office lobby, relishing the click of her heels echoing in the cavernous space. Lights activated as she passed through the office. Her first meeting wasn't for an hour. Meeting her team for the McGregor file began the day at eight, then a video call for the Palliser file. Marco and Ashleen were assigned to the McGregor project, and they walked her through their plans for their first meeting with the operations manager. She coached them on a few last-minute points, but they had prepared well. The CFO for Palliser was a tad on the stuffy side, but Jill predicted she could win her over with a timeline that would come in much faster than she requested.

Satisfied with the morning, Jill caught Omar to join her for lunch to discuss her approach to the CMR file.

"Oh, you're going to love it," he said, gesturing with a French fry. "That's my area of expertise."

A piece fell into place. That would be why Angela paired her with Omar as her orientation buddy. Clever Angela, always planning ahead. "Well, I'll be picking your brain as I go. I did a bunch of reading on the weekend, but grants are new to me. I'm meeting one of the owners this afternoon for a first review."

"Anytime. And," he said, turning mischievous, "you'll have to tell me if he's cute. I broke things off with Samuel this weekend. Hot but dumb."

"You need to date people your own age," Jill teased. Hot but dumb boyfriends? Omar and Sophie would get along great. "Besides, I'm not setting you up with a client."

"Why not? It's not my client," he retorted, and Jill rolled her eyes in feigned exasperation.

Later, teeth brushed and crumbs swept to remove any lingering traces of lunch, Jill scanned her file one last time before her meeting.

Nicholas Martin, co-owner of CMR Environmental, looking to secure funding for a new remediation technique his business partner had developed.

Biochemistry. Because why wouldn't her very first grant writing assignment be on her favourite topic? Jill winced as she pulled up her notes.

I don't need technical knowledge, she reminded herself. *I learned about Peruvian export tariffs. I can make myself learn chemistry to get through this.*

Footsteps sounded down the hall five minutes before their meeting time. She gave him bonus points for being early and stood to greet him as he entered the boardroom.

Alright, she had expected a nerd. Last year, she had consulted a civil engineering firm through a software upgrade, and every one of them had been adorable dorks. If one of them got a paper cut, it wouldn't bleed until they secured an *Injury, paper cut, bleeding* release form, for approval.

The man in front of her had dark eyes and a brilliant smile that looked like it had benefited from orthodontics. Well-tailored charcoal blazer over an athletic frame, light grey trousers, and a sweater that looked expensive. His credentials were included in the client package, so she wasn't surprised at how young he was, five or so years older than her. Omar's reminder popped into her mind, and she wondered if he was into dark-haired, bro-y looking guys. She kept her internal grin under wraps as she figured an engineer might fit half the requirements of the hot-but-dumb type Omar kept falling for.

"Hi, Nicholas. Jill Northrop. It's a pleasure to meet you." She shook his hand and motioned for him to sit, thanking her past self for putting on the heels and coming in only a couple inches shorter than him.

"Excited you're working for us on this. Call me Nick," he said as he reclined in the boardroom chair with casual comfort.

Even after being out of Montreal for several years, she caught the trace Québécois accent stilting the cadence of a few syllables. Right, the file showed he was a fellow McGill alumnus. The different faculties and five years separating them likely meant they didn't cross paths with the same people on campus, but if she needed an icebreaker, she could find out if they had frequented the same pubs. He seemed friendly enough that wouldn't be an issue.

"Your work sounds promising," she said. "Is your business partner joining us?"

"Should be. His last field visit wrapped early, but he's always late." Nick looked past Jill's shoulder and broke into a smile. "Speak of the devil, here he is now."

Jill turned, processed what she was seeing for a millisecond, and felt her stomach plummet to the tips of her pointy shoes.

TWO

This can't be happening.

The worst part from the most challenging class of her hardest year of university. Filling the doorway and striding into her boardroom, late, snow melting from his knitted beanie and flannel-clad shoulders onto the carpet.

This was Nick's partner? Had his name been on the file? She had reviewed the contract from front to back. Nick's name peppered the documents, but the CMR partner had been simply listed as Dr. Campbell.

The man now standing in her office hadn't been a doctor then.

"Hi, I'm Alex. Pleasure to meet you." His voice was deep, softer than the tyrant who barked instructions at her in labs. Clearly, he treated people like actual humans if he wasn't trying to terrorize them. Maybe just people he needed something from, and right now, he needed something from her.

Her legs remembered the professional thing to do would be to greet him, and so she stood, numb. He towered over her, even in her lucky stilettos, her eyes level with his jaw. The humiliation of running bodily into him after fleeing the lab and leaving her professor's office swept over her with fresh heat.

He reached out to grasp her hand, large and warm, even coming in from the snow. A shock bolted from their clasped hands to her sternum. He tilted his head, eyes crinkling at the corners. "Do we know each other?"

Jill tried to hide her disorientation as a flicker of recognition, and the bright smile she pasted on felt more like a rictus. "You seem familiar, too. We'll have to figure that out sometime."

Oh, yes, can't wait to reminisce about old times.

He still hadn't let go of her hand. "And you must be ...?"

About to have a heart attack.

Fuck. This was happening.

Snap out of it, Northrop. Don't let this dick throw you off. She firmed her grip on his hand and gave it a perfunctory shake before extracting her fingers from his. "Jill. Northrop. I'll be working with you on your proposal. For your grant. And the venture capital funding."

Smooth.

Alex stepped back a pace and pulled off his beanie, running his fingers through the mussed auburn hair plastered to his head. "Nick says we need the help, so ..." he trailed off, shrugging one shoulder noncommittally.

So, he wasn't as interested in being there as she wasn't interested in working with him. Made sense he would wear jeans and work boots to a meeting with a contractor then, while his partner had arrived looking like a professional.

She motioned for the three of them to sit, perching at the front of her chair and fanning out her notes. She'd done this dozens of times. She could do it again. She crossed her legs and wound her ankle behind her calf to stop her foot from bouncing. "You must have a lot of background information for me to review. How about giving me a bit of context?"

Nick sank back into his chair, clapping his hands together. "Alex, this is your brainchild. Why don't you do the honours?"

Alex turned to Jill. "What do you know about environmental remediation?"

About as much as an hour and a half of googling could supply. "'Environmental remediation is a process that removes contaminants from soil, sediment, groundwater, or surface water,'" she recited from her notes. "'It is subject to extensive regulations, and remediation may be based on human health and ecological risk assessments.'" She looked over at Nick, hoping he'd take over.

"Great." Alex nodded. "Sometimes remediation is recommended, sometimes it's legislated, and focuses on pollution prevention, health protection, or productive use. Our work focuses on the latter two, specifically tier one remediation sites. Tier one guidelines are generic; they are developed to protect the more sensitive end of the range and can be used at most sites without modification."

This guy sounds like a textbook, Jill thought, then flushed, as she essentially regurgitated Wikipedia to a man who was probably cited on the very page she'd taken her notes from.

"Bioremediation uses a living system to remove pollutants," Alex continued. "Think fungus, microalgae, bacteria. It's a newer field, and slow. It can take decades to clear a site. We've developed—"

Nick interrupted, "—he's developed."

Alex waved him off, "—a genetically-modified, self-limiting microalgae for bioremediation that works in situ for heavy metals. Usually it takes ten, twenty years to remediate a site." He paused, trading a glance with Nick. "I think our technology will get that down to eighteen months."

Wow. An order of magnitude faster. And if it was proven, likely less expensive, too. Venture capitalists should be all over this.

"I'm not well-versed on the specifics of your field, but that sounds promising." More than promising. It sounded groundbreaking. She turned to Nick. "Why hasn't this gone directly to VCs?"

"We tried. We've only conducted lab tests so far—"

"—and we don't have proven scalability—"

"—and the venture capital firm we're talking to is excited but won't commit until we can put together a better proposal—"

"—and the federal grant will give us the infusion we need to run a pilot project and get the data to convince the VC."

That was a lot of contingencies. Jill tapped her pen to her lips. "Are there any barriers with the federal grant?"

"Not directly," Nick said. "It's more that we have a lot of competition. I've submitted five grant applications, and nothing. All levels of government are prioritizing climate and environmental sustainability, but funding is limited. The serious start-ups are working with people like you to give them an advantage. I want to keep the playing field level."

Alex looked at Nick, exasperated. "If you'd have said that the first time, I wouldn't have fought so hard against hiring a consultant."

"I did," Nick said. "You didn't listen."

Alex's look of exasperation turned into a scowl.

Aha. There was the dick she remembered. And he hadn't wanted to hire her. Great.

Hello, deep end, she thought. *Omar, I hope you're ready to play lifeguard.* "Blackburn has an excellent track record with both government grant writing and private ventures." It was true. Blackburn did. And she was going to work her ass off to add to that successful track record, even if it meant getting her mother on the phone for chemistry lectures.

Okay, not that.

Jill forced a small grin, keeping her mask intact. "I'll be working beside you the whole way. I'll set up a couple of fact-finding sessions to make sure we target the best grants, and then we align the outcomes of the grant request to feed into what the VC is looking for."

Nick raised his brows in triumph at Alex, who grunted in response. Agreement? Dismissal? Jill couldn't tell.

At least Nick is in my corner, she thought. This was going to be an uphill battle.

"I'm looking forward to getting started," she continued, lying through her smile. "Let's begin with granting options and timeline."

Jill ignored the tension gripping her shoulders. While Nick handled the non-technical answers, Alex replied for all information directly related to the technology and grant needs. As the meeting progressed, it dawned on her that while Nick was more invested in her expertise, she needed to work far more closely with Alex. Every time they made eye contact, heat threatened to crawl up her cheeks. After a while, and he sat back in his chair, arms crossed over his broad chest with his mouth in a firm line.

It took the entire meeting to recover the remnants of her composure. Her secondary list of notes was scrawled out long-hand, ready for review with Omar to check her logic, but the file looked to be straightforward. As they got close to the end of their time, Jill messaged Eileen to reprint their contract to add Alex's information and signature. She was about to ask them to stop at the admin assistant's desk on the way out when Eileen replied she was swamped and would she please, please, please come by and pick up the file? Jill shot back a quick confirmation and stood to excuse herself.

"This is a solid start," Jill said. "If you'll wait here a few minutes, I'll be back for signatures."

Jill navigated the twisting corridors to the front desk, turning the last hour over in her mind. Nick seemed perfectly reasonable. Alex was going to be impossible.

I've dealt with lots of assholes before. Hell, I've dealt with this *asshole before. I've got this.*

Less than a minute later, contract in hand and ready to turn the last corner to the boardroom, their hushed conversation reached her in the hall.

"Positive. She was in that class I TA'ed at McGill."

"Wait, the one that …?"

"Yep. Think I almost failed her. Glad we aren't hiring her for her deep affinity for chemistry."

Jill stopped dead outside the door, cheeks flaming. Definitely still an asshole. She squared her shoulders and turned the corner to face them, chin high. Nick looked surprised. Alex looked mortified.

"Nick, thanks so much for coming in. It was a pleasure to meet you." She turned to look Alex directly in the eye, handing him the file. "Eileen has highlighted the areas for your review. Please return it to her on your way out. I'll see you next week," she said, and spun on her heel without walking them to the front desk.

Her office door wasn't fully closed before she was texting Sophie.

shitcrapfuck

???

Client from hell

Ooh let me guess ... entitled man-child who has driven the family business into the ground needs rescuing

Do you remember that brutal first year chem class?
My client is our TA

Her phone crowed three seconds later.

"Shut the fuck up!" Sophie shrieked.

"I know, right? This is—"

"The dude with thighs like a Greek god and the dreamy green eyes?"

Jill gaped. This was not the response she'd expected. "I was going to say 'the worst?'"

"He was so fucking hot! What was his name? Alex?"

Dr. Campbell, now. Jill made a noise that sounded like *ungh.*

"The way he used to roll up his sleeves?" Sophie continued with barely contained lust. "I could've chewed every inch of those forearms."

Come to think of it, this was the most Sophie response. "I was too busy trying not to fail to see any of that!"

"I don't know how we got anything done in that class."

"You didn't get anything done! You failed, and I barely passed. Which was mostly his fault. Do you remember those labs?"

"No. I blocked them out."

"Exactly. Completely unreasonable."

"Come on. Was it really his fault? Even if it was, that was years ago," Sophie prodded. "Don't kill me for saying this, but chemistry wasn't your strong point."

"Well, clearly," Jill muttered.

"So, was he still a complete dick? Yelled at you and stomped around barking instructions like the good ole days?"

No, but it was only a matter of time until that side of him came out. Jill plucked at a piece of lint on her otherwise immaculate pants. "I heard him tell his partner he was glad they didn't hire me for my chemistry skill." It stung. More than she would have thought.

"That's not why people hire you and you know it," Sophie said firmly. "You're not an expert in logistics and you knocked that one out of the park."

"He's going to be impossible to work with."

"Wouldn't you be? He and his partner have a lot riding on this."

"He was dressed like he came in off a farm." Nick did say Alex had come in directly from a field site, but she opted not to relay that.

"Like a dirty farmer or a sexy farmer? A dirty, sexy farmer?"

"I'm trying to be miserable here."

"Why do you have to be so committed to holding a grudge?"

Jill made a face at her phone.

"I know you're making that face." Sophie clicked her tongue. "That was a long time ago, Jillybean."

The anxiety she had struggled through all semester. Breaking it to her mother she was changing her minor. Hustling for extra credit in other classes to salvage her GPA. She made the face again. "Wasn't that long ago, chicken wing."

"Do you need comfort or advice?" asked Sophie.

A hug, she thought. Her next several months would be full of long hours poring through technical documents explained in the most condescending way imaginable. An exhausting marathon of keeping up her professional exterior to mask her discomfort. All while babysitting a moody dick and navigating a file that was new territory for her in a field that triggered PTSD.

Cool.

Angela had assigned the file to her with growth in mind, but she couldn't have planned for this scenario.

"Neither," Jill sighed half-heartedly. "I've got this."

She had years of experience hiding her feelings.

—

The pom-pom trend of a few years ago taught Jill the right attire for volunteering went beyond wearing things she didn't mind getting dirty. Between huskies lunging at swinging puffs and cats attacking swaying fringes, the temptation to eat her clothes was overwhelming. Now, she stuck to a strict wardrobe of retired running shoes, old jeans, and a small rotation of sweatshirts. Today, she had donned an old long-sleeved concert tee shirt and a pair of second-hand jeans she had over-dyed lilac on a whim. She thought they were cute for weekends. Connor had said she looked like an Easter egg and refused to speak to her when she wore them. The jeans had sat, unworn, in the back of her closet for over a year.

Turns out, the experimental lilac jeans were extremely cute on the weekends, shielding her from errant claws, rough concrete floors, and the early spring winds that sent chilly gusts searching for faults in her clothes' defences. She hunched out of her jacket, keeping one hand firmly on the leash with a wiggly puppy on the other end.

"Morning, Travis," she said, smiling brightly at the shelter's volunteer coordinator. The quiet man who made Sam Elliot look like a city slicker had greeted her at the front desk her first day. Faded jeans over cowboy boots, a paisley shirt with dome fasteners, and from the state of his salt-and-pepper hair, there was a cowboy hat on the premises. Jill silently bet herself if he'd been wearing his hat, he'd have tipped the brim at her. She had been instantly charmed.

"We got a new girl," Travis said, motioning her to follow. Jill wasn't sure if he meant a new volunteer or a new animal. "Want to meet her?"

Jill followed him through to the pens, her thoughts drifting to the week she had. A flicker of anxiety popped into her chest whenever she replayed the end of her meeting with Alex.

"My boss assigned me a new project. It's a bit different than what I'm used to," she said, trailing a few paces behind. "I met my new clients this week. It's … going to be a challenge."

Travis kept walking. "You keen on it?"

Jill paused. "Yes."

"You reckon you gonna learn from it?"

Another pause. "Yes."

"If you climb in the saddle, be ready for the ride," he quipped.

She smiled at his back, turning his words over. She had moved to Calgary for a new start, and part of doing new things was facing challenges. She wouldn't let one minor bump veer her from her plan, and she filed the latest Travis quote away to share with Sophie later.

The cacophony from the enclosures reached them from down the hall. There she was, shivering in the corner of her pen, ears down and tail tucked.

"Man dropped off while you were out. Not aggressive, but real scared. She's gonna need some care."

The frightened dog looked physically healthy: probably a shepherd-pit bull mix, with a smooth black-and-tan coat and clear amber eyes that followed Jill's every move.

"What's her name?"

"I ain't repeating what he called her."

She looked at the sweet girl. "Let's call her Daisy." Jill sat down outside the pen's closed door. She didn't have any other plans this morning. A bit of quiet company for her new friend would do them both some good.

"How about we sit together for a bit?" Jill spoke softly to Daisy, who hunched further into the corner. "It's okay. We can take our time."

THREE

The night before her first day at CMR, she did some extracurricular research.

Nick Martin. His LinkedIn profile highlighted his professional engineering designation with a couple of years in industry before creating the start-up with Alex. Lots of Twitter posts sharing a billionaire's motivational quotes. Jill repressed the urge to roll her eyes.

Dr. Alexander Campbell. McGill undergrad and graduate studies. University of Calgary for his PhD. Aiming for the overachiever award, also a P. Eng. No social media, not even an old Twitter account for her to stalk, but several academic papers turned up in her sleuthing, both as co-author and lead author. Even her mother would be impressed. Out of morbid curiosity, Jill bit her thumbnail and checked the citations.

Of course. Not like Jill needed to tell her mother her work had been cited again. She had a Google alert notifying her whenever her work showed up in research. The knowledge that her daughter was working with him would send her on either an *I told you so rant* that it could have been Jill doing that work, or a lecture that now she was nothing more than an assistant.

Her mother's words, not hers. Jill exhaled forcefully, willing the headache to pass before it set in.

Within minutes of arriving at CMR the next morning, she saw Nick was right: they needed help. Clients hired her to untangle knots and fix problems they had created, but this was next level. From what she could tell without comprehending the reams of data sheets, Alex's technical work looked meticulous. Rigorously recorded and tracked soil salinity, sodicity, and pH values to an exacting precision, each site carefully tagged and categorized.

The same level of care did not extend to the rest of the business.

"Alex is a brilliant research scientist. It took me forever to talk him into starting CMR," Nick had said her first day in their office. "His problem is in here. I usually don't let him touch non-field paperwork like contracts, but I was out of town when our file was due. He filled it out and didn't even include himself in it. Given that he didn't want to hire you, I'm impressed he completed it at all."

The sticky notes in varying colours and sizes decorating the perimeter of Alex's monitors and the haphazard pile of paperwork balancing on the corner of his desk were going to make her break out in hives.

"Would you consider doing a process audit before we start?" she asked. "It could make this a lot easier."

Nick waved a lazy hand. "Organized chaos. We know where everything is. At least, I know where I put everything I do, and Alex knows where everything is that he's done." He smiled charmingly at her. "Besides, this'll be fun."

This'll be a wild goose chase.

Just as much information lived in Alex and Nick's heads as on their networks, printed files, and random external drives. So, much to her chagrin, Jill booked three days a week at CMR, a short drive or a decent walk from her downtown apartment. The converted house in Inglewood had creaky hardwoods, scuffed walls, and two banged up desks. With no other options and Alex nowhere to be found, she sat at his desk her first week, trying to not touch anything, her feet dangling above the floor.

"Do you want to give me a heads-up if you want me to leave when you bring clients through?" Jill asked, perched at the front of the huge chair.

"I don't bring clients here," Nick said with a laugh. "I only bring clients to our lab space. Looks more professional."

Fair enough. She thought the Inglewood office was rather homey.

Alex had passed through once her first week. When she scrambled up, he motioned for her to stay, saying he was just dropping off samples. On her second Monday, a new workspace had sprouted up over the weekend.

Well, not new. A spindly, antique desk with a muted honey gleam and a stubborn drawer, an upholstered chair tucked under it. It was actually the perfect size: big enough to hold the two new monitors that had appeared along with the desk; small enough to nestle between the two men's stations.

"This is fantastic." She spread her open windows across the screens, grateful to not hunch over her laptop anymore. "Thank you."

Nick shrugged. "Alex must've brought everything in on the weekend."

Surprisingly considerate, really. Even if it was because he didn't want to share his space with her. At least they had that in common. She didn't want to share her space with him, either.

Apparently, he didn't want to spend his time with her, either.

Jill checked the clock for the fourth time. Alex was late. Really late. For their first meeting. He had been out in the field all week and she couldn't do anything without the information locked in his brain. They had barely started, and already working with him was as impossible as she feared.

Traffic sounds flowed through the front door and creaking floorboards announced his belated arrival, and she turned a stormy look at him. Nick was right when he said Alex couldn't be relied on for anything outside the lab.

So, the good doctor graces me with his presence. How benevolent.

He looked like he had just rolled out of bed, all wrinkled flannel and sleepy eyes. He obviously hadn't shaved during his days on the road—the scruff of his beard had come in slightly feral and redder than the tousled auburn waves on his head. He gripped a large thermos like a lifeline, shirt sleeves rolled back over thickly muscled forearms. Through her peevishness, Jill made the mental note to tell Sophie some things hadn't changed.

"Good morning," she said curtly, and raised her perfectly manicured brows in question. "I hope I can count on some of your time today?"

Alex halted halfway through the door, looking slightly stunned. He looked down at his rumpled shirt, ran a hand over his chin, and back at Jill. "I, uh, are we meeting?"

Really? She had sent the request days ago. "Yes."

"When?" he asked with grimace.

An hour ago, but if someone was going to act like a jerk in the office, it wouldn't be her. Anymore than she already was acting, anyway. "Whenever you're ready, I need about two hours. Please," she added.

"No problem," he said, looking relieved. "Can you give me, ah, forty-five minutes?" He turned to leave, then waited for her response.

She gritted her teeth and forced a smile. "Great. I can work on a few other things in the meantime." Nothing as priority as the information she needed from him directly, but clearly he didn't care if they got the grant.

Okay, that was harsh, and she didn't need to rub it in. Even if she wanted to.

His broad shoulders dropped several inches. "Okay. See you soon." He swigged a gulp of coffee, dropped some files on his desk, and left as quickly as he'd arrived.

Jill closed her eyes and smoothed a flyaway lock of hair behind her ear. She didn't want to get off track so early; the grant application deadline wasn't going to move for Alex's inability to read a freaking meeting invite.

"Told you," Nick said. "Don't worry, I'll make sure you get what you need."

"Thanks," she replied, and busied herself with sorting files until his partner returned.

A little over an hour later, Alex was back. Hair still damp and clean-shaven, he had changed into clothes which at least looked like he hadn't put them on straight off the floor.

Nick's eyes flicked to Alex as he crossed over to Jill's workstation. "Nice shirt," he said, smirking at his screen.

Alex levelled a flat look at Nick. "Thanks." He pulled up his chair next to her, leaning his elbows on the desk and looking down at the scattered documents. "Okay, I'm all yours. What do you need?"

A light charge sparked through her torso. He had sat close enough his thigh almost brushed hers. Close enough to feel the heat radiating off his body. She sucked in a breath and inhaled the clean scent of soap and pine that clung to his skin. An inexplicable shiver ran over her, and she crossed her legs tightly.

Alex clocked her movements and shifted his chair over. "Sorry, didn't mean to get in your personal space."

Focus, Northrop.

"I've gotten as far as I can on my own," she said, clearing her throat. "Can we work through R&D and Demonstration? I need more information on the pilot scale."

Yes, information on the pilot scale. That's why they were meeting.

They were farther along than she'd initially thought. She showed him what she'd found and where she needed his help, and he added comments and corrections, growing animated as he went. It was surprisingly endearing, seeing this person she had pegged as a dick exuberantly detail his work like a proud parent showing off photos of their kid. She shut down that train of thought and focused on the list of work to go.

"I've researched successful grant applications, and you'll have the best shot using two of these three methods," she said, pulling up a few tabs on her browser.

"That's not what I used in my thesis," he said, frowning.

And how'd that turn out on your last grant applications? "But you're not trying to appeal to academics here. There'll be a mix of bureaucratic and technical people on the review panel. I recommend this for the technical reviewers," she pointed a finger at the screen, "and this for the non-technical ones. The Watson project used these successfully."

Alex leaned forward, elbows on his knees, squinting at the screen in front of them. "Oh. I didn't think about that."

Obviously. But she held her tongue and waited for him to work through it.

After a moment of furrowing his brows at the screen, his frown resolved. "That makes sense," he said, looking at her with a mixture of appreciation and satisfaction. "Nick, what do you think?" He looked over at his friend's empty workstation, then turned back to Jill. "When did he … did you see him leave?"

Jill shook her head, surprised he'd managed to sneak out without either of them noticing. Her lips quirked without her permission. "I didn't know he had a stealth mode."

Alex barked out a laugh. "Usually I get a running commentary on his every move. If this keeps up, I'll put a bell on him."

Jill caught most of the giggle as it burst forth.

What am I doing? This person is not my friend.

She rearranged her smile to Resting Professional Face. "As long as he's back for our meeting at eleven." She glanced down at her phone to check the time. It was fifteen minutes to noon. Jill gaped at Alex, aghast. "I didn't hear the reminder notification," she said, scrambling through the pop-ups on her screen. She'd gotten so caught up she didn't even notice the creaky floorboards or slamming door.

Alex gave her a small grin. "Maybe he'll be lucky enough to get some of your time this afternoon?"

A memory of yelling jumped into her mind, and she hunched her shoulders out of instinct. "I'm sorry. I deserve that," she said in a small voice.

He shook his head, looking at her carefully. "No, it's my fault. If I hadn't been late, you would've gotten the two hours you needed from me, and you'd have been on time."

Jill stared at her hands. It wasn't a memory of Alex yelling that made her flinch, but Connor. He would have called her an idiot—or worse—making her work off a debt of guilt until he said she was sorry enough.

Here was Alex, making light of her mistake and taking responsibility so gracefully. And she'd thought he was being the rude one.

She tried to come up with a breezy reply, but found it hitched in her throat. Even months later, it caught her unawares. The dull torment of living with Connor springing up at the most unexpected times. She busied herself with the files on the desk, willing the tightness in her chest to dissipate.

Alex drew his brows together. "Are you … is everything okay?"

"Yes!" she said as brightly as she could muster. The crack in her voice was so small he probably missed it. She scrambled to grab her phone and jacket, rushing to the front door. "I need a walk. I'll be back after lunch."

"Okay." He looked as though he were going to ask something else, and instead said, "See you after lunch."

Jill stepped outside, inhaling the crisp air deeply. The knot that had grown in the pit of her stomach hadn't waned. Was she going to have a panic attack?

No, this was different. Blunt and heavy, not sharp and nauseating. She let out her breath through pursed lips, exhaling for a count of five. How long would she be fighting this? Any random conversation triggering a visceral memory. It knocked her control off-centre every time.

It hasn't even been three months. It's going to take time.

She typed into her phone's search bar, grimly eyeing the results: *there are seven therapists near you!* Her health spending account had lots of room left. It was time to go back. After adding a reminder to book a session, she reset her shoulders and turned down the street, counting on the walk and thin spring sunlight to soothe her in the hour before she had to head back.

—

Tzatziki spilled from one end of the oversized wrap while lettuce escaped from the other. Elbows on her knees and a napkin between her butt and the sidewalk, Jill took another enormous bite, relishing the falafel like she hadn't eaten a huge breakfast sandwich from the coffee shop down the street hours earlier. It was Monday, after all. She'd been ravenous since yesterday's long run, once again needing the extra day to make up the calories she hadn't been able to consume the day before. Besides, she could stand to put on the few pounds she'd lost over the last few years.

Jill and Omar's standing Monday lunch date was mutually beneficial. She brought questions from her prior week with Alex and Nick and got to stuff her face with wild abandon, and he had a willing partner to try new food trucks as he extolled the virtues of lunch meetings.

"It gives you a chance to catch up as you wait for food. You can buy time to think about your responses while you chew, and it's a humanizing activity," he said. "It's hard to take yourself too seriously when you have a mouthful of food."

Wiping a smear of sauce from her cheek, Jill couldn't help but agree.

"And your files are good?" Omar asked.

"Great. Marco and Ashleen are doing a solid job on the McGregor file. She's a little nervous to share her ideas, even though they're almost always excellent, and Marco is so afraid of being 'that guy' he only ever speaks after she's spoken first. The Palliser audit is a slam dunk, and the CFO already loves me."

"And what's new in the world of the Disorganized Duo?"

Despite Nick's assurance the chaos was organized, Jill had yet to find any order. She caught a drip of sauce before it landed on her pants. "Besides the fact that they're missing six weeks of receipts from seven months ago? Not bad."

"It's a good thing you're on that file," Omar said, half-seriously. "I'd have told Angela to put someone else on it if I got stuck with that mess."

"You'd have that luxury," Jill pointed out. "I can't decline my first grant because conditions aren't perfect."

Hello, career limiting move.

"Fair point," he conceded.

"Anyway, Alex came around on my recommendations, and Nick goes with the flow." She studied a corner of her wrap. "I think they need a process audit."

Just last week, Jill had spent half an hour with Alex dragging out of him the full list of licenses and permits CMR needed, then another hour hunting through network folders for copies, before Nick remembered they had saved them on two external drives. If the previous week's frenetic hunt for information was any sign, it didn't bode well for the rest of their proposal.

"What are you going to do?"

"I'm going to bring it up with Alex," Jill said after a moment of thorough chewing. "Nick seems to think they're fine, but Alex has been pretty receptive to my ideas."

Surprisingly receptive. He had spouted her entire "it worked for the Watson project" argument nearly verbatim when Nick had asked about the communications plan. She didn't know if she was more surprised at his memory or the warm glow she'd felt that he'd taken her advice so seriously.

Omar nodded his approval. "Good plan, and great job of planning to pitch a service package."

That isn't why I'm suggesting it, Jill thought. Would they think she was trying to upsell them? Sure, it would cost money, but it would really help them. Alex was so committed to the success of his technology that he had to be on board for something that made perfect sense, right?

FOUR

"Not interested." Alex leaned back from the desk with his arms crossed and a furrow between his brows.

Jill wasn't even a minute into her speech. A filing and retention policy. A naming practice for key documents to prevent mysteries like ACNM-Siptec-FINALV3-Copy(2).doc, which neither Alex nor Nick could identify until they opened it. A shared calendar so they could plan, well, anything.

She had left her earbuds at home during her long run the previous morning, forgoing her favourite playlist to rehearse. In every way, the audit was an excellent idea. He didn't let her get through her second bullet point.

I gave up listening to the new Beyoncé drop yesterday to practise and you won't even listen? Jill thought, taken aback at his hard "no". Keeping her tone level, she tried again. "May I ask why you don't think this would work?"

"We've found everything we've needed."

"It took us three days, a million emails, and a billion phone calls to get the copy of your patent. We still don't know where the last grant application was saved. If it was saved."

"It'll take a bunch of time we don't have."

"It'll save a bunch of time in the future."

"We've managed fine so far."

"You're a science guy, right? You know entropy? Your office looks like a tornado ran through it because you're letting it fall to entropy," she said through gritted teeth, pretty sure she was using the word "entropy" right. She gestured at the mountain of stuffed binders, half-empty filing boxes, and loose thumb drives. Thumb drives!

He drummed his fingers on his sizeable bicep, working his jaw. "I need some sugar."

"You … what?" Her laugh came out as a kind of cough, thrown by the abrupt change in conversation.

"It's been a long afternoon and I need a break. Going to grab an ice cream." He cleared his throat. "Come with me?"

Her blood still coursed from their exchange. A pleasant stroll wasn't exactly topping her list of preferred activities right now. Especially not with him. She pressed her lips together and exhaled sharply.

"Please?" he prodded. "My treat."

They had worked through lunch. Again. A break would be useful to cool off. In more ways than one. Ice cream wasn't the nourishment she needed, but she could grab a smoothie on the walk. "Fine. I could stretch my legs."

The late April day was unseasonably warm, tempered by a clean, cool breeze flowing off the river, the sun already pulling west in the sky. The lunch crowd had thinned, but the pathway bustled with cyclists, scooters, and parents pushing strollers. It wasn't shorts weather yet, and her weather app showed snow next week, but today she'd left her jacket at home on the short drive into CMR.

By the time they reached the storefront minutes later, ice cream sounded like the perfect antidote to their heated conversation. Jill stepped into the shop, lifting the stray bits of hair from the back of her neck and letting the air conditioning cool her. She leaned over the scuffed counter to consider the selection of quirky artisanal flavours: lavender Earl Grey, honeyberry, pancake batter … but the orange creamsicle called to her. Alex was already devouring his double scoop of chocolate as he paid for their cones.

Alex led them to a nearby bench sheltered by a grove of spruce. The sun's unexpectedly intense rays attacked both her rapidly melting ice cream and her unsunblocked skin, and Jill gratefully rested against the weathered wooden slats. With one hand occupied with her ice cream, she lifted the front of her shirt with her free hand to encourage air flow. She must look like a mess, with her hair coming out of its knot and sweat beading her neck. She concentrated on trying to catch the ice cream drips before they covered her fingers. It wasn't high on her list of priorities to end the afternoon sticky and covered in ice cream.

"It occurs to me," Alex started, "that we've been working together for over a month, and I don't know a thing about you."

Just the way I like it. "Ask me anything."

He drew himself back. "Where are you from?"

"How do you know I'm not from here?"

"Are you?"

Touché. "Toronto."

"Ooh, centre of the universe. That's a strike against you."

Really? He was going with that overplayed joke? She raised an eyebrow and sucked the tip of her thumb to clean a rogue drip.

Alex looked pointedly away, a flush creeping up his neck. "Ah, did you have any pets growing up?"

"When I'm done with that question, do you want my mother's maiden name and the street I grew up on?"

He cast his eyes down to his own melting cone. "Yep, childhood best friend's name, too."

Play nice, Northrop. He's obviously trying. Jill relented. "No pets. My parents would never let animals in the house." When she would get home from volunteering at the animal shelter, she had to do laundry right away so she wouldn't track any hair or dirt into their home's pristine interior.

Getting her ice cream in a cone was a terrible idea. No one could look professional while licking. Next time she'd get a cup. Not that she planned on making it a habit to go on regular ice cream dates with him.

"We always had cats growing up," he said, "but I love dogs, too."

A crack formed in her icy resolve, and her opinion of Alex stepped up a couple of notches.

He continued, "Siblings? I have an older sister who has strong opinions on every facet of my life."

She shook her head. "Only child, but I only suffer from a few only child afflictions," she said. "Used to getting my own way," she weighed out on her free hand, "but still good at sharing," balancing with her ice cream laden one. "My turn. Favourite snacks?"

He raised his ice cream cone as if he were toasting her with it. "I'm a sucker for anything sweet." He raised his brows for her turn.

"Salty, spicy. Nachos. Chips. But I'll never say no to ice cream," she said, saluting him with her cone before taking another taste. It might be the best ice cream she'd ever had. "Next time, I'm trying the lavender Earl Grey."

"I haven't had that flavour." He drew a breath and met her eyes. "Favourite class in university?"

Ah. So, they were talking about the asshole-shaped elephant in the room now. Jill set her shoulders and walked through the open door. "I had lots of favourites, but my least favourite was chemistry," she said crisply.

Let's see what he does with that.

Alex puffed out his cheeks. "I owe you an apology. That conversation you walked in on was not what it sounded like."

"Are you saying that you're sorry I didn't understand you," she asked, crossing her ankles, "because that's not much better."

Alex grimaced. "This isn't going how I'd hoped," he said. He started again. "Can I be completely honest with you?"

Jill nodded warily.

"I remember you from university."

"There were two hundred people in that class alone. How do you remember me?"

"Not all of them left the lab crying."

Oh. Right. A flush of heat rushed up her neck that she hoped he would think was from the afternoon heat. "I bet a lot of them did."

"Everyone was upset in that class," he admitted. "I was going through a lot of personal stuff. Trying to get into my PhD program and had taken on responsibility for two hundred first years. The professor was consumed with a study, and I said she could be hands-off and trust me with the class. And I was wrong. I was completely overwhelmed." He looked at her again. "I'm sorry. I'm sorry that I was a shitty TA and you had to deal with the fallout from a couple of shitty months in my life."

Fuck. This was making it a lot harder to hate him. She licked a dollop of ice cream from her finger. "In the spirit of honesty? I dropped my science minor after that class. My mom's a biochemist. She wouldn't speak to me for a month after I told her."

Alex tilted his head, eyes closed against the clear blue sky. "That's what I meant. The whole you not having an affinity for chemistry thing? That was my fault."

Nope. Not his fault. Being in his class didn't help, but her mother could take that honour. It wasn't fair to let him keep carrying it. She sighed.

Sophie was going to be so proud.

"Hey," she said, and rested her fingers on his arm. Her stomach swooped unexpectedly, and Alex looked down at her hand.

"I won't lie and say it wasn't a terrible time for me," she said, carefully withdrawing her roaming hand to pin it between her knees, "but that was never going to be my passion. I found the path I want to be on. It's okay. No hard feelings."

The tension drained from his shoulders and his features eased into relief. "We don't need someone for their technical background."

He gestured at himself. "I have that. I need your skills on this. I was, um, a bit hesitant to bring in outside help."

Jill smirked. "A bit?"

"Okay, a lot hesitant. But working with you has been great. I can't imagine doing this without you. The grant," he added quickly, and then, quietly, "Thank you."

A little box deep inside her opened, and the grudge she'd carried for years dissolved in a rush. "I'm glad to help."

And she had the perfect way to do that.

Alex seemed like he was in a good mood. She ran her tongue over her teeth and braved her pitch one more time. "And if my skills suggest doing a process audit …?" she trailed off.

"Mmfph," he grunted, but his lips might have quirked.

That wasn't the hard "no" he started with. She could try again later, hopefully before a freak avalanche of poorly stacked records boxes buried her in their storage closet. At least now she was pretty sure that if she did get buried, this new Alex would rescue her.

"Thank you," she said, finishing the last bite of her cone. Suddenly, the next several months working with him seemed a lot more promising. She dropped her professional mask and smiled up at him—her real smile—and nudged his shoulder with her own. "That was delicious."

He blinked at her slowly and broke his gaze away from hers to stare at the river, his ice cream melting over his fingers. "Anytime."

—

So…
Evil Alex might not be evil

Shocking. Why?

An apology. For his dickishness
in uni.

That wasn't an "I'm sorry you feel that way" apology

Like an actual "I was a dick and you didn't deserve that" apology

There are real human men who know how to do that?

Not sure if he's human yet

So when you talked to him instead of leaning on a nearly decade old grudge, it turns out he's not a dick??

I didn't say he wasn't a dick. I just said he wasn't evil

Then he said they couldn't be doing this without me

Be still my ovaries

Still think he looks like a Viking had a baby with a lumberjack, then left the subsequent child to be raised in the forest by wolves

Wait is that a bad thing?

lmfao

PS his forearms say hi

A meme of a Victorian woman on a fainting couch popped up on her phone. Jill snickered as she switched her phone to silent and stashed it in her bag.

It was still early. The Humane Society wouldn't close for another hour and Daisy might have gotten lonely since Jill had seen her on the weekend. She didn't usually go in during the week, but she had time to stop at her apartment after work to change, and she wasn't hungry yet after her late-day ice cream. Plus, she'd be close to that Thai place Omar mentioned, so she could grab takeout on her way home.

Besides, it's not like she had other plans.

Jill stopped to chat with another volunteer at the front desk and made her way through to the dog enclosures where Travis was saying good night to the animals.

She looked over to Daisy's pen, not seeing anything from where she stood. "She wasn't adopted, was she?" she asked quickly.

"Nah. Just hiding."

Tucked into the corner, paws on either side of her nose, Daisy looked as if she hadn't budged since the weekend. Her amber eyes showed white at the corners as she tracked Jill's careful movements.

Jill chewed the corner of her lip and leaned back on her heels, arms hugging her knees. Daisy's food dish was full. "Is she not eating?"

"Not when nobody's near."

She wanted to do something, anything to help soothe the scared girl. "Can I leave a toy in her pen?" she asked, hoping Daisy would begin to recognize her scent and associate it with comfort.

Travis passed Jill a stuffed chew toy, and she made a show of petting it and speaking kindly to it. She placed it carefully in the pen, and Daisy didn't flinch when she opened the door.

That was good.

"Okay, Daisy, I'll see you in a couple of days. Good girl." She hoped someone at some time had called her a good girl. Or maybe it was better if they hadn't, and she could associate it with a safe person.

Jill followed Travis from the enclosure, leaving the dimmed lights on behind them.

"Is there something I can do?"

"She's gonna need some time. Sometimes you need to go slow to go fast."

Jill grimaced. Patience wasn't her strong suit, but she had to go at Daisy's pace, not her own. She had told Daisy they could take their time.

It was so much easier to give advice than take it.

—

The mouth-watering scent of Thai red curry already infused her kitchen. She added the takeout receipt to the growing pile on her counter, wincing as she mentally tallied the week's expenses.

I can't keep doing this. Meal planning starts tomorrow, she thought, preventing the promise from fleeing her brain before the curry could hijack her motivation. She scooped the last grains of rice from the takeout container and peeked in her empty fridge.

Note to self: look up how to meal plan.

A dozen easy recipes on Pinterest later, her phone rang in her hand, and she winced when she saw the name on the caller ID blocking the screen.

Crap. She couldn't let another call go to voicemail.

How should she answer? Excited? No. Affectionate? Not their style. Tired? True, but that would lead to questions. Steeling herself, she tapped the green accept button.

"Hi, Mom," she said, landing somewhere between subdued and polite.

Cold, but truthful.

"Jillian dear, so good to finally talk to you," her mother's simpering tone seeped from across the country. "I thought you had forgotten about me."

One hand clutched the phone to her ear, fingers digging into her temple, the other hand gripping her chair. "It's good to talk to you, too. I just got home. What's up?"

Her mother proceeded to recite the events cataloguing her friends' lives. Or rather, which of her friends' children were getting promotions, getting married, and having babies. All the things Jill should be doing, and one out of three wasn't good enough. Jill made all the appropriate affirming noises in the right spots. Familiar guilt swirled in her stomach, for not living up to her mother's impossible standards, and for wanting the call to end already.

"You know, I had coffee with Deborah on the weekend," her mother said, and Jill's guilt froze into something altogether different.

Deborah. Her mother's best friend. Connor's mother. Who had, without a doubt, enabled—or at the very least, ignored—her son's awful behaviour.

"Oh?" she replied, voice sounding hollow, even to her own ears.

"Connor really misses you. He hasn't been the same. I know you two aren't on the best of terms, but you should call and check in on him."

It was barely a suggestion.

And that would mean unblocking his number. Conceding any ground she had gained in setting her firm, no-contact boundaries. His words piercing her armour like a knife.

"Mmm," said Jill, willing her tone to remain neutral. "Hey, I'm starving." *You're a terrible daughter,* she thought, looking at the empty takeout container. "Thanks for the call. Tell Dad I said hi. Love you both."

Jill could picture the expression her mother was almost certainly making, a subtle twisting of her mouth, displeasure radiating through the call. Jill promised she'd call soon and hit end slightly faster than what could be interpreted as civil. She'd hear about that the next time she took her mother's call.

A wave of exhaustion hit her out of nowhere. She abandoned the meal planning list she hadn't yet started and put down her phone in defeat.

Thirty-four hundred kilometres between them wasn't nearly enough.

FIVE

"We've looked there already."

"What about the other drive?"

"Full of backups from last year."

"Are you sure?"

A pause. "No."

Jill and Alex were elbows deep, metaphorically in the network drives and physically in the filing cabinets. Their financials could generously be called a disaster. At least, she thought they were a disaster. She couldn't find corroborating backup information to confirm.

About three years ago, Alex and Nick had started CMR on the back of a napkin. Jill put fifty-fifty odds the napkin was either crammed into a records box with another pile of documents waiting to be shredded, or had been tossed out with something else incredibly important.

Today, they hunted for payment confirmation of a pending license renewal. Alex had entered the transaction into the wrong account, reversed using the right account, re-reversed with the wrong account, and then entered with the wrong total.

"Now you see why I don't let him near the books anymore?" Nick asked.

Alex sent a mildly offended look at Nick. "I'm sitting right here, you know."

Nick gave a shrug that Jill read as, *well, he brought it on himself.*

Jill silently agreed and hid a smile. "Okay, can you check the folder again and I'll start digging in the storage room?" she asked. "I think I saw a box from that month."

"Um, I reused lots of boxes when we moved from our old location," Alex said sheepishly. "Not sure how many I relabelled."

That was going to add hours—days, maybe—to their search. If it was there at all. She stared at him in silent bewilderment. "How? How did you get through a PhD?" she finally blurted.

"Slept his way through the dissertation committee," Nick deadpanned, without looking up from his screen. "Ow! What?" he asked when a flying pen struck him in the shoulder.

Jill snickered and turned to Alex to await the retort.

"Apologies for my colleague who was apparently raised in a barn." Alex prepared to launch another pen and narrowed his eyes without malice at Nick. "I refuse to acknowledge such slander and will point out that all of my lab and test results are in impeccable order."

"I'd report you to HR for abuse in the workplace, but we are HR, so…" Nick stood and unplugged his laptop. "I'm going to grab a coffee and set up at Rosso for a few hours."

Alex muttered something in French, just loud enough for Nick to hear, then added, "Bring me back a chocolate croissant?"

Nick extended a specific finger and slammed the door behind him, leaving them alone.

"Do I need to ask for a copy of your doctoral degree for this business case," she asked, smiling slyly, "or do you not know where that is either?"

A flush crept up Alex's neck. "In storage at my mom's house. Haven't bothered to take it to my place yet."

"I'll trust you on that." At least it was one less thing they'd need to look for. Jill eyed the storage closet with dismay. It might offer passage to another dimension. She'd been in there once, exiting dusty and empty-handed, but sure she had seen things that would be needed in future stages of the grant. Now knowing the boxes may be mislabelled, she dreaded to think of going through each one meticulously.

Nick had said the chaos would be fun. Odd he was never here when the fun was to be had.

"Okay, wish me luck," Jill said with stoic determination. "If I'm not out in two hours, send a search party."

Alex looked resigned. "Hang on, I'm coming."

A few weeks ago, she would have bristled, reading his sigh as exasperation with her. Now she knew he was making time to help her, even if it meant doing something he avoided. It felt … good. She ducked her head and ignored the flare under her ribs.

The storage closet was a reverse Tardis, apparently far smaller on the inside. Rickety metal shelves occupied most of the space with boxes stacked two deep, dustier even in the month that Jill had been in there last. Today was not a good pencil skirt day, but at least her lucky stilettos would give her the extra inches to peer higher on the shelves. Perhaps it was a better idea to dress down a little more for days at CMR. Alex and Nick wouldn't mind, she was sure. Nick occasionally wore more formal attire when meeting with prospective clients, but Alex rarely broke into office casual territory. Even today, Alex had on well-worn jeans, scuffed Blundstones, and a light blue cotton shirt. With, of course, the sleeves rolled up.

At least one of them was dressed for moving things, and it might be satisfying to order him around to get payback for the hours of fruitless searching they'd done. The thought of watching him follow her commands sent a ping zipping through her chest, and she turned her focus to the shelves.

"How on earth did you collect this much stuff in three years?" Jill murmured, struggling to budge the boxes behind the outward facing row.

He shifted beside her in the cramped space, angling the box so she could read the label. "It's not all ours. Some boxes were here when we leased the place, and we didn't get rid of the old stuff."

Jill turned to him, her jaw dropped in disbelief. How this man's brain worked was a complete mystery.

"It's not as bad as it sounds," he said hastily. "The banker's boxes aren't ours. Those are the old ones. Ours are all the light brown boxes." He looked hopefully at her.

She closed her eyes. "Is there any chance you may have repurposed their boxes for your records?" she asked evenly.

"Um …"

She exhaled quietly through her nose. "No problem. We can do this," she said out loud, and shifted into organization mode. "Okay. You start high, I'll start low. When you come across stuff that isn't yours, can you bring it into the office, and we can tag it for shredding?" She gestured at her skirt and heels, giving him what she hoped was an apologetic smile. "I won't be much help on moving boxes. I'm not dressed for heavy lifting."

His gaze followed her motion, then snapped his eyes to the shelves in front of him. "No, you are not." His voice came out tight, clearly annoyed at her. Nick had said he hated the office management side of their work and here she was, springing this mind-numbing chore on him, and getting him to do the grunt work.

"I'm sorry, I'm derailing your afternoon," she said, shaking her head. "You must have a million other things to do." The stacks of boxes suddenly looked mountainous.

"No," he said quickly. "Let's do this."

"Oh, thank god." Jill sagged in relief, and the grin Alex gave her turned into another surge of heat. She packed away the entirely unwelcome feeling and sank down to her heels to busy herself with the first box. She swallowed, working to free her throat. "I'll start here."

Alex pawed through the boxes on the top shelves, moving some, dragging a few out to the main office, and Jill stood to relieve the pressure from squatting so long. She stared out into the main office, watching his shirt strain against his thick arms and broad back, maneuvering the heavy boxes like they were stuffed with feathers. Her pulse increased and she felt her breathing speed up.

She must have stood up too fast. That was all. She dipped her head and closed her eyes, hands on hips.

Recentre. Inhale slowly, exhale deeply. Repeat.

"Not in that one."

Alex's deep voice was right beside her, and she jumped with a yelp. His sleeve brushed against her bare arm as he reached for the next box, and the heat came flooding back.

Alex's lips curled in a half smile. "Maybe I'm the one who needs a bell. You okay?"

"Ha!" Jill said, fanning herself with her hands. "Yep, fine." Totally fine. She shone a bright smile up at him to prove how totally fine she was. He ducked his head and grabbed another box.

Good. The sooner they got through this, the better.

The storage space slowly gave up its hoard, mostly trash with enough treasure to keep it interesting. Jill dug to the back of an untouched shelf, shimmying a box forward. The faded label showed the right date … "Hey, I think we have a winner," she said, unbalancing as she spun to call him over.

Alex turned at the same time, and the narrow space between them dissolved. A shiver raced across her skin where the solid warmth of his body pressed flush against hers. Her hand caught against his chest, fingertips counting his heartbeats each second they pressed together. His palm pressed to her waist, steadying her, and she felt his fingers grip her slightly. Her lungs stopped working, and she slowly lifted her eyes to meet his.

Alex stared at her, expression unreadable. He blinked twice. Slowly.

"Ah, sorry," he said, the vibration of his voice rumbling through her fingers and up her arm. His words stirred the hair by her ear, goosebumps travelling down her neck to battle her rising heat. He shifted away as much as the confined space would allow and Jill willed her hand down to her side.

His hand was gone from her waist. "Let me get that." He pulled the box from the shelf and exited the tiny room, leaving a cold space in his wake.

Jill stood, mute. Her fingertips and waist still glowed from his touch. She drew a shaky breath and exhaled slowly.

Lather, rinse, repeat.

She should go back to her workspace, casually smash her forehead into her laptop, and snap out of whatever this was. Maybe not.

She rubbed her hands up and down her bare arms. Okay, she should say something. *How weird was that?* No, too awkward. *Sorry, remembered a quick errand … be back in a month!* Ugh, no, deadlines and professionalism and all that.

"Jill?" he called quietly from the other room.

I'll just join my client and have a completely clever and graceful conversation. Everything is completely normal. Absolutely nothing weird. Straightening her posture, she convinced her feet to move her out of the storage closet.

"You were right." He looked down into the open box in front of him, transaction copy in his hand. A faded receipt, smaller than her phone. All this trouble for one flimsy piece of paper.

"You found it."

"No, you found it." He cleared his throat and turned, looking at the chaos of the office. "I'm sorry for this mess," he said. "We've been so busy for so long. I mean, I'm not complaining. I'm glad being too busy is our problem, rather than the other way. This just wasn't a priority."

Jill shrugged. "Don't worry, I've seen worse."

"Really?"

One precariously stacked box slowly slid off the desk and exploded its contents across the floor.

Thanks, universe, for the assist in making my point. She covered her grin behind her knuckles. "Actually, this might be the worst."

Alex smiled down into his crossed arms. "You planned that."

"My powers are mighty," she agreed. Then added, seriously, "If, when, this becomes a priority, I can help."

The look he gave her was slightly less stubborn than before. More progress.

Taking great care to avoid touching him, Jill plucked the single sheet of paper from his grasp. "I'll add this to the application file."

She wound her way back to her workstation then, putting up walls around her brain to block out the past five minutes in which nothing weird happened, tracked, filed, and checked the box. Nothing like sinking into a good list to take her mind off things. She stared at the cursor flashing on her monitor.

Why wasn't it taking her mind off things?

Footsteps stopped in the doorway, Nick opening and closing his mouth like a fish, a bag holding presumably a chocolate croissant clutched in one hand. "What did you do to the office?"

—

Sooo the single worst thing that has ever happened to anyone happened to me today

Worse than when I sent nudes to a co-worker instead of my fuckboy?

Okay maybe not that bad

Jill paused, fingers hovering over her phone. What exactly had happened? She accidentally bumped into her client? Offices are small. Things like that happen all the time. But practically embracing, touching, not inappropriately, but … intimately … with every molecule between them charged. The same heat rose up her neck as the scene replayed itself for the hundredth time that hour, and she exhaled through pursed lips to collect herself.

A close-ish encounter with not-so-evil-Alex in a storage closet

Spill

She put down her phone and paced her living room, fanning herself with her hands. It had been hours ago. She hadn't gotten anything done for the rest of the day. Going back to hunt in the closet was out of the question. Instead, they had both stayed glued to their desks, silent. Nick made a few brief attempts at conversation but gave up with Alex's one-word replies and Jill's polite but hardly more extensive answers. She'd left as early as she could, murmuring she'd see them next week.

She tapped out what she hoped was a suitably casual reply.

Tight space. No room to move. Just a bit of full frontal body contact.

There were hands.

And eye contact.

Well that sounds hot as fuck

Jill resumed her pacing. It was mortifying. It was awkward. Heat prickled under her skin even thinking about it.

I guarantee you it was not hot. This is a client who was completely pissed I gave him a bunch of extra work.

Then I made him move stuff all afternoon and we made a mess

So he was following your every
command? You made a mess?
Hot

I can't tell you anything

Tell me more about the hands
Where were they

Shut up

Love you!

Any sense of order around the Calgary climate eluded her. The city blended clouded skies, concrete towers, and dusty sidewalks into a wash of greyscale, but a green haze in the branches swaying overhead hinted at a lushness days away. Tightly closed buds of white, pink, and purple promised a riot of colour to accompany the new leaves. Even in the middle of May, she had left her apartment that morning wearing one of her old Toronto spring uniforms, but the wind cut through everything she wore, necessitating a full clothing swap, and she went home to change before she had made it halfway down the block.

Good thing, too. The morning chill hadn't broken by the time they were getting lunch. She and Omar grabbed wraps from the Halal food truck and marched to the Blackburn office break room for their weekly debrief.

Ashleen and Marco wandered the halls and Jill pulled them into the break room to join her and Omar. They sat like owls, all wide eyes and turning heads, uttering the occasional "who?" when Jill or Omar dropped a name. Sure, they were new in their careers, but she was only a year older than Ashleen and a few years younger than

Marco. She added getting them to break out of their shells to her to-do list.

"They must have had a competition to see how randomly they could store things. I think last week almost convinced them they need to get their work in order." The memory of the awkward moment with Alex in the closet jumped into her mind again, as it had so many times over the last week, and she hoped the flush creeping up her neck didn't get past her collar. Omar might be a little too interested in hearing about the storage closet. "I need to leave the heels at home if we're going to dig in."

"They don't have you moving things, do they?" Omar asked, brows furrowing. "You're not a grunt for hire."

"I'm happy to help. And besides, I'll be glad to get off my butt and move around a little more." And burn off some of the nervous tension that always built up when she was there. She turned to her quiet protégés. "How are things coming with the McGregor account?"

Marco and Ashleen exchanged a look. "What do you do when the balance sheet doesn't balance?" asked Ashleen.

Jill grinned. "If the balance sheet doesn't balance, it's just a sheet," she said, repeating a quip her mentor had passed to her and they snickered at the height of accounting humour. "First, backtrack and find the error. Also—one of my favourite parts—sit down with the owner and learn about their business. See if you can do a site visit. You'll be amazed at what comes up when you see the work in action."

Honestly, that might be a good idea for herself. She had locked down so much of the grant outline, but there were a few missing pieces to complete the work. Nick would surely be willing to help with the details, but she doubted Alex would want to put himself in another situation like last week. The thought of more time with him in close proximity made her stomach give a disconcerting squirm.

She would put that off as long as possible. Preferably until the end of time.

SIX

The city must have been holding its breath, waiting for the May long weekend to pass. The weekend itself was a snowy mess, which Omar said was Calgary's traditional last screw-you from winter for people making outdoor plans. Then the next day erupted into a rush of spring and the city transformed. While the cherry blossom season in Toronto was beautiful, it was short. Calgary bloomed in synchronized waves of crabapple and hawthorn and rowan and lilac over weeks that shaded from fuchsia to pink, white to purple, perfuming her morning runs and lunchtime walks. Even from her apartment window, she could see the river had risen dramatically over the past several days. Photos from a few years ago had shown her neighbourhood under water, but Ashleen assured her that the river levels always rose this time of year and it probably wouldn't flood again. Probably.

Jill pulled into the Humane Society parking lot later than her usual time, checking in quickly with the front desk and making a beeline for Daisy's pen. The dogs started barking as soon as her footsteps sounded on the floor. She paused and gave them each a greeting as she made her way down the line, a scritch through the enclosure's wires for the dogs that were safe to touch and a calm word for the ones who needed more space.

Daisy was in her usual position, crouched on her belly, paws framing her nose, but as Jill came into view, the nervous dog's ears twitched up, and … did it? Yes, the tip of her tail gave the tiniest of wags. Jill's heart leapt, and she resisted the urge to swoop in for cuddles, instead sinking down in front of the enclosure. Daisy flexed her paws, stretching forward, and Jill cooed in reply.

Travis walked by, his hands thrust in his pockets and smiling from under his moustache. "I think she's been waiting for you."

"That's because she's a good girl who knows her friends," Jill said matter-of-factly, smiling at Daisy. She turned to Travis. "What do you need me to do today?"

Travis sent her to help Rachel, one of the other volunteers, clean out the cat area. They spent the next hour dodging errant paws and giving chin scratches between wiping out litter boxes, Jill listening to stories about Rachel's MBA project and Rachel listening to stories of CMR. Cleaning duty was never Jill's favourite work, but the staff were so appreciative of the time it freed for them to focus on other things. More importantly, the animals were more comfortable, and it gave her time to visit them all. Not a fun task, but a great outcome.

She dropped her rag. That was it. Focus on outcomes. That was how she could approach the audit with Alex again. Jill attacked the remaining feline crates with renewed energy, already planning how to approach the conversation one last time. If he didn't bite, she'd drop the issue. It was their business, and they didn't have to take her recommendations … whether or not she was right.

After a last sweep of the area, she made her way back to say goodbye to Daisy. On cue, her ears perked as Jill entered the room, but she hung back seeing Travis showing around a young family. The parents crouched in front of a pen of a young border collie, a little boy blowing raspberries at the dog and receiving a mouthful of kisses in return. On the other side of the room, Daisy's brows twitched as she looked from the boisterous boy to Jill.

The border collie had been at the shelter for a week, but him finding a family quickly wasn't in doubt. Smaller, younger dogs often found homes faster than the bigger dogs. Especially bigger, pit bull mixes.

She lowered herself in front of Daisy's pen, the room quiet once again, and the tip of Daisy's tail gave another tentative wag. Jill turned to check the clock behind her, then stopped herself. Why was she checking? She didn't have anything else to do today. She silently chided herself. She had been here for three months and had made no effort to make friends in her temporary city. She wasn't sure she knew how anymore.

It had happened without her noticing. Connor, isolating her from her friends. Restricting her social life to orbit his. Making her friends inconsequential, then an inconvenience, and suddenly, there had been no one left in the city that had been her friend alone. Now, finally away from him, she was free to. She thought of the remaining length of her contract. It would be awfully lonely without some social life.

"Well, Daisy, you'll still be top of my list," Jill promised. She hesitated, then opened Daisy's pen. She had moved glacially with Daisy over the last several weeks, leaving treats and sharing lots of soft words, but not making any moves to reach out. But now Daisy stretched to the open door, nose snuffling by Jill's fingers. Carefully, slowly, Jill rubbed under Daisy's chin, and the dog who had cried with nerves in the corner for weeks gave her a whine of happiness.

Several minutes later, Jill walked back through to the feline pens. "Hey, Rachel, I'm heading to Mission for a coffee. Want to join me?"

—

Jill had a new routine. Every morning, she opened the weather app on her phone to see what season she was walking into.

Saturday had been a textbook spring day. Brilliant blue, cloudless sky, with a temperate breeze rustling new leaves. Coffee with Rachel had been a great idea. The hours on the coffee shop's patio sped by and left them both slightly sunburned and over-caffeinated. Jill realized how much she missed having the carefree conversations of her own friendships, not monitored by Connor.

Now two days later, even with the calendar assuring her it was the last week of May, she huddled in the CMR office, shoulders wrapped in a chunky knitted sweater and fingers clutching a chai latte. Overnight rain had slowed to a drizzle by morning but the cold clung to her bones, despite her fortifications of wool, instant oatmeal, and spiced tea.

Nick's demeanour only added to the chill in the air. Despite his earlier assurances working in chaos would be fun, he had quickly turned sour when the actual work got underway. He disappeared, pouted, or dragged his feet, every time she asked for anything. Jill was forcefully reminded of the people in her university study groups who claimed to thrive under pressure. Invariably, they didn't.

Instead, Alex had stepped up. The man who had initially resisted hiring a consultant, who didn't want to get involved with the non-technical side of their work. From information to late nights, Alex had been there, giving her everything she needed.

A disconcerting glow filled her whenever she thought of it.

Today's task was compiling financials. Not fun, but not onerous, either. It was like she'd suggested he get a root canal. Nick sat across the room and glowered at the list Jill had emailed him.

"It shouldn't take too long." She and Alex had done the hard part already, digging up all the prior years' documents. Hours of tracking down scattered tax records and cobbling together the full picture from disparate spreadsheets. Still, Alex had worked steadily beside her without so much as a tired glance.

His eyes flicked up, then back to the list. "Are you sure we need this now?"

The grant checklist is right in front of me. Do you think I'm lying to you? She cleared her expression. "Yes, this is everything we need for this phase. We don't need commercialization plans until the VC proposal, so I've excluded that from our current work list."

"Isn't this what we are paying you for?"

She blanched at the unexpected rancour in his tone. "I'm putting together your funding application," Jill said, keeping her tone level. "I don't have system access. You need to run these reports to complete it."

"Fine. I'll get it to you by end of day."

"Thank you. Send me the reports as you generate them." She forced a smile. "We're almost there."

And they couldn't afford to waste time.

Jill turned back to her screen. Now what? She had blocked her entire day to build the budget. She fiddled with the mouse. Nick had been the one to push for the consultant. Maybe he was the one who needed the handholding, not Alex after all. An image of her sliding her hand into Alex's flashed in her mind, and her stomach fluttered.

"How can I help?" she chirped, trying to shove the mental image away. "I can't run these reports for you, but we can work through these together."

Nick drummed his fingers on his desk. "Sure," he said, after a moment's pause. "Come here."

Jill bristled at the order but crossed to his desk. No sense in quibbling over politeness with deadlines looming. She pulled up her chair and focused on the shared screen.

Nick's humour slowly improved as the to-do list shortened and the completed items grew. He fiddled with a couple of the reports, constraining some time frames, but those would need updating before she drafted the proposal for the investors, anyway. She let it slide and instead hammered through the remaining items.

She glanced at the clock. Alex was usually in the office by now. Tomorrow was his field day. Nick usually took their client meetings, so he wouldn't be with clients. Maybe he was at the lab running tests?

"Earth to Jill?"

Jill jumped and turned to Nick. “What? Sorry. Where are we?”

“That’s the last one.” He dropped a sheet in front of her and pointed at the file saved to the folder. Nick’s sudden mood swing gave her whiplash, his most winsome demeanour on display and smiling at her as if he had known all along it would be an easy task.

Jill blew out a breath. The last hour and a half had been exhausting, but worth it. She gathered the completed file, the budget section waiting for her to dive in. She considered making a joke about how it wasn’t as bad as he had made it out to be but decided against it. Sour Nick might make another appearance.

“Perfect.” She waved the file, determined to keep up her energy. “We’re in the home stretch now.”

“Home stretch? Are we winning?” Alex filled the door frame, a box tucked under one arm. Stray raindrops clung to his hair, a few auburn locks falling across his forehead. He nodded at Nick as he crossed the room and sent Jill a smile that sent a rush sweeping through her.

She clutched the folder tight to her chest, unsure if it was wise to risk the walk back to her desk with her knees as loose as they suddenly were. “It’s still raining,” Jill bit her lip, mentally cursing her lame observation.

“A bit.” He lowered the box, straightening the edge so it aligned with the corner of his desk. “Reran some sample sets this morning. Didn’t notice until I left the lab.”

Nick tilted onto the back legs of his chair, lacing his fingers behind his head. “Well, while you were playing with your test tube, Jill babysat me all morning. Totally kicked my ass.”

Well, at least he admitted he’d been difficult about it.

“You missed all the fun,” Nick drawled, and continued in rapid French that ended with a grin that strayed into smarminess.

Oh, so now it was fun? Didn’t seem like it an hour ago. Not having gone past high school French almost a decade earlier, Jill couldn't follow anything more than a few words, but whatever he'd said made Alex noticeably tenser than he had been a moment ago.

"Oh?" he said, and Nick deflected the dagger-eyes aimed at him with a wide grin.

Why Nick wanted to rile him up was beyond her. "Last reports for the grant ready to go."

Alex pumped the air with his fist.

"Home stretch, not finish line," Jill reminded him, not trying to contain her smile. "I still have to put it together, then we need to do final reviews."

Fortunately, Alex's reaction to more work was far more positive than Nick's had been. "Alright, let's go." He grinned easily at her, running his fingers through his damp hair, and the weakness in her knees returned.

Nick put on his jacket and announced he was picking up sushi. After getting their orders—spicy tuna sashimi and dynamite rolls for Jill and a double bento box for Alex—he left the two, promising a quick return.

She focused on the files spread out before her and considered where to begin. It was her first grant, but it wasn't her first consult. With the federal application nearly complete, the work of the proposal for the venture capitalist loomed ahead. Nick had dragged his feet when she asked for the commercialization plans. It probably hadn't been done yet. There was one surefire way to make the second half of her time with CMR better, and neither Alex nor Nick was going to like it.

No time like the present to bring it up.

"So, it's been challenging to get some of the work I need out of Nick. He talks like he is all on board with the work, but when it comes to doing it …" No, too personal. She paused, unsure of exactly how to say it. She left the comment dangling and switched to a new approach. "We could have months between when we submit the grant application and when we hear from the feds."

Alex narrowed his eyes at her, clearly predicting where she was going.

"We can use that time to put everything in order. Once you have proper systems in place, it'll save Nick from doing work he hates, you won't need to worry about anything important going missing …"

From the flush that crept up his neck, she wondered if their hunt in the storage room crossed his mind. The memory of his hand gripping her waist had dominated her thoughts ever since, no matter how hard she tried to shove it in a box.

"And a process audit will get us there."

Jill nodded her head firmly. "From what you've told me about your new tech, CMR is going to get big, and you'll need to have more than you and Nick. It will be far easier to bring new staff on board, and in the meantime, you'll benefit from improved processes." She caught his gaze and held it. "It's a smart play."

Convincing clients usually made her excited, but the rate her pulse had increased was much higher than what could be attributed to her love of workflow and task management, and she trapped her shaking hands between her knees.

Alex exhaled forcefully, a pained look on his face. "Do you have any idea how much I hate that kind of stuff?"

The bubble of tension popped, and Jill burst out laughing. "Yes, Alex, I've been working with you for three months. I know exactly how much you hate that kind of stuff." She grinned with growing excitement. "But I love that kind of stuff. I promise it will only hurt a little."

He huffed out a laugh. "I'll hold you to that." He scrubbed a hand over his chin and snuck a sideways glance at her. "You knew I'd get on board with this eventually, didn't you?"

"If not now, it would have been soon." She quirked her lips in a smile that was maybe a little smug. "I'm tenacious."

"Oh, really?" he said in mock surprise.

She pointed at herself. "Only child. I told you I'm used to getting my way."

"I'll remember that."

Jill smiled, equal parts satisfied and relieved. "When do you want to run it by Nick?"

"Today, but let's get some food in him first. I'll bring it up after lunch."

Jill didn't think Nick's mood swings had been a case of the hangries, but she was inclined to stack the odds in her favour.

Twenty minutes later, Nick strolled in with provisions and the three descended on their meals. The two men discussed a few client files and Jill kept her head down, steadily working her way through her sashimi. Finally, after Alex speared a last piece of katsu pork, he put the idea of an audit in front of Nick. He remembered all the points she had brought up, even from their first conversation. A few times, he looked to her for confirmation on a specific point, but she had the feeling it was so she could speak to the more appealing outcomes of the work.

He trusted her opinion. He was completely in her corner. A rush of warmth flowed through her.

Nick, not so much. "Is this just a way to bill us more?"

Jill was used to direct questions from clients, but Nick's shit today was piling a little too high. "If you put my recommendations in place, you'll make it back by the end of the year." She stood to leave. "Why don't I let you two discuss in private?"

"No. You've got a lot to do this afternoon, and we're on a deadline."

"We've all got a lot to do, Nick," said Alex, brows drawing close. "Jill's brought forward a great idea. I think we should do it."

"So, we're going to fall over ourselves to do what she says?"

What? Since when were recommendations orders? Sure, she'd been persistent, but this was the first Nick had heard of them. She sat, nonplussed at his outburst.

Alex barked out a short stream of French Jill couldn't follow.

"Ah, you're right." Nick rubbed his face with both hands. "Sorry if you were offended." He let the front legs of the chair hit the floor with a bang. "Well, it sounds like you two have a make-work project. Keep me posted. I have to meet with a potential client this afternoon and make us some money."

"Nick—"

He strode out the door, calling over his shoulder, "She's all yours!"

Footsteps faded, a door slammed, and Jill and Alex were left looking at each other.

"That was extremely uncool." Alex frowned at the empty doorway, sounding as perplexed as Jill felt. "I'll talk to him."

She would have asked if Nick's mood swings were common, but from Alex's reaction, it sounded like this was unusual. But after all the time she'd spent dragging work out of him, she was rapidly running out of any benefit of doubt she was willing to give.

—

Jill flopped onto her couch and tucked her feet under a blanket, her mind seesawing. Alex agreed to the audit, and convinced Nick they should do it. But Nick was acting even grumpier. Alex respected her ideas. Nick disappeared more and more during the day. She'd get to keep working with Alex longer. Side by side, hours at a time, to—

Jill bounced up to lap her living room. She needed a distraction.

It would be late in Montreal, but her friend would almost certainly still up. Sure enough, her call connected halfway through the second ring. Sophie sang the opening bars of her ringtone to her in greeting and Jill joined for the last lines.

"It's been three days since you've called me," Sophie scolded playfully.

"Just trying to make you miss me."

"Well, it worked. Guess who's coming to Calgary?"

Jill squealed and did a little dance in her seat. "Ah, *ma poulette!* When?"

"Two weeks. My boss was scheduled to go to the Canadian Women in Marketing Conference, but when I found out it was in Calgary, I convinced her to give me her seat. Conference ends Friday, and I booked my return flight late Sunday so we can spend the weekend together!"

It had been ages since they'd seen each other. Jill had driven to Montreal for Sophie's twenty-fifth birthday, and with Kyle flying up from Boston, the three of them spent a raucous weekend full of laughter and inside jokes. Jill had felt easy and free and whole for the first time she'd left university.

At least, when she wasn't thinking about dealing with Connor when she got home.

Sure enough, he had sulked for weeks after she got home, moping around their apartment, complaining about everything from her missing his friend's housewarming party to the weekend being a waste of money. He had been furious that she had shared a hotel room with Kyle, even though Sophie had been in the room with them, and never mind that she and Kyle had slept in the same bed a hundred nights in university with nothing but friendship between them. She stopped texting Kyle, and never went back for another visit. When Sophie tried to come to visit her in Toronto, Jill knew Connor would throw a fit. She couldn't dredge up the strength to deal with it, so she had made an excuse that she was too busy with work and wouldn't have time, feeling like she was going to throw up the entire time she lied to her friend.

But now she didn't have to manage Connor's tantrums.

Jill thought she might cry in relief.

She added the dates in her calendar app as soon as they hung up and sighed with happiness. She was going to see her favourite person in two weeks. She couldn't wait.

Plus, it didn't hurt that now she had something to look forward to and keep her mind busy. Two weeks would fly by.

So long as nothing else happened before then, everything could keep going according to plan.

SEVEN

"Are you sure?"

"Yes. We're ready."

"We have everything?"

Jill smiled. "Everything."

Silence.

"Did we … I mean …"

"I'm positive."

"Wait, we should check one more time."

"Fuck, if you don't do it, I will." Nick pushed back from the desk, nervous energy radiating out of every pore. "Hit submit."

"We have all the attachments." Jill kept her voice calm. Reassuring. "We've checked that we have every file. Twice." She resisted the urge to rest her fingers on his arm, to pass a bit of her confidence to him. "But if you want, we can check again."

Alex rocked to his feet. Now both men paced the office, Alex swinging his arms and Nick cracking his knuckles, floorboards creaking and groaning in a staccato rhythm.

If there hadn't been so much on the line for Alex, Jill would have thought it funny. Cute, even. In a purely platonic way. The hours they had put in, the late nights poring over a single sentence, the entirely too many sushi runs. Putting their heads together and figuring out problems. The last months had been amazing. Fun. And, well, Nick was fine.

So much had gone into this moment. Nick had submitted for other, larger grants in the past, but it didn't matter, because every one had been declined. The grants weren't the right fit. Jill had scoured the options until she found the perfect grant. Not the biggest, but the best. She had put all their years of work together into a neat, professional, and—hopefully—persuasive package to convince the federal government to grant them up to two and a half million dollars.

Two and a half million dollars. This, no matter the outcome, would change their future.

Either they'd get the grant, and they could pursue developing a revolutionary technology that could advance the field overnight, or they'd continue taking certification sign-offs and one-off contracts that would have Alex driving all over the province. And a potential solution to an existential environmental problem would sit on the shelf, unproven. At least, until they ran out of money. CMR barely broke even. Sure, there might be other grant opportunities, but this one was perfect. The timing, the scope, everything. This was their best shot.

The application closed in three days. They had time. If the men needed to work out a bit of tension first, five more minutes wasn't going to hurt. Nick wore a groove in the space between their desks as Alex lapped the perimeter of the room. Jill waited, almost patiently.

The website was loaded. Files attached, ready to go. Alex took one more lap around the room and dropped heavily into the chair beside her, pressing his fist tight to his mouth.

"Okay. Do it."

"It's your work," she said, and nudged the mouse towards him. "It should be you."

A maelstrom of emotions swirled on his face, eyes wide and fixed on the screen. She wanted to pull his fist away from his mouth, unclench his fingers and put his open palm to the mouse. Instead, she bumped his shoulder with her own, and he looked down at where their shoulders touched.

"I haven't been this nervous since I defended my dissertation."

Jill pressed her lips together to hide her grin. "Was it because you slept with everyone on the committee?"

Nick stopped in his tracks and bent over laughing so hard Jill thought he'd give himself a hernia, and Alex let out his own strangled laugh.

"God, I hope you know he was kidding." With a glance to his friend, then to her, he clicked submit, and slumped forward onto the desk with his head buried in his forearms.

Nick blew out a breath and bounced on the balls of his feet. "Okay. What now?" He ran a hand over his face, staring at the back of the monitor like he could see into the interwebs to watch the submission en route to Ottawa.

"Now we wait."

"Can't wait." Alex's muffled voice came from the mound of arms and shoulders beside her.

"You can." Jill stood, pushing her chair under the desk. "Applications close in three days, so they'll be reviewing soon. We might even find out by the end of August."

More muffled groaning.

"So, now we ..." Nick trailed off.

"Take a couple days off," Jill finished, gathering her things. "You don't have clients until Monday. It's good timing."

Nick found one last uncracked knuckle. "You don't need to monitor our schedules. We're not that hopeless."

An entire backlog of unentered forms begged to differ.

"You guys are kind of hopeless. But seriously, you'll need energy when that grant comes through. Take a break."

The shoulders beside her gave a lurch as Alex sat back, scrubbing his face with his hands and wearing a mildly anguished expression.

He looked surprised she was standing and glanced at her bag slung over her shoulder. "Are you leaving?"

There was something more behind the question in his voice that Jill couldn't place, but it caused a stir somewhere between her lungs. "I was going to head home?"

"Oh, sure."

Jill didn't miss his disappointment. He looked completely lost.

Oh, of course, he did. He had been working so hard for so long, he didn't know what to do with himself without a task in front of him.

She knew all about needing distractions. She could fix that.

"You know what? This was a big day. We should celebrate. Let's go eat in an actual restaurant instead of over our desks." She braced for a "no, thanks." He probably had a life outside of work. A girlfriend to spend time with. Not that it was any of her business. She crossed her arms over the flutter in stomach.

The anguished, wistful expression softened into tentative relief. "That sounds great."

Nick's head popped up from his phone. "Can't. I'm meeting Cass."

"Cass?" Alex looked surprised. "Didn't know you were still seeing her."

Nick looked like he had taken a bite out of a lemon. "I won't be, if I bail on her again."

Jill couldn't help the smile spreading across her face. "Looks like it's just me and you."

"Yeah," Alex said, his own smile mirroring her own. "Looks like."

"I know just the place."

—

She pulled him down a bricked back alley and through an unmarked door to a secluded patio, he obediently followed her every turn. Strings of lights draped overhead glowed faintly against the sun, plants winding their fronds along the wrought iron trellises. Muted traffic noises punctuated the strains of faint blues music floating by from a nearby pub. The deck held a half-dozen tables, all but one occupied with people enjoying happy hour glasses of wine and pints of beer. They settled into the last open spot, away from the chatty crowds enjoying a late spring afternoon away from work.

"How did you find this place?" Alex said, regaining his bearings and his remaining tension slowly looking like it was dissipating.

Jill shrugged, all nonchalance. "I have my sources."

Note to self: Thank Omar for bringing me on his never-ending quest to find all the best spots in town.

This most recent best spot in town had frosty beer and loaded nachos. Jill's malty amber ale was rich, almost sweet, and so smooth she promised herself to savour it slowly.

Alex didn't appear to have any interest in self-control. He closed his eyes and downed half his pint in one go, and she watched the muscles of his throat work as he tipped his head back.

"Sorry," he said with a gasp, wiping a smidge of foam from his lips. "I don't usually do that. I'm just ..."

Exhausted, drained, stressed ... "Thirsty?" Jill offered, and his shoulders lurched with suppressed laughter.

They both started their second pints as they got to the end of the nachos, and Jill ordered more food. Alex descended on the wings with the same gusto he had with the nachos. Sophie might have some competition in the chicken wing department.

Jill snuggled into the bar stool's plushly padded seat. "You're from here. And U of C has a great environmental sciences program. How did you end up at McGill?" she asked before shovelling the last guac-laden nacho into her face.

"My grandparents. My mom's family is from Montreal. They offered to pay for the first two years of all the grandkids' undergrads and gave us a place to live as long as we were at university. Only house rule was that we spoke French at home. And I figured, why not? I didn't have a better plan. Didn't even know what I wanted my major to be. Plus, my grandparents are amazing. Almost all of my cousins took them up on it. It's worked out well, except for two of my younger cousins who had to share a room when they started the same year, but they loved it."

Jill thought of her own small, loosely knit family. An uncle on her dad's side, two much older cousins that she had met a handful of times. She had always looked with envy at people's sprawling families. When her family would visit their cottage in the summer, she'd escape to the neighbours' cabins as soon as they arrived, spending the weekend with the herds of other kids, pretending they were her brothers, sisters, and long-lost cousins. She had thought she had gained that with Connor's family, with his two older brothers and nieces and nephews. None of whom she had seen since New Year's. Not that she wanted to, except for the kids, who she missed like crazy.

"That sounds amazing," she said wistfully.

"It really was." He paused. "I almost didn't make the requirements to get into McGill."

Jill feigned shock. "What? The brilliant Dr. Campbell? A lowly B plus student?"

He shrugged a shoulder. "I coasted through high school. All I cared about was hanging out with my friends and playing rugby. Anything that kept me outside. But once I got to university, everything clicked. I mean, once I was dialled into environmental sciences, the U of C was a lock. Turns out if I'm doing something I love, I'll put in the work."

"It's like the opposite of what we were told growing up. Not if you find a job you love, you'll never work a day in your life, but when you find it, you'll want to work harder than you ever have in your life."

"Exactly."

She spun her pint glass on the table, condensation leaving interlocking rings on the tablecloth. She had lived through one aspect of her life dominating everything. Then she had tried to bury herself in her work, and still found herself unfulfilled. Something missing. "But I don't know if that's true. At least, not for me," she said. "I don't want to only be my work. I want more than that."

His jaw tightened, nodding as if moving through water, before sitting back. "What about you? Why McGill?" he asked finally.

"Both my parents went there. That's where they met. It was part of their plan for me as long as I could remember. I had scholarships for two other universities, and I didn't even consider them." Her parents wouldn't have forgiven her. She kept her eyes firmly on the tablecloth, thinking back to planning her university course loads with her mom as early as her first year in high school, her extracurricular activities carefully curated to her best advantage.

"I wouldn't change it, though." She tipped her head. "It was amazing. All of it. And it was the most fun I ever had in my life."

"But it put you onto a career where you have to work with people like me," he said, grinning.

She huffed a smile, and she told him about her work, other clients, what she loved about it. The challenges, the problems she solved, the industries she learned. Sometimes it was a box-checking exercise, a governmental hoop to jump through. Other times she helped companies level up, turn around failing operations, enter new markets. Alex snickered when she shared the story of a retiring plumber trying to leave the business to his son, who hated—literally—getting his hands dirty and thwarted every attempt at his father's succession plan. Alex howled when she told him about a client who had been trying to start a black-market exotic pet import behind his fertilizer distribution company. When the owner's unsuspecting daughter had brought Jill through on a tour, they'd nearly been trampled by a herd of fluffy camelids.

"He had been so proud of his amazing deal, but the original buyer backed out when alpacas showed up instead of the vicuñas he thought he was ordering," Jill gasped, wiping her eyes. "I don't know if he was more embarrassed or furious when I reported him. Then I contacted my volunteer supervisor at the Humane Society. We didn't take the animals, but we placed the animals in refuges."

"You volunteered with the Humane Society?"

"Still do. Every Saturday."

"Of course, you do," he murmured.

"Yes," she said, a bit defensive. She wasn't sure if she needed to be indignant or not. Connor used to complain it cut into their time, that it was already on her resume, and she didn't need to do it anymore. That she should at least be spending that time doing a side hustle, like him, not giving away her time for free. Eventually, she said her work looked highly on volunteering to get him off her back, though he still tried to get her to move her shifts to times that were more convenient for him.

She stuck her chin out. "It's fun. Fulfilling."

"I think it's great. Why didn't you stay in Montreal for grad school?"

"I was accepted to York. My dad went there, and my mother—" didn't care where she went, as long as it was a good school. It wasn't chemistry, so it didn't count. "She wanted me closer to home."

Jill didn't mention it was to push her and Connor back together.

"I had great friends there. I miss them," she said instead.

"Do you keep in touch with anyone?"

"Just Sophie. She's still my best friend." Jill smiled down at her hands. "She was in the same chem class as me. She was a bit more forgiving with your teaching style."

"Must not have cared much about chem if she thought that was okay."

"You have no idea. The only chemistry in marketing is the metaphorical kind," Jill replied with a small laugh before she sobered. "The others? I mean, we swap texts on birthdays, Christmas sometimes, but … no, we don't keep in touch."

Her heart dropped as she thought of Kyle, her adopted big brother, her partner in crime. The one person she could gang up on Sophie with. Because Connor had argued over every phone call, every visit, every comment on a social media post. In the end, she hadn't been strong enough to fight him. It was a miracle she still had Sophie.

She shook herself. "How about you? What do you do when you aren't saving the environment?"

"Don't have a lot of time for much else than work."

Did that mean he was too busy for a girlfriend? Jill chugged the last of her beer to prevent herself from asking.

"I try to get to the gym a couple times a week, usually get there once," he continued. "Have dinner with my mom and sister's family once a month. Still play rugby, but all I do is pray we don't make the tournament playoffs and I have to skip a bunch of games and let my team down."

"Has that happened before?"

"Oh, no, we're terrible—" he paused while Jill stifled a snort of laughter "—but we might this year. I just play to see the guys, stay in some kind of shape." He let out a heavy sigh. "You know what you were saying before? About wanting to work hard?"

Jill nodded.

"I love this work, but I haven't taken my nephews swimming in three months. I can't keep working eighty hours a week. I need to pilot my research in the field. And we need the VC investment to make it happen."

"So, no pressure, right?" she said with a grin.

"Little bit of pressure." His eyes crinkled along the lines that were becoming increasingly familiar to her, and there was something different in the smile he gave her. "Might take me a while, but when I'm sure of something, I usually get what I want."

A tremor ran under her breastbone, and she gripped her empty pint glass. She half-held her breath as she squeaked out a high-pitched laugh. "Guess I'm not the only tenacious one?"

"Guess not," he said. "I've done what I can to make it happen, but everything is riding on this grant. For the first time, I'm feeling good about what we submitted. That's all thanks to you."

Jill broke her gaze and clasped her glass, heart knocking against her ribs.

Nothing. It was nothing. She was reading into something that wasn't there. He was talking about the grant. His research. That was it.

"Last call," the server said, passing by their table, and Jill jumped in surprise. The lazy afternoon sun had long dipped behind the buildings, the light breeze no longer carrying the heat it had hours ago.

"Shit! I mean, shoot! I'm sorry," she said. "I didn't mean to keep you so long."

"You didn't keep me. I needed this. I, ah, thanks for staying," he said. "Besides, it's good to be out before I hit the road."

"Oh, right. You're going away again." Jill felt a light pang of disappointment and quickly chalked it up to having to delay their work.

"Yeah, I'm due for a cycle at a few sites." His enthusiasm seemed to dim.

What had she told Ashleen and Marco? Learn about your client's work? This might be the perfect opportunity, and great timing before she started the audit. Even if it meant she'd be doing the opposite of what she said she'd do: avoid extended periods of time with him in tight spaces.

No problem. It would be fine.

"I've been thinking, I'd like to learn more about your operations. Could I … I mean, if it made sense … would you be able to show me some of your sites?"

Alex lit up, eyes widening. "Yes! I'm going through the eastern and southern sites. It's a full day of travel, but we'll stop lots and it's a gorgeous drive. I think you'd really like it." He looked into the middle distance as he worked through his plan, then added hastily, "If tomorrow works, I mean."

Tomorrow. Not a lot of time to prepare. Her mind flicked to the awkward tension from their close contact in the storage closet. And then whatever tonight was. Not that it was anything. Just a casual multi-hour dinner between coworkers. She wasn't sure a full day with Alex was safe, but she couldn't help but beam at his infectious excitement. "I can make tomorrow work. I'll clear my calendar."

"Great." He smiled at her. "I can't wait to show you what I do."

"I know what you do!"

"Not like this. I want to show you why it matters."

She stuck the last chicken wing in her mouth and signalled for the bill. "His treat tonight," she said to the server with a grin.

Alex took his card back and took a deep breath. "It's, ah, pretty late. Can I walk you home?"

Yes, that would be lovely. Jill frayed the edges of her napkin under the table. "Oh, no, that's okay. It's out of your way."

"Please let me order you an Uber, then?"

"Oh, um," she stammered. That knocking between her ribs was back, joined by a heat in her cheeks. "You don't have to—"

"It'll make me feel better if I know you get home safely," he said. "Please."

Of course. How many times had she checked in with Sophie to make sure she'd gotten home after a late night? That was something friends did. Maybe that's what she and Alex were, now. Friends.

The glow of friendship usually felt warm, not feverish.

"Okay, thanks." She tucked the feeling away and let a friend do something kind for her.

EIGHT

Most things woke her up easily. It had been like that for as long as she could remember. Night sounds, flickering lights. Her own busy brain. Everything made four straight hours of sleep a rare event.

Dorm life should have been hell, but after a lifetime of disrupted sleep, the chaos of living with a hundred other people barely made an impression. In second year, Sophie had raved about her cannabis sleep gummies and convinced Jill to try them. Once. The combined couch lock and paranoia left her frozen, staring at her dorm room ceiling all night, and she swore them off forever.

Her father thought she might grow out of it. First it was growing pains, then puberty, then the intensity of university. Didn't matter, he had assured her, it would pass.

When she moved in with Connor, he complained he could feel her lying awake, disrupting his own sleep. He bought noise cancelling headphones—for himself—and had blackout curtains hung in their room, saying it would be the best thing for her. While the darkened room certainly removed one potential disturbance, it always made her feel oddly disconnected from the outside. Invariably, she'd either huddle away from him in bed, or get up early anyway and sneak out of their bedroom to spend her mornings in the relative peace of the living room.

His mother had cornered her one Christmas and tried to send Jill home with a week of her temazepam. "It's fabulous," she'd raved, one hand gripping an elbow and the other gesturing with her third glass of Chardonnay. "Just try it."

"I'm not sure I should take something without a prescription," Jill had whispered, and the room went silent. On the way home, Connor had scolded her for disrespecting his mother and embarrassing herself.

Sleep that night had been worse than usual.

This morning, after a few fitful starts in the night, the much more pleasant early June sunrise eased her awake. She luxuriated in bed for a few extra minutes, the golden light filtering through the gauzy curtains while she waited for her alarm clock to go off. After a joint-popping stretch, several yawns, and one coffee later, she tucked herself at her kitchen island and logged into her laptop to clear her to-do list.

Update email to Omar - *sent*

Update email from Ashleen and Marco - *read*

Reply to the aforementioned update - *complete*

Useless meetings - *declined*

Important meetings - *rescheduled*

Final report to Angela on the Palliser file - *submitted*

Reorganizing her day to fit in the last-minute road trip – *done.*

An hour and a half later, she stepped out of the shower and stared at her closet. This was her first environmental site visit. She still had her steel-toed boots from her work with Elgern Logistics, but she didn't think those were necessary, pretty sure Alex would have told her if she needed protection on this trip.

Jill caught her bottom lip between her teeth. She could text him, but it was barely after seven. Besides, he wouldn't want to have a fashion conversation with her. What was he usually wearing when he came in from field days? A small rotation of fleece shirts and jeans, sturdy but not construction-rated footwear. Once he came in wearing a snowy white lab coat and a scowl. Later, he said it was only because clients were on the tour and Nick made him wear it. Jill privately thought it was a good look on him—the lab coat, not the scowl—but kept her mouth closed and buried her head in her work.

So, casual, workwear type stuff. Steel-toed boots weren't required, but neither were stilettos. Sitting in a car most of the day would mean comfortable, but not sloppy. These were field sites, so there weren't going to be other people she'd be meeting. It would be Alex and her. All day.

Don't overthink this. It's a site visit. No big deal.

Twenty minutes later, she had rolled up her jeans, slid into an old rec softball team jersey (Big Bunts emblazoned across her chest—the team Connor harangued her into quitting because her games conflicted with his family dinners), cotton jacket, and her Chelsea boots. Then stripped off her softball jersey, unsure if she wanted to invite Alex to check if her bunt really was as big as advertised (*also, note to self, look up softball leagues*). And not like mattered at all, but she had a fitted cornflower blue tee shirt that made her skin glow and eyes sparkle.

A text from Ashleen popped onto her phone as she pulled the tee shirt over her head.

Stop emailing before dawn! It
stresses me out

Sorry! I'm out of office all day and
wanted to get back to you.

Besides it was way after dawn :)

Haha don't worry we got this!

Yeah you do! See you tomorrow

Jill grinned as she slid her phone into her bag. Ashleen and Marco had gelled into a powerhouse team and were cruising through their file. She should include that in her performance review.

On the fast track for management, indeed.

It was still early. She was always early. The first in the CMR office in the mornings, with Nick showing up around eight and Alex stumbling in a couple hours after that. After a week of working with them, they had cut her an extra key, so she wasn't stuck on their schedule.

She checked the time again. There was time to walk to the office and still pick up coffees and breakfast. And if Alex still hadn't shown up, she could get a bit more work done while waiting.

Instead, when she walked up to the office ten minutes early, Alex had just parked, looking like his usual dishevelled morning self and unfolding from the most beat-up, lemon-yellow Volvo wagon she'd ever seen. He launched himself forward when he saw her, his sleepy eyes lighting up.

"Morning," she said cautiously. Her eyes flicked from him to the relic in front of her. "Is that safe for road trips?"

Alex patted the dented hood fondly. "Absolutely. Anni-frid has been around the province hundreds of times and across the country a dozen. She hit half a million kilometres a couple years ago."

That mileage didn't really ease her worry, but that wasn't what caught her attention. Jill raised her brows. "Anni-frid?"

"You know … the ABBA singer? Volvo, Swedish? My mom named her." Alex shoved his hands in his pockets. "It stuck."

Well, that was unexpectedly endearing. "I thought you'd be driving an electric car, or at least hybrid."

"One day. But I have student loans, and Anni-frid's still going strong."

"If you say so, I'll let you and Anni-frid give me the grand tour." Jill squinted into the vibrant morning sun and held out a chocolate croissant and coffee. "Two sugars, one cream," she said, and he accepted the offering of caffeine and sugar with a groan.

"Fanks," he said around a mouthful of croissant. "Jus' wo' up."

"I figured you'd need it."

Alex spread a map—an actual paper map, since cell coverage was choppy in the rural areas—over the hood of his car, rolled up his sleeves, and showed her the plan. The familiar scent of soap and pine reached her, and she found herself quietly inhaling as she leaned towards him to follow the route. He was in a version of his work site uniform: green plaid cotton shirt and worn denim, his scuffed Blundstones dwarfing her own boots. Peering at the map beside him, standing so close, she became acutely aware of the missing extra height of her stilettos. If she shifted a bit to the left, even as he leaned over the hood of the car, she could slide her shoulder comfortably under his arm.

"So, what do you think?" he asked, looking at her expectantly.

"What? Sorry, can you show me that again?"

He had them out at sites all day. First, east out to Drumheller, a stop on the way southeast to Redcliff, another stop on the way west to Foremost, through Lethbridge, the two more stops on the way to Pincher Creek, before heading northeast to home.

"Full day, about nine hundred kilometres—" so that's how Annifrid earned her miles "—and with our stops, we should get back into town just after dinner," he said.

There were circles and symbols inked across the province. Jill traced along their route before hiding her nail-bitten fingers into her fist. "You have contracts at all these sites?"

"Yep. Site audits. Some using current tech. Right now, we bid on pretty much anything. We're so new we can't really afford to be picky on location," he said, returning the map to the glove compartment. "We don't have licenses for the States yet … of course, you know that." He turned a lopsided smile on her that turned her belly liquid. "But we've got a bit of work in BC, and a couple of sites in Saskatchewan. We've grown a lot in three years."

Jill bit down the urge to say that they hadn't properly filed a document in those three years, but Alex caught her face and held up a finger.

"I don't know what you're going to say, but don't!"

"What? I wasn't going to say anything!" she said, all wide-eyed innocence.

"You're losing your game face," Alex said, looking down at her with a wry grin, and she found she didn't care much to hide behind it again.

"I'm collecting samples at a few sites, readings at others," he continued, throwing his jacket into the back seat. Boxes that looked like coolers—for samples, mostly likely—were strapped down with bungee cords in the wagon's cargo hold. Other than his jacket and a small duffel bag, the car was spotless.

At least his mobile office was organized.

Jill was opening the passenger door when Nick pulled up behind them, revving the engine of his shiny cherry red pickup. She slid her professional mask into place as he jumped down and sauntered towards them with his thousand-watt smile.

"Alex, my man, what are you doing up so early?"

Alex leaned on the door. "Bringing Jill around to see a few of our sites."

"When did you two plan that?" Nick's eyes flicked past Alex to where Jill stood.

"Um, last night?" Alex said.

Nick's smile showed every one of his teeth. "Well, that's a great idea. I'm sure Alex has a lot he'd like to show you."

The car heaved as Alex shifted his weight on its frame.

"Too bad I couldn't clear my calendar. I would have loved to come," Nick continued. "Maybe I'll give you the tour next time and Alex can take the clients."

"We have to get on the road," Alex said. "I'll give you site updates tomorrow."

Jill ducked into the safety of the car, releasing a quick breath. An entire day stuck on a tour with Nick? Not a tempting prospect. Not that spending the day with Alex was tempting. It was just for the operations tour. Purely educational. She swallowed that train of thought along with a bite of her blueberry muffin.

Alex dropped into the driver's seat and the engine coughed to life, compelling Jill to peek at him out of the corner of her eye. Nick knocked on Alex's window, still grinning widely, and Alex cranked down the glass.

"It's not too late to change your mind, Jill. My truck has air conditioning. And power everything."

"Can you please sign off on the grant checklist? I'll add it to my file tomorrow," Jill said through a terse smile, and Alex levelled a flat look at Nick as he cranked the window back up.

The streets had emptied from the morning rush, and they swept past industrial plants and into open farmland. Within an hour of leaving city limits, farmer's fields morphed into arid plateaus and rocky hoodoos, earth flowing from sand to ochre to rust in stark contrast to the vibrant azure sky and its smattering of fluffy little clouds. Then the car would hit a rise, plateaus would swallow valleys, and the world became a patchwork of shrubs and grasses.

The car slowed, the tires rolling over from the smooth hum of asphalt to the crunch of gravel. Alex navigated down a back road and pulled over on the unmarked stretch of dirt, hopping out of the car and popping the trunk.

"This used to be an old natural gas site. Pump jack used to be right over there." Alex pointed in the distance. "The towns are moving to renewables, wind mostly. I'm part of a panel that'll sign off on this site sometime next year."

"So, this isn't CMR work?"

"Nah, this just brings in cash. As P. Eng.'s, Nick and I can both sign off on external site remediation or investigate compliance. So no, it's not our tech, but it helps keep the lights on while we get started."

He recorded a few more readings, bagged and sealed the samples, all the while explaining the site and process. He dropped his hand to the back of her seat, twisting to look over his shoulder while reversing down the narrow road, and she shivered as she turned her eyes to track the landscape beside her.

Each site had its own story tied to the land. To the people who had worked and lived there. Who wanted to keep living there. Alex shared what each site had been, what it needed, how long it was going to take. To Jill's great relief, there was very little chemistry talk at all.

After Alex shut down her suggestion of sushi ("Not here. Trust me," he said gravely), they made a brief lunch stop at a hole-in-the-wall diner, then pulled up to a gas station in Medicine Hat. She got out and leaned on the door well while he refilled the dwindling tank.

The morning had been beautiful. Fascinating. The work that Jill had been coordinating began to fit into place, islands of information sliding together like tectonic plates forming new continents, and the VC proposal made so much more sense. She pushed a stray lock of hair away blown free of her ponytail, looked around the area, and started with recognition.

"Ooh! I know where we are! I stopped for gas here when I drove to Calgary!" She turned to Alex with inordinate pride in her discovery.

He looked at her, surprised. "How long have you been here?"

"For as long as I've known you, plus a week."

"You're brand new here? Have you been to any of the places we've driven through yet?"

She shook her head, ponytail sweeping past the collar of her jacket.

"Do you want to take a couple of detours? It's a long day, but …" He paused, "Unless you, ah, need to wrap up early. If you have plans tonight. Or a boyfriend to get home to." He studied the gas pump keypad in deep concentration, the lightest flush of red slowly creeping up his neck.

Her chest swooped with one of those rushes that were becoming decidedly less unexpected. "No, I don't. Have any of those things." She locked her gaze on a fascinating sign on the other side of the gas station, promising two for one windshield wiper fluid with every fill-up. "I'd love you to show me." Purely work related. Getting to know the area. Research.

Or something.

The day rolled by with the miles, villages and hamlets disappearing in the rear-view. The sun followed their progression west, occasionally obscured by voluminous pearly clouds stacking into the stratosphere. Badlands gave way to fields again, new corn reaching beyond the horizon's edge, and the mid-afternoon sun poured over her. She curled up like a kitten in a sunbeam. Alex had tuned the radio to some station playing a mix of classic hits—he had already apologized for the broken CD player, and the car didn't have an aux plug-in—and the soft music and road noise faded into a comfortable silence.

A sudden thump lurched Jill upright. The mountains stood a lot closer than they had a second ago. She blinked rapidly and looked sideways at him through her lashes.

"Did I fall asleep?" she asked, then hesitantly, "Did I snore?"

Alex smiled, not taking his eyes off the road. "Think I lost you about twenty minutes ago. And no, you didn't snore."

"Why didn't you wake me up?"

"Figured you needed it."

She smoothed her hair. "Sorry, I just—"

"Nothing to be sorry about. You didn't miss anything."

"Thanks." She always needed sleep, and hours on the road stretched ahead of them. Oddly, it didn't seem too long.

His hand rested casually on the top of the steering wheel, sunlight slanting through the side window, illuminating the hair on his arms in an auburn haze. He had freckles, just a few, she would have sworn hadn't been there a few weeks ago. Across the bridge of his nose, too, with a few more dusting the ridge of his cheekbones. Fine creases at the corner of his eyes and lips that deepened whenever he smiled at her. Tendons that rippled under his skin as he shifted his grip.

"Jill?"

"What?" she said, snapping out of her reverie.

"Fall back asleep with your eyes open?" he asked, a small smile on his lips.

Shit. She'd been staring, and that was the second time today she'd zoned out. Her sleep last night must have been worse than she'd thought. "I guess I'm still waking up. Did you ask me something?"

"You've been here three months. What brought you here?"

Jill shrunk into the worn seat. This could go a lot of different ways. She'd only ever talked to Sophie about it. "Short version or long version?"

Alex glanced at her with a curious, open expression. "Long version."

"I was looking for a fresh start. My firm offered me a transfer. For a year. Permanent if I like it." Jill hesitated, turning her water bottle over in her hands. "I had left a … not great relationship. I tried living with my parents as I got settled, but …" She sighed, her mother's passive-aggressive comments floating to the front of her mind. "I figured, the more space between us, the better."

His brows drew together. "Bad boyfriend?"

Here we go. "Can I be blunt?"

Alex nodded.

Jill stared at the ramshackle barn on the edge of the horizon. "He was manipulative, possessive, controlling, and I know lots of people have it worse. Much worse. But …" She took a steadying breath. "Remember when I told you about friends drifting away?"

"What happened?" A thundercloud settled over Alex's expression.

"He isolated me from almost everyone I cared about. I didn't even realize he was shrinking my world. All of a sudden, I didn't have anyone."

"Even your parents?"

She gave a grim laugh. "They love him. Still do."

A photo still hung in her parents' hallway. A snapshot taken at a friend's wedding the first year they had gotten back together after university. They looked like a stock photo of Happy Young Couple. Jill, in her flowing afternoon tea dress, hair long and loose over her shoulder, and Connor with his crisp grey suit and looming posture, dominating the photo. Looking back years later, that wasn't her real smile. She had still been trying so hard to please him, to please her family. When they got home from the wedding, Connor complained about the food, how people were dressed, how tacky the decorations were. How her dress made her look sloppy. When she moved back with her parents after leaving him, she had begged them to take the photo down. They brushed her off. She looked so pretty, and why would she want to forget how good things could be? That didn't help assuage the guilt and regret that faded memories of better times had been the only things she had clung to for so long.

"Our parents have been best friends since university. His family moved back to Toronto from New York when Connor started high school, so we didn't meet until we were teenagers. But our parents had this dream of their kids getting together. And when we were in high school, it was cute. And when he didn't get into McGill and I thought we were going our separate ways, I was relieved."

In the weeks after she had left him, it dawned on her that was the turning point. When she had achieved everything he thought he should have gotten. The grades. The scholarships. The score career position right out of school. Connor had still done more than so many other people who didn't have the same opportunities. Degree, just not from his or his parents' choice of university. Good job, although not immediately in his field. Jill had been proud of him, but his resentment towards her festered. Instead of raising her higher, he tried to drag her down, below him. Where he thought she belonged.

"I wasn't allowed to bring a carbohydrate into the apartment for years because it would ruin his perfect diet and his perfect six-pack abs. He wouldn't let me eat sugar outside our home, either. Said he could smell it on me."

"Jesus."

"I can't believe I still have Sophie. I think she stuck around because …"

"She loves you and knew you needed her?" he said, voice soft and soothing.

"Yeah." She leaned on the console, fingers pressing into her lips. The bruises on her arm where Connor had grabbed her that night, dragging her from the room to seethe at her in private, hadn't faded for two weeks. Each blue imprint a reminder of what he had done. What he would've done again. She hadn't told her mother, or even Sophie. She had been grateful it was winter, so she could wear long sleeves without question. That she had to factor his violent outburst into her wardrobe choices, even once, made her sick to her stomach.

She weighed her next words carefully. "I'm glad of two things. One, that I got out when I did. I don't want to think about what could have … anyway. And two, that he didn't care about my work. He never talked about it, asked about it, so he never knew enough about it to make me doubt that part of myself." She looked at Alex's stony profile. "I'm really good at my job. I trust my instincts and I know how to get shit done. But he took all my confidence outside of that and tore it to shreds."

His jaw clenched as he worked to get the words out. "Does he ever bother you?"

"No," she whispered. "I've blocked him on everything." It barely mattered. Her mother delivered a running commentary, forcefully updating her every time they spoke. Along with how Jill should live her life differently. She shivered.

Slowly, Alex reached across the console, stopping his hand an inch from hers. Without hesitation Jill closed the distance and slid her hand into his.

Was that an overshare? Heavier than the *I came for work* spiel he was probably expecting when he asked the question. But it was so easy. Peaceful and warm, and she let herself soak up his solid comfort.

She was about to tell him if he ground his teeth any harder, he'd crack a molar, but she swallowed the words. He'd let her talk. He gave her the space for it. Instead, she said, "Sorry. That was a lot."

"Please don't be sorry." He exhaled, softening his grip on the steering wheel. "My parents got divorced my first year of grad school."

"What happened?" she asked, half-turning in her seat to face him better.

"Don't know. They never really told me or Gemma why. Dad was up in the oil sands a lot, my mom down here. I think they grew apart and figured it out when we left the house. My dad always told me the most important thing a man could do was take care of his family. Then one day he's calling me, telling me he's leaving my mom. A week later, my girlfriend broke up with me."

Her breath caught in her throat.

"Then my thesis advisor moved. Left me to figure out everything on my own. I had to completely scrap my thesis plan. Everything I thought was solid in my life was yanked out from under me in a week. All that fear, people leaving, of not knowing what to do. I was a raging asshole for months. Got in a fight after practice with a guy on my team, who said some extremely close-minded shit about my sister and her girlfriend. My coach lost it on us. Asked Gemma if she'd come in so my teammate could apologize to her face to face, and he cried the whole time. Two years later, he cried at her wedding." He paused. "Gemma was furious with me. Told me to get my shit together and kicked my ass into therapy."

Thank you, Gemma, for looking after your brother. "Your sister seems like an amazing person."

"She's a stone-cold boss," Alex agreed. "Therapist gave me a ton of work to figure it out."

"That must have been so hard. Dealing with all that."

His smile wavered between self-conscious and rueful. "You saw exactly how hard it was. I wrote most of your course materials in the middle of all that. I should not have been writing lessons for new students. I had signed up for it, but I was completely out of my depth."

Her first impressions of him so many years ago. Glowering, moody, and unfair … was replaced by heartbroken, hurt, and overwhelmed. She looked down where her fingers entwined with his and squeezed.

It was still on her list of things to do. To find a new therapist in Calgary. She had seen a counsellor a few times in university, when her mother wasn't there to say it was all in her head (*where else would it be?* she'd always wondered) and she had started to unpack years of baggage. Her mother's narcissism, her father's submission to his wife's will—and her guilt that she let herself get sucked back in when she returned to Toronto four years later. Then, after leaving Connor, she had a few sessions. Just a start. If she were ever to admit it to herself, going back would have meant dealing with everything she had ignored. Maybe now, with the energy and space and clarity she had lacked for so long, she could peek into that neatly packed baggage she had hidden away.

She drew a deep inhalation and let it out in a long sigh. "I think I'm overdue for some figuring stuff out, too."

"Look at us, doing the work." Alex smiled down at their fingers, then his brows drew back together. "You're only here for a year?"

For the first time since arriving in Calgary, that certainty wavered at the edges. Jill couldn't put her finger on why. "I don't know," she said, and withdrew her hands to tuck under her arms.

—

They pulled off the highway onto a township road, driving straight into the late day sun. Some landmark invisible to Jill's eye must have come into view and Alex pulled them down another back road. The coral and violet rays blazed on the vibrant green fields, the sky deepening into cobalt, piles of white clouds turning grey with the creeping hours. The winds gusted down from the mountains and Alex squinted up at the gathering clouds as he led her out among the waving grasses.

"There are always industry lobbyists who push back against environmental requirements. Costs too much money," he listed off the excuses on his fingers. "Cuts into margins, takes too long, crowds them out of markets they want to get into."

"And your tech will remove barriers."

"Time, anyway. Decades ago, this field was a quarry. Really lax environmental protocols back then, and it sat for years, completely wasted." He ran his hands over the waist-high stalks, heads flowing between his fingertips. "I led a team here during my post-doc. Cleared the entire site in less than two years. Now, it's prairie again, but if my tech had been used—I mean, if it was around back then—we could have been eating food from this land ten, twenty years ago."

Jill pulled her cotton jacket closer around her ribs, smiling up at him. "You're doing incredible work. I'm glad I get to be a little part of it."

"Me, too." Alex took a last look at the landscape before them. "Let's get back on the road. We have an hour before we reach our last stop."

The light shifted as they continued west, prairies rolling into the foothills of the Rocky Mountains, blue shadows long behind them. It was hard to tell if the sun had dipped behind the mountain peaks yet, or if it had hidden behind the now overcast sky. Even though it was still light, she checked the time on her phone and started at the late hour.

"This last stop is quick," he assured her. "I'd skip it and get us home faster, but I really need this sample today."

"Don't worry. I'm having a good time," she replied. "I mean, this has been really helpful." Alex shot her a light smile, and it might have been the changing light, but she thought his cheeks flush.

After half an hour of lurching down an unmarked dirt road, the day finally declared its intention to reverse seasons, and the windshield caught its first flecks of white. Jill leaned forward, gaping at the accumulating flakes.

"Is it snowing?" she asked weakly.

"Mm-hmm."

Jill looked at him in disbelief. "It's June!"

"Welcome to southern Alberta, where you can get all four seasons in any month."

She choked out a laugh as the sky released a flurry of perfect cotton balls.

"If it makes you feel better, we can get tee shirt weather in January …" he trailed off at her expression. "Um, at least it isn't hail?"

Alex pulled over minutes later, and despite the dropping temperature, Jill followed him to the location and accepted his offer to collect the last sample of the day. Fastening the lid, she handed the container back with a satisfied flourish.

"See, chemistry can be fun," he said. "Maybe you missed your calling after all."

"That's like playing in a sandbox."

"Sure, a toxic, hazardous sandbox—" and seeing her horrified expression "—kidding! We only visited end stage sites today. I wouldn't bring you anywhere dangerous."

I know you wouldn't, she thought, but tried to look angry anyway. "That. Was not. Funny."

"It was pretty funny," he said, and brushed the snowflakes from her shoulders.

The Volvo accumulated at least an inch of snow in the minutes they had been away. Jill squinted back the tire tracks on the dirt road they had come in on, already obscured. "Are the roads into town going to be okay?"

Alex finished clearing the last of the windows and threw the snow brush back into the trunk. "Oh, sure. Might take us a little longer to get home, but it'll be fine."

It was not fine. Anni-frid had decided she'd driven enough that day.

Alex tried starting the engine again. Not a click. Not a thump.

Jill looked resolutely out the windshield, voice level. "Is there a problem?"

"I'll call AMA." He swallowed. "If my membership hasn't expired."

Okay. Easy fix. She had a membership, even if Alex didn't. She whipped out her phone.

No bars.

They were in the middle of a field, in the snow, hadn't seen another soul in at least an hour, and they couldn't call for help. A sliver of fear pierced her chest. "Can you fix it?"

"I'm not that kind of engineer."

The phone shook out of her hand and clattered to the floorboards. They were stuck. She had to do something. Anything. Her brain raced to find a solution.

"I'm so sorry. This has never happened before." Alex spoke to her from the far end of a long tunnel, his voice barely audible over the rushing in her ears. "Jill, are you okay?"

It couldn't be more than fifteen kilometres to the main road. She ran that all the time. There'd be cell service. Eventually. She could fix this. Her hand fumbled on the door handle, and she sprinted from the car.

"Wait!" Alex was out of the car and beside her in a second. "We have to stay put. It's still snowing, and we don't know how far it will be to get service. It's going to be pitch-black out soon. We won't see anything."

They were stranded. In the middle of nowhere. With no help on the way. And there was nothing she could do. Her throat constricted, and she turned her widening eyes to Alex.

"Hey." He looked down at her, voice steady and low. "I have an emergency kit in the trunk. We can camp in the car. I've done it before."

Her stomach roiled. She was going to throw up. She swallowed hard and her breath whistled through her windpipe. When she tried to draw breath again, the world greyed, and she felt herself tilt.

"You're okay. You'll be okay. I'll keep you safe."

A pressure on her arms, holding her upright. She felt her butt hit something and suddenly, she was sitting, her head between her knees.

"Breathe, Jill." His voice was strained. "Breathe for me."

Inhale slowly, exhale deeply.

There's nothing I can do. But I'm safe. I'm safe. He'll keep me safe.

She raised her head, blinking slowly. She sat in the passenger seat of the car, her feet in the gathering snow. Alex knelt in front of her with a dusting of snow melting in his hair.

Heart rate, slower. Breathing, deeper. Stomach, calmer. Her extremities were usually freezing after a panic attack, but her hands were tucked between his, warm, shielded from the chill. All normal. It was over.

But he'd seen it.

"How long was I..?" she managed to say.

He shook his head. "Are you okay? How do you feel?"

She blinked, trying to think of something. "My feet are cold."

He gave a shaky laugh. "Mine, too."

They struggled to stand, stamping their feet, still holding each other for balance. Jill looked down and withdrew from their joined hands, tucking her fingers under her arms. Even though he'd stopped her from running, the aftermath of the panic attack felt like she'd sprinted for an hour. She wearily coaxed her voice into producing a whisper. "What now?"

He blew out a breath, looking relieved. "I'll fold down the back seats. It's not the Four Seasons, but it's better than sleeping in the front. And," he said, rummaging in his pack and extracting a bag of chips, "I have snacks."

Alex was right. Any sane person would stay put until morning. She tried to smile and reached for the chips, the bag rustling in her shaking hands. She firmed her grip until her knuckles turned white and looked down at her dinner: jalapeño lime chips. Spicy. Salty. He remembered. A corner of her lip curved, and she nibbled corner of a chip as he cleared the cargo hold of the uncooperative Anni-frid.

Night landed in a rush, snow materializing out of the black above them. It would have been stupid to try to run for cell service. She would have been stuck in the dark and cold, lost, wearing only a flimsy jacket, and she cursed herself. She wiped the traces of chips from her hands on the clean snow, crawled into the back of the wagon, and was halfway through braiding her hair before she realized Alex was closing the hatch from the outside.

She dropped the partially braided strands. "Where are you going?"

"I'm sleeping up front."

"Wh-why?"

"I'll crowd you. I'll …" he trailed off. "The front is fine. Really."

He had pushed up the front seats as far as they could go to drop the back seats flat. He wouldn't fit behind the wheel, let alone be comfortable enough to sleep. Jill dropped her chin to her chest and had her second stupid thought of the night.

"Wait." This was a terrible idea. "There's lots of room back here." No, there wasn't. "We'll both fit." Not going to think about how close that fit will be. "Besides—" she clamped her lips shut before she could add "then we can share body heat."

Stop talking. She should stop talking.

Alex wavered, looking from the front seat to the space beside her. "I don't know …"

"Please?"

He dropped his hands from the hatch and wiped a hand over his face. "Promise you'll elbow me if … just promise you'll elbow me."

The felted blanket completely covered her, and he said it covered him. It didn't. She could see his arm sticking out the other side. He plastered himself to the far side of the cargo hold, and Jill scooted over as far as she could, creating a small island of space between them.

The dark country night descended around them, so quiet Jill could almost hear the snowflakes landing on the roof. Heat radiated off him even across the few inches separating them, and she rethought her insistence they share the space. His immediacy was overwhelming. Of course, it was. He was a huge man lying right next to her, no matter how hard they were trying to keep space between them. If she said she changed her mind and asked him to please sleep up front after all, he'd be in the driver's seat before she could finish the sentence.

No, that would be her third stupid idea of the night. It was going to be weird no matter what. She might have to hold her pee all night. He might snore. She might snore. Besides, it was freezing. Really, far more practical to have him beside her. For warmth. Besides, if anyone should sleep up front it should be her. It was his car, after all, and—

Stop overthinking, Northrop. That's not going to help.

No use in trying to make herself fall asleep, but no sense in stubbornly trying to stay awake, either. The rise and fall of Alex's breath lulled her with its steady rhythm, and she stopped fighting the tendrils of sleep that curled around the edges of her consciousness. She tucked her arms tight to her chest and prepared for another restless night.

NINE

Jill was unusually relaxed. Deliciously warm. And exceptionally comfortable.

I never sleep in, she thought, as the thin morning light washed over her closed eyelids. *What day is it? I can sleep a few more minutes ...*

She inhaled a cozy scent and shifted on her side, trying to stretch the sleep from her stiff muscles, only to feel her movement blocked by a large, solid mass. She froze, and the events of the previous night flooded back.

Broken down car. Chips for dinner. Panic attack. A night in the aforementioned broken-down car. Now, she found herself fully draped across Alex.

Who was lying there awake.

Looking at her.

From underneath her.

Jill bolted upright, her cheeks flaming.

"Hi," he said, his husky voice filling the tight space. He looked at her cautiously, as if she were a deer ready to flee if he spooked her.

"Oh, hi, good morning," she stammered. She gave a weak smile that probably looked more like a grimace and gestured at his torso. "I'm really, really sorry about that." She snuck a peek at his chest where her cheek had been resting seconds ago and cringed. A tiny drool puddle. Barely noticeable. Maybe he wouldn't see it.

"It's okay," Alex said, shifting so she could finish disentangling herself. He glanced down at the miniature pond she'd left on his shirt, and her flood of embarrassment threatened to drown her.

She wriggled her way seated before huddling back as much as the cramped space would allow. Her hair had fully escaped her braid in the night, and she ran her fingers through it to tame it as best she could. Her elastic was lost among their wrinkled clothes or tucked under the emergency blanket. The thought of looking for it and finding some other lost accessory—an earring, or a bobby pin—snuck up like a sucker punch to the gut. He said last night he'd slept back here before. She wondered who else had slept here with him. And how recently. She fixed her stare out the rear-view window and tucked her knees up to her chin.

"Um, breakfast?" he asked, pulling protein bars out of his emergency kit. He rubbed at the dark circles under his eyes and stifled a yawn.

After a protein bar each and another failed attempt at starting the car, they agreed the best plan was for them to walk into cell range together. A knot unclenched in her chest. She didn't love the idea of waiting at the car alone and didn't think she could give the needed directions to roadside assistance if Alex had stayed behind with the car and samples. The fact that she would be spending more time with him had nothing to do with it.

Snow had fallen fast and thick overnight, layering a blanket of white that hushed the sounds around them. A few lazy flakes still came down, dotting the patches of blue sky breaking through the clouds. The temperature already rose enough that snow thawed into glistening drops on the leaves, and the last flakes melted in her hair and trickled in icy streams down her neck. A sudden warmth enveloped her, and she sighed as the scent of pine, earth, and something else delicious reached her nose.

I'm wrapped in nature. Soft flannel brushed her cheek, and she realized what brought the relief.

"Wait, no—"

"Please, you're shivering." Alex adjusted his jacket more snugly over her shoulders, his breath fogging around him. "Besides, I run hot."

She knew. She'd tucked herself against his warmth all night, and another shiver that had nothing to do with the cold ran over her skin. She stuffed that feeling down beside the thought that she was maybe glad to spend more time with him, and her protest stalled on her lips. Instead, she nestled her nose deeper into the collar of his jacket and focused on her boots trudging through the snow.

Not in the plan. This was definitely not in the plan.

After several increasingly soggy kilometres, Jill's phone pinged several different tones—texts, missed calls, and yes! Glorious cell service. She let out a whoop and fist pumped, hoisting her phone aloft in celebration. Alex dropped his head back and closed his eyes before pulling out his phone to call for rescue. After a series of directions that Jill would have never been able to keep straight, he furrowed his brow, grunted, and signed off the call.

"Good news and bad news."

Jill shifted from foot to foot, hugging his jacket across the fluttering in her chest. "Good news first."

"We got lucky. There were a ton of accidents last night."

Which could have been us, she thought. "Which means they have a lot of cars to pull out." Jill chewed her bottom lip. "How long?"

"Could be an hour, could be six. Probably more," he replied, shoving his hands into his pockets. "Nick could be here in two if I call him now."

It wasn't a hard decision. Between waiting for the tow truck, and the drive back to town, eight hours without real food, a toothbrush, or more than a bush to pee behind would be miserable. Even if it did mean two hours in a truck with Nick and his power-everything euphemisms.

"That would be nice of him."

Alex called Nick, finishing up with confirmation that yes, he owed him after this. "He's on his way. We'll be having lunch at home." Alex shoved the phone in his pocket, looking relieved. "If you're okay to be out of cell range again, we should wait at the car. Nick knows the site, and this snow is going to make a mess when it melts."

The hour-and-a-half return trek to the car flashed by. Then there was just time to kill. They wandered around the area and restacked boxes. Alex named the mountains in the distance for her, and Jill pretended her mind wasn't racing. Finally, he opened the wagon's hatch and she hopped up, feet out of the slush and legs dangling over the edge. Alex dropped his weight beside her, and the wagon heaved in protest.

"I need to change the shocks," he mused.

"Shocks?" Jill said, voice strangled. "You need … shocks."

A panic attack after getting stranded in the middle of nowhere and a mess of nerves in the aftermath. His car wouldn't start and their feet were soaked with slush. She hadn't had caffeine in over twenty-four hours.

And he needed shocks.

The bubble finally popped, and insane peals of laughter racked her from head to toes. She bent over her dangling feet, clutching the tailgate for support and gasping for air. Alex waited with arms crossed for her outburst to end, but every time she looked in his direction, she started again, cheeks and stomach aching. After a minute, or maybe two, with Jill whimpering giggles as she struggled for control, he nudged her knee with his.

"Are you done?"

She hiccoughed once and sniffed. "Absolutely not."

His gaze was fixed on his crossed arms. "My dad bought this car for my mom when she came home from the hospital with me," he said after a moment. "This is the first time Anni-frid has let me down."

She nudged him back, pushing against his solid thigh, shoulder brushing his. "I don't think she let you down. She kept us safe overnight."

"You're being far more understanding about this than you need to be."

She should say something. Something funny, like *Sophie would laugh if she heard you say I was understanding.* Jill parted her lips, but nothing came out.

Her eyes found their way to his crossed arms, biceps flexed against the expanse of his chest. The Storage Room Incident (which had taken on capital letters in her mind) pushed to the forefront of her consciousness, competing for real estate with the memory of waking up not two hours ago cradled against every nook of his body. She wondered what it would feel like to let her hand explore more than just the contours of his torso. What his arm wrapped around her waist would feel like. She wondered what it would feel like to have his other hand wound through her hair.

He turned to her, and she mirrored his movement as if moving underwater, slow and languid. He was so close. Her pulse kicked up as she felt his heat, the movement of his breath, the rise and fall of his chest. He swallowed, eyes searching her face and her centre of gravity shifted as she leaned into his warmth.

The crunch of tires on gravel snapped her back to her surroundings. She reeled back, launching off the wagon's open back and coming to a standstill at the passenger side door, breathing through constricted lungs and hearing her pulse pound in her ears.

What the hell was she thinking?

She wasn't thinking. She had nearly kissed Alex.

She watched the melting snow running in rivulets down the window. No. That couldn't be right. She was mistaken.

She gulped a breath. It wasn't a panic attack. Panic took her out of her body. Cold. Everything drowned out by the rush of blood in her ears, lungs constricted, her vision reduced to a pinprick at the end of a tunnel.

Now, she was very much in her body, with every nerve ending on fire. She rubbed her hands over the spot where their arms had touched, and fresh heat surged through her.

She was stressed. He was tired. He certainly wasn't thinking that. Neither was she.

The pickup skidded to a stop several feet away. Nick jumped down and crossed the slushy road, paper bags and a tray with to-go cups in his hands.

Jill peeked out of the corner of her eye. Alex stood frozen in place, head still turned to where she had been moments before, his shirt strained across the breadth of his shoulders.

"You two had an exciting night." Nick sauntered over, mouth stretched in a shit-eating grin. He turned to Jill. "Told you it would be better to wait and come with me."

"We're great, thanks. Yep, we're safe. Glad you asked." Alex straightened, pressing his thighs against the car to stand, and the car lurched in response. Jill repressed an insane bubble of mirth ready to burst forth.

"Provisions, as requested." Nick's smirk remained firmly in place. He tossed a bag at his business partner, who caught it one-handed, before passing Jill a similar bag and one of the cups. His eyes travelled down to her feet and back up. "Don't you look cozy."

Jill stilled, holding the bag and cup in front of her like a shield. Of course, she was still wearing Alex's jacket. What would be the least weird option? Tear it off? Leave it on? Walk to Calgary over the next day and a half to avoid this conversation?

Alex levelled a pointed look at Nick. "She was cold. I wasn't." He turned to Jill, voice softening. "Keep it until you're warm."

She nodded and squeaked out a thank-you as she accepted Nick's offering. Pickle juice soaked the sandwich and the coffee might have been lukewarm an hour ago. The calories didn't seem worth the hassle, but she forced herself to swallow a bite.

Obviously, she had imagined it. Whatever didn't almost happen minutes ago. Alex looked perfectly calm and unfreaked out. Because there was nothing to freak out about.

Alex grimaced as he took a bite of his own sandwich while Nick pulled the truck around to bring the two vehicles nose to nose. Ten minutes and several unsuccessful attempts to start the ancient wagon later, Alex shook his head, disconnecting the jumper cables linking the vehicles.

"Well, it was worth a shot." Alex stuffed the cables into the car's storage.

Nick looked at Alex like he was crazy. "You wouldn't have seriously gotten behind the wheel of that thing again?"

"No, I shouldn't be driving." Alex yawned, rubbing his face with both hands. "I got about seven minutes of sleep last night."

Jill nearly choked on her last bite. He must have been miserable, stuffed back there with her. Maybe she elbowed him. Or snored. Maybe she made him uncomfortable. A wave of guilt washed over her. She had slept like a log, out for the entire night for the first time since … she couldn't even remember. All while Alex suffered through the night. She shot him a wide-eyed look, and Nick's smile grew.

"Oh, really. Why's that?"

"Hey, Nick?" Alex said, pleasantly. "Shut the fuck up."

"Ooh, testy."

"Did you bring your hitch?"

"I'll tow you to town on the condition you let me bring that rusty sack of bolts straight to the junkyard."

Alex glowered, but there was a twinge of something else in his expression that sparked Jill's empathy. Given the history of his formerly trusty ride, this was not the time to have this conversation.

"Maybe she just needs a bit of work?" Jill offered. Alex's expression softened, and her stomach fizzed in betrayal. Jill hauled the walls up around her and briskly turned to Nick. "Thanks for coming to get us. Anything I can do to help and get us on the road?"

Turned out she was pretty useless with the hitching process but did help transfer a few sample boxes to the bed of the truck. Alex offered her the front seat, but Nick sniggered, reminding him he didn't fit in the back. Jill was only too happy to accept the back seat, faking the illusion of distance for the return trip. She'd have more than enough room, but Alex would've been smooshed. Plus, the thought of having Alex sitting behind her for two hours did things to her thought paths she didn't want to travel down.

Walls, Northrop.

It was one of those trucks that needed the front door to open to gain access to the rear door. That was probably for the best. She wouldn't be tempted to throw herself into traffic to get away from Nick's weird mood. Or her own. Alex opened the passenger, then rear doors, and Jill climbed up into the back seat, painfully aware her ass would be fully displayed in his face.

Cool.

She scrambled in as fast as she could and sat ramrod straight, staring at her hands pressed tightly to her lap. Alex shut the door behind her, the truck lurching as he swung up to the front seat. Even through her nerves, Jill couldn't resist murmuring, "Does the truck need new shocks, too?"

He exhaled through his nose, chin to chest. She could tell he was smiling, even from the back. Nick displayed an unfortunate ability to turn on his powers of observation at the most inopportune time, glancing between the two of them. She shrunk against the seat and pulled the jacket higher around her neck. Nick gunned the engine, and Jill turned on her mental timer for the two hours until the ordeal would be over.

As soon as they were in cell range again, a new chorus of pings hit her phone, and she descended on the notifications flooding in. A few emails from work (Ashleen sent the final sign-off docs for a last review—which looked great—and Omar asked if she had seen the federal government's updates on the clean growth strategy webpage—which she had), a handful of texts from Sophie (three for plans for next weekend, two about her date last night, and one asking why Jill hadn't texted back yet and she hoped it was because she was having sex with a cowboy), and another voicemail from her mother.

Guilt twisted her stomach. She had let her mother's last two calls go to voicemail again, with a text to say she'd call her later. She gripped the phone, hearing her mother ramble about another brunch with Connor's mother (hadn't Jill called him yet?), she had forgotten to mention she had a contact for the McGill Calgary alumni chapter (so good for networking), and do remember to call (your father misses you). Jill exhaled and wearily deleted the messages one by one.

Alex spoke over his shoulder. "Everything okay?"

"Mothers. You know." Jill's mouth twisted slightly. "Mine's a bit ..." Strident, overbearing, and controlling came to mind, but she stayed silent.

"Much?" Alex offered.

If she had been thinking straight, she would have caught it before she said it. Jill laughed grimly. "That is an exceptionally kind adjective to describe Lizanne Saigner."

Nick snatched a glance in the rear-view mirror, and Alex twisted fully in his seat.

"Hold up. Saigner? As in the Saigner-Pickering Protocols?"

Shit. It was bound to come out eventually.

Jill sighed quietly. "The one and only."

"I've cited her work—" Alex tipped his head back "—dozens of times."

"I wrote a paper on the S-P Protocols in my undergrad," Nick said. "Holy shit."

"Your mother is Dr. Saigner," Alex said, turning back to the front. "That explains her fit when you dropped chem."

"Yeah." Jill shrugged out of the jacket and passed it to Alex over the back. "Thanks. I don't need this anymore."

They passed car after car in the ditch on their way into the city, telltale skid marks showing the cars' careening paths off the road. Jill shivered, grateful it hadn't been them, followed by the surge of heat remembering waking up draped over Alex, chased by the guilt that she had made his night miserable.

You are a mess. She closed her eyes and pushed the thoughts down. She could sort it out later. Much later.

The snow had almost disappeared by the time they hit the city limits. A few patches of white clung in the shadows, but the roads and sidewalks glittered with the snowmelt in the sunlight. The city had a weird time-out-of-place feel, where everyone busily went about their lives, while Jill occupied a carved-out bubble as a detached observer.

Alex jumped out of the truck before it came to a full stop outside her apartment, and her feet were already on the ground before her brain realized she had taken his proffered hand to step down. Jill slowly withdrew her fingers and clasped them in front of her, and he thrust his newly released hand deep into his pocket. A series of unreadable expressions crossed his face, his jaw working as if he were swallowing the words he wanted to speak. He glanced in the truck's cab before shutting the door. He reached out as if to touch her, instead letting his hand fall to his side.

"Are we … I mean, are you okay?" His deep voice was pitched lower than usual, full of concern, and the knot of tension that had built between her shoulder blades over the last two hours transformed into a nervous stammer between her lungs.

Yesterday had been … great. Even fun. Until the breakdown. And the panic attack. Waking up like they did. No wonder she felt so off. Then, whatever that was this morning. The definitely not almost-kiss. Which she wasn't thinking about. And neither was he. Because there was nothing to think about.

Okay, Northrop. Calm, cool, and casual.

She leaned in, face solemn. "I have never, ever, eaten a more disgusting sandwich in my life."

Alex blew out a laugh. "That was pretty vile."

"I'm not sure I'll recover."

"Call me if you need a ride to the hospital." He gave a dry chuckle, then asked, "Seriously, you'll call me if you need anything?"

"What I need is a shower and a toothbrush. But thanks." She hesitated. "I'm sorry I didn't let you sleep last night. If I snored or elbowed you or, you know. That can't have been …" she rambled. She tucked her fingers under her arms and resolutely avoided his eyes. She should stop talking.

"Jill …"

"I'll see you next week," she said firmly and escaped into her building. Alex remained on the sidewalk, still watching as she entered the elevator, and she stared at her shoes all the way up to her floor.

It was nothing. Nothing happened. She overreacted. She just needed a couple of days to get some distance and the entire weirdness would blow over.

If the knocking in her chest was any sign, that was highly unlikely.

—

"Overnight? With a client? A male client?" Ashleen's huge brown eyes widened further. "My mother would kill me. Then resurrect me, give me a lecture, and kill me again."

Marco laughed. "My wife would straight up kill me. Male or female. If I left her alone for an entire night with the baby without telling her where I was, you'd never see me again."

"It wasn't on purpose. We didn't have cell reception. I couldn't call anyone."

"We need a plan," Omar said. "If we don't hear from each other within twenty-four hours of a text, send out an Amber Alert."

"Amber Alerts are for kidnapped children."

"A Jill Alert then. When a co-worker has been kidnapped into the foothills." Ashleen slurped her pho. "I'd have turned this role down if I had known sleepovers were a part of the job description."

"It's part of the 'other duties as required' clause," Marco said.

"I'm never telling you guys anything again," Jill muttered into her soup.

Ashleen and Marco's assignment had wrapped successfully that morning, with full sign-off and submission. With her own project submitted and waiting for results, Jill declared the four of them needed a celebratory lunch. Which was obviously different from the regular lunches they already had every week, because Jill said so. Plus, she was paying.

Her favourite power duo had, there was no other way to say it, crushed their first file. Sure, it had been straightforward, as Angela had promised, but it had come with a few left hooks that the two identified and solved with Jill's help. With Ashleen fresh out of university and Marco brand new into a career change, this had been the perfect confidence booster for the newest members of the team.

After a lifetime of having praise diverted from her, Jill adamantly believed in giving recognition where it was due. Her mother had a preternatural knack for taking credit for Jill's success, either fully or through insinuation. When Jill had been accepted to McGill, her mother whispered to her social circle it was because she had pulled in favours, even though the university didn't have a legacy program. Of course, it could have nothing to do with Jill's top of class GPA or years of volunteer service. Or how when she had been hired on at Blackburn, her mother had said with an indulgent smile that it was name recognition, even though they didn't share a last name and Angela had no idea who her mother was.

"Your commitment to your role is admirable, but I think we can agree that sleepovers are over and above the call of duty. And we don't want to encourage Jill to send more early morning texts," said

Omar, looking at Jill with mock severity, and Marco enthusiastically bobbed his head.

Jill raised her soda water. "To Ashleen and Marco, who will take on all the work so Omar and I can sleep in. Congrats!"

"To our awesomeness," Ashleen agreed, and the four clinked glasses. "Seriously, though, we couldn't have done it without you."

Jill beamed. Sure, they needed a bit of coaching, and she'd got them asking the right questions, but the success belonged to them. Angela had passed along the glowing post-consult feedback from the clients and had herself congratulated Jill on her leadership through the project, but seeing Ashleen and Marco so proud and energized was the best part. She sipped her water and let the bubbles and the moment wash over her.

Until someone shut off the oxygen in the restaurant.

"Jill!" Alex strode up to their table with a bag of takeout in hand, wearing a look of surprised pleasure and a navy suit that he had absolutely no business looking that good in.

The perfectly tailored looked like it could barely contain his physique. The jacket strained across his shoulders, a light blue shirt snug across his chest. Clearly, the weekly rugby matches and sporadic gym sessions were more than enough to keep him in resplendent form. She had no idea that body was under his worn jeans and casual flannels.

Actually, she had an awfully good idea that body was under his clothes. Waking up plastered against him mere days ago, sublimely cozy and warm and relaxed.

Jill was sure she had opened her mouth to reply, but oddly, nothing came out. She snapped her mouth shut, cleared her throat, and tried again.

"Oh! Alex! Hi!" Too cheerful. It was too cheerful. Marco and Ashleen exchanged a look that was not nearly subtle enough for Jill's liking. Heat licked up her neck and she tried not to stare.

Alex tracked her gaze and grinned self-consciously. "I know. Ridiculous, right? We're meeting a new client today. Nick made me wear it."

Ridiculous was not the word that came to mind. She pressed her lips together in a smile she hoped didn't look manic, grateful that some kind soul had turned the air back on in the room. "And he still put you on lunch duty? Rude."

"That's what I said, but with more swearing. Anyway, I remember you saying this was a good spot." Alex rolled his shoulders against the confines of the jacket, tugging on his sleeve. He inclined his head at the group. "Work lunch?"

"Oh, right!" She launched into making introductions, because apparently her brain needed a script to make it through the next few minutes. Marco smiled broadly, Ashleen did an exceptional impression of a clam, and Omar aimed a sideways look at Jill she was positive would come back to her later.

Alex turned back to Jill. "Since we ran into each other, can I steal you for two minutes?" The look he gave her was light, with something else cruising below the surface.

Oh, good. More alone time.

She ignored the knocking in her knees and excused herself, weaving between the packed tables and noisy chatter of the lunch crowd, following him to the front of the restaurant. She wasn't exactly sure where she should rest her eyes, but where her gaze landed certainly wasn't appropriate. At least he couldn't see her staring this time.

If anyone asked, she'd say she was just checking the tailoring of his pants.

The restaurant's entryway had barely enough room for the two of them. Because of course it did. Jill squeezed in after Alex and peeked back at her table through the vestibule's red and gold curtains. The trio blinked in unison at her from the table. She resisted the urge to yank the curtains closed.

Alex leaned against the doorway, looking slightly helpless. "How are you doing?" he asked, voice low. "I mean, after …"

Oh, she was fine. Super fine. She hadn't been thinking about every moment non-stop since walking through her apartment door four days ago. Not about having a panic attack. Or the impromptu camping trip. Or drooling all over him. Or the not almost-kiss that she had completely misread and was surely something innocent.

"I think we can agree," she started, weighing her words carefully, "that was all very …" Inappropriate? Confusing? Embarrassing? She inhaled, trying to ignore the swirl she had avoided examining, but his woodsy and warm and something else scent derailed her train of thought. He was looking at her with such care, so close she could feel his warmth, and the flimsy construction of her carefully guarded exterior crumbled around her.

"I'm so sorry," she blurted, heat rushing up her neck. "I slept all over you like you were my own freaking pillow!"

"I don't—" he started.

"I *drooled* on you!"

"It's okay …"

"I heard you tell Nick you had a terrible night."

"It wasn't a terrible night."

"And I made you sleep with me. I mean, in the back. Oh, god." *Stop talking, Northrop.* She slammed her mouth shut and buried her face in her hands.

"Jill," he said in a strangled voice. "You didn't make me do anything."

"Why didn't you push me over?"

Alex opened his mouth and closed it without answering.

And I nearly kissed you. She shut those words before they could tumble out but couldn't catch the next ones. "And I had a panic attack." She lowered her fingers to press her lips. "I'm sorry. You shouldn't have had to deal with that."

"You have nothing to ..." His posture shifted and the line between his brows softened. "I'm just glad I was there."

Dealing with panic attacks—uncommon as they were for her—was unpleasant enough. To put it extremely lightly. The first time she had one in front of Connor, gasping for breath on the bathroom floor, he had complained she was being dramatic. For almost three years, she had thought he was right. And Alex wanted to help her through it.

A knot between her shoulder blades slowly released. "Thanks."

"So," he looked at her cautiously, "you're not mad?"

"Wh-why would I be mad?"

His cautious look morphed to incredulity. "I got you stuck out there. Overnight. All of that was my fault."

"Oh!" Jill dropped her shoulders. Suddenly, even with her heart racing, she jumped at the chance to sidestep her nerves. "Can't you tell? I'm furious. And I'll find a way to make you pay." She narrowed her eyes at him, trying, and failing, to look menacing. "It will be creative."

"I'll watch for that." He smiled at her uncertainly. "You're really...?"

"I'm good. Really." Really-ish. Not really. Why did he have to be looking at her like that? She nodded briskly. "Are you? Good?"

He nodded, clearing his throat and tugging on his sleeve again.

The last of Jill's tension escaped in a high-pitched giggle. "You really hate wearing suits."

"It's not that," he said, frustrated. "I can't get the stupid sleeve buttons done up. They're so—" he huffed a sigh through his nose "—fiddly to do up one-handed."

"Here," she said, stepping into him and taking up the sleeve. He helped her. She could help him. Easy.

"So that's why you roll up your sleeves all the time," she said as she nimbly fastened the ornery buttons. Her fingers grazed his wrist, and she froze. He looked down at her with an odd expression, eyes dark and lips parted as if he was about to say something that wouldn't come out. Maybe something he was too polite to say.

If the flush hadn't left her cheeks yet, it would have come rushing back. She had just apologized for being way deep in his personal space. And she was way in his space again. She tucked her wandering hands into her underarms, hoping her deodorant would hold up against the prickle of heat twigging under her skin.

"Welp, all done." She took a quarter step back, about as much as the space would allow. Jill made a mental note to scout potential locations so she and Alex could avoid spaces smaller than a metre square. Which seemed to happen a lot.

"Ah, thanks," he said, still looking dazed.

"Yep. No problem," she clipped her words, voice coming out higher than it should. "What are friends for?"

"Yeah, friends ..."

Before the charged silence could stretch any longer, Jill straightened her spine and tore her gaze from his, glancing at her table. All three stared openly at them. Awesome.

"Since I'm good and you're good and everything is good, I'm going to get back to my team." *And hide under the table for a couple hours.* She hesitated, still holding her breath, then turned on her heel and left him standing in the entryway.

Jill ignored the three faces waiting expectantly and the eyes she was sure were fastened on her back. Carefully, she spread her napkin on her lap and concentrated on sipping her pho.

"I take it back," Ashleen said. "I'll do sleepovers."

"Me, too." Omar tracked his eyes to Jill, brows raised.

"I won't, but I get it," Marco said cheerfully.

"Who wants dessert?" Jill asked. "I could go for dessert."

"I told you to tell me if your client was cute."

"How about doughnuts? Anyone?"

"That guy's a scientist? And a doctor? My mother might not kill me for bringing *that* white guy home." Ashleen rubbed the side of her nose. "Actually, she'd still kill me."

"Or ice cream? Village has their new flavours for the month out."

"Ooh, the lime coconut flavour is amazing!" Marco said.

"Ice cream it is!" She would buy him all the lime coconut ice cream he wanted if it ended this conversation quicker.

While Ashleen and Marco debated non-dairy options, Omar leaned in. "What was that little sidebar?"

"We're starting the audit draft next week. Thanks for your help preparing my pitch." Jill scooped the last spoonful from the bottom of the bowl. "By the way, all three of you need to lower your eyebrows before they permanently join to your hairlines."

—

The murderous cacophony reached her even before she had opened the front doors, which meant Switchboard and Kevin were fighting again.

Rachel was in with the felines, cleaning out the food trays and litter boxes. The vocal kittens were in a temporary enclosure as she worked, attempting to kill each other without causing any real harm.

"You need to learn manners," Jill said to Switchboard, who displayed all his fiercest kitten teeth in response.

"Miao!" He punctuated his opinion by licking the glass.

Travis loped into the room, rainbow bandana knotted loosely around his throat. Jill wasn't sure, but she thought there was an extra giddy-up in his usual easy stride.

"Happy Pride Month," Jill said and her favourite cowboy twinkled his eyes at her.

Rachel shut the kennel door and wandered over. "If the summer doesn't convince you to move here permanently, nothing will," she declared. "Concert season, Pride, and Stampede?" She glowed with the anticipation of the upcoming festivities and waved her hand dismissively. "There's no way you're going back."

"It's going to take a bit more than a few parties for that."

"You haven't seen our parties yet."

"I reckon you'll like it alright." Switching gears, Travis said, "You were on the road during the storm."

She had recounted the trip to a few people, each group getting a different edit. Her team, who didn't learn the specifics of the sleeping arrangements. To Angela, who had asked for surprisingly few details after Jill apologized profusely for missing a day of meetings and not replying to email for a full day and a half. And, of course, to Sophie, who had drilled her when she sensed Jill wasn't dishing the full story, eventually extracting every minute detail. Including the almost-kiss that didn't happen.

Her parents—and by extension their entire social circle—didn't need to know anything.

Rachel and Travis could get a short version. Jill focused on the terrifying kitty in front of her. "Long day, learned a lot, got stuck."

"That's a fine Travis impression you did there. Where'd you get stuck?"

Shit. She should have skipped the last part. "About two hours out of town. We had to sleep in the car overnight."

"And this was with Enviro Guy, right?" Rachel gave Jill almost the same expression Omar had days earlier. What was it with everyone and these looks they were giving her?

"Mm-hmm."

"So, this rando drags you into the middle of nowhere and strands you overnight?"

"Alex isn't a rando. I've known him for months." *A little over three of them, in fact, if I don't include one traumatizing semester of university.* In retrospect, it wasn't as traumatizing as she had thought for so long.

No, it had been traumatizing, but now she knew why. "He had an emergency kit, food, blankets." She listed on her fingers. "We were safe."

Travis tugged the corner of his moustache. "Well, at least he ain't all hat and no cattle."

"That's what I was thinking?" Jill said, exchanging a bemused glance with Rachel, who shrugged. She made a mental note to check the cowboy idioms webpage she had bookmarked a few weeks ago to translate some of Travis's more arcane expressions.

"He took care of you when things got rough. You're above snakes. All that matters."

A warm glow blossomed in her chest. For all the things she had worried about that night, her safety hadn't been one of them. Sure, she had a panic attack, but she didn't have panic attacks out of fear. Those were about loss of control, not danger. She couldn't fix the problem, but he promised to keep her safe until they could solve it. She trusted he would.

If she hadn't felt safe, she wouldn't have slept.

"Hmm." Rachel let the word float into the air and the twitch in Travis's moustache hinted a smile.

Her mind skidded off any potential interpretation of … *this.* She tucked the little glow into a neat box, stacking it beside the other emotions she was ignoring and swore she'd sort through some other time.

Jill pulled up a neutral expression. "Yep, all good. Anyway, I'm going to give Daisy some belly rubs."

As she left the room to see her favourite girl, she told herself if she did this right, she could ignore this until her year in Calgary was up.

TEN

The king size bed was pristine in its neatness, white sheets still tucked at the edges, with only the fluffy pillows tossed out of place. The Saturday morning sun was already well up and the west-facing windows reflected the sun's rays onto the surrounding buildings. If she sat up, she would have seen the Rockies in the distance, the last snow of winter still clinging to its peaks. Jill lounged with her fingers laced behind her head. She couldn't think of anyone else she'd rather start the day fighting with.

"I am not going for vegan brunch."

"But it's so good!"

"If there are no eggs or whipped cream, it's not brunch."

"You'll love it, I promise." Jill dialled up her puppy-dog eyes. "I would never lie to you."

"*Non,*" Sophie held up a finger, "and you can't make me."

Jill peeled off the sheet mask, Face the World written in fancy gold script on the forehead, and disposed of the gooey plastic before rifling through another one of Sophie's conference swag bags. "You still haven't forgiven me for that wet tofu scramble, have you?" she asked, and Sophie's normally beautiful face contorted into a grimace as she faked a dry heave.

"Ooh, nice lip balm." Jill continued her search through the conference goodies: pink earbuds with kitten faces; laser pointer with different colours to toggle through; insulated water bottle that would have been great when she was stranded with Alex. "Are you taking all this back?"

Sophie pulled out a few items tagged for sponsored posts then waved her permission to pillage the rest, and Jill cackled at the score.

Sophie had insisted that the best way to spend the weekend would be for Jill to move into her hotel with her. Jill, never one to pass up housecleaning and chocolates on her pillow, had an overnight bag packed before she had ended the call. She had left the Blackburn office early Friday afternoon, set her phone to forward calls to voicemail for the weekend, and raced across downtown to meet Sophie at the conference hotel …

… and clung to the person who cared most about her in the entire world for the first time in a year and a half, swallowing the hot tears that threatened to spill down her cheeks. Alex's words from their road trip came back to her: Sophie, among everyone, had stayed by her side through everything. No judgement. No pressure. Only unwavering support, unconditional love, and an uncanny ability to see through any facade Jill attempted to put up.

A weekend with her little chicken would be perfect.

As Jill created her treasure pile—merino socks! Tech-compatible running gloves! Her only takeaways from the last finance conference she attended was a cheap calculator and a bad cold—her phone buzzed on the blankets beside her.

Alex.

Her stomach turned a lazy somersault. Despite assuring Alex she was fine and cool and totally okay, running into him at the restaurant only proved how not fine or cool or okay everything was. The fizzing and swooping she had packed away shifted and rattled in their tidy boxes, demanding her attention. Texts from the source of her turmoil only made it harder to ignore.

She picked up her phone and installed a look of casual indifference to keep the grin off her face.

I need to take more days off. I got to Rosso before the lunch rush and they had lemon cakes left

Imagine having a Saturday off :)

Also those lemon cakes are fire

Your friend's in town this weekend, right? What are you two doing?

Sophie peered over her shoulder. "You should invite him out with us tonight."

·A traitorous flush crept up her neck to her freshly moisturized cheeks. So much for the look of casual indifference. "No, that'd be weird. Also? Privacy?"

"You're funny." Her sparkling eyes narrowed to catlike slits. "It won't be weird. Do it. I'm always right."

"No. Alex is having his first real day off in months. He doesn't want to spend it with me."

"He's texting you."

Jill swallowed. It was nothing. He was probably bored. Or being polite. Her fingers hovered over the keys. *My friend leaves tomorrow. Do you want to come out with us tonight?* Deleted it, and typed it back out. Deleted it again.

She turned her phone to silent and pitched it onto the bed. "There's a coffee place nearby that has amazing lemon cakes. Let's grab one and figure out where we want to go for brunch."

One of the many benefits of having Sophie around was the instant wardrobe expansion. Even though Sophie had more boobs and Jill had more ass, the two women wore almost the same size, with polar opposite shopping habits. Jill had the sense that she was putting on a new personality with the uncharacteristic clothes. She rummaged through Sophie's suitcase and pulled out a coral pink romper, a vintage green shirtdress, and a pair of yellow ankle pants, holding all three options up for her friend's assessment.

"That shade of green is all wrong for you, and the pants need washing." Sophie pointed to the romper. "That will look ridiculous. Like, stupid good. Now, what did you bring me?"

Jill paused her struggle to do up the romper's back zipper, pulling out a pair of white sneakers and wiggling the shoes in a little dance.

"You were supposed to bring me those lilac jeans of yours," Sophie grumbled good-naturedly, slipping on the sneakers and buttoning the green shirtdress.

Jill basked in Sophie's affirmation of her excellent taste. "Too many kitten claw holes. Besides," she replied, eying the lineup of impractical shoes at the door, "I knew you'd need something for walking."

Sophie was right. The romper looked great on her.

Between Connor's aversion to enjoying delicious food and her anxiety-induced suppressed appetite, her clothes had started to hang off her body. In the nearly six months since leaving him, some of the angles she had developed had softened, and the romper's silky fabric swished against her arms and thighs as she turned side-to-side in front of the mirror. He would have said it was too short, too low-cut. An urge to pull it off welled up in reflex. Jill smiled and smoothed her hair loose over her shoulder. She looked—no, she *felt*—fantastic.

Suck it, Connor. I'll wear whatever I want. Especially if it's low-cut and short.

Half an hour later and armed with lemon cakes and double Americanos, Jill promised Sophie they'd find all the eggs and whipped cream she could want. With the Stampede weeks away, businesses had already started their country decor. Bales of hay, temporary wooden fences, and all manner of equestrian tack were stacked in doorways and lining patios. Sophie gleefully posed by the decor, pulling Jill in for selfies against the leather saddles and sequinned cowboy hats.

"If you'd have told me it was Stampede already, I'd have made room in my bags to bring home cowboy boots," Sophie said, posting the photos to her various social media feeds.

"You know you can have boots shipped home, right?" Jill asked, and grinned as her friend's brain got hijacked by the possibilities.

Calgary put on its best show for her friend. The river sparkled like it had been filled with sapphires overnight, bordered by aspens and cottonwoods shivering vibrant green in the light wind. Spring was ready to tip into summer, and the sun high overhead held a pleasant heat that made Jill glad she had chosen the light, breezy outfit. The swishy fabric had a barely-there feeling that had her checking that she had remembered to put something on. Families and runners packed the river pathway, Jill and Sophie making way for the former and being skirted by the latter. It was so crowded that she didn't notice him until he was right in front of her.

Of course, he looked a little different than usual. Not so much the fitted rugby jersey and shorts, but one toddler on his shoulders, little hands gripped under his chin. A second toddler hung off his arm, giggling wildly as Alex lifted the boy off the ground like he was performing a bicep curl. Two women flanked him, one woman pushing an empty stroller and the other trying to grab the hand of the boy clinging to Alex's arm.

He saw her seconds later, his face going completely blank, his gaze travelling down the length of her body before snapping back to her face.

"Hi!" Jill's voice came out all breathy, as if she'd just finished a tempo run. "What are you doing here? I mean, what's up?" She slid her hands over her hips, looking for pockets to hide her suddenly sweaty hands. Not finding any, she crossed her arms instead, then tried clasping them in front of her, and finally landed on gripping the strap of her bag.

He blinked. "Day off." The little boy on his shoulders kicked his heels into Alex's broad chest, hard enough to knock loose a response. He gave a lopsided smile. "Boss's orders."

Her heart did its second inconvenient flip-flop of the day and her blood fizzed up to her cheeks. He was still flushed with laughter, the corners of his mouth curving along those familiar lines. One muscular forearm anchored the feet of the boy around his shoulders, jersey pulling across his chest and biceps, and the snug shorts flexed over his thighs as he shifted from foot to foot.

The woman pushing the stroller looked like a miniature version of Alex, all auburn waves and open smiles. "Alex, who's your friend?"

Alex had apparently gone selectively mute, silently gaping while Sophie vibrated beside her. Jill sucked in a deep breath and plastered on a bright smile.

"You must be Gemma! Alex has said so much about you!" Jill waved, unsure if shaking hands would be weird. It would probably be weird. She redoubled her grip on her purse strap to prevent her hand from flailing. "I'm Jill. We work together."

"Oh, you're Jill!" Gemma stretched Jill's name out over a couple of extra syllables, her smile widening. "It's so nice to meet you. This is my wife, Bea, and our boys, Jake and Henry."

The little boy on Alex's shoulders ducked his head to bury his face in his uncle's hair, while the boy hanging from Alex's arm roared and tried to flip upside down.

Alex found his voice. "We were at the zoo. Henry liked the lions."

"And I'm Sophie. Thanks for the tip on the lemon cakes. We got the last two. Anyway, we saw your text earlier. We, in fact, don't have any plans tonight. You should come out with us!" Sophie's smile mirrored Gemma's. "I've never been to a cowboy bar," she added, so very helpfully.

Jill kept her smile rigidly in place as she swivelled her head to level a panicked look at her very best friend in the entire world, who fluttered her lashes back.

"Alex, that sounds like so much fun," Bea said with her own grin, gripping her son's hand as he pulled his feet up to swing between them. "You should go."

"Ah, what about dinner?"

His sister looked at him like he was stupid. "Go after dinner, old man."

"Oh, right." Alex looked as stunned as Jill felt. She gave him a weak shrug.

"Fantastic. It's a date." Sophie smiled triumphantly and looped her arm through Jill's. "Well, wasn't this lucky?"

So, so lucky.

Jill's mouth opened and closed. She gave one last look at Alex, hoping to convey … what, she didn't know. "It was great to meet you all." She managed a genuine grin for the two boys. "I like the zoo, too. My favourite animals are the polar bears."

Henry responded with a bigger roar, and Jake lifted his face out of Alex's hair with a shy smile.

"Nice to meet you." Sophie waved her fingertips at the group, before turning to Alex. "Text Jillybean when you'll pick us up tonight. I know you have her number."

Alex choked on a laugh, a smile spreading wide. He mouthed *Jillybean?* at her, and her stomach completed a full pirouette.

It really was a shame. Truly. She had loved Sophie for so long and now she was going to have to commit a felony.

She forced her free hand into a stilted wave, eyes wide with embarrassment as Sophie pulled her away, Alex turning to follow her as she left. As soon as they were out of earshot, Jill hissed in Sophie's ear, "I am going to *murder* you."

Sophie looked unforgivably smug. "You wouldn't make it in jail. Besides, now we have plans."

"You are unbelievable."

"Believe it, sister."

In the restaurant, after their table had been cleared, Sophie begrudgingly admitted the vegan brunch was delectable, and excused herself to the bathroom. Jill pulled out her phone the minute her friend was out of view.

Her fingers paused over the keys. She had to let Alex off the hook. He clearly wanted to stay in tonight and visit with his sister and her family. Hadn't he said how much he missed spending time with them? She couldn't pull him away the minute he had free time.

As she dithered, bubbles appeared under his name. Her heart skip-stepped and she held her breath, waiting.

Pick you up at 10? What's
the address?

The fizzing returned to flood her body. She tapped out the address to Sophie's hotel, and before she could change her mind, added:

I can't wait

She watched the bubbles appear. Stop. Reappear. Held her breath again.

Me too

Don't laugh at my
dancing, Jillybean

A pleasant embarrassment washed over her, fingers and toes tingling as she read his words, even as she swore she would never forgive Sophie for anything ever again.

I am going to murder her

Will you visit me in jail?

Every day

Sophie dropped into the seat across from her, smiling like the cat who ate an exceptionally delicious canary. Jill slammed the phone face down on the table so fast she was sure she'd cracked the screen.

"How funny is that? He texts you this morning and then we run into him not two hours later?" Sophie laced her fingers under her chin. "Seems kind of like fate."

Jill rolled her eyes, willing the flush to fade from her cheeks and heart rate to slow. "I don't believe in fate."

"That was pretty fate-y, if you ask me."

"No one's asking."

"I'm just saying it looks like the universe is sending some signals. The closet, the car, the impromptu sleep-away camp. Now today?" Sophie took a dainty sip of coffee. "Something is going to happen."

"Nothing is going to happen."

"The way you were eye fucking him when we ran into him?"

"I was not!" Had she been? Shit. "Well," Jill continued loftily, "he's an objectively good-looking man."

"So were a lot of guys we saw today, and you didn't stare at any of them."

"I did not stare!"

"Right into those big green eyes of his."

She replied without thinking. "They're dark blue, with gold around the iris."

"Oh, are they now?"

Jill snapped her mouth shut. Oh.

No.

Sophie patted her hand, still smirking in the successful maneuvering of her checkmate. "We can talk about that when you're ready. Right now, let's save us both some time and admit you have nothing to wear tonight, and I don't have anything else clean."

"I thought you'd be ready for a random night out?"

"Of course, I'm ready." Sophie brandished her credit card. "I'm ready to go shopping."

ELEVEN

Jill chewed her thumbnail, staring at the clothes Sophie had strong-armed her into buying. She couldn't do it. She couldn't go out like this. She couldn't let *Alex* see her like this.

"Why are you biting your nails?" Sophie asked. "You look great."

Sophie had been right. Jill didn't have anything to wear. She had put her foot down at the sparkly gold bandeau top (which Sophie immediately added to her maybe-pile) and the black pleather mini skirt (which was barely longer than the bandeau), but she had ended up with these cute strappy heels on sale and a cropped red halter top and white denim pants and oh god there were at least two inches of her midriff showing.

Jill tried to pull down the halter top's hem to cover the strip of skin and succeeded only in adding a display of cleavage.

Shit.

"If you had pulled this out of my closet, you wouldn't have blinked," Sophie said reasonably. "This is librarian adjacent. You could teach preschool in this outfit."

Jill inspected her reflection doubtfully. "You and I know very different preschool teachers."

"Do you want a cardigan, Grandma?"

Jill brayed out a giddy laugh and turned resolutely from the mirror. It was a quarter to ten, and she hadn't even tried to see if she could properly sit in the pants. What if she couldn't sit? What if they gaped in the back and her underwear showed? Oh god, what colour underwear was she wearing? Did it show through her pants? She spun to the mirror, scrutinizing her backside for any visible evidence.

"Why are you so nervous?" Sophie's tone was perplexed. "You like this guy. Why the stress?"

"I don't like him. I mean, I like him, but I don't *like* like him. We work together," she replied, straightening her spine and adopting a neutral expression. "I just don't usually socialize with clients."

"Okay, we're still there? Alright." Sophie rummaged in her handbag. "Make sure your phone is charged before we go."

"Good idea." She checked. Fully charged, as usual. She paced the room, trying to think of a task. She'd already chewed off and reapplied her lipstick half a dozen times, and her wallet was in her purse, and …

"Sit down. You'll make your feet sore before we even get there."

Jill obeyed, perching on the corner of the bed and trapping her hands between her thighs. Wait. She could comfortably sit. Jill twisted to look behind her. No visible underwear. One of the many taut threads of her nerves relaxed slightly.

The buzzing of her phone beside her tightened about seventeen more nerves. Jill stared at it like it might bite if she moved too suddenly.

Sophie shook her head and tossed her the phone.

Downstairs in an Uber. Black
Honda Civic

Jill chewed her lip before tapping out:

Down in 5

Sophie smiled at her patiently. "Let's go have fun. And fix your lipstick."

Alex jumped out of the front seat to open the door for them, and Sophie slid past him into the front before he could protest. Alex dropped into the seat beside her and leaned into the space between them to whisper, "Is it okay if I say you look fantastic?"

So did he, in dark denim cuffed over Doc Martens and a bottle-green button-down shirt. Jill's eyes drew to the apex of his collar where the top button opened to a dust of hair, then failed to repress a smile at his bared forearms.

"You know," she leaned in to whisper back, "back in university, Sophie used to drool over the way you rolled up your shirt sleeves like that."

His voice was a low rumble at her bare shoulder. "But what did you think?" he asked, and every synapse in her brain short-circuited.

The rest of the ride to the club was mercifully short. Sophie, bless her, kept a steady stream of charm flowing with Alex, the driver, and Jill each in turn, to keep the ride from lapsing into silence. The bouncer took one look at Sophie and waved them to the front of the line. Jill shrugged a shoulder at Alex and mouthed *sparkles,* before following her friend into the club and beelining for the bar.

"My treat this time," Jill said as she tapped her card for their drinks, and Alex quirked his lips at her, putting his own card back in his pocket.

Sophie raised her glass and voice above the noise. "To my best friend and a new friend!"

Glasses clinked and before the others had lifted their drinks to their lips, Jill drained half her martini. The bitter, savoury cocktail burned on the way down, softening the edges of her frazzled nerves and she turned to Alex, eyes watering. "I'm really …"

He grinned. "Thirsty?"

"Something like that," Sophie said with a smirk and pulled her towards the music.

Country music would never be her favourite, but Jill had to admit that it got people moving. Guitar twang and driving beat stoked the crowd into an energized throng and she let herself get lost in the lights and rhythm. The tension that had followed her all day ebbed away as she danced with Sophie and the string of men her friend had pulled into their orbit. She tried to pull Alex to the floor a few times, but he insisted he stay put at their table to guard their drinks.

Another song ended, and Jill dragged her chair closer to him. "You're not dancing." He must be so bored, babysitting their drinks against some potential roofie-wielding asshole. She leaned in close to be heard above the music, crossing her arm over her maybe-cleavage as she did. "Are you having a good time?"

"Yeah." His gaze travelled up her arm, stalling where the straps circled her neck. "I'm having a good time."

She toyed with her glass, the last sips of her first drink swirling at the bottom. "When I finish this, will you dance with me?"

"Going to need another beer before I'm dancing," he said, a smile catching the corner of his mouth.

Jill pushed away from the table, returning minutes later with a second drink, and slid it in front of him. "No rush. But I want a dance."

The DJ started layering hip-hop over the country tracks. Sophie drunkenly yelled with every song "I love this one!" her accent appearing with her increased blood alcohol levels and continued to grind with a man clad in head-to-toe denim. Jill laughed and lifted her hands to the lights overhead, the disco ball throwing rainbows over the mass of bodies. A blond guy in a sweaty polo shirt beside her smiled conspiratorially with her reaction to Sophie's exuberance. Polo Shirt leaned in, hand gripping her shoulder as he spoke something garbled into her ear.

"What?" Jill yelled over the music, leaning away from his voice.

His other hand landed on her hip, his mouth closer to her ear and releasing a whiff of sour breath. "I said, you're fucking gorgeous." His hand snaked up her wrist as he tried to loop it around his neck. Jill faked a smile and twisted away, turning her attention to the DJ spinning a Rihanna track over another country song she didn't recognize.

"I could watch you move all night," he said, the wheedling voice in her ear again.

Take a hint, dude. "No, thanks." No smile this time. Not even a fake one.

His hands assailed her waist and he ground his pelvis against her ass, even as she stiffened and glared at him. *This fucking guy.* She tried to pull away and resorted to the lie told by countless other women before her. "I have a boyfriend."

The invasion continued as if she had stayed mute, but before she could elbow him in the solar plexus, a solid arm pulled her away. Jill's eyes followed the arm up to Alex's dark expression, who towered over Polo Shirt and barked out hard words she didn't catch. Polo Shirt blanched, hands held up in front of him, and backed away.

Alex watched him disappear into the crowd and dropped his arm as soon as he was out of sight. "He won't bother you again."

She hated it. That so many guys only backed off when they thought a girl belonged to someone else. That "no" wasn't enough. That she needed a rescue at all.

She also hated that Alex's arm was no longer wrapped around her.

"I could've taken care of it myself," she said, rubbing her hands where it had been a moment earlier.

His brows drew together as he looked down at her. "But you don't have to."

A prickle started behind her eyes. Besides Sophie, there weren't a lot of people who had her back. Now she felt like she might have one more. She lifted herself onto her toes and twined her arms around him, leaning into his solid warmth. Just a hug. Friends hugged all the time. Slowly, carefully, Alex circled his arms around her waist and pressed his jaw to her temple.

She wasn't going to cry, but she couldn't bring herself to let go. Not yet. She took a deep breath to bring space into her lungs. "What did you say to him?" she asked into the hollow of his neck.

His jaw unclenched as he dipped his mouth to her ear. "I let him know what would happen to him if he didn't leave you alone."

"What was that?"

"Doesn't matter. It worked."

"I'll get you to tell me one day," she said, and even with everything, felt a tiny bubble of laughter fill her chest. She could only imagine what Alex could have said to make him back off so quickly. She almost felt sorry for him. Almost. Jill tightened her arms. "Thank you."

"I promised I'd keep you safe."

She was. Safe. And that was her cue to let go. She slid back to her heels, his hand lingering on her waist a half-second longer. She ran her fingers through her damp hair. "Would you please grab me a bottle of water? I'll be right back."

Jill tugged Sophie into the bathroom, the blunted noise spiking as the door opened and closed. Her friend slurred lightly as she called through the stall door.

"All these guys think I'm going to remember who they are the next time I'm in town," she said, deleting the numbers she'd added to her phone.

Jill bent over the sink with hands covered in suds, her heartbeat fluttering like a hummingbird.

Inhale slowly, exhale deeply.

She rinsed her hands and put her hand on her heart to will it to slow down. She pasted on a grin for Sophie. "Can you blame them for trying? You're pretty amazing."

"True." Sophie squinted at her, as if she could crack open Jill's brain and make sense of the jumbled contents. "Are you okay after that creep? I was on my way to knight-in-shining-armour you, but someone beat me to it."

"Ugh, you know." She paused, not sure how to untangle the emotions bubbling up. "Alex helped."

Sophie levelled an inscrutable stare at her. "Helped. Okay." She bounced with the muffled music, eyes on the door.

"Go collect some more hearts, or numbers, or whatever. I'll be there in a minute." Jill shooed her out and Sophie planted a kiss on her cheek.

She lifted the hair from the back of her neck and pressed cold water to the crook of her elbows. Her feet were sore, her ears were ringing, and the hummingbird wings should have slowed down by now.

But she had at least one more dance.

The black sheet of Sophie's bob bounced as she spoke intently to Alex, gestures punctuating the points Jill was too far away to hear. Alex nodded as she spoke, arms crossed tight across his chest, absorbing her every word. His eyes flicked up as Jill came into his line of sight and his shoulders released, his serious expression softening as she approached. Sophie swung her head to follow his gaze before turning back and stabbing a finger into his chest repeatedly with her closing comments.

Jill could recognize Sophie's meddling expression anywhere. She gave her friend a skeptical look as she approached.

"What's going on?" she asked carefully.

"I was just telling him the Canadiens were going to destroy the Flames the next time they play," Sophie said sweetly, and skipped past her to the dance floor.

"That's entirely believable," Jill called to her friend's retreating back, already absorbed into the throng of dancers, leaving them alone in the crowd.

Alex silently offered Jill the requested bottle of water, which she accepted with a small smile, looking anywhere but him. He had barely moved, looking like he was waiting for her to say something, his attention focused on her as she sipped the chilly water. Not knowing what else to do, she passed him the bottle, brows raised in offer.

He took it from her with a cautious smile. "Are we sharing drinks now?"

Jill's brain stalled for the millionth time that night. "I mean, we did when we got stuck overnight? And I don't want to waste it? And you look hot? I mean …" The words stumbled as they left her mouth. "Never mind."

Why didn't sinkholes appear on command?

"Jill, relax," he said, corners of his eyes crinkling as he tipped his head back to drink. Her eyes trailed on the column of his throat, and two simultaneous thoughts raced across her neurons.

The first thought was zero times in history had a man telling a woman to relax achieved anything other than the opposite of the desired outcome.

The second thought was, *oh, shit.*

One of the tidy little boxes she had hidden deep away rattled open, and out of it escaped the knowledge of how much she liked watching his eyes crinkle when he smiled at her, and when he spoke close enough his breath rustled her hair, and when he made her laugh with his self-deprecating humour. And how she wanted to press her lips to the pulse beating just above his collar.

The hummingbird in her heart quickened in response.

She was not relaxed. She was the opposite of relaxed.

He placed the empty bottle on the bar behind him and leaned his mouth to her ear. "Do you still want that dance?"

She nodded mutely, trying to parse her new realization, and let him lead her by the hand towards the music.

The music pulsed around them, the floor bouncing under the feet of dancers. She closed her eyes to hide from her thoughts. To escape into the music, to flow with the urgent tide pressing on all sides. To let the rhythm work its magic and let herself think the flutter in her heart was from the noise and lights and movement around her. She braved opening her eyes and broke out into a face-splitting smile.

It looked like he had a completely different song playing in his head, arms stiff at his sides and feet leaden. His concentration was etched across his furrowed brow, jerky movements nowhere near the beat of the music. He stopped his feet dead, a sheepish grin on his face.

"Told you I couldn't dance."

She hid her smile and leaned in to reply, but the music downshifted in tempo, and Alex lightly gathered her arms up to circle his neck without waiting for her reply.

"I think Sophie asked the DJ to play something I could keep up to," he said, the first bars of a slowed down version of "Jolene" receiving a cheer from the crowd. "Can I have one more?"

She was extra super not relaxed.

The languid song stretched around them. Without the need to find a beat, or maybe because she was close, his motion slowed and steadied, and she felt fluid pressed along the length of his body. He smelled like pine and clean sweat and she buried her nose in his neck.

"Jill?" he murmured into her hair, a shiver erupting along her neck where his breath stirred. His thumb grazed the strip of bare skin on her back, sending a companion surge to meet the one racing from her neck.

He had to feel it. The goosebumps where he touched her. Her shiver under his hand. Her heart pounding against her rib cage, pressed next to his. She let her hand drift over the nape of his neck, waves damp in the heat of the room. The lips that moved against her ear a second ago were level with her eyes, and as she tilted her head back, she saw a trace of her red lipstick standing out stark against the green of his shirt.

The colour was a stop sign. A yield, look both ways. Do not proceed.

In less than seventy-two hours, she was going to be sitting across from him. In his office. Him paying her to be there.

There was no denying it this time. No misunderstanding. She had been about to cross a line she couldn't come back from.

"Oh. God. I'm sorry," she said, pulling herself away. Confusion swept his face as she widened the gulf between them. "I'm so sorry." She pressed her hands to her open mouth. "I should go."

"Wait …"

Jill wound her way through the crush of bodies lost in the music, lights blinding her. Her hand clasped Sophie's arm as soon as she was close enough. "Can we get out of here?"

"But what about—"

"Please."

Sophie focused her blurry gaze. "Let's go."

She pulled up the Uber app as she followed her friend to the exit, searching for the fastest pickup available. Her eyes met Alex's from across the room, and he took two steps towards her before stopping. Fingers shaking, she confirmed the order, and a text banner popped up.

She shoved down the emotions roiling in her stomach and opened the message.

What just happened?

Inhale slowly, exhale deeply.

What could she even say? She tried a few responses. *I'm sorry I tried to kiss you. I'm tired. I didn't mean it.* But deleted them all before she hit send.

She didn't want to lie.

A staccato ring burst from her phone, echoing her racing pulse. She hit the red decline button without looking.

Sophie pulled her into the waiting Uber, brows drawn together in confusion. "Jilly?"

The bubbles appeared again.

Will you let me know you got
back safe?

Jill switched her phone to silent and clasped it between her palms.

The ride seemed longer on the way back to the hotel. She followed Sophie in a haze, through the lobby, up the elevator, into the room, the insulated silence of the soundproof walls pressing in. Jill carefully undid the straps on her new sandals and returned them to the shoebox before sliding onto the top of the bed, knees hugged to her chest. Sophie returned from the bathroom ten minutes later, face scrubbed of makeup and fluffy hotel robe in place of her glittery clubbing clothes, and cajoled Jill to complete the same routine.

Fresh out of the shower, hair wrapped in a towel and robe cinched around her waist, Jill eyed the makeup wipes saturated with red stain and thought of her lips skating near his neck as she leaned towards his mouth. So close. If she'd leaned in the smallest bit …

She braced her hands on the counter and let her head hang. Oh, she was in deep.

"Soph?" Jill crept out of the bathroom and curled into a ball, face down on the bed. "What did I just do?"

"That's what I've been waiting for you to tell me."

The bed dipped as Sophie scooted beside her. Jill rolled onto her back, pulled a pillow over her face, and said nothing.

"You should let Alex know you're with me at the hotel."

A charge shot through Jill's veins. "How do you … what?"

"Unlock it for me." Sophie took the phone from Jill and tapped out a quick message, hit send, and tossed the phone on the bed. "Done. I told him you're alive and you'd call him tomorrow. Now, what's going on?"

Jill swallowed against a dry throat. If she said it out loud, it would make it real.

Who was she kidding. It was already real.

She squeezed her eyes shut and spilled. "I almost kissed Alex."

"What do you mean, 'almost'?"

"I mean I almost. And then I didn't."

She wasn't drunk; she'd had the one drink hours ago. Then what? Why? Sure, they had spent a lot of time together over the last few months. And he was smart and funny and her stomach tied in knots when he smiled at her and oh, shit.

Not in the plan. Falling for Alex was not in the plan.

Okay. Time for a new plan.

Jill sat up abruptly, the towel coming loose from her hair. This was fine. Not a problem. She could compartmentalize. She'd been doing it for years. Put it in a box, lock it, and drop it in the Mariana Trench. "This'll pass. I can keep it to myself."

"I don't think you can hide this."

"Why not? I don't need to say anything. I didn't do anything. I'll—"

"Jilly." Sophie looked at her with a mixture of patience and amusement. "This is not a secret." She pulled out her phone and confronted Jill with an undeniable level of evidence.

Every photo Sophie had taken that night. Every video. Alex watching Jill as she left the table. His eyes hooded, lips parted, staring at her as she leaned in to mug the camera. His body turning to her like the tide following the moon. And Jill. Her hand on his waist as she laughed into the crook of his neck. Leaning over the table to whisper in his ear. Eyes shining with a smile she hadn't worn for years.

"He was watching you all night," Sophie said. "You left the dance floor every other song to swoon all over him."

Jill scrolled through the photos with mounting panic, stopping at a video Sophie had posted. The frame was square on Sophie kissing denim guy, wearing the cowboy hat she'd stolen from him. But in the background, Alex sat head down, leaning forward on a stool, one foot on the floor and the other on the bottom rung. Jill stood between his legs, hand on his arm as she whispered, smiling into his ear, his hand clenched in a fist by her hip, clearly restraining himself from making contact. She felt her body lean to the side as if she could find his hand on her hours after the fact, and her heart responded with a violent need to be known.

"You've been ignoring what you want for as long as I've known you. Just say it."

Jill leaned forward, gripping her head between her hands. "Oh god, Soph. This is so wrong. Alex is a client. I just got out of a mess of a relationship." Jill flopped onto the bed, wet hair splayed in tangles around her. "How did this happen?"

"People fall for each other all the time." Sophie rubbed her feet, yawning. "It's kind of the opposite of a problem. I mean, besides the whole working together thing."

"Fuck."

Sophie snorted. "Take all that other stuff away. How does he make you feel?"

"He makes me feel …" Nervous, excited, giddy. Warm, safe enough to share her story with him. And she wanted to share more. She had been shut down for so long in a desperate act of self-preservation. Alex reminded her not only that she had emotions, but she wanted to explore them. With him. "Soph, he makes me *feel.* What am I going to do?"

"Right now, you're going to do nothing," she said gently. "Go to sleep and talk to him tomorrow."

Jill pulled the covers over her head. Sophie was right. About the doing nothing right now part, and the talking to him part. Not about the sleeping part. There would be no sleeping tonight, but at least lying in bed, awake for hours, might give her the chance to make sense of her feelings and everything would be clear in the morning.

TWELVE

Omar peered down at the project closeout checklist, trying to find the best font size on his laptop to project to the shared screen. After watching him squint for months, Jill had finally convinced him to get his eyes checked. He still hadn't forgiven her for being the catalyst for him getting reading glasses as if he wouldn't have needed them if she hadn't mentioned it.

When she told him they made him look distinguished, his nuclear glare had nearly disintegrated her.

"And the application was submitted in full?"

"We needed almost all the contingency time, with their files the way they were, and they were pretty nervous to finally send it in, but we got it in on time." Jill's leg bounced under the table. Alex had nearly made her dizzy with his circling the day they'd hit submit, and the memory of his nerves triggered a surge of empathy that went well beyond what she was willing to admit to Omar. She gripped her arms across her torso to still the fluttering in her stomach.

"Sometimes the last step is the hardest," Omar said cautiously. "Sounds like you handled your clients well."

I am handling my client the opposite of well.

She'd been right. She hadn't slept. She had watched the buzzy red lights on the digital clock beside her flick through the night, anticipating a wave of anxiety. Instead, the fluttering in her stomach kept it at bay, like there was room for only one overwhelming emotion at a time. She had the twisted thought she might've preferred the panic attack. She knew what to expect with those.

In the morning, Sophie had convinced her to check her phone instead of pushing her breakfast around her plate. Jill had steeled herself for a barrage of messages, but Alex had sent only one last text after Sophie had let him know they were at the hotel: a simple thanks for letting him know she was safe, and to please call him tomorrow.

Once, when she was with Connor, Jill had forgotten to charge her phone before she'd left the apartment. Before she had realized her oversight, Connor had tracked her down at work, scolding her for her stupidity and for making him worry. When she finally plugged it in, she had over twenty texts and eight missed calls in the span of a few hours. Later, the admin assistant lightly suggested that Connor had perhaps not said the kindest things about her when he called. Jill had covered for him, again, laughing it off as a misunderstanding. Turned out, he had been trying to get a hold of her because he couldn't find his lunch bag. Which later he found in his gym bag. And he called her careless and irresponsible when she got home that night. How could she let him worry like that? What if something had happened? He just loved her so much and she didn't even care. He checked her battery life every morning before work for the rest of the month and made her text him every morning when she got in. She hadn't let her phone battery drop below half charge again.

At the sight of that single unread message, one of the hurdling balls of apprehension rolling around in her stomach had dissolved. Still, she hadn't trusted her voice to call, so she spent twenty minutes composing a text that essentially said she was awake. Her phone had chirped in her hand almost immediately with Alex asking to meet her that day. She had used the excuse that she was busy with Sophie—which was true, although Sophie said she'd be fine to go to the airport early—but they could meet after work Monday. She hoped the extra day would buy some time for the universe to drop the magic answer in her brain.

Then, Jill had spent the rest of Sunday ignoring the events of the previous night, and Sophie let her. Which was well enough, as her jittery nerves and accelerated heart rate accompanied the running commentary in her mind all day.

I'm a walking HR complaint. It's too soon after Connor. I could leave in a year.

But the questions that kept floating to the top …

What if he has feelings for me? How did I not realize this sooner? Why didn't I kiss him?

"Get out of your head, Jillybean," Sophie had said when Jill dropped her off for her red-eye late last night. "For once, let your heart do the thinking."

Jill nodded, with no clarity on what to do.

Clattering keys yanked Jill back to the longest day of her life and she snuck a peek at the time. Four o'clock. She was meeting Alex in two hours and the universe hadn't delivered her answer.

Well, crap.

"And the VC proposal?"

"Pending while we wait to hear on the grant. In the meantime, I've started drafting audit recommendations. Hopefully, we can complete it while we wait to see if we're successful with the grant."

And won't this be the most fun couple of months as I hide my apparently incandescent lust while we set file naming practices and organization standards. The Storage Room Incident had become decidedly more tame in how much unintended physical contact they had in the weeks since, but looking back, it was the first time Jill had sparked. Times when she found herself watching him, engrossed in his latest reports, a look of singular concentration dominating his features, and her eyes would flit to the nondescript door leading into the closet. Spending more time in the tiny space sent parallel tremors of delight and dread along her spine.

Omar looked at her with shrewd eyes. "Well, congrats on a great first file. I'll submit the project as materially complete, but we'll leave it open for follow up when we hear on the grant." He clicked through several more screens and pulled up the client feedback forms. "Let's get the satisfaction survey out by the end of the week."

God, this keeps getting better. Of course. The survey that Angela was going to scrutinize in review of Jill's first grant application. The one that her boss had said was critically important to the company as they rebuilt their name consulting for the environmental sector. What the hell would it say? *Top-notch understanding of our needs, exceptional ability to integrate multiple data sources, but absolutely no respect for personal space and tried to make out with me. Twice. Three out of five stars.*

"Cool. Great. Can we send it now?"

Jill closed her office door, leaning against the smoky-grey privacy glass. The floor had emptied, but she couldn't chance running into her team before she left. Ashleen noticed everything out of the ordinary, and Marco had no filter when it came to asking questions that crossed his mind. Omar had spent the first half of their meeting joking with her as usual while they completed the forms, then, after realizing she was acting like she had teleported in from another planet, tried to subtly probe for information. Even his innocuous, well-intentioned questions had rattled the facade of calm she had cobbled together.

She checked her phone for the hundredth time in the last twelve minutes. One hour to go. Jill had asked to meet somewhere in public. The Peace Bridge would be teeming with people enjoying the last days of spring as the season rolled to summer. She was confident—well, she thought she was confident—that Alex wouldn't do anything unreasonable, but her years with Connor had warned her not to take that for granted.

Fifty-nine minutes to go.

The Peace Bridge was a half-hour walk from her office. If she pressed her face to the glass in the office kitchen, she could see it from here. She could leave now and wait for him to show up. And let her thoughts spiral there instead of here. Brilliant plan! At least the walk might work out some of her tension.

She pulled her hair back into a low knot, ducked into the bathroom to brush her teeth, and sneaked down the empty hall. She glanced down at her white sneakers and had a fleeting wish for the extra three-and-a-half inches of confidence of her lucky stilettos. She had thought about wearing them that morning, but the half-hour walk to the bridge would have been ridiculous. The heels reluctantly went back in the closet.

The walk did nothing to clear her head. She fiddled with her playlists, trying to find something to distract her. Instead, love song after unrequited love song competed with the noise in her head until she yanked out her earbuds and shoved them to the bottom of her bag.

She wasn't ready. She didn't have an answer. And if she screwed this up, her work, his work, everything could go wrong.

Come on, universe. Give a girl a break.

Zero breaks from the universe.

Alex sat on the edge of a concrete bench, half an hour early, his long legs stretched in front of him and eyes down on the phone he was slowly turning over in his hands. Jill paused in her stride, her vibrating heart sending resonant waves through her body as she let her gaze sweep over him. She couldn't see his expression, but the tight angle of his jaw and rigid line of his shoulders made her yearn to smooth her hand along both to release the tension. He squinted into the sun as he scanned the crowd and pulled up straight as he caught sight of her.

No turning back now, and no more running away. She squared her shoulders and put one foot forward, then the other, until she was beside him, alighting on the bench a foot away from him. She crossed her ankles, tucked a stray lock of hair behind her ear, and clasped her hands in her lap.

Okay. Here goes everything.

"Hi." She made herself meet his gaze and the warm glow she had tried to pack away burst from its box.

"You're early." His voice was husky, a low rumble in his chest.

"So are you."

"I didn't know if you'd come."

"I wanted to talk, too."

What she was going to say yet, she didn't know.

"You pushed me away." It looked like the words were out before he could stop them. He closed his eyes and worked his jaw. "When we were close. I thought you were finally going to …" His shoulders rose and fell. "But then you pushed me away."

Okay, so jumping right in.

All night, all day, she played out versions of this moment in her head, hoping the answer would land fully formed into her brain. Thinking and planning hadn't worked.

She twisted her hands on her lap. "I didn't practise anything."

"What?" He blinked at her.

She tried again. "I didn't practise anything. I don't know what to say. I've been thinking about—" she waved her hand "—this. All weekend. And I don't know what to say."

"Okay, let's start there." The deep breath he took came out ragged. "Is it a good 'this?'"

A warm rush pooled in her belly as she contemplated "this" for the millionth time in the last forty-one-and-a-quarter hours. It was definitely a dangerous "this."

I might be gone in a year. A lot can change in a year. It's too soon after Connor. That was six months ago. We work together. I don't want only work together. I want …

"If …" He stopped. "If I've misread things. Or if I've made you uncomfortable, or if you want Nick to take over and you don't want to see me—"

"No!" she blurted out. That was not what happened. And definitely not what she wanted.

"Jill," Alex said, eyes pleading. "Tell me what you want."

Every muscle fibre trembled as she willed herself to answer. To be honest. With him. With herself. What would happen if, for once in her life, she stopped thinking and let her heart do the talking? If she opened her mouth and listened to what came out?

"I really want to kiss you."

All the angles of his body released as he brought his hand up to her cheek. "Thank god," he chuffed out a sigh. "Please."

This time, she leaned in.

When she pressed against the fullness of his mouth, catching his lower lip between her own, the noise in her head was replaced with a song. He tasted like salt and chocolate, and she traced his tongue with her own. Her hands found their way to his hair and the sound he released low in his throat fanned the heat in her belly into wildfire. Electricity surged where his fingers traced the base of her throat and she broke away to draw a shuddering gasp, taking his breath with her.

His shoulders rose and fell as his fingers continued to swipe long strokes on her neck. "That was …"

"Yeah." She rested her forehead on his, the edge of her nose lightly brushing his cheek. "Really not enough." Her nails gently sketched the knotted muscles at the base of his neck and the responding shiver that erupted under his skin had her pulling him to her again.

Melted. She melted towards him. Letting his lips chart the contours of her mouth, his hands slide to her waist and up her ribs. His light stubble was just a little rough, and she brought her fingertips to line his jaw to touch the same roughness her lips felt.

Her heartbeat thrummed along every line in her body and the warm glow that claimed its space in her core forced her doubts aside. The questions were still there, but subdued. Less demanding. Like they would be patient for the answers.

When she broke away a second time, her rapid breath matched his, and a charged silence stretched between them.

After several heartbeats, Alex cleared his throat. “So, I think it’s a good ‘this,’” he said from a place deep in his chest and Jill collapsed into his neck, stifling her laughter into the collar of his shirt. So what if she got lipstick on it? More would end up there soon.

Days, weeks, months of tension poured out of her. All the worrying and denial and working herself into knots. Was just over. And she was a little scared, sure. Okay, a lot scared. But it felt *so good.*

When Jill caught her breath, she pulled back, her pulse still singing in her ears. She looked down at their clasped hands, his thumb stroking the top of her fingertips, and met his eyes again with a nervous half smile on her face.

“Alex,” she said, “I’m kind of freaking out.” She refocused her eyes around her, and a different heat flooded her body. Her smile spread as her blush consumed her cheeks. She had purposefully chosen an extremely busy location for the audience. “And everyone is watching.”

He blinked and looked around the crowds as he brought her hands to his mouth. “I’m not sorry about that last part.” Still, he pulled back reluctantly, and continued, “But I don’t want you to freak out.”

“Oh, no. That’s coming,” she replied, and his chest hitched with a laugh. “But not now.”

“So.” The new heat in his expression sparked a stutter in her chest. “Can I take you to dinner tonight?”

“Like a date?” Her cheeks were starting to hurt with all the smiling she was doing.

“Yeah. A date.”

She twined her fingers with his. “Absolutely.”

They had eaten dinner together dozens of times, but tonight, everything felt different.

Now it made sense her pulse quickened when their gaze met. How he found a way to touch her at all times. His hand on the small of her back when he followed her into the taqueria. The length of his thigh firm against hers as they sat waiting for their table. The first time Alex slid his arm around her waist it sent such a shock through her centre she jolted in response, and she held his arm in place before he could withdraw.

"You surprised me," she said. "I need a bit of time to get used to this."

"Take all the time you need. I'm in no rush."

It wasn't weird. Or awkward. The air thrummed with this new thing between them and her trust with him hadn't changed. Instead, a playfulness she'd buried long ago surfaced, and she leaned into it.

Jill sipped her soda water, elbows on the table and chin in her palm. "I need to know where you learned to dance."

"I recall specifically asking you not to laugh at my dancing." He picked up his phone to scroll. "I have proof right here."

"I'm not laughing. I'm just asking."

"You might be amazed to learn that dancing isn't really my thing." He scratched the angle of his jaw with his phone and the urge to feel his stubble under her lips once more jumped under her skin and she nearly crawled over the table.

"I love dancing, but I think my days of clubbing are mostly behind me," she said instead. "But Soph really wanted to go, so …" she trailed off with a *what-can-you-do* shrug.

"… so we both went dancing to make someone we care about happy," he finished.

Jill ducked her head to hide her blush behind her soda. One more thing she wasn't used to. The kisses must have freed a flirty streak in Alex. Or maybe he had game. She wasn't sure what to do with it. "Can I ask what she said to you?"

"Some interrogation about my intentions. A bit of light threatening." He paused. "Mostly coaching."

Called it. Definitely her meddling expression.

"That sounds like *ma poulette,*" she said, and Alex snorted his Sprite.

"Your what?" he said, tears coming into his eyes, which could have been from either his laughter or the soda he irrigated his nasal passages with.

"You know? My chicken?"

"I know what it means," he said, wiping his eyes. "But, why?"

So, Jill told him about the night she, Sophie, and Kyle had a chicken wing eating contest, and while Sophie had been the last one standing, she hadn't been able to eat chicken since.

"So, if you ever hear a rooster call from my phone, you'll know it's *ma petite poulette.*"

"In that case, I'll change her text alert on my phone, too."

Jill clicked her tongue, shaking her head with a wry grin. "Trust that girl to get every cute guy's number."

"You think I'm cute?"

The hummingbird in her chest stretched its wings again as she realized this was something she could say now. She nudged her toes on the side of his leg under the table. "Yes," she said. "Really cute."

Now he hid behind his soda, tips of his ears going rosy and looking incredibly adorable. Could six-foot-two, burly men look adorable? Apparently, this one could.

"She told me to text her if I needed an assist."

"Be warned, she doesn't understand the concept of boundaries. But she has pretty good instincts, and she talked me off a ledge Saturday night." Maybe Sophie was clairvoyant, or Jill was far more transparent than she thought. Either way, she might not be sitting here if her friend hadn't held her hand as she had run up against the brick wall of her feelings.

"I'll have to send her flowers or something."

"She deserves it, but if she gets flowers before I do, I'll flip a table."

"Might send her flowers first just to see that." He toyed with her pinky finger. "Do you like getting flowers?"

She opened her mouth to reply and hesitated. "I don't know," she said. "I don't think I've ever … No, wait. My dad gave me flowers when I graduated from McGill."

"Hang on," he said, his expression slightly appalled. "None of your boyfriends ever gave you flowers?"

Boyfriend. Singular. "Ah, please let's not talk about exes." No time to let Connor intrude on their evening. And even though she didn't think of herself as a jealous person, hearing about Alex's past loves was near the bottom of her list of things to discuss at exactly this moment.

"Right, no." He resumed playing with her fingers. "Okay, you get flowers first."

"You don't have to do that."

He just gave her a soft look, and once again, her body heat rose.

Her phone vibrating on the seat beside her jarred her attention away from how the light slanted through his eyelashes—a pleasure that had been cut short the last time she caught herself admiring his features—and smiled at Sophie's text popping up.

What the fuck happened? Did
you talk to him yet??

… right above the banner announcing another voicemail from her mother.

Not tonight. She flipped her phone over with a groan, but not before she started at the time on the home screen.

Nine-thirty. In twelve hours, she and Alex were going to be at work.

One of the niggling questions shook itself loose from the others and floated to the top of her brain. Jill frowned at the pork belly taco that had done nothing wrong to her and picked off the last leaves of cilantro she'd missed.

"I'm having a great time, but can we talk about something practical?"

"Of course," he said, twin lines appearing between his brows.

"Tomorrow?" She let the word hang between them. "When we're at work?"

"Oh, right." His shoulders hunched against his shirt, pulling across the breath of his chest. Now that she had the permission to look, she revelled in studying the lines of his body.

Get a grip, Northrop. Focus. "This is kind of one of my freak-out things. I mean, I have a job to do, and I'm going to spend half my energy trying to not kiss you."

He closed his eyes and took a deep breath through his nose. "Walking right by that, because that is not what we are talking about right now," he said, more to himself than to her. "Okay, same. What are you thinking?"

"I think we should set some ground rules. Around office behaviour."

He covered his smile with his Sprite. "Like, no more shenanigans in the storage closet?"

The fantasy she had cultivated over months sprung easily to her mind. Of him following her into the tiny room, closing the door behind them. Pushing him against the shelves, hands in his hair as she dragged his face down to hers. His hands sliding down her waist, exploring … the fantasy that didn't have to be a fantasy anymore. She huffed a laugh from under her palms and squeezed her thighs together. "You, too?"

"Every day since."

"Not helpful right now," she said, her tone undercut by her reddening cheeks. "Okay, rule one. No touching in the office."

"I hate it. What else?"

"Or flirting."

"It's not flirting," he said, stroking her palm. "It's just talking."

"Alex."

"Okay. No flirting at the office."

She took a deep breath. "I think you should tell Nick. He might want a say if there's a potential conflict of interest in his company. Not like this is a conflict of interest. More like a personal relationship that we'll need to make sure there's no perceived bias. Not like this is a *relationship* relationship. We've just had one date. And even though you've hired me for this work and are in a position of authority over me. And I'll be suggesting ways to change how you run your business that you're going to hate. The grant is already submitted, so we're clear there. And we'll be doing a process audit, not a financial one, so there won't be a professional sign-off needed. But I still need to talk to my HR department and check our policies. Make sure I'm not breaking any fraternization rules. Crap, I really should've done that already." She cut her rambling and pressed the heels of her hands against her eye sockets.

Fuck.

Concern replaced the humour on his face. "Jill, hey …"

And what if whatever was happening between them went south? What if they had a few dates and he decided he didn't want to see her after all, and she had to act like everything was fine until the proposal was complete? What if he saw how much baggage she was carrying and didn't want to deal with it? She wouldn't blame him. She barely wanted to deal with it.

She curled her fingers into fists and dug her nails into her palm. God, she was falling apart over nothing, and he was going to think she was this fragile little …

Sophie's advice flowed back to her. *Get out of your head, Jilly.*

Her voice came out tiny. "I'm overthinking this." She exhaled slowly. "Don't worry. I'm not going to have a panic attack."

"I'm not worried." He paused. "Can I hold your hand?"

She nodded, extending one hand to him, the other propping up her head.

He closed his hands around her fist. "I said we can take this slow, and I meant it. You drive, okay?" He worked her hand open, holding her fingers open against his palm, and she hitched a laugh. She had wanted to do the same thing to him mere days ago to soothe his jangled nerves. She lifted her head to meet his eyes.

"I'll tell Nick tomorrow. Do you want to be there?"

Absolutely not. "Sure. Yeah."

"Okay," he said. "Since it's not office hours right now, can I walk you home?"

"Yes," she said, smiling. "That would be lovely."

THIRTEEN

The next morning was aggressively bright at a quarter to eight as Jill walked to the CMR office. The extra shot of espresso had been overkill. The last thing she needed was to be jittery on top of tired and nervous. She downed the high-octane brew and prepared for the day she was walking into.

Sleep last night had been predictably light. The kiss Alex had left her with on her apartment steps had done nothing to help her fall asleep. He had the good sense to break it off after a few seconds—she certainly wouldn't have been able to—and she stumbled into her apartment where she wandered for a few aimless laps before collapsing on her couch. Even though it was past midnight in Montreal, she sent a series of texts to Sophie:

Omg we kissed

I'M FREAKING OUT

Call you tmr xoxo

Jill tried to follow an evening relaxation yoga video on YouTube to wind down. When she clued in that the instructor had moved two asanas past the pigeon pose she was still holding, she gave up and took a shower, wishing she could have cranked the cold at that time of night. At least the leisurely fifteen extra minutes she spent with the shower head took the edge off.

A bit.

Her morning began at two, four, and finally five a.m. when she admitted the little sleep she had was over and rolled out of bed. She extended her run that morning to work out some of her nerves, then cursed herself, remembering she had her first softball game with her new team that night. Way to show up fatigued from an impromptu seventy-minute run, on top of what was going to be an emotionally charged day.

She also should've taken into consideration Alex didn't usually show up to the office until after nine, sometimes ten. The road trip had been an exception, and he had looked drowsy as he pulled up at eight. On time, for once. For her. The realization brought a smile to her lips.

So now she got to sit with Nick for the next god knows how long and work away like everything was completely normal until Alex showed up.

This is fine. Everything is fine.

I'm a professional.

I've got this.

She would start her project outline and chat with Nick like everything was super cool and super normal until Alex got there, and then she could let Alex take the lead on how he wanted to bring it up with his business partner.

Easy.

Except that when she walked through the front doors, Alex sat slumped in his chair with his chin down. The muscles of his chest flexed against his crossed arms, fists pressed into his biceps, testing the shirt's structural integrity. His legs kicked out in front of him, feet crossed at the ankles and thighs filling out the denim. The urge to see if his lap was as comfortable as it looked popped into her mind, closely followed by the wonder when she would eventually be brave enough to explore him with more than her eyes.

Also, lap-sitting probably fell under Rule One, no touching at work.

Following her own stupid rules was going to be harder than she thought.

Taking great care to walk silently, she crept up as close as she dared without alerting him.

"How many times have you hit snooze already?" she asked from six inches away, and he jolted out of his nap.

"Holy shit," he said, laughing as he started to wrap his arms around her, before pulling back and stuffing his hands in his pockets. "You scared the crap out of me."

"Maybe I'm the one who needs a bell," she said, tipping onto the balls of her feet and wishing she could have gotten that hug. Technically, they were in the office, but office hours wouldn't start for another ten minutes. It hadn't been a minute and she was already looking for loopholes. Starting down the road of technicalities would be a very steep, very slippery slope.

She begrudgingly backed up a pace. "How long have you been here?"

"Not long. Five, ten minutes. I tried to get here earlier but . . ." He yawned expansively and scrubbed his hand over his face. "Anyway, I wanted to be here when you got in."

"Thanks." Something pleasant squirmed in her chest. She wondered if this sweet streak of Alex's was just a best behaviour act that would fade over time, and the pleasant something in her chest tempered slightly.

Half an hour later, the uneven floorboards creaked with sharp steps, and Jill popped her head up to look at Alex, who smiled and turned to the door.

Nick entered the room with a full scowl, pulling up short at Alex already in place.

"'Sup."

This was going to be a treat.

Alex cleared his throat. "Have a minute?"

He looked between Jill and Alex, a smirk layering over top his scowl. "What?"

"So, Jill and I are …" He looked at her with a self-conscious smile. "I guess we didn't talk about that part."

They really hadn't. For all her talk about being transparent with the people she worked with, they hadn't figured out any details. Not that she regretted it. They had spent their time doing other, more engaging things. And she wouldn't have traded it, even now that they'd have to improvise whatever their "this" was.

She simultaneously cursed him for putting the ball so firmly in her court and appreciated him for not putting words in her mouth.

He did say she could drive, after all.

She focussed on Alex as she replied. "We're going to spend some time together outside of work." Short, simple, truthful. She turned her attention to Nick and pulled up her Resting Professional Face. "I felt like it was important to disclose that in case you have any misgivings about us having a social relationship."

Nick raised his brows at Alex and blinked slowly. "Well. I'd usually ask you what you think, but you probably aren't doing much of that right now."

Alex jerked back like he had been slapped. "You know—"

"—that this has been coming for some time. Good for you." Nick looked torn between smug and resigned. "I just don't want to deal with," he tilted back as if he would find the right word stuck to the ceiling, "anything."

Had it been that obvious? How they'd looked in Sophie's photos was one thing, but she hadn't acted like that in the office. Had she? Jill shoved her embarrassment aside, because right now, she didn't want to lose her shit. That she—that Alex, who poured unfathomable amounts of energy into his work—would act in a way to harm their work set her brain ablaze.

With her calm outside voice, she said, "Alex and I agreed on some ground rules to ensure that whatever goes on between us stays separate from any work I'm doing for CMR. I don't need to be on-site this week to draft the audit outline. I can work from Blackburn and give you both time to discuss. If you would prefer a different consultant work with you, I can hand your file over to a colleague."

Nick leaned back and sucked air between his teeth while Alex threw a dismayed glance at her.

"Let me be clear." Jill looked directly at Nick, a coil of tension winding up in her shoulder blades. "I want to work on this file. Your work is incredibly exciting, and I think I can get you across the line. Let me know what you decide."

Angela might not be happy with her gamble. Blackburn didn't have a bunch of people twiddling their thumbs waiting for projects to keep them busy. If it came down to it, Jill could swap files with Omar. The financial analysis he had been assigned wasn't his favourite work and Jill could wait until the next proposal file came along to get the experience Angela wanted her to have.

If Angela still wanted her to track to leadership if she fumbled this.

Fuck. One more thing she hadn't thought of.

The sigh that erupted from Nick had to be for dramatic effect. "No. It's fine. You guys are big kids." He turned his scowl to his screen, and Jill stifled a grimace as her insides unclenched. "But don't, you know, make it weird."

"That's the plan." She snuck a glance at Alex, who looked so genuinely relieved she had to fight the urge to squeeze his hand in reassurance, in direct violation of Rule Number One. Again.

She plugged in her laptop, a bit rattled from the conversation and looking to channel her nerves into the audit. Best practices. Risk reviews. Internal controls. Heaven.

As she pulled up her templates folder, her pocket buzzed.

Alex. At his desk less than two metres away, trying to look fascinated by his screen.

That went well

Jill pressed her lips together to stave off her grin and resolutely kept her eyes off him.

Better than I thought tbh
Can I take you to lunch?

How about breakfast? We can go now

Schooling her face, she flicked her eyes to him trying to frown at his phone while the corners of his mouth turned up. She bit the inside of her cheek and failed to quell the humming in her chest. Was asking him to go for lunch violation of Rule Number Two? She'd never flirted by text before.

Actually. That wasn't true. The brief exchange she and Alex had on Saturday afternoon had been pretty flirty. A lot flirty.

Well, shit. Everything was going to be this side of suggestive now.

Following her own stupid rules was going to be harder than she thought.

"It's been four minutes," Nick said, his voice breaking into her thoughts. "And you guys are not subtle."

—

Jill slept in the next day. Almost six a.m. Not her usual restlessness making her sleep in—she had only been up for an hour in the night—but the aching in her body from the new activity had knocked her right out. She gingerly stretched, pushing her hands up against the wall behind her and relishing the soreness in her throwing arm.

The co-ed softball team eagerly welcomed her into the fold, especially keen to add a new female to help keep them on the field with the gender ratio. They had lost by a couple of runs, but it had been warm and sunny, and they went out for beer after. One of the guys on her team had chatted her up a bit, but veered from flirty to friendly with good grace when she mentioned she was seeing someone. Jill was sure the little flutter in her chest as she mentioned it reflected on her face, trying as she might to stay low-key. When she got home, she had created a group chat with Sophie and Alex and sent a photo of herself posing with the bat.

She hadn't forgotten. It was more that she had pushed down how much fun she always had playing with a team. Any team. After her mother made her quit volleyball in high school because she thought her daughter was too short to excel beside the five-foot-eleven glamazons, Jill joined the cross-country team instead. A solo sport, sure, but still had the camaraderie of a group choosing to collectively put themselves through agony. Connor had passive-aggressively guilted her into giving up softball so she would be free to attend things he deemed important. Like going for dinner with his family—which she didn't love, but understood—or going to the gym with him—which she hated.

Jill set her espresso maker on the stove and scrolled through her calendar. The day was fully booked, but two appointments stood out to her:

9:00 a.m. - New client assignment w. Angela

2:30 p.m. - Call HR

The best part of her day was going to happen first, and if she was as smart as she pretended to be, she'd shift her call with HR before she met with Angela so she could go into that meeting informed. Get everything out of the way in one fell swoop.

What was the expression? If you have to eat a frog, do it first thing in the morning?

8:00 a.m. - Call HR

Then, added a placeholder:

4:30 p.m. - Call Mom

Last appointment of the day, but she could only eat so many frogs at once.

Another voicemail from her mother had shown up since the weekend that Jill hadn't responded to yet and putting it off wasn't going to help. And if she called just before her mother's Pilates class, she could cut the call short and still tick the box.

That Daughter of the Year award would arrive any day.

Two hours later at Blackburn, she sat with her office door closed on hold with the corporate human resources line, an intranet site open to the code of conduct page.

Jill chewed her pen cap to splinters as she scrolled. Lots of information on relationships between peer employees (no issue, but don't let the relationship interfere with work). More on relationships between people of unequal status in the organization (can't work in the same department). Even more on relationships with a direct report (someone is being transferred. Or fired).

Two concise lines on fraternization with clients.

First, as long as the nature of the contract didn't involve legal counsel, it was permitted.

Check. Jill had nothing to do with the law department, so she was clear.

Second, disclosure of the relationship was mandatory.

She had figured on that last one, and would've disclosed even if it hadn't been required, but seeing it in black and white sent a frazzle of nerves zipping through her chest.

Disclosure: pending.

The HR advisor picked up moments later and confirmed what she had read. One of the worries that had swirled in her brain separated from the pack and dissolved. Jill wasn't breaking any rules.

She still felt like she was going to throw up.

Angela Blackburn was her boss, mentor, and idol. A self-made entrepreneur who had prioritized hiring women and people of colour in a field dominated by white men. Who had recognized something in Jill two years ago when she was deep in Connor's sway. Who had given her a lifeline. A place to find and grow her strengths. Jill wasn't sure she would have had the confidence to leave if she hadn't had her work. The thought of disappointing Angela her made her want to puke in her inbox.

And now Jill sat in the boardroom, stiletto-clad foot bouncing under the desk, waiting for Angela to show up. The footsteps from down the hall spiked her blood pressure, but she fixed a pleasantly neutral expression on her face and stilled her vibrating extremities. Angela swept into the room, looking fresh even after her three-and-a-half-hour flight.

"Jill, always great to see you. How are you settling into Calgary?"

"Oh, it's great. Love the team here. Making friends and joined softball again."

"Excellent. Have you planned time off this summer yet?"

She hadn't even considered it. What would she do? Go to Toronto? Who would she see? She didn't have friends there anymore. A week sitting with her parents would be the exact opposite of restorative. While she was beginning to fill her life here, she didn't think she had enough to fill a week or two yet. And as much as she would love to spend every minute with Alex, he was incredibly busy. Besides, she would not rebuild her life around someone else. Danger lay that way.

But there was someone else she missed. Someone she hadn't seen in far too long. If he would see her.

Kyle.

Would he want to see her after she ghosted him after the trip to Montreal a year and a half ago? He had sent her texts for weeks after she got home. Connor had finally lifted his contact info from Jill's phone, telling him to leave his girlfriend alone. The texts stopped.

She could try. She wanted to try.

"I might have an idea," Jill said. "I'll book some time off."

With a nod, Angela pulled up a few slides to hand Jill her next file.

No stalling, Northrop. Do it now.

"Before we start, I should inform you I have a social relationship with one of my clients," Jill recited the speech she had composed the night before. "I checked policy and confirmed with HR that there are no conflicts to navigate." She held her breath. Stop talking. Short, simple, truthful. Just the facts. Not doing anything wrong. Everything is fine. Super fine.

At least she was rambling in her brain and not out loud.

"Thanks for letting me know." Angela hadn't looked up. "Inform HR if anything changes."

Jill blinked. "Th-that's it?"

"Well, it's not ideal, but you wouldn't be the first. We'd have to juggle a couple files if it comes to it, I'm sure, but that's why we have policies in place," Angela said, lifting her eyes from the screen. "I trust your judgement."

That makes one of us.

The rest of the meeting passed in a blur. Whatever the policy had said, Angela's opinion mattered most. Knowing she wasn't blowing anything by having a relationship with Alex nearly winded her with relief.

Back in her office, with a more complex file to lead Ashleen and Marco through, a new meaty financial audit, and a weight off her chest, she pulled out her phone and hit send on a quick note to Alex to let him know she wasn't getting fired and a celebration emoji, when a new text from her mother popped up.

Jillian, call me.

Her mother never sent texts. She checked them—Jill saw the read receipts—but always said that it was a lazy way to communicate. Really, though, her mother wanted to control the conversation.

This was rare. Two voicemails and now a text? What if something had happened to her dad?

She glanced at the clock. She could reschedule her next meeting. Dialling with one hand, she dragged her meeting block to eleven with the other. The call picked up on the third ring, and her mother's saccharine voice met her ears.

"Jillian, so good for you to finally call me back."

Jill braced her arm across her torso. "Hi. I'm sorry. I was busy. I'm sorry. What's wrong?"

"Nothing's wrong, other than my daughter avoiding me." Her mother laughed like Jill was the silliest thing in the world. "I'm checking in to see if anything is new?"

The air left her lungs in a rush. Maybe if Jill reached out more her mother wouldn't need to play this game. The familiar swirl of guilt roiled in her stomach. "Oh. Thanks for checking in, I guess. Things are good. Good and busy. Same old, same old. You and Dad are okay?"

"Oh, of course we're fine," she said, and Jill's chest tightened as her mother's voice pitched up into the sickly-sweet register that preceded an ambush. "But I was talking to Deborah the other day, and she said it looks like you are seeing someone already?"

Jill tried to suck in oxygen through a windpipe that had been clutched by a fist. "What?"

"Did you at least let Connor know? She said he sounded so upset."

"No, I don't …" Her words came out from the end of a long tunnel. "I … I don't need to update him on my life anymore, Mom."

"I know you two still aren't on the best of terms yet, but it really would have been the polite thing to do."

The stale silence lengthened. Jill's bitten nails left bright red half moons on her palm.

"And who is this person you jumped into dating already? It's not serious, is it?" The sound of sucking air through teeth reached through the phone.

"I … no … I don't know …"

"I didn't realize I was such a terrible mother you couldn't tell me these things," her mother replied, voice wispy and wavery, and the old guilt stirred up.

"You're not. Of course, you're not. There's not much to tell." The words felt like sand, dry and gritty and clogging her mouth. "Sorry, I have a meeting. I just really wanted to finally call you. I'm sorry. I'll call you sooner next time."

She ended the call and sat, frozen. It might be a world record. Zero to borderline in a minute-and-a-half.

She was not going to panic.

How? When? Jill wasn't talking to anyone in Toronto. And it's not like Sophie would have dropped Connor a friendly heads-up text.

Wait.

Sophie.

She pulled up the videos Sophie posted Saturday night. The tinny sound of the club piped through the phone's speakers as Jill landed on the video with her and Alex in the background. Looking intimate. Heads together, leaning close. A surge of heat cut through the ice surrounding her core, and she wished she could hide herself in his arms.

She clicked on the post and swiped through the comments. And she saw it.

grind_cman_grind: who teh fuck
is that with jill

A single drop of icy dread slid down her throat and landed like lead in her stomach. With shaking fingers, she forwarded Sophie the screenshot with the text:

911 pls call

Her phone crowed twelve seconds later.

"Shit. Oh, *shit,*" Sophie hissed on the other end.

The tunnel was already shortening and the fist gripping her throat released. No panic attack. The wave of relief alone was enough to make her feel dizzy. Still, her throat clicked as she tried to swallow and stated what Sophie already knew. "Connor saw the video."

"I'm sorry. I didn't know he followed me." Sophie sounded horrified.

How could she have known? It's not like Sophie kept tabs on all hundred and seventy thousand of her followers. And Jill didn't even know until now that Connor was still paying attention to her. Jill drew a long, deep inhalation and released her exhalation through pursed lips.

"I'll take it down. I'll block him. I'll report him," Sophie continued. "Oh, shit. I'm sorry."

None of that would really do anything now. He knew. And it shouldn't matter that he did. They weren't together anymore. She didn't owe him anything.

Her water glass was empty. Her second favourite coffee mug was half full and lukewarm. Jill took a swig of the tepid coffee with a grimace. "There's nothing to be sorry for. Can you just block him? He hasn't actually done anything. I panicked. I—" she groaned "—fuck me."

Jill put her head down on her desk after she ended the call. He would have found out eventually. She just wished it had been on her terms.

You were right. This is too soon to be seeing someone.

Her phone jangled beside her. The crazy thought Connor had somehow broken through her blocking him because she had spoken about him popped into her brain, and she cautiously checked the caller ID.

Alex.

He had never called during the day before. Was this a work call, or just to hear her voice? Did he do that? It seemed like a thing he might do. She didn't know if she was worried or excited, landing with one foot on each, a flutter in her stomach vying for dominance over the lead weight.

Wait. It was Thursday. When he wasn't on the road, Thursday was lab day. He was usually unreachable. He wouldn't be calling to put tabs on her whereabouts, would he? The thought burned like acid in her brain, and she shoved it down.

Alex isn't Connor.

If she took any more deep breaths she'd hyperventilate. She squeezed her eyes shut, crossed her legs tightly, and looped her foot around her ankle as if she could bind herself up tight enough nothing could escape.

"Hi! Alex! Hi! What's up?" That was cheerful. Perfect. She could hold it together for a few minutes.

His voice came through, slightly muffled over the whirring and clicking in the background. "Hey, I'm glad you aren't getting fired and we should celebrate, but what's the emergency? What was that screenshot you sent?"

The flutter in her chest morphed into a drumming and she pulled the phone away from her ear to check her messages. She didn't send the screenshot to Sophie. She sent it to the group text, right under the picture of her swinging the bat, her smile a mile wide.

If she squeezed her eyelids any more tightly, they'd fuse together.

Shit.

"I am so, so sorry." She had apologized too many times today. "I didn't mean to send that to you."

"Okay, but it looks like … what is it?" Alex's voice was laced with growing concern. "Jill?"

Cover. Lie. Deflect. The instinct was overwhelming. This would have been a trap from Connor. A way to box her into an answer he could use to twist into a way to manipulate her. She had spent too long doing that. It didn't belong in this new chapter of her life.

Alex isn't Connor.

She added a scrunched face to her list of wound-up body parts. "That's, ah, my ex? I meant to send it to Soph. You weren't supposed to see that," she finished lamely.

Whirring and clicking filled what would have been the silence on the call, then, "I can't leave the lab until eight, but can I see you after? Will you be okay until then?"

Tears pricked behind her eyes as an overwhelming rush of relief washed over her, and she realized she was nodding before she remembered he couldn't see her. "Please come over tonight."

—

The rest of the day provided a perfect escape. Meeting blurred into meeting. Lunch turned into something forgettable from the vending machine. By the time she had gotten around to reheating her coffee, the four-thirty reminder to call her mother popped up and a layer of frost creeped around the edge of her throat. Ashleen had to call her name more than once—how many more, Jill wasn't sure—before she hummed an agreement to an idea that had already escaped her thoughts. Hours later, the motion-sensor lights ticking off notified her the office had emptied around her.

She checked her phone. Almost seven. Loads of time before Alex would be over. She needed another task to keep her busy a little longer. Something like grocery shopping. She hadn't been since before Sophie had been here. The entirety of her fridge contained yellowing kale, a half-empty container of yogurt, orange juice, and an assortment of hot sauces.

Armed with a basket and a vague idea of what to buy, she stalked the produce section for new recruits to be sacrificed to the abyss of her fridge. Bread? Yes. Toast was easy. Peanut butter? Definitely for toast. Even better from the spoon. Yogurt? Always.

It was the pasta aisle that did it. She stood, paralyzed by the burden of deciding between a jar of roasted garlic or Italian herb marinara, and a crush of fatigue anchored her to the spot.

Why? Why did he have to intrude on her here? Alex and Connor shouldn't occupy the same space in her mind. And why did she have to be so weak? People broke up all the time, left hostile comments on their ex's and ex's friend's posts, bitched about them to their moms. Other people didn't have near panic attacks any time their ex's name showed up in print. She glanced hollow-eyed at the items in her basket, placed it carefully on the floor, and left.

She didn't bother turning on the lights as she walked into her apartment. Or hang up her clothes, brush her teeth, or wash her face. She dragged herself straight to her bedroom, stripped her clothes, and crawled under the covers.

God, she was so tired. She didn't even feel mad. Or anxious. Just heavy. Her mind emptied as she stared blankly out the window at the still bright sky until the jangling of her phone jarred her upright. She pushed her mess of hair back and blinked stupidly at the incoming call.

Shit. She completely forgot. Alex was here. Downstairs.

She buzzed him up, tying her hair into a ponytail and wiping away the mascara smudges.

Cool and relaxed, dishevelled but in a chill-and-sexy way. Yep, that's me. I can do it.

Throwing on a tee shirt, shorts, and a bright smile, she opened the door, holding onto the facade for a full half second until Alex's face crumpled her resolve.

She didn't have a chance to answer before she was enveloped in the warmest, most solid hug she could remember. She stood on tiptoes, wrapping her arms around his neck as far as she could, and let his heat replace the heaviness with comfort.

"What's wrong?"

"I've had a day," she whispered, "but I'm feeling better already."

"Tell me."

He followed her into the living room, and she sat facing him on the couch, tucking her hair behind her ears and curling up into a ball in the corner.

"It started so good. There is no issue with HR, and Angela was completely chill about it." She attempted a tired smile. "So, I guess that means I won't get fired. Yay."

He returned her light smile and squeezed her ankle.

"And then I got a text from my mother. Which freaked me out because she never texts. And I told you how my ex's parents and mine are really close?"

He nodded.

"He saw this video that Sophie had posted from the other night online, and he told his mom, and she told mine. It's a freaking gossip mill."

His brows drew together in confusion. "Video? What video?"

She retrieved her phone from her bedroom and sat beside him again on the couch. As she brought up the post, he wrapped an arm around her waist, pulling her into him, and the tension winding her insides softened as she melted against his solid warmth.

He studied the video, replaying it twice. The filters Sophie had added had done nothing to hide what was happening between them. He fiddled with the phone one-handed before turning it upside down on the couch.

"He used to get really angry when I talked to other people, and I told you about how he …" she trailed off. She stared at the phone as if she could see the video continuing on loop. "I hate seeing him bleed over into this part of my life. I want it behind me." She tucked her knees to her chest and buried her face in her arms. "I don't want to have baggage. I want to be easy. I just really like you and I shouldn't be talking to you about this."

No one wanted to hear about exes. Cocooned into herself as she was, she couldn't see his face. After a long minute, she mustered the courage to ask, "What are you thinking?"

The increasingly familiar rise and fall of his chest beside her felt like meditation. "That I'm glad there's half a country between you," he said, finally, one hand propped on his knee, the other tracing a circle on her shoulder. "And I know you're not going to be easy. I saw your audit outline yesterday."

She thwacked him with a couch pillow, her first genuine smile in ten hours breaking through.

He wrested the pillow out of her grasp to thwart further attack and fiddled with the fringe. "I'm glad you told me," he said softly.

She wouldn't have, if she hadn't panicked and sent the text to the group instead of only Sophie. The reflex to protect herself overriding any thought of allowing herself to be vulnerable. But Alex hadn't gotten mad. Or flown into a jealous rage. She searched her gut, listening for the wisdom of her instincts she had silenced for so long, and heard a tentative whisper saying *trust.*

For the first time in a long time, it felt safe enough to listen.

FOURTEEN

Well before sunrise, her stomach asserted its displeasure at her missing not only dinner, but lunch, the day before. She raided the slim contents of her fridge and hid the yellowed kale in a smoothie, blending it with the last of her yogurt and frozen blueberries into an abhorrent concoction.

I could be eating peanut butter and banana toast right now instead of choking down this green mess.

Well, no sense beating herself up for her crash at the grocery store last night. She had spent enough time beating herself up and packing away her emotions. At some point or another it always came out, no matter how tightly she sealed those boxes. And just being with Alex, him listening, with no judgment, no expectations, had been so good. Only a little scary to open up.

He had stayed long enough to make sure she was okay, then heading out well before she might interpret him hoping something more would happen. He left her with the lightest brush against her mouth, and even though a significant portion of her body had asserted a strong desire for more, she reasoned during several middle of the night awakenings it was best he left early.

If her dreams were any sign, it was definitely best he left early.

Her face contorted as she choked down the last of the smoothie and chased the dregs with a swig of coffee.

Note to self: mandatory trip to the grocery store today.

Second note to self: seriously, look up meal planning.

Even at the turn of a Toronto summer with soaring humidity, she would've donned tights, stilettos, and a blazer five days a week. That morning, she pulled on the violet wrap dress that hadn't seen the light of day since her last year of university. More appropriate for the weekend, sure, but her favourite white sneakers looked great with it, and almost everyone she passed on Ninth Avenue on the way to CMR wore similarly casual attire befitting a temperate June morning. She only mourned her row of unworn shoes a bit.

Jill looked up from her monitor when the front door opened and tried not to look disappointed when Nick strode in. It was still early, but she couldn't help it.

"Hey," she said instead with a smile.

"Morning!" Nick fiddled with the thermostat, sending a blast of air conditioning over her bare arms. "Found an article you might find interesting. I'll forward it."

"Thanks. Appreciate it," she said, surprised.

That didn't take long, she thought. Three days to chill out over Jill and Alex's mini bombshell they were dating? Nick had looked more resigned than surprised when they told him. Less of a bombshell and more of a no shit, Sherlock moment. Apparently, everyone except saw "this" coming. She shrugged into the cardigan she left draped over her chair and refreshed her inbox.

To: AlexC@cmrenvironmental.
ca; jill.northrop@blackburn.com

From: NickM@cmrenvironmental.ca

Subject: fw: Leading Edge: Stay away from
office romance

A&j - we should add a fraternization policy to the
audit plan

> *There are a few happily-ever-afters, but romance and work rarely end well, often resulting in a strained office atmosphere, loss of productivity, and ...*

Jill snapped her head up, mouth open to see Nick trying to suppress a smirk behind his hand, then bursting out laughing.

"You should see your face," he said with a final self-satisfied snort. "Jesus, Jill. I'm kidding. Just don't keep him up too late. He's got a lot of work to do."

"Haha. Right," she said, and wished for a turtleneck to pull over her cheeks.

After two hours of willfully ignoring Nick's presence and drilling through a swath of her notes, Alex's heavy tread sounded down the hall. She lifted her eyes to see him filling the door frame, and with Nick's email in mind, reigned in her smile to something workplace appropriate.

"Hey," she said, aiming for the same tone she used with Nick.

"Hey," he said, his own tone sending a burst of heat under her ribs and felt her smile breaking through. So much for workplace appropriate.

Alex frowned at Nick, punched a few buttons on the thermostat, and the icy air shut off. "Morning. We agreed on twenty-three degrees."

"What? It was hot," Nick said.

"Then take off your jacket," he replied, booting up his laptop. "How'd the meeting with that new lead go yesterday?"

A few minutes later, Alex spouted off a quick burst of French Jill couldn't follow but made Nick laugh again, which might have been *don't be an asshole,* because *don't be a duck* didn't make sense. A minute later, a reply popped to the top of her inbox, to Jill only:

> AlexC: should we add an anti-fraternization policy to the audit? Just make sure you don't box us out of seeing each other :)

Hiding a grin behind her screen, she replied:

jill.northrop: I'll do some research, but I'm not going to recommend policies that may leave your future employees unprotected.

AlexC: Unprotected against what?

jill.northrop: What if you get another sweet, guileless contractor in here who gets swept off her feet?

AlexC: Have I swept you off your feet?

Nick would have to turn the A/C back on if the temperature kept rising like this.

jill.northrop: Hypothetically.

AlexC: Well, hypothetically, in this specific case I'm good with sticking to a data point of one. But Nick is a wolf. We'll need a tight policy.

Jill finally understood what Sophie had droned on about in university, not being able to concentrate. The minute Alex arrived in the office, her attention was divided by the work in front of her and watching the light catch his auburn eyelashes. With a quick confirmation she wasn't sending to their group text, she discreetly sent a note to her favourite little chicken.

Fucking forearms, amirite?

I didn't even know

The gushing water, flexed bicep, and skull emojis contained the entirety of Sophie's response. Alex's head popped up at the muted crowing and smiled as he returned his focus to his work.

At least she wasn't alone. His gaze travelled her body, leaving a singed path in its wake. More than a few times, asking Nick to repeat himself on things that should have been easy answers. But they stuck to their Rules. Nothing broken. A little bending of Rule

Two, with some suggestive banter through email, but nothing that put them in the penalty box.

So far, they had kept it together for three whole days. They deserved a ribbon.

The spreadsheet she had been building for hours swam at the edges and her neck was stiff from the morning's reviews. The state of their reporting continued to amaze her. And infuriate her. And how much a person could mess up an income statement through a combination of lack of background and a reckless disinterest in accuracy in the entries.

It was a good thing he was cute.

She stood, wrapping her hands behind her neck and arching back, releasing the tension that had built up through the morning. If they had been alone, she would have put a bit of zhuzh into it, just to get a rise out of him. But as it was, Alex made no effort to keep his eyes off her. She could probably brush her teeth and get the same reaction.

The thought of him leaning against the doorway, arms crossed over his bare chest and smiling as she brushed her teeth sent a rush of heat through her body.

She needed to keep her thoughts PG, too.

"I need a break."

"Yep." The legs of Alex's chair scraped the floorboards before the words fully left her mouth. "Ice cream?"

She turned to Nick. "Coming?" she asked, trying to politely put as much "please don't" into it as she could.

"No," Nick sighed. "You two go ahead."

"Great," Alex said. "Back in half an hour, tops."

Nick rolled his eyes and smirked at the ceiling. "No rush."

Outside it was warm, bright, and loud, and none of it made an impression on her. She didn't want to be presumptuous, but Alex didn't look like he'd protest a minor detour. So, when she suggested a scenic route off the main avenue to get away from the noise, he let her drag him behind a construction barrier. She slid her hands up to his jaw, pulling his lips down to hers, and pressing the length of her body along his.

"Very good morning," she said when he pulled back to plant a row kisses up the side of her neck. The wind cooled where his lips had been, a counter to her rising heat. Her body shifted of its own accord. Fingers sliding through belt loops. Hips pressing forward against him. Her mouth found the corner of his, and she sighed as she tasted him again.

The low groan that rose from deep in his chest made her want to rip his shirt off, but he eased himself back like he was moving through mercury, as if loath to put space between them.

"Sorry," she said, breathless. "Too much."

"Nope. You are not too much," he said, voice tight and eyes closed. "Just … give me a minute."

She leaned forward on her toes, arms twined around his waist. Heady with the scent of him, she whispered below his ear, "You feel amazing."

"Not helping."

She giggled into the join of his neck and shoulder, which was rapidly becoming her new favourite place, before relenting and yielding him the space he needed. For now.

In line at the ice cream shop, Jill shifted to the left, sliding her arm around his waist and tucked her shoulder neatly under his. "Huh, I do."

Alex turned and looked down at her, a quizzical smile curving his mouth.

"I remember wondering one time if I'd fit under here." She gave a little shrug. "Looks like I do."

He squeezed of her hand around his waist, his Adam's apple bobbing as he looked away. "You fit me perfectly," he said quietly.

The river levels had dropped like Ashleen had promised, its flow meandering around rocks and corners. Breeze and birdsong replaced street noise, but not the humming in her veins. They found a stone bench beside a playground, a couple of moms chatting nearby while their kids raced on the slides. Parking themselves in front of an audience was a solid tactic to make sure they kept their hands to themselves.

"This was my dad's thing," he said, his double-scoop of chocolate already half devoured. "If he wanted to talk about something important, he'd always do it over ice cream. He said it put some sugar in your system and gives you something to do with your hands."

I'm thinking of some things I could do with my hands, she thought, pleasantly shocked with herself. This wasn't her. Or at least, it hadn't been her. Had she buried this part of herself, as starved as she had been for so long? Easier to pretend it wasn't there or had Connor flattened yet another way she sought joy? Or was it all new, with Alex waking up something new in her, like the urge to run her hands over him …

PG thoughts, Northrop. The food comments sounded a lot like one of Omar's first conversations with her. These two would get along well.

She leaned on the heel of her palm and caught the lavender Earl Grey ice cream drips with the tip of her tongue. "Is there something you want to talk about?"

"Wondering how you're doing. After yesterday," he said, letting the sentence hang there. An open invitation. She could choose how deep to go, brushing it off or diving in.

"Actually, not bad." She tucked her leg under her. "Thanks for coming over last night. It …" *made me feel safe. Cared for. Like I matter to you.* "… it made me feel better. Talking to you."

He caught her hand and dropped a light kiss on her shoulder. "Good."

She truly did feel better. Not so heavy, but she didn't want to drag it out again, and jumped on a topic change. "Speaking of feeling better, Nick doesn't seem to be too bent out of shape with us anymore."

"Oh, that. I don't think Nick was mad at *us,*" he said, a mirthless grin twisting his mouth. "He told me about his date last Thursday."

Jill searched her memory. "The one with Cass?"

"Yep. But the date wasn't with Cass. It was with Jess, and he texted her instead. When he got there, both of them were waiting for him. Together."

Jill made a *yeesh* face.

"Anyway, neither of them want to see him anymore," he said, "So he's, ah, sour right now. He wasn't exclusive with either of them, but I guess it's different seeing it than knowing it."

Right. Being exclusive. Alex might be seeing other people. Or want to see other people. But of course, he could be. He was smart, good-looking, and funny. And kind. Considerate. And the man could kiss. There'd be flaws in there somewhere, but nothing of the deal-breaker variety had surfaced yet. He might want options in play while the two of them got to know each other. And there'd be no shortage of women who'd want to be that option.

Was it too early to ask? Not that she'd ask him not to. Just that she'd know where she stood. And plan accordingly.

"So, are you …" she trailed off.

"Am I what?" He gave her a curious look.

Jill studied the bench under her hand. "Are you seeing other people?"

"Oh. No," he said, low and earnest. "I don't want to see anyone else."

"Me, either." Her chest unclenched and she gave him a wry smile. "Do you remember when I said I was good at sharing?"

"Only child, but only some of the traits? Yep."

"Well, I don't think I'm *that* good at sharing," she said as he laughed. It had been years since she had started a new relationship, and the couple of flings she had at university didn't prepare her for this. She'd have checked with Sophie for the basics, but Jill didn't think Sophie had been—or wanted to be—exclusive with anyone the entire time she had known her. "I didn't know that was something I should ask."

"Well, I'm sure there's going to be lots of things we'll need to ask. Like do you like pineapple on your pizza?"

"No, but I have people I love in my life who do," she replied, repressing a shudder at Kyle's obsession with pineapple and olive pizza.

"I think it's an abomination, so no conflict. Do you like surprises?"

She pushed Connor's ambush out of her mind. "I'm fine with surprises, as long as I know about them well in advance. You?"

"I think the right kind of surprises can be great, but I've noted your position. What kind of date can I take you on this weekend?"

"What if I said 'surprise me?'"

"You," he said, "are a study in contradictions. I love it."

The little voice tentatively extended permission. "I trust you," she said.

"Okay." The single word came out soft at the edges, sounding like *thank you*. "What are you doing tomorrow?"

"I'm at the Humane Society in the morning. I missed volunteering last week with Soph in town, and I don't want to miss another one."

"And I've got a game in the afternoon. After?"

She nodded, stretching into the glow in her chest. "Maybe I can stop by your game when I'm done? I don't know anything about rugby, but I'm a quick learner."

His eyes crinkled with the smile that already promised to be her undoing.

—

"Did you miss me? I missed you! Were you a good girl?" Jill rubbed Daisy's ears in gentle circles, taking the doggy kisses full on the nose.

Her favourite girl hadn't grown shy in Jill's absence in the two weeks since she'd seen her. Daisy had improved so much. At least, she had with women in the shelter, letting them get close, taking her for walks and learning how to be on leash. She was still fearful of men. It wasn't demeanour, or size. Even Travis, the kindest and gentlest person Jill had met and barely matching Jill's height, had just started being met with a nervously wagging tail and curious ears.

She finished showering her buddy with love and rejoined Rachel, who fervidly soaked up any morsel of detail Jill shared.

"I knew it," Rachel said, gleefully scrubbing the floor of the enclosure. "It was written all over your face. You were being so cute trying to deny it." She pitched her voice up to mimic her. "'We were stranded under the stars and we had to cuddle for warmth and he was a perfect gentleman and I absolutely am not crushing on this guy.'"

"I didn't say any of that," Jill said, hiding her grin as she wiped the litter box. "And it was snowing anyway, so there weren't any stars."

"That's not the detail to pick out of that."

"Are you sure you shouldn't go into law?"

Rachel cackled. "No, thanks. Even if I can't find a job when I graduate, my dad would kill me if I racked up more student loans. He'd edit the Wikipedia entry to be a photo of me beside the entry for Failure to Launch. So, as I was saying, details …"

"You know," Jill said, "if you think it would be up your alley, you should give Blackburn a call. Lots of variety. Good environment—" she gestured to herself "—fabulous team."

"Are you serious?"

"Yes, I'm serious. You absolutely should've gone into law, but yes, also serious about calling Blackburn." Jill transferred Kevin and Switchboard to their kennel, who did an admirable job not murdering each other and earned themselves each a scritch on their chins. "I can ask talent acquisition to pull your CV if you want."

"That would be amazing! Can I ask you questions? Do you think I'd like it?"

"From the sounds of your thesis project, you'd love it." She could practically see the wheels spinning in Rachel's head. "And now, I'm going to wash my hands of cat litter and go watch my … Alex's game."

Boyfriend? She rolled the word over in her mind. It seemed too early to define what they were. But it felt closer to the truth than "that guy" she was seeing. Maybe she'd keep that to herself a little while longer.

He'd said he was in no rush. Maybe he wanted to move slow and she needed to back off.

Or maybe, she could stop overthinking and trying to control everything in her life for once.

Sure. Because she was so good at that.

FIFTEEN

If she didn't want to miss the game for the second weekend in a row, she didn't have time to run home and change first. Jill grimaced at her chewed up jeans and holey tee shirt, and drove to catch the last half of the game straight from her shift at the shelter.

She had spent a half hour the previous week looking up rugby positions, rules, and other terminology so she wouldn't be completely in the dark. Rugby was played on a pitch, not a field; had halves like soccer, not quarters like football; but it was kind of, sort of, played more like football. Ish. And they didn't wear helmets. Okay.

Then, one of the other volunteers had asked to switch shifts, trading Jill's early morning time for his mid-afternoon slot. She had tried to make it last weekend. The first real weekend of summer hadn't decided if it wanted to be summer yet. Wind shifted the gunmetal sky into changing patterns, the breeze stubbornly kept the temperature in the low teens and whipped her hair around her face. Between showering, changing, and driving out to the pitch, she had arrived in time to watch the teams shaking hands after the game. Then Alex had needed to go home and change after, anyway. It would've been just as easy to wait until later in the afternoon when they had planned to meet. Still, getting a quick smile and squeeze from his hand made the trip worth it.

Jill had floated through the last week, swimming with long, languid strokes across the days as she let her hesitant inner voice assert itself. First quiet, then confident. Alex had sent cryptic texts all week, whether he was sitting across from her at the office, or at night when she was at home watching Netflix. When she had asked what they'd be doing, he replied the only surprise would be that it wasn't a surprise.

Since their phone call almost two weeks ago, Jill hadn't heard anything from her mother. Or, more importantly, from Connor. Sophie had blocked him as promised. Jill had still pored over Sophie's posts for any suspicious comments and came up with nothing. She couldn't quite shake the thought he'd create a new handle and lurk, but it didn't matter. He knew. And, as she said to her mother and reminded herself daily, she didn't owe Connor updates on her life anymore.

Besides one awkward conversation with an HR advisor who struggled to ask for details without getting too specific, telling her co-workers at Blackburn had been less of a news story than she expected. Marco and Ashleen had exchanged a triumphant look and an indiscreet fist bump under the table. Although Jill couldn't be certain, she thought she heard Marco saying he won the bet and coffee was on Ashleen for the week.

"And you were telling me not to date clients," Omar had joked over lunch. "But I called it. The way you were looking at him that day?"

Jill had blushed into her miso soup. "So I've been told."

"Not that I blame you. He's very—" Omar had made expansive hand gestures.

"—gentlemanly?" Jill had finished with a pointed look.

"Or something," he said with a snicker. "I still don't know what we'll do with their feedback survey." It had come back with "very satisfied" across the board, and Omar had arched his brows at her. "I mean, really."

"Nick completed the survey," Jill said defensively, "and he and I are strictly professional."

Professional at best. After his initial peevishness with Jill and Alex's relationship had cleared, he had swung back to monosyllabic answers and slow responses on her information asks. With everything going on in the office and not wanting to cause any more waves, she sucked it up in the hopes his mood swings would, well, swing.

Alex had started coming into the office later than his usual time. Nine, ten, and once, even eleven. It wasn't because of Jill. They almost never hung out late at night. Only once had they stayed out long, extending a game of pool to the best four out of seven. Even with Jill throwing every underhanded distraction she could think of into play, he thoroughly trounced her. She was home by eleven, alone, and plotting activities she had a chance of winning.

But the late mornings became a Catch-22. Jill could concentrate on her outline and recommendations, but with Nick scowling in the background. When Alex showed up in the morning, Nick defrosted enough to act like a human being. But then, there was Alex. Who drew her focus like a magnet. Who continued to abide by Rule One but was unable to follow Rule Two. She had to remind him it was in his best interest to let her work, and he relented. A bit.

She picked apart the previous week as she drove to his game. They had weeks, or even months, until they would hear news on the grant, and Jill's audit recommendations were ready. And when she pitched it, it would be the first meeting since Jill and Alex started dating, and apprehension flitted around the edges of her gut. Not with her recommendations. Those were solid. But once again dealing with Sour Nick and veiled comments he might make when Alex wasn't around. Then there was the worry of the work she'd pile on Alex's plate he would hate doing.

One of her doubts squirmed in its resting place, reminding her she hadn't dealt with it yet.

Unlike last Saturday, today the sun beat down on the pitch as if making up for missing a weekend of summer. Jill sat with Marta, a visibly pregnant woman she'd met briefly last week and whose boyfriend played on Alex's team. Parked under a beach umbrella with a lawn chair and a hand-held electric fan, she talked Jill through the game. It would take a while for her to pick up the details, but it looked fun, if not a little nerve-wracking watching the players pounding into each other. After seeing what Jill learned was a ruck, she vowed never to play herself. But she loved watching Alex. He couldn't dance, but he could move, charging across the pitch with a power and agility that riveted her.

"Look at that dump tackle. Disgusting," Marta said, grinning at her boyfriend being driven hard into the ground, then yelling across to him, "That's what you get for being so slow!"

Jill wasn't sure she could attain that level of casual indifference if Alex was tackled in the same way. Marta read her nervous expression and grinned. "Eh. You get used to it."

As the game progressed, the unfamiliar rules and plays blended together, and she lapsed into her conversation with Marta, who was extolling the virtues of potential baby names. Jill was in the middle of agreeing with Marta's preferred options, when without warning, she was lifted clear out of her seat.

Alex pinned her arms to her sides in a bear hug, dipping her back and holding her off the ground. He landed kisses all over her face and she squeaked, trying to gain purchase with her feet.

"Stop!" she cried through gasping laughter. "I smell like dog spit and cat food!"

The warnings did nothing to halt his onslaught. "I smell like a beast, too."

He did. Like fresh sweat, old uniforms, and that something familiar that flipped her heart over. He pulled back, a wicked smile turning the corner of his mouth. "Want me to stop?"

"Absolutely not."

He dropped one more kiss on her. "Hypothesis confirmed," he said. "I swept you off your feet."

A giddy thought rolled across her brain. In neon, fully formed. A chyron flashing in all caps.

She would take her clothes off with this man, very soon.

He raised a brow, a smile growing in place. "What's that look?"

"Nothing."

"Get a room, Doc," came a yell from across the field. A smattering of laughter followed, and he returned her to the earth, upright and feet planted, and she swayed with a heady rush.

"No fair," she said, wrapping her arms around his neck for balance. "I can't do that to you."

"You definitely do."

"If I still had morning sickness, I would throw up on you both," Marta said with a half-grimace, half-smile that clearly read *shit like that got me into this.* She reached her hands up to her boyfriend for an assist out of her chair. "See you next week, if Olivia hasn't shown up yet."

"Evelyn," her boyfriend insisted, hoisting Marta to her feet, "isn't coming for another six weeks." He turned to Alex. "Good game, and—" to Jill "—come next week. He actually hustled out there for once."

Marta waved as she waddled away, her boyfriend hauling the chair, umbrella, and miscellaneous other accessories and laughing off the rude gesture Alex tossed him as they left. Still breathing hard, he wiped his face with the hem of his shirt, exposing a slick expanse of defined stomach and a thread of hair that disappeared under the band of his shorts.

Jill resisted the urge to slide her hand along it and instead shoved her hands into her pockets to squint up at him. "You still haven't told me what we're doing tonight."

"Feeding you and plying you with wine."

"Am I wearing heels and diamonds, or the everyday pearls?"

"Nah, casual, I'd say wear what you've got on if you didn't smell like cat food."

She grinned, eyes dancing. "Fine. Unless you say otherwise, I'm wearing workout clothes. With holes." She chewed her lip. "What are you doing until then?"

"Shower, change." He checked the time on his phone. "I have a few hours of work to do."

Of course. It's not like his work had disappeared, and he was already probably putting in fewer hours since they had been spending time together. He had said he worked six-and-a-half days a week, and with a bit of quick math, he had put in far less than that in the last couple of weeks. Every minute he was with her was a minute away from work. He'd need every spare minute to keep up.

Once again, the conflict of interest between the two of them together sprouted fresh doubts.

She walked back to her car, telling herself not to worry about his time. He was a big boy. He didn't need her in his business.

Except now it was her business to be in his.

Shit, shit, shit.

—

With all the questions he'd asked her, she could have guessed it was a picnic date. Food, the outdoors, and time with Alex checked all her favourite boxes. He showed up late with an effusive apology and a backpack stuffed with food. It was fine. He'd texted to let her know. She grabbed the dessert he asked her to bring, laced up her sneakers, and they walked to the bluff overlooking the downtown core. Sunlight dazzled off the high-rise windows and snaking river, and the breeze ruffled the wild grasses around them. He unfolded the backpack to reveal a treasure of charcuterie, a powerful Barolo, and the most exquisite sandwiches she had ever eaten.

Jill tucked her heels under her on the fuzzy picnic blanket and captured a drip of pesto running down her wrist before it hit her sleeve. "Where did you get these?"

"Made them."

Her eyes grew round as she moaned with joy. "You can cook."

"This isn't cooking. This is assembling," he said, ears going pink. "But yes, I can cook."

"I should tell you now I don't cook. Not even a little."

"Come on," he said, stopping when she gave him a piercing look. "Not even pasta?"

"I have stirred a jar of sauce into boiled pasta," she said, and held up a finger before swallowing the bite of ham and ciabatta. "But I should clarify that I can't cook. I had after-school activities, so my dad could never teach me, then university … well, you know university."

"Lived at my grandparents' place in uni, remember? And grand-maman made damn sure all her grandkids could cook. Especially the boys."

"I love her." She plucked an olive from the board. She'd have to send his grandmother a thank-you card, then paused, momentarily nervous. "Is she still alive?"

"Yep. Eighty-seven and still ruling her retirement home and my grand-papa," he said. "So, no cooking after uni, then?"

"No, I … no."

Connor had demanded full control over all the food in their home, to measure the macros and ratios, not trusting Jill to properly fuel his body. Once, she had grabbed some breaded fish fillets on sale, and he had berated her for an hour that it was going to break him out of some zone he needed to be in. The reasons he needed to be in a specific zone at a specific time, he explained to her in excruciating detail, of which she could never make sense. After that, it was easier to eat the broiled chicken breasts and steamed broccoli he put in front of her and not fight.

"Well, division of labour. I've got cooking covered," Alex said, brushing a crumb from his thigh. "At least when I get home before nine."

He had been true to his word. She was driving. Alex hadn't initiated a single step in their growing connection, making no move until she had first. Her hand sliding into his back pocket would be met with his palm rounding the curve of her hip as he kissed her. Fingers climbing up the centre of his chest created the invitation for his thumb to brush the underside of her breast as he pulled her close.

Like playing with matches next to bone dry tinder.

But a few times. Like now. Perhaps when he wasn't as guarded. He made one of those off-hand comments. Like he was standing on the other side of an open door, inviting her to cross the threshold. It warmed, calmed, and shook her all at once. And the open, honest way he spoke stirred something as intense in her as any of his touches could. Like he wanted what was happening between them to continue. To move forward.

Into a future that might not be there.

Her contract was for a year. It might be made permanent. It might not.

She put the rest of her sandwich down and pulled her knees into her chest.

His brows drew together, and his voice startled her out of her thoughts. "I'm on the road all next week," he reminded her.

Right. The Western and Northern sites. A day across the border into BC. At least a day or two in Fort McMurray. A tour that would take at least four days. Longer, if he met with all the clients he should on the way.

She nodded, lips pressed in a line. She was going to miss him. And not just the new territory they were exploring. But his friendship. His self-deprecating humour. Equally happy to plan or follow Jill's whim. Or treats like tonight that were tailor-made to please her. The easy way they debated the best ways to spend a Sunday afternoon. Or spend a million dollars.

Even before they had started seeing each other, she missed him in the weeks he was on the road. The office would quiet, she and Nick working in silence in Alex's absence. Jill waiting for the time when Nick would leave to beat rush hour traffic and saying he'd work from home for the night, so she could finally put on some music while she wrapped her day. She never heard from Nick after he left. She'd still be getting emails from Alex for hours, whether or not he was on the road.

The thought pushed to the front of her brain. *Why doesn't Nick ever do the travel assignments?* Instead, she asked, "Isn't Anni-frid still in the shop? How are you doing the trip?"

Alex heaved a sigh, scraping a hand over his cheek. "They're still trying to hunt down a part. I'm borrowing Gemma's Subaru."

The question was out of her mouth before she realized she was saying it. "Isn't the truck Nick drives a company vehicle?"

He nodded.

"Why …" She chewed her lip, not sure if this would be overstepping. "Why aren't you driving that?"

The lines in his forehead deepened. "Nick drives the truck."

"But it's a company asset. It's supposed to support the business," she pressed, "and by driving your vehicle, or your sister's, you lose the write-off."

Alex blinked at her, looked like he was going to say something, then closed his mouth.

Oh, she definitely overstepped. "I'm sorry," she blurted out, chest tightening. "Forget it. I'm sorry. Sometimes I have a hard time turning off work brain, you know? Maybe we need Rule Three? No shop talk outside of work?"

"Jill, it's—"

"You know," she said, latching onto a diversion from her blunder. "Blackburn is having a client event for Stampede. Ashleen has been hyping it up for weeks. Do you want to go? I mean, I've obviously never been before. And I'll have to do a bit of schmoozing with clients, and of course Nick is invited, too. And it'll give me something to look forward to when you're back?"

"Honestly?" He shook his head, smiling to himself. "Nick would love it. Sure, let's go."

The anxiety tightening her chest released. He wasn't mad at her for overstepping. Fight averted. And the Stampede event did sound like fun, even if it meant sharing the time with Nick, but it would be worth it.

"Okay, we'll have to be on good behaviour when we're around my team, but we can peel off after a bit and have fun by ourselves."

"Now I'm on board."

SIXTEEN

You should've left me your cowboy boots

I'm going to Stampede, baby!

Kyle: those boots look like blisters waiting to happen

Sophie: Yeah!
Cowboy Coachella!!

Trust Sophie to have her priorities straight.

Jill scrolled through the images Sophie had sent in rapid succession, a gallery of hash-tagged posts from last year's Stampede for outfit inspiration. All the women wore combinations of crop tops and Daisy Dukes, or peasant blouses and jean skirts. Men wore tight denim in varying stages of distress, and either going full Canadian tuxedo or an alternative Hawaiian shirt over a tank top look. Everyone wore a cowboy hat, and nearly everyone wore cowboy boots.

Sophie: If I didn't have a crazy week, I would be on a plane so fast! Amuse-toi xoxo

ps I can't wait for Boston

Kyle: maybe next year we'll come to calgary

After several days of wavering, she had finally called Kyle, then spent the next two hours crying and laughing and catching him up on her life. And him catching her up on his. Finally landing the job he wanted. The new woman he had gushed about on their visit to Montreal a year and a half ago was now his fiancée. Thinking about moving out of the city so they could buy a condo, and Jill squealed when he said they wanted to start a family. Jill floated the idea of her coming to Boston, and he immediately added Sophie to the call. Plane tickets were booked before they hung up.

She had paced her apartment for five minutes, repeating *Alex isn't Connor* until she worked up the courage to call him and let him know her plans. When she did, he simply added the dates in his calendar, said it sounded like fun, and he was glad she was reconnecting.

He had sounded sincere, too. That it wasn't an issue. Her travelling on her own. With a friend—a male friend—he didn't know. She didn't need to ask permission. That he was happy for her to be doing something for herself.

This was how it was supposed to be, and not for the first time, she winced at how long she let Connor do that to her.

No, his actions were not my responsibility. That was not my fault.

Jill switched her attention to her screen, tapping the end of her pen against her teeth. Nick had been remarkably chill all week, even with Alex not around to act as a buffer. She chalked it up to him looking forward to the Stampede event. Or because she hadn't asked him for any work recently. That was about to change.

Her outline was complete. A novella of recommendations far beyond the original process audit that would streamline their work, implement efficiencies, and make things easier for when they hired staff.

She didn't know who was going to hate it more. Alex, for having to get his shit together for anything that wasn't directly linked to lab and fieldwork; Nick, for having to do something other than schmoozing clients; or Jill, being the proverbial messenger.

It wasn't a conversation to have without Alex in the room. They needed to hear it at the same time. Even if they hadn't been dating, she would have wanted the Alex Buffer in effect for this meeting. He'd had her back for months.

She dropped the calendar invite for the middle of next week, a couple of days after the Stampede event. Maybe the party would butter Nick up a bit and make the recommendations go over more easily. Jill pushed away from her desk, glad Nick wasn't back from lunch so she could sneak out.

Without luck.

Nick trudged through the main doors as Jill was sliding her laptop into her bag.

So close.

"Glad you caught me," she lied. "I'll be at Blackburn for the rest of the week, so I'll see you at the event next Tuesday?"

"Fine, but I need to ask you something."

Jill put her bag down on her desk. "Is this about the meeting next week? I attached an agenda—"

"—No," he said, cutting her off. "It's about Alex."

She crossed her arms, a thread of tension winding in her stomach. "What about him?" she asked.

"Did he tell you he missed a deadline last week? Clients with a site up north? All the data was ready, but he didn't get the status update in on time," he said. "We won't lose the client. But still."

Alex hadn't said a thing. The thread wound tighter.

Nick drummed his fingers on the desk. "He's never missed a deadline. Ever. And now …" He swept his arm towards her.

Shit. Last Saturday, when he would have normally spent the morning working, taking a quick break for rugby, then working the rest of the afternoon and night. Instead, he tried to cram in a couple of hours of work and spend the evening with her. And even though she hadn't said anything to him, she had still been upset that he had been late.

"I've been his friend for a long time. I moved here to get this company off the ground with him. It has been a long, hard road for us, and it has taken us everything to get here." Nick sat with his arms crossed, chewing the inside of his cheek. "I also know he hasn't been in a relationship—shit, I don't think he's gone on a date—since he and Kate broke up."

Alex had never brought up any of his exes. Jill drew a quiet breath.

"I don't know if I want to tell you to not distract him when we are so close to getting what we want, or tell you not to break his heart. Maybe both."

"Nick, I—"

"—what I'm saying is don't fuck this up."

The tension threaded through her stomach pulled tight, cutting the organs it crossed. Nick was right. She had thought only about what this might mean to her and spared no thought to how Alex would be affected.

You are so selfish.

Mute, she shouldered her bag and measured the steps she needed to leave the room.

"See you next week," he called to her back.

—

Jill flicked through the options on Netflix, the titles sliding off her brain as she scrolled past. A heaviness had lodged firmly under her diaphragm after Nick's lecture, only retreating to the background when she buried herself in her other files for the afternoon. She fiddled with the remote and eyed the time. Alex would be at the hotel by now, even if he was still working. She could make it fast.

The call picked up on the first ring.

"Hey, what's going on?" His voice came out in cheerful but tinny tones of speakerphone, along with the occasional key clack and mouse click in the background.

She wished he was holding the phone closer, to let the richness of his voice caress her, then pushed the silly thought aside. He needed to spend his attention on keeping up with his work, not coddling her.

"Hey." The single word was gossamer fine, and she cleared her throat to try again. "I just wanted to hear your voice."

"Just a sec." A few seconds of shuffling, then rich tones caressed her ear. "How's that?"

She closed her eyes as the sound suffused her with warmth, and she snuggled down into her couch. "Better. How's the trip?"

"Cold and mosquitoes. It's ten degrees and I'm getting eaten alive."

"Sounds miserable."

"A little more miserable than usual. How was your day?"

Jill shifted. She didn't want to begin lying now, but this was not a conversation for the phone. "I had to deal with a difficult client. It was a little frustrating."

"If they're anything like me and Nick, I can't blame you for being frustrated."

Got it in one. "Well, one of you can be a handful," she said, smiling. "Just wanted to say hi before I went to bed."

"And I've got a ton of work to do before I turn in. I'll let you get a good night's sleep?"

Jill huffed a small laugh. "I don't have many of those. I'll have to tell you about my lifelong battle with insomnia when you get back."

"Well, I've only seen you sleep once, but it didn't look like you had any problems," Alex said, words curling at the edges. "And I had a pretty close-up view."

"Ah, mmm …" The sense memory of the morning washed over her. Loose and secure in that moment between waking and realizing where she was: the odd juxtaposition of blissful peace in the back of a broken-down Volvo. She hesitated a moment before saying, "That was the first time I slept through the night in about three years."

"Oh."

She spoke before the silence could grow. "I just wanted to say good night. I know you have a lot of work to do." That Nick would blame her for if Alex blew another deadline. And Nick would be right. She fiddled with the fringe on her pillow. "Can I call you tomorrow?"

"Of course. Call me after eight," he said. "Now I feel weird saying sleep well, but try to sleep well."

"I always try."

She landed on a show she had started a couple months earlier and dialled Sophie to watch with her, swapping increasingly outlandish theories on the plot line while Jill bitched about Nick and Sophie bitched about a new client, with a few thoughts about Stampede wear thrown in.

An hour later as she brushed her teeth, Jill realized for the first time in a long time, she had a shitty day that ended pretty well. Some heaviness lingered, and the cuts from the tightened threads across her insides still smarted, but she had offloaded some of the weight and soothed a balm over the deeper cuts. A year, or even six months ago, she would have packed the troubles down into the density of a neutron star and hid it away.

She would have hidden it from Connor so he wouldn't have anything to hold against her later. Telling her they were first world problems, and she should deal with it. If she were really lucky, he would monologue about how his were actual problems.

And today, nothing was solved. But she talked to people she cared about instead of turning inward. The things she wanted to—needed—to talk about weren't buried.

Doing good, Northrop.

—

Ashleen blurred into a series of shoulder shimmies and finger snaps. "I knew it!" she squealed. "I love Angela."

"About time," Omar said, pecking out a text to his newest boyfriend. "I've been waiting to book it the hell out of here."

He had hinted about the annual company tradition for a week and the confirmation just came through. After the event tomorrow night, Angela was giving everyone in the Calgary office the rest of the week off.

"There are three types of Calgarians," Omar said, filling Jill in on the strategy of the locals during Stampede. He held out one finger. "Those who live, eat, and breathe it." He pointed the finger at Ashleen, who shimmied again. He held up a second finger. "Those who GTFO," and turned the finger to himself, then held up a third, "and those who pretend it isn't happening then whine about downtown traffic for nine days. And every group thinks they're right."

"We're right," Ashleen said, staring off into the middle distance with shining eyes. "I can't believe we get the rest of the week off!"

Jill opened her calendar app. Sure enough, Eileen had already gone through and rescheduled everything to the following weeks. She would usually be excited not having to wade through her appointments, except for her meeting with Alex and Nick. She'd been eyeing the date with a mixture of anticipation and apprehension, both ready to pitch her recommendations and nervous about how they would be received. Delaying the meeting would only extend the dread and halt the work she wanted to start.

With a sigh, she dropped a note into the rarely used group text between the three of them.

My schedule has been rearranged.

Do you two want to meet tomorrow instead or push it to next week?

Then, to Alex:

Blackburn has the rest of the week off after tmr

I wonder what trouble I can get into unsupervised for a few days :)

Her fingers hovered over the keys, wanting to add that she would love to see him if he had time, but she already had the answer to that question. The two responses to her first text came within seconds of each other, with Nick's first:

I dont care

Followed quickly by Alex's:

Can we do next week?
I'm swamped

Jill grimaced. No surprise. It could wait. Ashleen had hit a few snags in her file, and with Marco off on vacation, she needed support. A couple of her own clients were overdue with some information requests she could follow up on. And it would be nice to not have a day booked back-to-back for a change.

A borderline suitable-for-the-workplace curse shook Jill from her thoughts, and she and Ashleen raised their brows at the source.

"Peter," he said, "wants to spend the entire week at Stampede." He tapped a quick reply and dropped his phone on the lunch table with a look of genuine disgust on his face. "Well, that was fun while it lasted."

"Did you break up with him over text?" Ashleen asked, shocked. "I thought that just happened in movies."

Jill snickered. "It's not even the first time I've seen it happen. Once, I saw him break up with a guy because he ate too fast."

"It gave me indigestion to watch him," Omar replied. He gave a theatrical sigh and looked up at the ceiling. "He was cute, too. Anyway, what about Alex's partner? Nate? Is he coming tomorrow?"

"Nick, and wrong team." She spied Ashleen leaning forward and held up her hand. "You want nothing to do with him. I wouldn't let him near any of my coworkers."

"Fine. My aunties are giving me until I'm twenty-seven before they start setting me up."

Now that's a good plan, she thought, and steered the conversation to logistics, where and when to meet the following night.

Another text banner popped up with the accompanying buzz. She hid her smile as she pulled it up.

I'm sure you'll find lots of trouble
to get into :)

I'll be in town by 7. Can I
see you?

She chewed her thumbnail. Alex had been on the road for six days, but Nick's warning rang in her ears. Alex would only get farther behind in his mountains of work if he was with her tonight.

I have to run errands tonight

And find something to wear

I've been told cowboy cosplay
is mandatory

True. I'm not sure they'd let you in
without it

Ashleen and Omar were debating vegetarian options to request for the caterer. Her inbox was clear. She had nothing to distract herself with. It had been a long six days; he could say no if he didn't have time. She bent over her phone and cursed her weakness.

Can I text you if I get done early?

The one-word reply appeared almost instantly.

—

If Sophie had it her way, Jill's butt cheeks would be hanging out the bottom of a pair of micro shorts and her boobs spilling out of a crop top. She turned in the tight dressing room, holding up the phone so Sophie could dismiss every one of Jill's outfit choices through the FaceTime call.

"The red halter top you wore when I was in town would work."

"Not in front of my boss and clients, thank you very much."

"Fine, but if I had your ass, I wouldn't take those shorts off."

"Taking them off might not be an option," Jill grunted as she tried to peel them over her hips.

"Go with the dress!" Rachel called from the other side of the stall door.

Jill tugged until the denim shorts pooled around her ankles and blew a strand of hair out of her eyes. "Definitely going with the dress."

"Coward," Sophie said with a grin.

"Yep," she replied, but added the shorts to her purchases. She wouldn't wear them, but, ass or no ass, Sophie would slay in these.

"Okay, you're done," Rachel said, smiling. "Now, go see your man."

The familiar giddy rush floated through her stomach. Her man. She couldn't wait.

Jill pulled up to a humble, cream-coloured bungalow a few minutes away from the CMR office. The late evening sun slanted through the dust and leaves of the ornamental trees lining the patchwork of new builds and mid-century homes. A group of kids bashed their hockey sticks on the asphalt down the street, and the muted wheels of a freight train screeched in the distance.

She skipped up to the front door, partly because her yoga shorts and cropped tee shirt provided little coverage against the cooling night air, and partly from excitement to see him in the first time in almost a week. Four crisp raps, and seconds later footsteps could be heard on the other side of the door, then she was lifted over the threshold in one fluid motion.

Maybe her toes were on the ground. Maybe they weren't. Either way, her legs wouldn't have been able to hold her up. She let his mouth crush the breath from her, a wild throng pulsing through her centre and escaping her lips in a hush.

"I missed you," Alex whispered against her lips, fingers winding through her hair.

"Hi," she breathed. "I missed you, too."

And she thought she should stay away tonight. Stupid.

Alex pulled her into him, chest expanding as he inhaled for a long moment. "Why do you always smell so good?"

She leaned back to meet his eyes. "Even when I get back from the shelter?" she asked, a wide grin splitting her face.

"Mmm, especially then," he said, and buried his nose to her neck with exaggerated snorting noises that sent ticklish sparks racing down her body.

Eventually her kicking forced him to put her down. He raked his eyes across her body, and she felt oddly pleased her oldest clothes got an appreciative look. A blue light cast shadows behind him announced a computer screen was on. Nine-thirty on a Monday night and he was still working. Jill swallowed, remembering why she had planned to stay away.

She stepped back, smoothing her hair and pulling his tee shirt straight. "Do you have a lot of work left?"

He tore his eyes away from her legs and tracked her gaze to the flickering light behind him. "Ah, you know," he said, running a hand through his dishevelled hair. "Wrapping up a couple of things."

"I'll let you get back to it." She stood on tiptoes to leave him with a last peck, which he lengthened into something sweet enough to scramble her thoughts.

"Stay?"

Someone else had made unilateral decisions for her for years, with no respect for what she wanted. He wanted her to stay. She looked past his shoulder into the blue again. "You'll tell me when you want me to leave?"

He tugged her hand to follow him past the table where his laptop had gone into screensaver mode with a second screen flickering beside it, through to the living room, pulling her onto a beat-up couch beside him. More boxes were stacked in the living room, but moving boxes, not records boxes; some empty, some half full of binders. No pictures hung on the walls, and small TV sat on a box against the far wall, unplugged, with more boxes stacked on it.

She tucked herself close, wiggling her feet under his thigh, and running her nails along the nape of his neck. "What are you working on?"

"Finishing an article review while I'm waiting for an analysis to run," he said, eyes closed. "Site report is due tomorrow."

"What's the article for?"

"Bioreactive organoclay. Peer review."

"Is that …?" she said, searching her memory for any mention of that in the background information she had read on their files. "That's not your area."

He shrugged a shoulder, eyes still heavy. "Worked with a few researchers when I did my postdoc. Co-authored a few papers."

"On top of your own research?"

He hummed in assent.

"And that's separate from CMR?"

Another hum.

She traced the knotted muscles at the base of his skull. "How do you find time for it all?"

"I have been very busy," Alex said, "for a very long time."

The thought percolated up to mention Nick's comments to her that morning, but she shoved it aside. Jill looked around the living room, clearly little used, a layer of dust over most surfaces.

The dining nook she had passed through was in a similar state of forlorn unpacking, mismatched chairs stacked in the corner, just the one chair pulled up to the table beside his laptop. "When did you move in?"

"Couple years ago."

"You … what?" Jill pulled her hand away, and he opened his eyes. "You're living out of boxes!"

He looked chagrined. "Guess I never got around to unpacking."

Her own apartment had been fully set up within a week of her moving to Calgary, and it only took that long because she had needed to furnish it. She couldn't imagine living in this chaos, and the filing system at CMR suddenly made a lot more sense.

She leaned in, put her hand to his cheek, and feathered a kiss over his lips. "This is foreplay, isn't it?"

"What?" he choked a laugh.

"Admit it. You brought me here because you knew if I saw this mess, I'd have to organize it." She rested her chin on his shoulder. "You're crafty."

"You are not unpacking my stuff."

"C'mon, I can help."

"No." The word came out clipped, but he couldn't keep the smile from his eyes.

She brought her fingertips back to the nape of his neck, tracing light circles with her nails. "Let me help, and I'll let you cook me dinner."

He grunted, and she smiled. She was winning.

"I'm offering to take an annoying chore off your list and let you impress me with your culinary skills. My standards are low. It'll be easy." Jill loaded one more point into her argument. "It'll make me far more inclined to spend time here."

He narrowed his eyes at her, the result being extremely ineffective as he was clearly struggling to not melt under the designs she traced on his skin. Jill filed away the secret weapon she discovered, and waited.

If nails on his neck was Alex's Kryptonite, organization porn was hers.

Perfect.

"You are a terrifying negotiator," he said finally. "Impressive, but terrifying."

"It's pretty great, right?" She beamed at him. "Told you I'm used to getting my way."

The half smile faded from his lips as his gaze dropped to her mouth. He rubbed his thumb along the column of her throat. "How else do you like getting your way?"

Don't overthink it. Before she could change her mind, she threw a leg over his. She was right: his lap was as comfortable as she thought it would be. With one large exception pressed firmly against her inner thigh. Her feather-light kiss deepened, and her heartbeat sped up as she let her hands wander over his chest. "Let's see what you'll let me get away with."

"Try me," he said, and wrapped his hands around her hips to draw her closer.

This wasn't the plan for tonight. She was supposed to be at home, getting ready for tomorrow. Reading alone, doing laundry, painting her toenails. Letting Alex recover after a week on the road.

This was so much better.

Jill rocked forward on the insistent ridge pressing against her thigh, and he released a moan into her mouth, leaning back on the couch to tip her forward into him. His hands worked their way up from her hips and under her shirt, releasing a shiver along her spine that had nothing to do with the cool night. Her breath caught in her throat, about to lift the hem of his tee shirt, when a metallic series of alarms erupted from the dining room, and she jerked back with a yip.

"What the …?" she asked over the scolding noise.

"You've got to be kidding me," Alex groaned and leaned his forehead against hers, breathing heavily. "Analysis parameters need editing. It won't stop until I fix it."

Jill slowly pulled her hands away from their wandering. Right. He was working late to finish a report due tomorrow. Nick would lose it if he found out she was here while there was another report delay. It wouldn't have surprised her if Nick had planted the alarm.

She freed Alex from under her, trying not to stare as he adjusted himself through his jeans, and let him tend to his high-maintenance analysis. She should really get to bed anyway and let Alex … analyze things.

She didn't know if she wanted to punt the laptop out the window or be grateful it stopped her from getting carried away. She crossed her legs, and felt her pulse between her thighs.

Punt it. Definitely punt it.

At the door, he stalled her for a last minute, a slow finger drawing up between her shoulder blades, the golden rims of his irises catching the last of the light. "What are you thinking?"

I wish I was staying. "I can't wait to see you tomorrow."

She sat in her car for a full five minutes in front of his house, trying to corral her thoughts as she blinked into the setting sun. It was getting harder to pull herself away. She didn't want to. She didn't have to.

For once in her life, she wanted to let herself get carried away.

On her way home, she stopped at the drugstore for one last errand.

SEVENTEEN

Omar twiddled his pen and glanced at the clock, and Jill refreshed her inbox for the millionth time that hour. Omar had warned her the Stampede turned offices across the city into ghost towns, and Blackburn was no exception. The office was empty except for the two of them, and she hadn't gotten a single client email herself all day.

Except from Alex. She frowned at the status updates that came in at two in the morning. On the one hand, she was relieved. He finished everything he needed to last night and submitted the report on time. But that meant he was up for hours after she left. She had long ago figured out he was a night owl, but the thought of him cramming in work after she had taken his time sent a selfish twist through her gut.

Omar smacked his pen down on the desk. "Wanna get out of here?"

Jill was already closing her laptop.

"Forty minutes," he said, packing his bag. "No more. I'm making sure Angela sees me, getting food, and shaking hands with the CIO for the new energy contract and I'm out."

"Give me the signal and I'll create a diversion."

She might need her own diversion tonight. She hadn't spoken with Nick since he cornered her last week. As much as she wanted to resolve it, she didn't know how. Or if he wanted to. His dismissive response to the meeting change could have been a genuine lack of concern for the state of their business—which was unlikely—or the result of one of his mood swings—which was probable.

And then there was Alex. They were going to be together, in front of everyone she worked with. Many of whom knew she was seeing him. Others who did not. It was one thing to tell people; it was another for them to see it. Angela wouldn't be as sanguine with Jill's relationship if he pulled a repeat of his post-rugby hypothesis testing and manhandled her in front of their other clients, plastering her with kisses as she pretended to fight him off.

Ask us about the Blackburn enhanced client satisfaction package!

Hey, extension of office
rules tonight?
no PDA?

Scout's honour

She quelled a flutter in her chest and added asking if he had actually been a Boy Scout to her list of things she wanted to learn and got back to her primary pastime: worrying about horning in on his finite time. The disclosure to Nick weeks ago of *we are going to spend some time together and see where it goes* had definitely gone somewhere. Fast. And only speeding up.

Too fast? She had orange juice in her fridge longer than they had been dating.

From the conversation last night, he had work, voluntary or not, outside of CMR. And he still carved out time for her. Something had to give. The recommendations list she developed would load reams of work onto him, on top of the work he had already committed to, in direct competition with her desire to claim more of that precious time.

Right. Only child. You've always been too selfish.

No intrusive thoughts today. *Not true. I am not too selfish.*

Also, note to self: check the expiry date on the orange juice.

She pulled on the light blue peasant dress she bought the previous night, a mid-calf length with ruffled sleeves and eyelets. The extravagance of boots was outside her budget, but she had a pair of sandals that would be fine and found a straw hat that Rachel said was cowboy adjacent and looked cute.

Jill had counted on the crisp Calgary air to keep the fluff in her dress bouncy and waves in her hair smooth, but an uncharacteristically humid evening clung to her like a second skin. In the short walk from her apartment to the Stampede grounds, the sweltering temperatures permeated every ruffle, and she gave up on looking fresh.

It's fine. He'll think I'm cute, even if I'm sweaty.

Ashleen dazzled in her gorgeous Desi-western mashup and radiant smile, indifferent to the sweltering surroundings. She broke off from greeting the growing crowd of people to their tent and seized Jill's hand.

"This is amazing," she gushed. "I'm the designated greeter and Angela is already here and I met our new clients a few minutes ago and they were so nice!" She had come a long way from the new recruit who was scared of her own voice a few months ago.

Blessings on the people who enjoyed this sort of thing, she thought, and leaned in for a quick hug. "Angela put the right person in charge of client welcoming. You look amazing."

She didn't need to check her phone anymore to know Alex would be late. Nick rolled in and dropped into a chair beside Ashleen, his most charming smile in place. Ashleen shot her a pained look and mouthed *so cute, are you sure?* but after Jill gave a subtle shake of her head, Ashleen followed her warning and walked a line between friendly and busy, bustling away as soon as it was polite to do so. Jill attempted a sincere smile at Nick and vowed to keep a spare eye on him.

When Alex arrived, half an hour later, the only thing that Jill registered was her heart sending her a clear message, which said, *well, that's it.* Nothing was different; he just looked like hers. He scanned the crowd, all edges softening as he found her, and whatever nerves she had thinking about the night evaporated.

His arm moved to wrap her close, but he stalled halfway, letting a smile crinkle the corners of his eyes instead. "Hi. I hate office rules."

"Me, too." She cleared her throat. Omar was right. An early exit seemed brilliant. "So, here's the plan."

"Shoot."

"I need to spend an hour with these people, and you need to stay away from me, and then I promise I will get you something sweet. Deal?"

His smile deepened. "Deal."

Three years ago, running her first marathon, she bonked at the thirty-kilometre mark. Blood sugar depleted. Muscles seized. Lungs on fire. Twelve gruelling kilometres to go. Five months of training distilled to the mental toughness of bearing the next sixty agonizing minutes, the memory of dragging herself across the finish line seared into every cell as the longest hour of her life.

This was the second longest hour.

She chatted with a few guys in comms about the new marketing campaign. She linked up with Omar to meet the new client he was working with. She staved off a mild panic attack when she walked by Angela and Alex in animated conversation. She convinced Ashleen to ride the mechanical bull, then used the excuse of wearing a dress to get out of riding it herself.

And seventeen minutes had gone by.

She sidled up to Alex and handed him a plate of mini doughnuts. "I saw you talking with Angela. Was it, um …?"

"She asked me how the grant and audit were going."

Jill clasped her hands behind her back, shifting side-to-side so her dress swished below her knees. Fine. He wanted to make her squirm a little. She wasn't going to fall for it. "That's—" she cast about for a way to keep him talking to her "—nice."

He scanned the crowd, the corner of his mouth twitching. "Aren't you supposed to be ignoring me?"

"No. Maybe." She bit her lip. "This is fun, right?"

"Nope. Go talk to your clients."

"You're a client."

"You told me to stay away." He popped another mini doughnut into his mouth, resolute in avoiding eye contact. "Just following your plan."

Sometimes her plans were stupid.

Nick materialized beside them, one hand shoved deep in the pocket of his inadvisably tight jeans, the other grasping a sweating bottle of Corona. "I'm going to bounce. See if I can crash one of the oil-and-gas parties." He downed the rest of the beer and set the bottle beside the recycling bin, tracking a line of tents with a bevy of Daisy Duke-clad butt cheeks mingling throughout. "No offence," he said to Jill. "They have better food."

Jill pasted a smile on her face. "None taken. Good luck with that."

Alex narrowed his eyes at Nick's retreating back. "He's been kind of weird lately."

Except for their initial client meeting, Nick had been a moody jerk the entire time she'd known him. Which, granted, was barely over four months, and she didn't really feel like bringing up the ambush he'd sprung on her last week. At least now she didn't need to keep him away from Ashleen. She took a sip of her Perrier. "Forty-one minutes to go. You remember Omar, right?"

Time did what time does, and passed. Slowly. Jill wrapped up a visit with the CFO from Palliser, with whom she was genuinely glad to catch up, said a few more goodbyes, then found Omar and Alex sequestered at a table between a bale of hay and a keg. Alex was gesturing with his can of soda in growing circles, while Omar nodded enthusiastically.

"I thought you'd have ducked out by now," Jill said. "Forty minutes is way up."

Omar jutted his chin at Alex. "The introverts found a corner and stuck to it."

She tilted her head at Alex. "What do you say, introvert? Ready to … what's a cowboy word? Mosey?"

"Ready if you are." He stood, slapping Omar's shoulder in a farewell. "Good talking to you."

"Same." Omar shot a knowing look at Jill. "Enjoy your week off."

The grounds slowly filled, people packing the spaces between games, rides, and vendors, and the scent of deep-fried foods and barn animals saturated the humid air. Loud families and kids shrieking with glee were replaced with louder throngs of revellers shouting with inebriation.

The minute they were out of eyesight from their party, she stepped up to her tiptoes and wound her arms around his neck with a sigh. "I've been waiting an hour to do this."

"You're worth the wait." Alex pulled her into him, nose buried in her hair. "You're so beautiful."

How long did they have to stay here?

Focus, Northrop. Calgary experience. Rite of passage and all that.

After a beat, he released her. "Okay," he said grimly. "What do you want to do? Rides? Weird food? They have pickled ice cream and deep-fried scorpions this year."

She shuddered. "Rides make me queasy, and I hate pickles."

"But you love salty!"

"And you love ice cream. Do you want pickled ice cream?" she asked, and it was his turn to shudder.

Alex stood resolute, one hand wrapped around hers, the other shading his eyes as he scowled over the crowd like a general evaluating a battlefield.

Jill caught her lip between her teeth. Not once had Alex suggested they do anything around large groups of people. Her giant introvert, indeed.

She wrinkled her nose at him. "This isn't really your thing, is it?"

"Ah …"

"Come on, tell me what you like."

"I like you."

"That's not what I mean," she said, blushing. "Spill."

"I hate crowds," he blurted. "It's so … they're so …"

"Noisy and hot and people pressing up against you and …"

He repressed a shiver.

"Do you want to get out of here?" she asked hopefully, and a ripple of anticipation wound through her.

His shoulders sagged. "Please."

The sun closed in on the edge of the horizon, and they wandered past the slow rush of people heading in the direction they were leaving, like tributaries feeding a river. She nudged their course of direction along. Waiting at a crosswalk, she slipped her fingers between the buttons of his shirt, searching for the soft thread of hair she'd discovered last week.

Treasure trail, she thought with a stifled giggle before he clapped his hand over her exploring fingers.

"Sorry." She tried pulling away. "You don't like it?"

"Yes. No. Yes," he breathed. "But not here, or—"

"Or what?" she teased, eyes dancing.

"Or I will have to stop myself from dragging you somewhere private."

There'd never be a better invitation than that. She flexed her fingers against his stomach and felt her playful smile turn into something altogether different. "Okay."

"What?" His eyes were dark as he searched her face.

Shit. Maybe it wasn't an invitation? Maybe his mind was somewhere else completely and he had work to finish tonight … "I mean, we can …"

Come on, Northrop.

She took a steadying breath. "Do you want to go to my place?"

"Are you thinking Netflix and chill?" he said slowly.

"No." She squirmed. He was going to make her say it. "I want to be with you tonight. All of you. Do you want—"

He smothered her words in a hard kiss that left her reeling, only stopping when the whoops and wolf whistles from a gaggle of passers-by reached their ears.

"Yes, I want," he panted against her ear, his breath warm on her neck while his hands roamed her shoulders, down her arms, tugging at her waist, sending shivers coursing through her centre. "Need to stop at a drug store. I don't have anything. I didn't know—"

"I did," she said. "Last night, after I left your place."

The look of elation that crossed his features made her throw her head back to laugh. He kissed her palm, already pulling her down the street. "Let's go."

The steps of her building were under her feet, and she was pinning him against the elevator doors until they slid open. Laughter bubbled in her chest as they stumbled backwards into the hall, thudding into the wall opposite the doors as she tried to corral her smile into something she could kiss him with. Distracted by his teeth on her neck, a frustrated growl left her lips as she struggled to unlock her door. Alex lifted his mouth long enough to slide the key into her lock for her, and they spilled into her apartment.

He pressed her hard against the other side of the door, mouths working to find rhythm, tasting each other's heat and salt of the night. Her hands wound around his shoulders, half for balance, half to feel the muscles flex under his shirt as his hands slid down and under her ass, hoisting her up to fit her body to his, her thighs wrapped around his hips. Through the vibration thrumming in her body, she was dimly aware of being transported across the room, being set on something high, his hands travelling up the length of her thighs and nudging the hem of her dress with each pass. She gripped his shirt to drag him close, rucking it up and sliding her hands under to feel the muscles rippling over his back. Her hands found their way to the band of his jeans, using it as an anchor to shift herself forward to fit more snugly against him and feel how ready he was for her, too. He dropped his mouth to her neck and palmed her breast, thumb brushing the sensitive tip and sending a current straight through to the heat growing low in her belly. She arched back and banged her head against the cupboard with a sharp *ow,* and he pulled her forward, laughing.

"Kitchen," she said, registering her surroundings for the first time. "Wrong room."

"Tell me where."

She gripped his shirt, dragging him with her as she stumbled backwards into her bedroom. He was gorgeous. All swollen lips and tousled hair and flushed skin, broad chest rising and falling as his darkened eyes drank her in. Her fingers found the buttons at the top of his shirt, undoing them one by one, pushing his shirt off his shoulders as her lips followed the edge of his collarbone. She charted the contours of his torso, the light dust of hair across his chest funnelled down and disappeared under the waistband of his jeans, and she fumbled with the buttons to follow the trail with her mouth.

"Wait." He pulled her to her feet, and his hands skimmed up her arms to the buttons at the top of her dress, then stopped, brow furrowing. "This isn't working. Why isn't this working?"

"Not real buttons," she said with a breathless smile. "What if you needed to undo them one-handed? It … it just slips on."

He sank to his knees in reverence and pressed his face to the buttons he just failed to undo. "You were thinking of me taking your clothes off when you bought this?" he asked, teeth toying with the hardened peaks of her nipples through the thin dress and heat bloomed fresh between her thighs.

Her legs were going to give out if he kept doing that with his mouth, and she leaned into him. "I've thought about you taking off my clothes lots of times."

His strangled groan clued her in that she said it with her outside voice. She swallowed a tight giggle and reached down to pull the flowy dress up, but he halted her movement again.

"Please, let me."

At her nod, his hands travelled over the curve of her waist to the flare of her hips, settling on her knees under the hem of her dress. "You're trembling," he said, and stilled his hands. "Are you—"

"—so are you," she said, voice shaky. "Don't stop."

The dress disappeared, peeled off in a breeze across her skin to reveal the only remotely sexy things she could comfortably wear for an hour in public. Eyes drunk, his gaze sent shivers of anticipation across her skin. His fingers slipped under the pink lace bra and pulled the fabric aside to take the tip of her breast into his mouth, and she inhaled with a sharp *yes.* "I might have thought of you when I put these on today, too."

"Holy shit." He lifted his eyes to her in sublime realization, smile widening. "You planned on seducing me tonight."

"Maybe a little," she said primly, trying not to blurt out exactly what she wanted him to do while willing him to take the rest of her clothes off.

Apparently, he could read minds. He deftly unhooked the clasp and slid the straps down her shoulders, her sexy undergarment plan being short-lived but effective. A rasp escaped his throat as he swiped the calloused pad of his thumb across one taut nipple, the other still drawn into the slick heat of his mouth and the trembling in her legs increased to a quake.

She gave up on trying to filter her thoughts and let them spill out. "I'm going to fall over if I don't get you in my bed right now," she whispered, hands unsteady on his shoulders.

"Goddamn." He let her push him backwards, folding at the knees when he hit the edge of the bed and dragging her down on top of him.

Her breath came in shallow gasps, her hair spilling around him, and hands braced against his shoulders. The thin fabric of her underwear left little barrier between them, and even through his jeans, there was no way he couldn't feel the heat between her thighs, his hands full of her ass as he ground against her. She worked the top two buttons of his jeans open enough to slide her hand in to grip his length and he shuddered out groan.

"Fuck, Jill."

Her smile spread and she lowered her lips to his ear, letting the peaks of her breasts dance across his chest. "Oh, Alex, if I'd have known you'd feel this good—"

It was like she'd pulled a trigger. Alex flipped her on her back, crushing her into the mattress, his mouth on hers and fingers edging her underwear down over her hips. She shimmied to speed their removal, and her last of clothing was tossed across the room. His hand travelled up the length of her calf, up the inside of her thigh, ending in a gentle stroke with his fingers along her folds.

He drew a ragged breath. "God, you are so fucking wet."

Her entire world was the heat building at her core and his gorgeous body pressing against her and her hips rocking into his hand. "Alex?"

"Love it when you say my name. Say it again."

"Alex, I don't think this is going to take very long."

"Fuck me. I'll go slow." He licked her nipple. "So slow."

"Can we go slow next time?"

"You're going to kill me," he groaned into her skin, sliding his finger over her clit, and after a minute, eased a finger inside her. He slowed at her sharp intake of breath, moving against her until she shook, and an embarrassingly short time later, he sent her on a rolling climax, her lips sealed to keep from crying out.

With the last waves, she locked her legs together to still his hands and pulled his mouth up to hers, succeeding only in kissing his teeth as he pressed his grin to her cheek.

"You just … so good …" Full sentences were overrated. And impossible to form with the blood nowhere near her brain. "… Oh my god."

"Glorious." He worked his hand free from the clasp of her thighs and stroked the plain of her stomach. "I'm going to find out everything that makes you move like that."

She let her head fall back to the pillow in bliss. She had an orgasm. Hard. She didn't think she would, not the first time they were together. That she felt comfortable enough with him to let go. And she wanted to feel more of him.

She struggled to shift from underneath him. Instead, he pinned her down with a palm to her stomach.

"But … condoms … bathroom counter."

He blocked her second feeble attempt to rise.

"In a minute," he said, the lazy circles of his fingers drawing out a line of goosebumps. She gasped at his tongue skating over the pulse point on her neck, and he planted a line of kisses down her neck, breasts, and over her stomach, leaving a trail of little fires as he went.

"Alex, what are you doing?"

"You said I could go slow next time," he said, burying his nose in the soft down between her thighs. "It's next time."

"What?" She can't have heard right, still halfway insensible from the aftershocks.

"I want to make you come again."

"I can't." She was barely hanging on already.

He prised her thighs loose, hooking one knee over his shoulder. His tongue travelled a long, languid path, and he smiled at the raw sound that escaped her throat.

"Bet you can."

She, in fact, could.

He set a fire that spread across her body, teasing and pulling back as the tension at the base of her spine built, her thighs aching as she chased her release, and she whimpered into the night.

"I'm not done yet," he said every time she got close, sliding his tongue more slowly.

Her entire centre clenched, and she choked out, "Please?"

He buried his face against her until she cried out, and this time when the waves crashed over her, the edges of the room went dark.

If she couldn't move before, she was boneless now, blinking away the stars that flashed behind her eyelids and hands fluttering uselessly at his hair. Finally, he relented, licking a drop of sweat from behind her knee.

"You are spectacular," he said, leaving her with a deep kiss. "Don't go anywhere."

A gasp of laughter escaped her. Not a problem. Her legs would never work again.

She heard fumbling in her bathroom, then seconds later he was back, tripping out of his jeans, kicking them to the corner and kneeling between her thighs once more. She struggled up to reach his mouth with her own while she wrapped her hand around his length.

Firm strokes, her tongue teasing his mouth, his breath hitching as he pulsed in her hand. The next time they were together, she wanted to explore every inch of him, give him back the same wickedness he had shown her. But right now, she needed him inside her.

"Please don't make me wait."

He swore as he tried to put the condom on the wrong way, righted it, and rolled it down. She sighed as he settled along her body, chest pressed against hers and ready at her entrance. He brushed a strand of hair from her eyes, lifted one of her knees and eased forward.

So gentle, so careful, and still she sucked in her breath as they joined. She whispered some words she couldn't recall against his cheek as he slowly retreated, pressed deeper, and again, until she opened to him, and he filled her completely.

He stopped, rigid, his face contorted in concentration. "Don't move."

She'd never move again if they could stay like this. Connected. Wrapped around him. Then her body arched into him, and she pressed her mouth to his to swallow his groan. After a beat, the hold on her thigh firmed, and he moved, slow and restrained, and it felt like heaven. She twined her arms around his neck, hips canting to draw him closer to match his dreamy pace. But he was a powerful man, and this was not all of him.

"I'm not made of glass," she said, and he jerked as she bit his lip a little harder than she might have planned. "Don't hold back."

"Definitely going to kill me." He slid a hand under her shoulder. "You need to tell me if I'm too much."

His restraint fell away. Each thrust a searing rush of pleasure deeper through her. She matched his rhythm, exhausted, exhilarated, clinging to him as tight as she could.

Her name was the last coherent thing he said, husky and ragged, and she closed her eyes to feel the words rumble through his chest. She couldn't move anymore. He locked her legs wide as he bore down on her, hands gripping her ass to angle deeper, the full weight of his chest crushing her breath from her lungs. The broad muscles under her hands coiled when he neared his release, and she dug her heels into his glutes until the tension poured out of him in a wild rush.

The air around them filled with his jagged breath and he rocked slower, slower until he stilled above her, chest heaving. Blood sang in her ears as he weighted her to the bed and she wound her fingers through his hair, damp with effort, wishing to stay like this all night.

Except she couldn't. He was crushing her, and she was going to die.

"Alex," she squeaked, "I can't breathe."

He pressed onto his elbows, lips on her temple as the last shivers coursed through his body. Jill filled her lungs, kissing everything she could reach, legs tangled and fingers clasped, together in the fading light.

"You are so perfect." His mouth moved against her ear, and he shifted off her and disappeared from the room.

It had never been like that before. So close, so focused on each other. She didn't want it to end. She twisted the sheet between her fingers until the bathroom faucet stopped, and footsteps crossed back to the room.

"Will you stay?" Her voice came out more timidly than she wanted, but maybe he would think she was trying to whisper. "If you want to, I mean."

He blinked at her with bleary eyes and passed her a glass of water. "I want to."

She huffed a small smile, trying to hide behind the glass. He slid into bed beside her and took the glass for a sip before setting it down and turning to her, stroking the hair back from her ear.

"Why so shy all of a sudden?" he asked, voice soft.

She looked away from him into the dark. Just because she knew she shouldn't be, didn't mean she wasn't. "A couple of weeks ago, when we went for ice cream," she started, hesitantly, "and we were saying there are things we'll need to learn about each other?"

When he made a low hum in his throat, she continued, "I just don't want to stop feeling so close to you after … but I don't want to get in your space if that's what you're used to … sorry. Is this too weird?"

"Wait, are you trying to tell me you're a cuddler?" he asked, the corner of his mouth curving. His chest hitched as he suppressed a laugh, gathering her close to him. "You slept nearly on top of me before we were even dating, within, no joke, half an hour of falling asleep."

"Sorry—"

"Don't be. I'm not. And I stayed up that whole night to make sure I didn't wake up spooning you and pressing a hard on against your ass." He nipped her fingers. "God, that night was torture."

"You said it wasn't a terrible night!"

He shrugged a lazy grin. "Didn't say it was terrible. I said it was torture."

The warm glow between her ribs melted the rest of the uncertainty with enough power left over to heat her cheeks, and she snuggled deeper into the crook of his shoulder. It wasn't the first time she fit herself into this spot, but it was the first time she did it with permission. And naked.

She pressed her lips together to stifle a laugh. "I nearly kissed you that morning after."

"Like I said." The low growl rumbled under her fingers. "Torture."

"Did you have feelings for me then?"

"Yep."

She stole her fingers back to trace abstract lines across his chest. "When did you think you might?"

"First time we went for ice cream," he said instantly. "Already knew you were smart and cute, but I also thought you hated me. Just wanted to apologize for being an asshole in university, so you wouldn't look like you loathed me."

"Loathe is a pretty strong word." She propped up her chin on his chest. "Accurate, but strong."

"And then you were really nice about it. And funny. And you didn't let me off the hook. That's the first time I saw your real smile, and knew I was in trouble." He looked at her sideways. "And watching you lick that ice cream? Also torture."

The flush in her cheeks deepened with the old embarrassment, coloured with a shade of delight. "I was so self-conscious about that."

"Trust me when I say it was not the last time I thought of that day."

Next time they went for ice cream she was definitely getting a cone. And eating it slowly. "If I hadn't … I mean, would you have asked me out eventually?"

"Mm-hmm. Just wanted to make sure of ..." he said, failing to stifle a yawn, and the next several words were incomprehensible. "Thank you for not making me wait that long."

Sleepy Alex. File this under one more way he looked adorable.

Reflections of streetlights shone on the windows of buildings outside her room, filtering through the curtains. The open window let in a warm breeze and street noise below, tires on pavement and the occasional holler from people leaving—or perhaps still heading to—the Stampede. It was hard to believe they had been among the throngs below less than two hours earlier. Now they were the only two people in the world, and her blood sang with the newfound connection between them.

She nudged herself up to brush her lips against his and dropped into a dreamless sleep.

—

She almost made it through the night.

Sometime around three, a discordant uneasiness jolted her awake and her breath caught as she tried to pinpoint the source.

She was in bed. In Calgary. Good.

And not alone. Alex.

Lightly snoring, bathed in shadow. Sprawled on his back, one arm thrown over his head, the other resting on her hip. With his scent on her skin and his heart beating under her ear.

The tension that startled her dissolved, replaced with relief and a wild thrum in her chest.

Maybe because it was new. Maybe it was because everything between them was really, really good. Maybe it was something else. But it had never been like this before. And not just tonight. A shimmering flow under her skin, each point of contact between them an active current.

She would have basked it in for the rest of the night if she didn't have to pee so badly.

After, she splashed water on her face, the bathroom tiles cold under her bare feet. She peered at her reflection. The skin on her neck and breasts red from his stubble. Lips swollen, hair tangled. Grey eyes tired, but bright. Glowing. She ducked her head.

Pump the brakes, Northrop. It is way too early for that.

She slipped on a tee shirt she had left on the floor the previous morning and silently slid between the covers, curling up with her back to Alex's sleeping form.

EIGHTEEN

Shafts of light pouring through the window warmed her awake, and her eyelids fluttered open.

Despite her attempt to put distance between them when she returned to bed, Alex had pulled her close in the night. Her back was flush against his chest, his breath stirring the hair at her neck and his hand up her tee shirt. His concern of pressing morning wood against her ass in the back of the Volvo had been well-founded. Rolling her hips against him to wake him up would be a luxurious start to the day, but a decadent soreness between her legs pulsed in protest at round two.

But if he was gentle with her, and they eased into it …

Damp heat spread between her aching thighs, and she swallowed a giggle. That pulse between her thighs wasn't a protest at all.

What's gotten into me? He'll break me on day one. I need to get the hell out of bed.

But she couldn't make herself get up right away, rolling to face him and giving herself over to the pleasure of looking at him in the light. Lashes flush against his cheek. The mole on his shoulder where her head had been resting the night before. A peek at a tattoo on his bicep when she carefully lifted his arm off her. The glow spread its warmth through her core, and after a few minutes she slid out of bed, grabbing some clothes and heading into the shower.

She left him a note when she went to the corner store—she didn't have any cream for his coffee, and they weren't in toothbrush sharing territory yet—but he was still fast asleep when she quietly unlocked her front door. Curled up with her second cup of coffee and a book, rustling in the bedroom an hour later alerted her to his impending wakefulness.

"Good morning." She sat on the edge of the bed, put two cups of coffee on the bedside table, and tried to make her smile look more relaxed and less shy than she felt.

He dragged her across the bed to bury his face in her thigh, eyes still closed. "Mm-hmm. What time is it?"

"A little after eight." She tucked a strand of hair behind her ear and twirled the end around her finger. "Did you sleep okay?"

"The best." His hand travelled over her hip, thumb splaying over her belly under her tee shirt. He rubbed his hand over his face and squinted up at her with a lazy smile that flipped her stomach upside down.

He was unfairly good-looking waking up.

"So …" Jill paused, casting about for what to say next.

"So," he confirmed. His thumb swiped slow waves. "How are you feeling?"

Amazing. Ecstatic. Scared as hell. Like I'm running full speed and I can't stop. Like I don't want to look at this too closely, or I'll jinx it. She let out a breath through pursed lips and let herself show a smile. "Good? Like, really good?"

A fraction of tension she hadn't seen left his shoulders, and he brought her wrist to his mouth. "Good," he said, softly.

"Are you …?"

"Oh, me? Fantastic. Better than fantastic," he said, covering his mouth with his hand. His eyes focused as they travelled over her body, and his brows pinched together in disappointment. "You're wearing clothes."

"I've been up for a couple of hours. I brought you coffee. And I got you a toothbrush. And there's a fresh towel in the bathroom if you want to shower."

He looked delighted and confused through his lingering sleepiness. "When did you get me a toothbrush? Never mind. I need to use it."

Ten minutes later, Alex staggered into the living room, pulling on his jeans and running wet hands through his hair, smelling like her honey-lemon body wash. He flopped onto the couch beside her and took the coffee from her with a groan.

She tucked her feet under his thigh and sipped her coffee. "I love this no-shirt look you have going on." She traced the ridge of his shoulder to his bicep. Shirtless mornings could be a tradition she'd enthusiastically support.

"It would be a good look on you, too," he said, toying with the flimsy material at her neckline and pulling her in for a searing kiss. Her insides sparked as his hand slid up her shirt. "What time did you say it was?"

Time to pump the brakes. "Um, time for me to kick you out?"

He pulled back. "What?"

She listed her day-off plans on her fingers. "I switched my volunteering from Saturday to this morning in—" she checked the time— "two hours, and if I want to get my run in, I should leave soon. Then me and one of the girls from softball are going for pedicures. And I still haven't gone to the library yet, so I'm going to do that, too."

Would he want to see her again tonight? She paused, half-smiling at him from under her lashes. "And I'm going to try to meet up with this amazing guy tonight, if he isn't busy?"

"You're talking about me, right?" he said, and defended her pillow attack one-handed.

"Yes, but keep this up ..." she threatened, smiling.

"In that case," he said, squeezing her hand and sounding placated. "I'll try to get out early."

"Don't worry, call me when you're done," she said, rubbing her thumb on his jaw. She felt lucky enough getting his time tonight already. She didn't want him to think he had to choose between her and work. Or give Nick more ammunition to blame her for distracting Alex even more. No matter how badly she wanted to push him on his back and straddle him like a stallion.

One night of Stampeding and she was going full cowgirl.

Oh. Cowgirl. That'll be fun …

Note to self: tell Sophie nothing of this train of thought.

She reluctantly untucked her feet from under his thigh. "I'll see you tonight? Hot date?"

"Hot date. On it."

"Now," she said, getting up and tugging him to a stand, "you need to get out of here so Nick doesn't—" she caught herself before she was going to say *give me shit again,* but managed to complete it with "—wonder where you are."

"For once, he'll be right when he grills me this morning." He looked down at her, smiling. "Don't worry. If he asks, I'll tell him I was up late working on data tables."

—

Jill floated through her day on a zephyr. Her run devolved into a meandering walk punctuated with a few bouts of jogging, a gentle fatigue in her muscles slowing her usual brisk pace, and she turned home after half an hour without regret. Not being her usual day to volunteer, the shelter was full of people she didn't know, which was just as well, so people wouldn't comment on her sappy grin. Kevin and Switchboard had been adopted, as she thought they would be as soon as they behaved, so she spent her time with Daisy, even taking her for a short, incident-free walk outside and rewarding her girl with copious kisses and snuggles. During pedicures, Jill steered the conversation away from herself and onto softball and her friend's new job. Any comments on why Jill looked so good she attributed to going to the Stampede the night before and having a lot of fun. Which was true, technically.

She wanted to keep this to herself a little while longer. She even responded to her friends' barrage of texts demanding updates with a benign reply:

Things are going well :)

Sophie: Oh shit that sounds gooooood

Kyle: he better treat you right

looking forward to hearing about this new guy

Sophie: You have NO IDEA how excited I am for you to hear about him :x

Between Kyle's overprotective big brother act and Sophie's divination skills, Jill steeled herself for the pending interrogation that would come with her visit to Boston.

She couldn't wait.

As much as she wanted to be with Alex today, the space to breathe was a relief. A chance to turn everything over in her mind. To peer under the edges. Test for faults. She wasn't being naïve (*because you have so much experience with men)*, or blind (*that's the definition of a blind spot)* but there wasn't a red flag in sight. And she had experience with red flags.

Sex with Connor had been antiseptic. Transactional, almost. Nothing intimate about it. They went through the steps often enough he could brag to his friends. But instead of bringing them closer, it left her feeling alone.

When they were in high school, she didn't have anything to compare it to. At university, she had slept with a guy in her class in second year a few times, which had been fine, and another guy in third year, which had been fun. But neither earth shaking.

Alex was shaking her world in seismic waves that was changing everything she thought she knew.

She put down the book she was failing to read. Nestled in a window well, the library's ceilings soared overhead. The glass panels let in shafts of light across the arched wooden walls, the cavernous space surprisingly quiet. The perfect place to let her thoughts glide across her mind and try to make sense of everything.

Travis had been one of the many people away from the shelter that morning for Stampede festivities, so Jill had avoided the twinkling eyes that would have seen right through her. Even so, she could almost hear his slow words saying, "If you go looking for trouble, you'll find it." And really, that was part of her job. Finding trouble. The mistakes, the chinks in the armour. The secrets that people tried to hide.

Stop. It's not going away overnight. It's going to take time.

And note to self: stop snoozing your reminder to book therapy.

A buzz from her pocket announced a new text, and the surge of pleasure at the sight of his name made her hide a grin into her hand.

I can get out at 7. Want to come
to my place tonight?
I can make more
than sandwiches

Seven had turned into seven-thirty, so Jill pulled up to his place at a quarter to eight. Late. On purpose. For a habitually early person like herself, it was as long as she could hold off setting out without her internal alarm clock blaring at her, but Alex's chronic lateness warranted time-delay tactics. Still, as she pulled up to his place fifteen minutes late, the windows in his house were dark. She was starting to text him when a silver Subaru parked behind her, and he scooped her out of her car to envelop her in a thorough embrace.

Not even twelve hours since she'd seen him, but she breathed his piney-woodsy-Alex scent deeply like it had been a month.

"I'm sorry." He released her after too short a time, running a hand through his hair. "I didn't have time to pick up anything for dinner."

She repressed a mild dismay. Late and disorganized. That's who he was. She knew what she was signing up for.

Instead, she clicked her tongue with a smile. "You tease. Here I was thinking you'd romance me with a decadent meal." She dropped a kiss on his throat. "Do I at least get to choose my flavour of ramen?"

"We're not eating ramen. I can pull something together," he said, brow furrowed, and repeated, "I'm really sorry."

A nerve pinged at her. "What's up?" she asked, trying to keep her voice light.

"Just feel like an asshole for being late. I set a reminder and everything," he said, turning an abashed smile on her that softened the ping from moments ago.

That's right, she thought. *He says he's sorry. And I think he means it.*

"You know, you could have asked me to bring groceries."

Alex grunted in response.

Even through his modest claim of throwing something together, Alex's kitchen was far better stocked than Jill's. Soon they sat in the mismatched chairs at the dining-room-table-turned-office, with a growler of IPA Jill discovered was not to her taste and plates of creamy pasta primavera that was.

"This is divine." She swirled a cherry tomato in the rich sauce, the flavours bordering on obscene in their decadence. "Whatever you are going for, it's working."

"My emergency meal," he said between bites. "Glad you like it."

This was his emergency meal? Hers was cereal and a can of tuna. "It's amazing. You'll have to show me how to make it."

"Mmm. I have a reputation as a terrible teacher to uphold. Easier for me to make it for you on demand."

She grinned as she speared another rotini. "You're going to spoil me."

"That's the plan."

Warmth flowed from her chest to her extremities, colouring her cheeks and making her fingers tingle. "I don't know what to say to that," she murmured into her plate.

"Don't say anything." He shrugged a massive shoulder. "Just let me."

He didn't have a dishwasher, so she washed, and he dried. The gentle ease of it flowed around her in a river. The light clatter of stacking dishes. The warmth of his shoulder beside hers. The sudsy water she pretended she wasn't splashing purposefully on his shirt, but since it was wet, might as well take it off. His arm reaching behind her to put the plates away, his hand teasing the nape of her neck as he moved past. His bare chest brushing against her shoulder blades, even with plenty of room behind them.

The rest of the dishes were left forgotten on the counter as she nudged him into the bedroom. And this time they lingered, slow, and Jill explored in all the ways she wanted to.

—

"What's your favourite memory from when you were little?"

The blue twilight and muffled voice of the Stampede announcer babbled through the open bedroom window, neighbourhood sounds having long since ceased. A fan planted in the room's corner lazily pushed air over their feet sticking out from the bottom of the single cotton sheet. Jill, while tired, was not even a little sleepy, and basked in the still-warm night.

His arm was curled under her head, thumb tracing circles on her shoulder. He stretched a leg free from the sheet as he considered.

"Probably tagging along after Gemma to her rugby matches. I always wanted to do everything she did, and she hated having me copy her all the time. Drove her crazy that I joined a couple of years after she did, but by that time she was already ignoring me. I was an incredibly annoying ten-year-old."

Jill had asked for a baby sister or brother every year for Christmas until she stopped believing in Santa. "Were you two always close?"

"When we were little, sure. We fought like crazy, but then Gemma hit high school and didn't want anything to do with me, and when I got bigger than her and my dad told me I had to stop fighting with her. It wasn't until she came back for Christmas during her first year of university that she realized how much she missed her baby brother."

"Well, you are incredibly missable."

"Not everyone holds that opinion."

The thought of little Alex trailing after his big sister squeezed her heart in a funny way. Did he have knobby knees and bird-like arms, or had he always been a solid tank? A ginger kid with hair darkening to that rich auburn as he got older? Smiling and happy even then, or wide-eyed and quiet tagging along after his big sister? "Do you have pictures?"

He brushed his lips against her temple in thought. "I'll ask my mom to text me a good one."

"Baby pics should look ridiculous. I want a bad one."

"She has more than enough of those," he said. "What about you? Favourite memory?"

"My family's cottage. We spent almost every weekend there in the summer, and at least one week in August. It felt like everyone in Toronto would flee the city at the same time, and it took forever to get there. But when we did, it was so beautiful. So quiet." And she could get away from her parents for a while. Not have so many rules. She scrunched the sheet with her newly purple toes, smiling. "By the end of the weekend, I'd be so covered in dirt my dad would say I didn't need sunblock."

He paused, a thoughtful look on his face. "What are you doing next weekend?"

Besides volunteering, her weekends were usually laid-back, with Alex starting to claim chunks of that time. "Nothing yet."

"Have you ever been backcountry camping?"

"I've never been camping."

"Never?"

"Cabins and chalets only. My mother would never sleep on the ground."

He shook his head. "It's wild that Dr. Saigner is your mother."

Jill drew the sheets up tight under her arms, and said nothing.

"You know," he continued, "she gave a talk at Yale my first year of grad school. Nick and me and a few others road-tripped down to see her."

That would have been the year Jill graduated from high school. Her mother had accepted the speaking request. Of course, she would. It was Yale. Even though she'd done loads of seminars and talks and everything there over the years. And never mind that she'd miss Jill's convocation and parent dinners and all the other celebrations that went with it. Jill had felt so selfish for wishing her mother could have been there, but hadn't said anything. She knew what the conversation would have been like without needing to have it.

"Oh?"

"Her research on nanotech geometry and drug delivery systems was incredible. Not my field, but Nick fanboyed over her for weeks after."

"I bet."

He pulled back. "You guys don't have the best relationship, do you?" he asked, carefully.

"Is this camping idea some new plan so you can get me stranded overnight again?" she said, flattening the sheet under her hand.

"You know you don't have to work that hard to get me to sleep over anymore, right?"

He squinted at her through the dark. "There's a spot in Kananaskis. Amazing views, beautiful hike. Been a while since I've gone. We could go for a couple nights?" He hesitated and added, "And if you hate it, we can cut it short."

"I think so, I mean, it sounds fun," she said, glad to pass the parental discussion. Then, planning brain took over, and lists of questions stacked on top of each other. Mostly of the can-you-hike-in-running-shoes and toilets-and-backcountry-camping variety, but she shoved them aside. "I don't have any gear, though. Or any idea what to bring."

"Don't worry about that. I've got everything. But you want to?"

Three whole days with Alex. She definitely wanted to, but a Nick-shaped doubt pinged her mind. "It won't be a problem to take the time away?"

"Nope. I can move a few things around." With the light lines between his brows, he sounded more confident than he looked, but still, his smile spread. "It's one of my favourite places."

"In that case, I'd love to." She could google what to bring. Maybe bear spray, or a sat-phone. She snuggled further down the bed, eyelids growing heavy. "On one condition. I'm driving."

—

Sometime later, her consciousness swam to the surface. Silence and darkness stretched through the open window. The night had sent a chill creeping over her body, and her fingers reached across the expanse of cool cotton beside her.

She sat up, pulling the single sheet to her chest. Faint clacking could be made out on the other side of the closed bedroom door, a blue light peeking along the bottom crack.

He crouched over his laptop in boxers and a rumpled tee shirt. The rustle of the sheet around her pulled his attention up as she shuffled over and he smiled with a slightly guilty expression, closing a few tabs before pulling her onto his lap. "What are you doing up?"

"I was cold." Jill leaned against him, stifling a yawn. "What are *you* doing up?"

"I won't be long." His hand tracked down her goosebump-covered arm. "Let me get you a blanket."

When she woke up the next time, he was tucking himself around her, and this time sleep pulled her under until the sun was up.

NINETEEN

Thursday evening errands involved cleaning her spotless car and getting an oil change, just in case. A bit of light googling to check what she should wear, and she decided her usual running clothes would be fine, including a fleece jacket—which if it hadn't been for the surprise snowstorm the night she and Alex were stranded, she would have thought overkill in the summer—and the merino socks she snagged from Sophie's swag bag. Then she culled half the clothes, figuring getting dirty was part of the fun. A quick trip to the grocery store to pick up the list Alex texted her, since he'd be glued to the lab all day and unlikely to get there before it closed. He forwarded her the route at her request, so she could map the altitude and check the driving time to the trailhead and best time to leave the city.

Which she couldn't figure out because he still hadn't told her when he'd be ready.

He had replied to her texts between tests after lunch when she had checked again what time they were leaving.

Relax! I have it under control

Not giving up control was one of her defining personality traits. It still didn't help her relax, but at least this time it made her smile. A bit.

After spending the last couple of nights together, she felt a little strange getting into bed by herself just after sunset. Not lonely, but

… missing him. A warm, excited feeling she wanted to lean into. She wondered if he missed her, too.

With superb timing, her phone chirped.

Just got home. If you're still up,
good night and talk to you in
the morning

The extra warmth she felt had nothing to do with the summer heat.

And, fine, it drove her crazy she still didn't know what time they were leaving tomorrow.

He's spontaneous, she thought. *Pro: camping trips for fun adventures. Con: Who knows when the adventures will begin? Tune in and find out!*

The next morning, a gaggle of pedestrians on their way to the Stampede blocked her exit from her parkade. A minute later, a parade diverted her seven blocks. At the end, she could have run to Alex's place faster. Maybe Omar was right and leaving town was the right plan. Maybe she should move out of downtown, rather than living smack in the middle of it.

Or maybe she wouldn't even be here this time next year and it wouldn't be an issue. She slammed the door on that thought as she walked up to his house.

Alex yawned as he answered the door in athletic shorts, the waistband slung low on his hips and chest bare in the early morning sun. Okay, he was just waking up, so they were leaving closer to lunch. No problem.

"Do you always answer the door like that?" she asked, sliding her cold hands up his back to exact a little revenge. "Or you trying to distract me?"

"You're saying I distract you?" he said, gritting his teeth at her chilly fingers.

"A little."

"Good. Come on. Almost ready."

A tent, sleeping bags, folding chairs, and other supplies were already piled in the kitchen. It looked like they were going on an expedition, not a weekend jaunt.

Jill added the groceries she had picked up to the stack of gear. "Isn't that going to be heavy?" Then, hoping she wouldn't regret her next question, "Do you need me to carry anything?"

"Nah, I'm not worried about packing light. We're only going fifteen kilometres. Besides," he dropped his voice to an over-the-top seductive murmur, lips brushing her ear. "It's your first time. I want you to enjoy it."

Cheesy? Sure. Spark-inducing? Oh, absolutely.

He Tetris-ed the entirety of their weekend supplies into a massive backpack and easily hoisted it out to her car. She nudged the pack with her knee. It had to weigh half as much as she did. Only fifteen kilometres. Clearly those thighs weren't built by rugby alone.

He handed her a second, much smaller pack. "Bea left this here. She won't mind you borrowing it."

"I guess they aren't doing tons of backpacking right now with their boys so young?"

"Nope, but next summer I'm taking those monsters on short trails. Big enough they can scramble around, small enough I can still carry them both if they get tired." An almost serene expression came over his face as he talked about his nephews. He had looked so relaxed when she and Sophie had run into them—well, until he saw her—and the boys clearly adored their uncle, with Henry climbing monkey-like on his arm and Jake perched high on his shoulders, Alex's forearm securing the kicking legs safely in place. Jill's lower belly gave an unexpected lurch at the memory.

She busied herself transferring her small stash of items to Bea's pack and settled the padded straps over her shoulders. "Are you sure you don't want me to carry anything else?"

"I'll let you know if we need to switch packs halfway," he said with a grin, and adjusted a couple of her straps until the weight balanced perfectly. "Looks good."

Once the packs were sorted, Alex was ready far faster than Jill expected. Connor getting ready to go anywhere had been an inexplicable ordeal every time, some frustration or another. He couldn't find his wallet. Or he needed to get changed again. And of course, somehow it always became Jill's fault.

"Where'd you go?" Alex looked down at her, startling her from her thoughts, his fingers brushing her arm.

"It's nothing. Why is Bea's pack here? Did she drop it off?"

"Oh, this is her place," he said. "She and Gemma both left a bunch of stuff here when they moved out."

Bea's place. She filed that bit of information away, put the smaller pack in the trunk beside Alex's massive one, and shut the hatchback door.

The highway out of the city on a Friday mid-morning was faster than any memory she could dredge up heading out to her family's cottage. It was probably that the trip was less than half the distance, not fighting for road space with the hoards of people fleeing Toronto. Maybe it was because she was driving and not stuck trying to entertain herself in the back seat. Maybe it was being with Alex, even as he dozed beside her. She wished for half a second he was driving so she could be passenger princess and stare at him.

Before long, they were as far west as Jill had ever been, and the looming skyline came up to meet them as they entered the park. Pavement gave way to gravel, jolting Alex awake, and the loose road slowed them down almost as much as Jill stopping the car to take pictures every time they saw mountain goats, or when Alex spotted a grizzly in the tree line. He assured her, twice, he brought bear spray.

Cars packed the trailhead parking lot when they arrived, sun positioned perfectly overhead, and Jill raised her brows at him.

"Day trippers," he said, handing her some hiking poles. "We might be the only people out there tonight."

He checked their packs one more time, double-checked their water, and motioned for Jill to lead.

"I don't know the trail."

"But this way you can set the pace. I'll let you know when we need to make a turn," he said. "Besides, now I get to look at your ass for the next four hours."

"So, when I'm setting the pace, should I stay out of reach," she widened her eyes and suffused her words with sweetness, "or let you catch me?" For good measure, she batted her lashes.

A wild gleam flashed across his face. "Surprise me."

"I like not being at work and we can break Rule Number Two," she said, standing on tiptoes to plant a chaste peck on his cheek.

He still looked dazed from her last comment. "Work is the last thing I'm thinking about."

It looked like it might be true.

The trail followed a serpentine brook through the valley before disappearing into a dense forest, distant creek sounds and bird calls filtering through. Their steps fell into a meditative rhythm as the mountain incline began in earnest, and the cool mountain air was a balm after the heat of the city. Returning hikers waved as they passed, looking tired, dusty, and blissful.

Suddenly, the path opened in a riot of iris-purple, buttercup-yellow, and flame-orange. Wildflowers waved in the gentle breeze, covering the meadow into the distance, framed by jagged peaks piercing the sky.

Jill stopped in her tracks. "It's so beautiful," she whispered.

"I was worried we might be too early in the season," he said, sounding relieved. "I thought instead of bringing flowers to you, I could bring you to flowers."

She swallowed against the knot that had formed in her throat, blinking rapidly. She was not a crier, so she wasn't going to do that, instead ducking her chin and pressing her hands hard into her hips. "Alex …" But nothing else would come out. Even that came out a bit watery.

How was he real?

"You like it?" He pulled her as close as her pack would allow and smiled into her hair. "Come on. A bit farther."

The trail through the meadow wound long in front of them, skirting the foot of the mountain, and Jill ran her fingers over the blooms as she passed. Eventually, the flowers were replaced by scrub and brush as the path followed the line of another valley. She turned to him, shielding her eyes from the sun.

"Thank you," she said. "That was … really sweet. I love it."

"You deserve flowers." He tucked a lock of hair behind her ear and kept the lead.

After a couple more hours, they reached the site. Two other tents were set up far enough away that they wouldn't overhear conversation, but perhaps hear other, unguarded things. Alex's mind clearly went in the same direction, and his voice into her ear sent a shiver directly between her thighs. "If you need to stay quiet, you can bite down on the pillow."

The indignation she wanted to reply with came out instead as scandalized glee. She teetered up to her toes, unbalanced by her pack, and wrapped her arms around his neck. "You're impossible."

"And an hour ago I was sweet," he said, shaking his head in mock dismay. "You have a terrible memory."

You can't keep anything straight, can you? Are you stupid, or are you losing it?

She tried to freeze her expression, even as the blood drained from her face and her fingers numbed. Her lungs couldn't draw a full breath and Connor's words echoed, him looming over her and shaking his head in disgust.

"Hey, what'd I say?" Alex firmed his grip around her.

Jill pasted on a brittle smile and pulled away. "Nothing! I just need to get this pack off."

"This doesn't seem like nothing." He released her with a look of reluctance. "Please tell me?"

Cover. Lie. Defl—

Alex isn't Connor. This isn't a trap.

Jill dropped onto a stump. She had told him a bit on the road trip, and more when she had dropped the screenshot of his comments in the wrong chat. But vague allusions. No details. Nothing that made it real. There would never be a great time. Might as well be now. She stared at the ground, tucked her shaking hands under her arms, and told him.

The constant surveillance. The one-sided arguments over imagined slights that would last for days. The shifting maze of rules she had to follow or deal with simmering rage, or silence. Then the love bombing. Being showered with sugary words and insipid gestures after a vulgar fight or nasty insult and leaving her reeling. The shame she felt for not leaving sooner.

"I'd just started the second semester of my master's. I got up one morning and went to take my birth control pill, like I did every day at that time." She levelled a hard look at Alex. "Every day."

The site set-up lay abandoned. Alex sat beside her, stoic in his sentry.

"He tried to convince me I took it the previous night. Said he saw me take it. And I dropped it. I didn't want to fight. Then two days later, it happened again. He said I was too busy and obviously I was overwhelmed with school. He said it was probably too much for me and he wouldn't be mad if I quit."

She leaned forward, clutching her elbows. "And I let myself believe he was right. That I was losing track of things. But I didn't drop out. I booked an appointment to get an IUD the day after it happened the third time. I told myself I was forgetful, like Connor said, but I knew. I knew he was trying to …" She pressed her lips together, still not able to say it out loud. "I didn't tell him. I just kept taking the pill and if he tampered with them again, it wouldn't matter.

"And I stayed. For two more years." She drew a shaking breath. "Sometimes I remember something or hear something—" Alex hunched beside her "—and I'll be right back there."

Alex sat crouched with his hands over his mouth, silent so long he had to be thinking of a reason to pack up and leave. A client he needed to reach, or a report he forgot. She tried to count to twenty of her dull heartbeats, lost track, and started over, desperate for him to say something.

"Why?" His muffled voice came out anguished from behind his hands. "Why would he do that?"

She shrugged. "He hated I was doing something he wasn't. I think that's how he tried to stop me."

Well, that was it. Too much. Too soon. It was still early. They could turn back tonight. Jill was steeling herself to offer him a way out, when he rubbed the heels of his hands hard over the ridges of his cheekbones, staggered to a stand, and wrapped himself around her.

"I'm sorry. I didn't know," he murmured into her ear. "I don't want to control you. I just want … I want to know you."

The wave of relief ached as it washed over her, and Alex shattered into fragments through her wet lashes. She swallowed hard to clear the tears before they fell, and her voice came out a ghost of a whisper. "Thank you."

This time his long silence didn't alarm her. His eyes searched hers, thumbs stroking her face. "I swear I will never hurt you. Do you believe me?"

She wanted to. More than anything. Something fragile shook in her heart.

"I believe you," she whispered, and he nodded, every line of his body held rigid as he stared into the distance. She broke her gaze away, tucking her hands around her ribs. "What are you thinking?"

Alex clenched his jaw and exhaled sharply through his nose, glaring out over the valley as if Connor might stroll into view at any moment. "That I've never wanted to punch someone in the face this much in my entire life."

"Um, please don't, but thanks for saying it," she said, surprised to find the corners of her mouth curving, and the murderous heat in his eyes retreated. She took a tentative step towards him and reached for his hand. "Can we forget about this? This is supposed to be fun. I don't want to be high maintenance."

"Letting me know what you need, what makes you happy? That's not high maintenance. And if it is," he said, firmly, taking her hand, "then be high maintenance."

He couldn't be real.

Maybe he is, said the voice, and Jill dared to believe.

The camp was in disarray. Tent laid out but not set up. Folding chairs still folded. Food stashed in dry bags, and suddenly the fifteen kilometres up a mountain caught up with her, and Jill became acutely aware of her gnawing hunger and cooling sweat clinging to the neck of her shirt.

Alex did two things in rapid order. First, he pressed trail mix and an apple into her hands, scarfing down a bar himself. Second, he pressed her into action. With both of them working, the assembly was completed minutes later and the nervous energy that consumed her burned off into a heavy fatigue.

After a quick look at the other tents for privacy, she stripped her damp shirt and sports bra and threw on a dry tee, and the chill that settled into her bones evaporated. If he thought of her bare skin in front of him, he didn't show it. Instead, he insisted the best part of camping was napping, any and all times of day. She could've sat in the sun. Read the cozy mystery novel or sapphic sci-fi novel she'd packed. Eaten more snacks. But between the hike and confessions, the escape into sleep sounded perfect.

With the sun still bright overhead, she toed off her shoes and crawled into the narrow tent. She was out before she could roll onto her back.

—

Barely a month ago, she'd woken up just like this. Sprawled over him in the back of his car, with her thigh thrown over his hips and cheek pressed into his shoulder. This time, though, his eyes were closed, fingers stroking her arm where it lay across his bare torso, and she flexed into the angles of his body in sleepy self-indulgence.

She loved the way he felt. Warm, solid. Firm, but with give. The body of a man who took care of himself and still ate spaghetti.

He would have known she was awake by now, her breath changing and body shifting, but he lay still, the rise and fall of his chest keeping her in a half-lidded stupor. There was no reason to wake—no tasks, no rush—and every reason to let herself sink into his comfort.

After several minutes of peaceful silence she whispered, "Remember the first time we woke up like this?"

"Mm-hmm."

"Is it still torture?"

"Opposite of torture." A small sound escaped his throat, and he smiled. "Same amount of drooling."

They mustn't have slept long. The sun had shifted slightly in the sky, casting them in a crimson light as it passed through the burgundy walls of the tent. Jill propped her head up on her hand, fingers of her free hand splayed over his stomach. Thinking of the Kryptonite she discovered, she traced her nails across his belly in the same slow strokes Alex was making on her arm. A gratifying array of goosebumps erupted as the muscles shifted under her fingers.

His eyes stayed closed, but his mouth twitched as he suppressed another laugh. "That tickles," he said, words vibrating up her fingertips all the way down to her toes.

Ticklish Alex. Another favourite.

She moved her fingers to the tattoo on his smooth skin of his bicep, following the ornate loops. "What does this mean?"

"It's a Celtic triquetra. Means a few different things, but I got it for its representation of earth, water, and sky."

"When?"

"Right after I started my PhD. Everything I was doing was so clinical. Felt like I was losing touch with why I started."

"That's beautiful," Jill said. Knowing what he wanted, marking himself with a constant reminder. "That you know what matters to you."

Alex opened his eyes, an odd look on his face. He looked like he was about to say something when his phone pinged from beyond the tent walls. The odd look on his face morphed into displeasure. "I try."

The phone pinged again, metallic and harsh against the organic surroundings, and his brows drew together. Jill had turned off notifications before they left, but was surprised they even had reception out here. She raised herself onto her elbows, and the phone vented a brash ring.

Alex was out of the tent, thundering over to the phone set on one of the camp chairs. He answered in terse tones and listened for a moment, pacing in tight circles. "This is not an emergency," he said, then spouted off a hard stream of French before disconnecting the call.

He answered the quizzical look on her face with one word. "Nick." He chucked the phone into his bag and dropped into the camp chair, which creaked in distress under the sudden weight. Jill feared for the integrity of the poor thing and lowered herself in the one beside him.

"I told him not to call unless it was important." Alex ran his fingers through his hair. "That was not important."

Jill crossed her legs under her and waited.

After a moment, he started. "I work a lot. You know that." Jill nodded. He took a deep breath and continued, drawing out the pauses between each word in a slow train. "That has, ah, not always worked out great for me."

Something flashed in Jill's mind she couldn't quite put a finger on.

"My last relationship ended because of it. She begged me for months to make more time for her. I didn't. She was a great person and deserved more than I was willing to give her. Eventually, she broke up with me, and I don't blame her."

Jill bit her lip. "Was that Kate?"

"How …?" Alex frowned. "Oh. Nick."

"Before Stampede. While you were on the road. I think it was mostly by accident." She skipped the part where Nick accused her of making Alex miss the deadline.

It was weirdly incongruous. Nick's display of concern for Alex, now disturbing him after apparent instruction not to call unless it was dire. She couldn't shake the sense that he was punishing Alex for taking time away. Or punishing her for being the catalyst for it.

Alex slumped low in the chair, his legs extended long in front of him. He looked out beyond the tree line, the sun casting a long shadow. "I've made a lot of mistakes. I don't want to make those same mistakes with you."

The flash turned into a light, and a worry that had floated unformed at the edge of her awareness coalesced. "Alex, we've been spending a lot of time together," she said, measuring her words. "When are you making up that time?"

The chair creaked under his shifting weight. "I'm fitting it in."

Leaving his place at ten, him itching to get back to work. Sending emails at two in the morning. Coming in later and later to the office.

Falling asleep as soon as he sat still. It wasn't sustainable. He'd make himself sick.

She pulled her legs up to her chest, wrapping her arms tight around them. "No."

His eyes snapped to hers. "No, what?"

"You love your work. You'll hate me for pulling you away."

"Jill—"

"You can't change your life for me—"

"I want to ch—" He stopped, and his voice softened. "I'm trying to make space in my life for you."

"And I need space, too."

He'd said it wasn't high maintenance to ask for what she needed. She could do this.

"I got out of something where my entire life was consumed by one person. And I like you. A lot. I think this could be something. But I need to build something new. And I really, really want you to be a part of it, but I need to build it around myself instead of around someone else. And I don't want to worry you'll resent me."

Alex sat unmoving.

"Can we be honest with each other?" she said. "I let you know what I need, and you let me know what you need? Even if it's space?"

After a long pause, he asked, "If you need space, we still have time to head back tonight."

It didn't feel like a threat, or a trap. It felt like a genuine offer.

"No. Even if I needed that, I wouldn't have the energy for it." A watery smile crossed her lips. "I want to be here with you, but I don't want you mad at me later for being with here with me instead of at work."

"I want to spend time with you," he said. "I'm barely spending the time with you that I want now. But I hear you. Space."

Jill adopted a deadpan expression. "But not so much space that you forget what I look like, okay?"

Alex looked at her for a moment, lifted himself out of his chair and sat on the ground in front of her. His hand circled her ankles, drawing her feet into his lap. "Sometimes you deflect with humour, you know," he said.

She felt laid bare, exposed, but she looked up. "It feels safer. Sometimes I feel you're giving me this best behaviour version of you. I mean, I keep waiting for something to go wrong. Or you to get mad at me for, I don't know. Something." She shivered in the late afternoon heat.

He nodded slowly, a muscle jumping in his cheek. "I really, really hate that guy."

"What's the opposite of a fan club? Foe club? You and Soph can start one of those," she said, and stopped herself. "Sorry. Deflecting."

He squeezed her feet still settled in his lap.

Jill fiddled with the loose ends of her braid. "I'm really nervous about screwing this up."

"Me, too." He didn't seem to care if her feet were still sweaty from the hike, hands working at her tender arches. "I want you to feel safe with me, to talk to me when you need to. But I don't want you to feel like I'm pushing you faster than you're ready."

She nodded and released her grip on her torso. "I don't know how to have these conversations."

"We're doing it right now," he said.

It was disorienting to be in the presence of patience. She didn't know if his hands caressing her calves or his gentle smile was more comforting. Right now, she needed both.

"We're going to need to get you hiking boots," he said, clocking her wince as he hit a sensitive spot. "Come on. I need a snack before dinner."

TWENTY

She fell asleep in her chair not long after dinner. Confessions and hiking were exhausting. Alex prodded her to crawl into the tent before the late summer sun dipped behind the trees and the evening cooled in the alpine air.

The next time she opened her eyes, the sky was already light beyond the tent's walls. The morning pressed crisp on her skin and she rubbed her sock-clad feet together, pulling the sleeping bag up to her nose. Alex, who radiated a small star's worth of heat, had kicked a leg out from the sleeping bag at some point in the night, and Jill snuggled into him to absorb it. For a minute, anyway.

Curse her tiny bladder and its devious plot to foil her coziness.

Alex stirred as she re-entered the tent and she nestled back into the space beside him.

"I should have slept with you months ago," she said into his shoulder. "You do wonders for my insomnia."

A chuckle resonated through him, and he covered his mouth with his hand. "Not a compliment I've heard before."

"I mean …" *I feel safe enough to sleep with you.* She bit off the rest of the words and rested her chin on his chest instead, making him tilt his head down to look at her through his tangle of lashes. "I didn't know you ever woke up early."

"I'd have gladly slept with you months ago, too, even if it meant waking up early," he said through the tail of a yawn. "As long as I get enough sleep, I don't usually get up too late."

If you aren't working at all hours of the night to catch up, you mean, she thought, and he squeezed her arm at her expression.

"Won't say I'll never work long hours, but I won't get stupid about it," he said, and she gave a tentative nod. "Want coffee?"

Jill dressed as best she could in the warmth of the sleeping bag, donning running tights and a fleece pullover before stepping into the mountain air.

Alex squatted with the coffee tin in front of the camp stove in flip-flops, shorts, and a ratty, waffle-knit Henley, sleeves pushed back up his forearms. The first rays of sun broke over the ridgeline and spilled into the valley, remains of the cotton candy clouds starting to lose their pink and blue with the fading dawn. Golden morning sun splashed across his concentrating form, highlighting the downy hair on his legs and arms, the stubble that grazed his jaw, the tousled waves that fell over his forehead. He tipped his knees forward into the dusty earth, turning a smile to her as she zipped the tent closed, and her heart tripped over itself and landed in her throat.

Dr. Alexander Campbell was the most breathtaking man she had ever met in her life.

She was in so much trouble.

The boiling coffee recaptured his attention. "It might be grainy, but chewing coffee never killed anyone," he said, handing her a cup as she settled in the chair.

She wrapped her hands around the mug, letting its warmth seep into her, and tucked her knees close to her chest. "Thanks," she eventually got out, words steaming into mist around her.

Alex dumped a spoonful of coffee whitener and sugar into his coffee and dropped onto the log beside her. "Now we need to talk about breakfast. It's the best part of camping."

"You say everything is the best part of camping."

"Part of my sales pitch," he replied. "Trying to get you to come out again."

It was going to be an easy pitch.

She'd need hiking boots, though. Running was decent cross training for hiking, and she had put double the kilometres under her on the road last weekend, but the uneven terrain had torched her feet, and Alex laughed as she limped around the campsite.

"Lesson Three. Bring camp shoes to give your feet a break from your hiking shoes." He extended his flip-flop clad feet out in front of him, cocky in his superior packing prowess as Jill padded around the dirt on her socked feet.

Lesson One had been to bring snacks. All the snacks. Sure, she had done the grocery shopping for the trip, but she didn't think everything was coming with them, and she gawked at the array of chips, chocolate, and treats he pulled Mary Poppins-like out of his backpack.

"Told you I wasn't worried about packing light," he had said as he housed a handful of cookies. "Besides, we need to refuel, and now we don't need to carry it back."

Lesson Two had been invest in good gear. That lesson might have been unplanned, as he said it scowling at his broken chair after dropping his ninety-something kilos into the flimsy thing. Jill had giggled behind her hands while comfortable in her own fully functional seat and snacked primly on her chips in sensible silence.

Jill tried to glare at him. "I see nothing has changed. Teacher still withholding information until after the test."

"Oof, that hurts," he said. "Probably not as much as your feet, but . . ." He caught her incoming swat. "Sit down. I'll clean up breakfast and we'll head to the lake."

Moving around helped. Despite his protests, Jill helped with the cleanup and eventually the stiffness in her legs and tenderness in her feet eased. Sort of. With teeth brushed and camp secured, she followed him—slowly—on the hour hike to the lake.

It could have been a postcard. Or a painting. Shale pinnacles still threaded with snow speared the cerulean sky and reflected in the milky turquoise water, smooth as a sheet of glass. Besides the adorable animals Alex said were pika squeaking on the rocks, a thin breeze smelling like dust was the only sound breaking the silence.

"Suddenly, my feet don't feel so sore," she said, turning to him, and her smile slid off her face. "What are you doing?"

She hated that she already knew the answer.

His shirt was already off, untying the laces of his boots. "Going in. And you're coming with me."

"That's going to be freezing!"

"No doubt," he said, "but it's great for sore muscles. You'll feel better when it's over."

"I don't … I think …" Jill stalled for an excuse. There had to be a good one, but her brain froze at the prospect of getting into the icy water. There was no chance the water was warmer than it looked.

"It's kind of a tradition for me." He reached out a hand, eyes crinkling with his smile. "Please?"

Her heart tripped again, and a terrible realization dawned on her. "Oh, no," she whispered.

"What?"

She pulled her shirt over her head. "I can't say no when you look at me like that."

"You should not have told me that," he said, delight spreading across his features. She wouldn't be able to say no to that look, either.

"Please don't use it for evil." It came out a little less funny and a little more vulnerable than she wanted. After their conversations yesterday, it was a step in the right direction.

His delight softened and he kissed her slow enough that she was certain she'd carry enough heat into the lake to warm it herself. When he broke it off, he let his earth-shattering smile return. "I would never."

Jill put her foot down at full skinny dipping in case other people showed up and kept on her bra and underwear. Alex had no such qualms and Jill, having zero objections to that, grabbed his hand as they inched their way to the water's edge, scree crunching under their bare feet and cool breeze reaching them from across the lake. A metre from the water, Alex pulled short.

"This is a glacier-fed lake," he said seriously. "I'll be freezing. I don't want to hear a single word."

She fluttered her lashes in confusion. "I have no idea what you're talking about. Is there a small problem? You're not shrinking from your promise to take me swimming, are you?"

She deserved it. She didn't even try to fight it. He flung her over his shoulder in a heartbeat, grunting when his feet hit the water, and the full shock of cold hit her seconds later when he submerged them in the frigid lake. She kept enough sense not to flail in fear of damaging any of his sensitive areas, and when they resurfaced, his chest quaking with either cold or strangled mirth, she wrapped herself starfish-like around his torso before he dunked them under again.

She had lived through more than one ice storm. Bitter winters with minus thirty windchill. A two-day power outage in which she, Sophie, and Kyle shared a bed for heat. But until that moment, she didn't know what cold could mean. Floodgates of every neuron, every inch of flesh, every one of her senses overloaded. The searing cold crossed deep into pain and her lungs heaved behind vocal cords sealed shut. Then going under, once, twice more, each time gripped him harder with every limb, finally releasing a blood-curdling scream and "Stop!" on the third time breaking the surface.

Alex staggered out of the water with Jill wrapped around him, unwinding her legs and collapsing once they hit the shore.

This was it. This was the end. Hypothermia. She pushed her hair back from her face, struggled to her knees, and screamed into her hands at the top of her lungs.

"That. Was. Horrifying!" she gasped through her chattering teeth and seizing cheeks. She crawled over to where he had sunk to all fours, shaking and laughing as he wiped away tears and lake water.

Her skin burned. Her fingers and toes flamed red with cold. Blood surged through her like fire. "Let's do it again."

Another plunge, this time under her own power with slightly less noise and a fraction of a second longer.

Confirmed. It was horrifying. But exhilarating.

Back on land, they soaked up heat from the sun from above and the rocks below. Rivulets of water pearled between the goosebumps pebbling her skin and her heart rate returned to a rhythm approximating normal.

"I don't know what you were worried about," she said, eyes wandering over his body. "Everything looks fine from where I'm sitting."

"Good thing I'm a confident man," he said as he pulled up his shorts, grinning. "My girlfriend thinks I look 'fine'? Guess I'll take what I can get."

"Gorgeous, powerful, stunning ..." Dropping a kiss on his shoulder for each descriptive. *Kind, funny, caring* ... She reached for more adjectives that felt safer to say out loud. "Swoon-worthy ... feet-sweepy! Mmm, so feet-sweepy."

"That's better," he said, the tips of his ears turning pink.

Girlfriend. The word fizzed under her breastbone. Sure, of course she was. But it felt so good to hear him say it. She grinned like a loon as she pulled on her shirt and the last of her goosebumps vanished, and she made the mental note to tell him how pretty he was more often. Given how often she thought it, it wouldn't be hard to remember.

Once Jill reapplied sunblock to their exposed skin, they lounged in the sun, gorging on their lunch of bread, cheese, and fruit. They held still so the pika might venture near, one coming close enough for Jill to snap a photo of the fluffy little animal. She stripped her socks off one more time, gritting her teeth and wading to her thighs for ten whole seconds in the glacial lake, conceding in good grace that yes, her legs and feet felt better after the ice bath, and Alex gave her a satisfied nod.

He took them down a different path back to camp, meandering through a forested valley surrounded by stands of spruce and pine and scatterings of phlox and bluebells. The air carried the sharp sap scent of the warm trees, and she leaned into him, closed her eyes, and let her nose tickle his neck.

"This is what you smell like. Out here. Like the woods. And lake water," she said. "I love it."

His neck flushed by her cheek, and he pulled her closer.

The cold had long seeped out of her bones by the time they reached camp, the sun pouring into the valley. One of the other sites had left while they were away, the other site sat silent with no one in view.

They were alone.

Jill snuck a glance at Alex, who was focused on kicking off his boots and downing a handful of trail mix. "Do you want to take a nap?"

"Not tired." He took a swig of water and stepped into his flip-flops.

Okay, less subtle. She bit her lip and tried again, sliding her hand under the hem of his shirt. "Me, either."

"Wh—*oh,*" he said, and launched the sandals off his feet and across the campsite.

Less hinting, more saying. She could work on her delivery.

They fought their way out of their clothes in a tangle of limbs, shaking the sides of the tiny tent with every movement. Jill stifled a giggle as she pictured what it must look like from the outside.

"We're making so much noise," she whispered hoarsely, and twisted her hands through his hair as he worked his mouth down her body.

"Is that a challenge? To see how much noise I can get you to make?" His lips traced her nipple in lazy circles, eyes gleaming in the low light.

Tell me what you want. She wanted to feel. She arched her back to chase the warmth of his mouth. "Yes."

"Challenge accepted."

He scooped one hand under her hips to angle her closer to his tongue, fingers of his other hand stroking her deep inside. Slowly letting the tension build in her belly, up her spine, until her eyes screwed shut and her fingers tangled her hair. His lips trailed over her clit in steady swipes, every pass sending her heels harder into his back, devasting her into complete compliance.

"Alex," she choked. She was shaking so hard he groaned, and the resonant vibrations pushed her over the edge. "I'm going to—"

The guttural cry ripped from her throat before she could hold it back, her orgasm shattering through her.

"Stop!" she gasped, trying to hold in the rest wild laughter that threatened to break free. "I'm done! Stop!"

He dropped a kiss on her belly button. "Think I won the challenge."

Actually, she was pretty sure she won. She pulled his mouth up to hers and giggled as the last tremors faded. "Sorry, I—"

"Don't apologize for how amazing you are."

The sun diffused hot through the thin fabric and bathed them in crimson. She lingered like salty nectar in his mouth, and she sucked his swollen lip, stroking his neck, his weight pressing her flush to the ground. Then, she wiggled under him until he rolled them over and she sat on her heels, hands trailing over his chest.

Alex reclined before her, drinking her in with darkly hooded eyes. She pressed his thighs apart and let her tongue trail over the rasp of his stubble, the cords of his neck standing out as she travelled down his body. Her nails skated the flexed lines of his torso, tantalizingly close to where he strained hard on the taut skin of his belly.

"Do I get to take the challenge, too?" She wrapped her fist around his girth, and he hissed series of profanities as she slowly pushed her lips down his length.

"Alex, if you're going to give me any chance to win at all, you have to be patient," she said a few minutes later. She sat back to admire him. His body packed with heavy muscle, tensed under her hands. Sun-kissed skin dotted with freckles. Everything, gorgeous.

She did want to tell him how pretty he was more often. She took a deep breath.

Don't be shy, Northrop. Just do it.

"You have a beautiful cock."

He jerked under her, and she smiled.

She gathered her hair into a ponytail and placed his hand at the base of her head to hold it back. One by one she licked her fingers, he tracked her every move, and she gripped him again with long, firm strokes. She took a deep breath. "I love how you feel inside me."

"Oh god."

The red shadows would hide her flush. "The only problem with having you in my mouth is that I can't say your name."

"Fuck me," he whispered hoarsely.

"Like this?" She dropped tongue down his length again, her fist at his base taking what her mouth couldn't, hollowing out her cheeks until a tremor coursed up his body and his head dropped back with a primal moan.

"Jesus, Jill."

Oh, this was fun. She pulled away to make him wait. "Is it torture?"

"Fuck. No. Yes. Please."

"Alex, I want you to watch me. I want you to tell me when you're close. I want you to come in my mouth," she said, and he lurched into her hand. "But I'm not letting you come yet."

At any moment, at any whim, he could take control, however he pleased. Instead, he gave himself up to her. Thighs tensed. Hands restrained in her hair. Eyes on her, hungry, as she demanded. And she revelled in it.

"Jill, so close," he managed to get out. She responded with a hand on his belly and took him as deep as she could until he broke like an earthquake.

Aftershocks still rolling over him, she retraced her steps up his beautiful, trembling body. The crease of his thigh, stomach, chest, and when she dusted her lips on his neck once more, he crushed her against him.

"I think we tied on the challenge," she said, smiling into his neck.

"That … I … love … amazing," he stumbled over his words as he tried to kiss her hair, grasping at whatever was under his hands, toes still curling against the sleeping bag beneath him, and Jill basked in his rapture.

Slowly, his clumsy pawing turning into gentle strokes, and she snuggled along the length of his body, and he tightened his hold.

"Stay," he whispered.

He wanted her close. It charged through her with a thrill that was terrifying and soothing. Alex had found her defences and was, whether he knew it or not, systematically dismantling every wall she had built around herself. At this rate, she wasn't going to have any protection left.

Her heart pounded against his. "I'm not going anywhere."

TWENTY-ONE

Long summer days meant the sun still hung well above the horizon when his shifting woke her, fingers caressing the skin rubbed raw on her neck. His brows drew together as the corner of his mouth raised a touch. "You're all red."

"It's just the light in here," she hedged, pulling his fingers from the sensitive area. "You were right, though."

"About what?"

"Naps are a pretty good part of camping."

Half an hour later, after Jill readily concurred with Alex's suggestion that they retest the hypothesis that "napping" may in fact be the undisputed best part of camping, she followed him gingerly out of the tent into the afternoon. Two more groups had set up camp in the time they had disappeared into their sanctuary hours ago, and she chose to imagine the walls of their tent were made of concrete rather than nylon.

Alex strung up a tarp for a makeshift shower, frowning a little at the scraped skin glowing hot on her thighs and breasts. "I'm going to tear you apart if I'm not careful."

Oh, if he only knew.

"Don't worry. Tomorrow morning, I'll rub my legs on you like a cricket and get revenge."

He snorted as he trickled a stream of water over her reddened skin. "I look forward to the exfoliation, but I might need to say goodbye to my annual January beard."

Feral, Beardy Alex? "I don't know if I want to miss that," she said, winding her arms around his waist. "Might be worth skipping a month of kisses."

"There is no way I'm going a month without kissing you."

And then they sat. Quietly. Jill curled up in the chair with her mystery novel while Alex dove into the sci-fi she brought as backup reading. A bag of chips torn open between them, sharing a can of warm ginger ale. Letting the sun trace its path in the sky and wind whisper in the trees, muted voices drifting over from the other sites. It wasn't as hard as it would have been a year ago. Not rushing from task to task. Not working to keep her mind busy. Or finding reasons to be alone so she could breathe.

What was hard was waiting to see if the peace would break. How, when, she didn't know. Even thinking about it might jinx it. Her brain provided a colourful stream of intrusive options, but she tried to let them slide off before they took purchase.

I'm doing really well. It's not going away overnight.

It was wearying to think of how long it might take, but not as much as it once had.

Alex had made no concessions to cooking from scratch for the weekend, and the simmering channa masala released a mouth-watering smell that drew a trio of campers from a neighbouring site to comment on it. Ten minutes later, the group returned with their own dinners in hand, unfolding chairs and cracking cans of beer. Alex hadn't made more than enough curry for the two of them, but passed their new friends extra naan to wrap their hot dogs in, and later, s'mores for all. Alex found he and one woman had gone to the same high school, albeit a decade apart, and laughed at the school probably not having a renovation since. Jill got a recommendation for a yoga studio near her apartment and swapped numbers with another woman to try out softball. The visitors left when the stars came out, and restful silence surrounded them.

She couldn't even remember how they got on the topic. Some circuitous route through graduations and landlords and killing houseplants. She plunked him down in front of her chair, working her elbows into the mass of knots in his shoulders until she ran out of steam, then wrapped herself big-spoon style across his back.

"How did you end up living in Bea's place?"

"Moved in when Kate and I broke up. Bea didn't have renters and I didn't want to spend a ton of time looking for a place."

"And it's still all in boxes. Two years later." Jill repressed a shudder.

"You may have noticed that organization is not my strong suit," he said dryly.

She considered his words. "I don't think that's true. You're incredibly organized with the things that matter to you. Anything in the lab. I've seen your reports. I mean, you can't file them to save your life—" he chuckled, a low rumble she absorbed through his back "—but the content is flawless. And you did a PhD. Those don't happen by accident." She sighed, snuggling tighter against his warmth. "Even this weekend. You organized all of it and we have everything we need."

"So far. We have a whole extra day here."

"Now who's deflecting?" she chided, bumping his side with her knee. "Do you remember when you said to me that when something is important, you put in the work?"

He hummed an assent in his throat, and one of those charges sparked her again. That dual sensation of his voice resonated in her ear and in her body at the same time.

"I was talking to my volunteer supervisor a couple days after we got stranded, and he said that even with everything, you took care of me that night. You were prepared to deal with an emergency, and we got through it fine and now we have a funny story."

He stayed silent a long minute and when he spoke again, his voice came out tight. "You had a panic attack that night. You were so scared. That was my fault."

She tightened her squeeze around him. "That was not your fault. I had a panic attack because I couldn't fix it. Not because I was afraid," she said firmly. She got up to sit in front of him, taking his hands in hers and searching his eyes in the flickering lantern light. "I have always felt safe with you."

"Good. I mean, thanks." He swallowed hard, Adam's apple bobbing in his throat. "That means a lot."

"It means more to me than you can know."

She turned his hands over in hers, broad palms and long fingers dwarfing her own. They had spent so much time together over the past several months. First, with bad first impressions and old grudges he coaxed her into putting aside. Then, forgiveness and friendship. Even as her feelings sparked and she sent him the most indecipherable and confusing signals, his patience and understanding. Now, this feeling growing between them. Through it all, from the moment he had walked through the door of her office months ago, he had shown unwavering kindness and respect.

"I haven't told you about when I left Connor." She hadn't planned on saying anything. But there it was. The words leaving her mouth as if she were musing on tomorrow's weather. Alex raised his head, but she kept her gaze firmly on their linked hands.

"Every New Year's Eve his parents have this huge party in their huge house with all their important friends and entire family. Clients, community contacts. Of course, my parents. Fancy clothes, fully catered. The whole deal."

The tailored grey sheath dress that once fit her perfectly had hung off her frame. The white gold choker of his mother's Connor had insisted she wear kept catching in her hair, and she swept up her tresses in painstaking curls so it wouldn't tangle in the intricate chain.

"It was almost midnight. I remember looking at the clock and being so tired after he yelled at me in the car on the way over and thinking I could go home soon. Everyone was gathered in the great room, waiting for the countdown to start. In front of everyone, he asked me to marry him."

Jill could still read Alex's expression through the darkness, guarded and careful, stiffening at her words.

"We had never talked about it. I had no idea it was coming. There were a hundred faces around me, everyone smiling and waiting for me to jump up and say yes."

It was part of the plan. Not hers, but someone's. Instead of following the script and saying what she was supposed to say, the word had stalled on the tip of her tongue.

"I froze. I saw what my life would be, and it scared me to death. It was a nightmare. Everyone's faces slowly falling, people whispering as I just stood there. I couldn't say anything. Connor's face ... He was so angry when he pulled me out of the room and said we'd talk about it when we got home."

His hand a vise at the base of her chin, hot breath an inch from her face. Seething, that after all the times he had told her to shut up, this one time he wanted her to say something, she stayed silent. Self-consciously, she rubbed the spot where the bruises had darkened her arm. A reminder for the first two weeks, unexpectedly making it easy to stay firm. "I told him I had to go to the bathroom. Instead, I snuck out to the car and drove straight to our apartment."

It had been surreal. Packing her clothes in her fancy dress, stopping only to leave his mother's necklace on her nightstand when she grabbed her passport. The elaborate curls in her hair falling out with the cold sweat prickling her scalp. Anything that didn't absolutely have to come with her was left behind.

"My parents let me move back in with them. I wasn't going to stay long. Just for a month or two until I got my own place. But my mother kept telling me I needed to try harder, be more forgiving.

She even tried to drive me back to his place once. Every time I talk to her, she tells me I made a mistake."

Alex's guarded expression slipped, and anger etched his features.

"I spoke with him that night when he figured out I had left and I told him it was over and I never wanted to see him again. That night was the last time I did. At first, I thought he made this big production of doing it at the party because he was so sure I'd say yes that he'd want an audience." She huffed a mirthless laugh through her nose. "Now I think he did it because he thought I'd be too scared to say no in front of other people. In a way, I guess he was right."

Alex sat staring at her, mouth opening and closing for long seconds. One hand went to her cheek, then the other, and he pulled his forehead to hers. "You are," he said, "incredibly brave. To stand up to him and get yourself out after everything you went through? That takes so much strength."

"Thanks," she said, lip warbling into a half-smile. "You sound like Soph."

"Sophie is smart and right and I like her more every day."

It didn't feel like best behaviour. It just felt like him. "Alex? I would really like a hug."

He shifted her into the cradle of his arms, her back resting against the breadth of his chest. If it was too good to be real, she wouldn't let herself think about it right now. But it seemed real, and she let the serene cadence of his breath soothe her.

"So that's why you don't like surprises," he said, almost to himself.

She stared into the fire and let a new tranquility settle over her. "I haven't had control over things for so long. I know that's not life. I know I can't control everything. But where I can, I want to take it back."

So far into the mountains, away from city lights, stars crowded the inky sky. The day had long lost its heat, but their shared warmth kept the chill at bay. Even after their full day outside in the sun and the trees, she was wide awake, and Jill stared unblinking at the Milky Way for the first time in her life.

TWENTY-TWO

Jill scoured her notes, scrutinizing the order of the slides. Switched slides sixteen and seventeen, then back. She changed the font. Changed it back. She could spiel off the process recommendations forwards and backwards while spinning a baton and riding a unicycle. No more review was needed.

Jill's leg bounced double-time under her desk. After weeks of delays, the meeting started in an hour. Nick had taken an impromptu trip to Montreal, so Alex picked up the slack. Alex didn't say it, but he appreciated the extra time before she pitched the recommendations, and Nick, well, he didn't care. Under their adoption of Rule Number Three, she hadn't brought it up when she left Alex's place two nights ago, saying she needed the next night to review. And besides, he'd be at the lab until late. She hoped he had checked his calendar.

Enough delaying, Northrop.

Resting Professional Face securely in place, Jill packed her bag, replaced her stilettos with sneakers, and swept through the office. She visited Ashleen and Marco, who spared a frazzled word for her as they wrangled their file. She spent a few minutes chatting with an advisor in talent acquisition and yes, they had received a new résumé from someone named Rachel and sure, they'd review it. Stopped to see Omar, who assured her the plan she outlined was solid.

"Good luck today," he said, and then in a lighter tone, "and say hi to Alex for me." He gave her a nod that had nothing to do with work. "He's a good guy."

The flush on her cheeks and the smile on her lips crept up. "Yeah, he's pretty great." She ducked her head and said, "I'll let you know how it goes."

Jill slipped into her stilettos half a block from the CMR office and stashed her sneakers into her bag. Sundresses and cotton shirts were left in the closet that morning. Today called for armour. Navy pencil skirt. Cream silk button down. A blazer, which she had carried over her arm all day because it was too hot to put on and why had she even bothered with it? The shirt was already sticking to the back of her neck. At least the slick knot she had pulled her hair into that morning remained in place.

Ten-oh-five. The cherry-red pickup was parked out front. Neither the yellow Volvo nor silver Subaru were in sight. Jill chewed her bottom lip, contemplating. Alex probably walked that morning.

Probably.

Twenty-two minutes later, Jill was back in front of the CMR front doors, this time with a tray of coffees, two muffins, and a pain au chocolat. No need to stop for a breath. She had been coming here for months. Just another day at the office.

It was not just another day in the office.

It would be the first time all three of them would be in the office at the same time in over a month. A lot had happened. Nick cornered her about distracting Alex. Her relationship with Alex had evolved into something completely different. Larger, deeper. She had opened up in ways she hadn't in years, or with anyone else. And now she would be recommending a slew of changes, some of which could be viewed as favouring Alex. Some that very much didn't. It crossed her mind that sleeping with Alex could conceivably be defined as "a change in relationship" she should bring to the attention of HR for conflict of interest purposes, but that wasn't going to happen right now. She had asked Omar to review her list, with names and titles scrubbed, to check for bias. He had suggested a couple of immaterial tweaks but otherwise endorsed her plan. It was go time.

Okay, one breath. She squared her shoulders and clipped through the front doors.

She thought it had been hard before. Thank god they had Rules.

Alex lifted his head at her entrance, eyes brightening and shoulders unwinding. "Hey."

A wave of warmth washed over her, and she swallowed the smile that threatened to split her face. "Hi, yourself." A finger brushed his when she passed him the coffee and he rewarded her with a secret look that made her heart stutter.

His gaze travelled down her legs and back up with a puckish grin. "Nice skirt," he said under his breath. Not nearly quiet enough for Jill's liking, and she pressed her lips together in a complete failure to remain impassive.

You're impossible, she mouthed at him, and his smile widened in response.

Rules, schmules. No one was perfect.

She turned to Nick, who was absorbed in his screen. "I come bearing caffeine and sugar," she said, setting down a second coffee and a muffin. He turned with his own wide smile, taking the muffin with cheerful thanks.

Nick was at the top of a mood swing today. Lucky bounce.

Jill plugged in her laptop, swivelled the second monitor to face the two men, and spent the next forty-five minutes outlining her recommendations for business improvement. Small things, like an actual cleanup of files and an IT upgrade. More expensive changes, like contracting a financial analyst and hiring part-time admin assistant. Seismic shifts, like relocating the office.

"There are benefits to this location," Jill said, "but you aren't taking full advantage of this space and it is costing you a lot of money. This isn't a priority consideration, though you should either leverage it better, even from a branding perspective, or combine your office and lab space."

The location was a huge convenience for Alex, and she hated it should be considered for change, but she wouldn't be doing her job if it wasn't on the list. At least he knew she wasn't only giving recommendations she selfishly chose to benefit him. She clamped down on the thought that she had left off returning the truck to a full company asset, given how well that conversation had gone down in private.

She advanced to the next slide. "Hiring a field tech in northern Alberta will cut down on your travel time and expenses, and let you more properly expand into that market. You are limited being based here without a permanent footprint up north. This will open more time to focus on the central and southern sites."

Alex wiped a hand over his mouth and looked something between hopeful and pained. The bi-monthly, multi-day treks up north exhausted him, but it would be hard for him to give up control of the work—an irony not lost on her. Nick glowered at the suggestion of hiring a third hand.

"You're getting in each other's way. Nick, you take care of the clients. Alex, you're in the field and the lab. When you two switch roles, inevitably it ends up causing issues." In her first month at CMR, twice she had seen meetings go out to the same clients with conflicting purposes, and once a site visited by each of them on consecutive days. "Until you hire an admin assistant, you need a task tracker to make sure you aren't duplicating efforts. That will help with your internal communications when you need to hire more staff, and when you have meetings with other prospective VCs."

"Wait." Nick spoke for the first time since she had started. "Why would I contact another VC?"

"It's common practice," Jill said, already clicking to the next slide. "Securing funding is far from certain. You should be speaking to a few firms to maximize your chance of a successful bid."

"We should?" Alex glanced at Nick.

"I have been developing a relationship with this group for a year. We're sticking with them. They're going to invest in us." An edge crept into Nick's voice.

"If it's certain, why do you need a proposal?" Jill asked, genuinely confused. "Also, the firm you've been working with has more history acting as an incubator, but I think with your position now, you might think about reframing your need for an accelerator."

Alex volleyed his eyes between them. "Incubator? Accelerator? For what?"

Jesus. Nick hadn't told him anything. Jill opened her mouth to explain, but Nick cut her off before she could start.

"Is that it? Everything you have for us?"

Ah. There was the Nick she knew. Jill corralled her expression. "I've organized the recommendations in order of priority and biggest impact, and by financial versus process. It's a lot to digest. Now, what questions do you have for me?"

Alex sat in contemplative silence for a beat. "Can we afford to hire people now?"

"No," said Nick, just as Jill said "Yes."

Nick pursed his lips. "We can't."

"You can," Jill insisted. "It will take some adjustments, but you can hire a part-time admin assistant and contract a field tech by the end of the month."

"Techs are expensive. We can handle the field work."

"*I'm* handling it, Nick." Alex pinched the bridge of his nose. "I can't do it all anymore." Jill ached at the fatigue in his voice. She tried to haul up a divider between her work and her boyfriend. It didn't work.

"We have a plan. We should stick to it."

"Your current plan got you here," Jill cut in. "It has been solid. Perfect for a start-up in its first couple of years, but you've outgrown it. And more work is coming. Put my recommendations in place and you'll be ready when it does."

Tension rolled off Nick in turbulent coils and he looked at Alex, arms crossed. "Alex and I need to talk."

Alex looked at Jill. A few months ago, his expression would have been unreadable. Now, she could see him trying to see if she needed backup, and perhaps get her to stay.

The former wasn't needed, and now was not the time for the latter. Nick's dismissal didn't faze her. Even with the sudden appearance of his sour persona, the pitch had gone far better than she had expected. She had delivered dozens of recommendation packages to clients, and not all were received with open arms and wallets. Sometimes even returned with light hostility. And clients always needed time to parse the details.

"There's no rush to decide on anything, however, the sooner you want to move ahead, the faster we can get you set up." Her laptop was already in her bag, and she decided against changing into her sneakers here. The armour could stay on a little longer.

Nick waved dismissively, but Alex caught her hand as she passed his desk, thumb stroking her wrist.

"I missed you last night," he said, voice low. "I want you with me tonight."

Jill's breath caught in her throat, and she nodded. It was hard to keep armour in place when he was looking at her like she was already naked. She had no idea how they were going to work on the proposal together.

She closed the office front door behind her. Her new favourite sushi place was two blocks away, and Omar had wanted to try it for weeks. She could fill him in on the meeting and hear how his financial analysis was going, while giving Alex and Nick some time to talk in private. Her phone was already in her hand to text him when a banner flashed on her screen.

Sushi could wait.

A spike of adrenaline split her in half, her stilettos falling like hammer strikes as she skittered back into the room. "Guys," she said, "it's here."

Alex's wary eyes showed he knew the answer already. "What's here?"

"I think we have an answer on the grant."

"What?" Alex croaked, and Nick's face blanked.

"Check your email."

This was it. Everything they'd worked for. Nick hunched in his chair. Jill clutched her elbows and forced herself to breathe. Alex dropped in front of his desk, kneecaps popping as they hit the hardwood. He cast a nervous glance between Jill and Nick, and after a few clicks, sunk onto his heels with his hands limp at his sides.

"What?" Nick demanded.

Jill peered over his shoulder, and her heartbeat slammed in her throat.

Holy shit.

"We got it," Alex said weakly.

"How much?" Nick's voice cut through the air, the hostility drained out of him, now all eager impatience. "What did we get?"

Alex turned to Nick, eyes wide. "All of it."

Nick's chair careened into the wall as he launched himself out of it. "Fuck yeah!" he howled as he pumped the air with his fist.

Jill stared dazed at the screen. Two and a half million dollars. More than enough to fund the studies to pilot Alex's research. Enough to keep CMR afloat. Everything they'd been counting on. It was going to happen.

"Alex." Jill's voice was a whisper. "You did it."

He staggered to his feet and crushed her in a consuming embrace. "You did it," he murmured in her ear, and a mixture of gratitude and relief coursed through her. Months of hard work with weeks of late nights and early mornings had paid off. Alex got what he needed, and she helped make it happen. She squeezed her eyes shut and let herself be swept off her feet.

"Thank you, thank you, thank you." The words tumbled into her hair, and he pressed a kiss to her. "You are incredible. I can't believe it. You did it."

His embrace stilled around her, and her feet met the ground again. Then she was being ripped away and being crushed in unfamiliar arms.

"Holy fuck!" Nick fairly yelled in her ear.

No kisses, thank god, and she let herself grin when he released her, thinking Omar wouldn't have minded the hug. She patted Nick's shoulder. "Congratulations," she said, and stepped away a handful of paces.

Alex gripped double handfuls of his hair as he blew out a long breath. Nick slapped him hard on his back. "My man, cancel whatever you were doing. We are going to destroy this town tonight."

Jill vowed she wouldn't let it show on her face what she guessed Nick's version of celebrating would be. And if that's what they wanted to do tonight, she would smile and tell them to have fun. They deserved it. But if she knew Alex even a tiny bit, whatever Nick had in mind wouldn't be high up on his list of fun times. Alex's reaction confirmed her suspicions.

"Nope," Alex said before Nick could detail his plan to wreak havoc. He released the grip on his hair, leaving it sticking up in wild directions. "I want to call my mom and my sister, go home and have a nap—" Jill studiously brushed a piece of lint from her shirt "—take you guys out for dinner, and not wake up hungover at three tomorrow afternoon."

Nick waved a hand, unfazed. "Fine. But we're charging dinner to the company. Neither of us will want this bill on our credit card."

—

The afternoon unfolded exactly how Alex wanted. He called his mom and sister, while Nick called a few people to share the news on his end. Jill forwarded the confirmation of grant success to Omar and Angela. A debrief calendar invite from Angela landed in her inbox a minute later with a note to take the rest of the afternoon off. Then Alex not-so-subtly told Nick he needed to rest before going out that night and Jill let herself be pulled out after him, catching the smirk on Nick's face as they left.

Sophie hadn't been wrong when she said they weren't the best at hiding "this."

Minutes later they tripped through his front door, his hand already sliding down her skirt's zipper.

"This is what you were wearing in the storage room that day, isn't it?" he said. "I've dreamt of taking this thing off you for months."

Once, Jill swore she'd never let herself be caught alone with him in there again. Now, months later, turning the fantasy into a reality sounded like an excellent idea after all.

A restful nap followed the extremely unrestful one. After a bit of logistical juggling, Jill rummaged through her closet at her place, trying to find something appropriate for the trendy restaurant Nick secured reservations for on short notice. Her hands paused over the grey sheath dress she had last worn at New Years and pulled it out of the closet …

… and dropped it straight into the donation pile.

Someone else would make wonderful use of it. Jill never wanted to see it again.

A couple hours later, in her violet wrap dress and a few cobbled together accessories, and Alex looking stunning in his navy suit, the elevator whisked them to the someteenth floor of a building Jill had walked by a hundred times on her way to work. The last of the late summer sun shone through the windows, spilling across the dark wood and supple leather, and Jill stepped into the heady, dreamy night. Like crossing a threshold, reality shifting into something new. Alex wrapped his arm around her to whisper in her ear and Jill startled at his touch.

"No rules. We're not at work," he said. "Don't make me keep my hands off you." Then, as if to assure her compliance, he added the *look*, eyes crinkling. "Please."

She bit her lip, fighting to keep the frisson skating across her skin from showing. "I thought you weren't going to use it for evil."

"I lied."

Nick was already sitting at the table with a date, a cherub-cheeked woman with an infectious laugh and such a sweet disposition that Jill thought she might contract diabetes by the end of the night. She liked her immediately, and squashed the uncharitable thought that Cass—she and Alex shared a surprised look when Nick texted he was bringing her—could do much better.

Alex faded in and out of awareness through cocktails, occasionally joining conversation with mumbles of "we got it" well into appetizers.

"You did," Jill confirmed. "Think of all that work you get to do now."

He turned a rueful look at her that made her heart squeeze, and she ran her nails along the nape of his neck, and he melted against her hand.

"Don't worry," she said. "I'll be there to help."

She tried so hard not to compare Alex to Connor, but sometimes the differences would be too glaring to miss. Connor had always avoided showing her any attention in public unless he felt a need to assert ownership, keeping her close around his friends and pulling her along at family functions.

Alex's touches connected them. An assurance. Whether they were alone or around others. Without a hint of possessiveness.

Jill had been stranded in the desert and it had finally rained.

Nick raised his brows once when Alex absent-mindedly brushed his lips over Jill's fingers as he studied the menu but appeared to rapidly accept the display. Or maybe it was another mood swing. Or Cass's pleasant demeanour had rubbed off on him. Whatever the cause, it felt so good to be open and celebrate a huge night.

Halfway through dessert, it dawned on her. Angela had minced no words with how important this file was, for Blackburn to re-establish its name in the environmental sector. Her first grant writing project was a success. Jill had delivered.

"Alex," she said, turning to him in her own daze, "we did it."

"Yeah," he agreed, squeezing her hand, "we did."

Three bottles of wine and five courses later, Nick prepared to head out for round two of celebrations. "Now the party starts," he declared, with Cass smiling wanly at the plan.

Jill hoped they had fun. She was already dreaming of her bed.

"You two are the cutest. I never met Alex before, but Nick talks about him all the time," Cass said, leaning into the bathroom mirror to adjust her mass of perfect chestnut curls and touch up her fiery lipstick. "I don't know what he was so worried about."

Jill held her face expressionless. "Oh?"

"I mean," Cass continued hastily, "Nick gets a little twitchy where Alex is concerned. They've been friends a long time. But I think he warmed up to you quickly."

That sounded like a heavily spin-doctored version of Nick's telling of that tale. Nick cared about Alex deeply, that much was clear, even if he had a weird way of showing it. How was this funny and kind person spending time with someone who was so, well, not?

"So," Jill started awkwardly, "you and Nick have been dating a while?"

A thin smile crooked Cass's cupid's bow lips. "Something like that." She gave a helpless shrug. "We can't seem to figure each other out."

How many times had Nick and Cass come together and split up? The doubt of the other person's feelings. Their intentions. Trying to fix things. Not knowing if it was worth it to fix things. Or maybe they were super casual, and they had friends-with-benefits'ed their relationship. From the look on Cass's face, Jill didn't think so.

"Well," Jill said after a moment, "I hope you figure out what is best for you."

Alex sat alone at the table, staring out at the night sky with flickering candlelight gilding his features. He turned as she came close, and the smile he gave her stopped her heart.

This brilliant, focused man who had worked so hard for so long, finally getting what he deserved. And she got to be there when it happened. They had done something amazing together. What else they could do?

The excited swimming in her stomach that had been her constant companion for months almost felt like background noise. A distant rumble of a freight train's wheels on the tracks. Then … *bam.* The train would barrel by, the unstoppable forward momentum knocking her back, a rush flooding her body, every nerve ending on fire. His patience as she worked through her fears. Giving her space to move forward in her own time. With care that at some point she had stopped thinking held conditions, and with that thought, the knowledge unfurled within her like a flower.

I'm falling in love with him.

For a split second, the urge to hide seized her, to run home and burrow under the covers until it passed. To run to him and confess *you're taking my heart and I don't know what to do.* Instead, she stood motionless to let the revelation wash over her, eyes wide and heart pounding.

Too soon. She wasn't ready. Not for this.

The touch he left on her arm left a shiver behind it. "Ready, Jillybean?"

She opened her mouth to reply and found her voice still caught. She nodded, hand hiding the pulse surely visible at her throat.

On the streets below, the night eddied around them, warm and calm in stark contrast to the storm within her. Soon, Alex would disappear into an avalanche of additional work, and she would leave for her trip to Boston. Maybe it would give her the space to figure out what to do.

It's okay, said the voice. *Let it come.*

It wouldn't wait for permission. She had no choice if it came or not. She just hoped she would be ready when it arrived. Maybe things would work out that neatly. In the meantime, it could sit in a box and wait until she was ready to deal with it.

Jill slid into the Uber's back seat, Alex beside her a moment later. Her fingers sought his on the seat between them and hoped the vibrations of the road masked her trembling hand.

TWENTY-THREE

Rachel pounced on Jill before the shelter doors had fully closed behind her.

"I have an interview!" she said in a breathless rush. "Next week!"

Jill sneaked in a hug around Rachel's hopping. "They only pulled your CV yesterday. They must really like what they saw." After months of listening to Rachel second-guess her work, in stark contrast to her thin but perfectly respectable résumé, a bit of deserved confidence boosting might do her some good. Sure enough, Rachel continued her little dance as Jill added, "Do you want to review interview questions?"

She did. For almost an hour.

"I'm insanely jealous. Furious," Rachel said, when she ran out of questions, tossing the ball down the enclosure's length.

"For the vacation part or the Boston part?"

"Yes."

Fetch was a work in progress. Daisy had locked down the "chase" portion, but bringing the ball back? Not so much. Dust and dog slobber formed a revolting slurry on her lilac jeans. Wiping her hands on them helped neither clean her hands nor make her jeans any worse. Jill trotted to the far end and coaxed Daisy into dropping the ball, ears perked and tail batting the side of the fence, ready to bolt after her prize. She raised her non-ball wielding hand parallel to the ground in the sit command to which, being the goodest girl, Daisy obeyed, and was rewarded with the next toss of the ball.

After spending a quiet night at Alex's after their impromptu celebration, he had dropped her off for volunteering that morning. She had briefly considered running from his place to the shelter and burn off some of her nervous energy, but the thought of having her sweaty, running short-clad legs bared to nails and claws convinced her to accept his ride. And he was due to pick her up in ten minutes.

Which was why when she checked her vibrating phone, she started in surprise he had already arrived for her. She was about to text back he was never early, but stopped. Sure, he was late a lot, but he always let her know. And when it was important, he was usually early. Even when it meant he dragged himself out of bed to meet her, like when they were going on their road trip, or when they were telling Nick about their relationship. Oh, right, and the day they met to figure out where Jill's mind was after she panicked and abandoned him at the club.

A thread of guilt twined her stomach. Back when she first left Connor, her therapist had coached her about absolute thinking. *Always* and *Never* were dangerous thoughts. A new fear added itself to her list: her old habits could derail what was happening between them.

One more thing to work through, Northrop.

She really needed to get into therapy again.

Taking a deep breath, she chewed her lip for a moment. Daisy had finally warmed up to Travis. She could take it slow if Daisy didn't want to meet a new human. Specifically, a male human. She hit send.

Want to meet my girl?

She led Alex past the front desk, a little wave at Rachel as she left, then down the hall and into the adoption area where Travis said they could try to introduce her.

"You'll need to be really slow. And gentle," she said, almost biting her thumbnail before remembering where her hands had been. She puffed out her lips instead. What else would make Daisy comfortable? "Wait at the doors first so we can see if she's okay with it? She'll approach you if she is."

"Slow. Gentle. Let her make the first move." His mouth quirked. "I can do that."

She couldn't look mad, no matter how hard she tried. "Did you just—?"

"Hey, it worked once."

He really was impossible.

Daisy was curled up on her blanket, tail thumping at Jill's reappearance, scooting across the floor next to her. Alex edged into the doorway before easing down to the floor, his knees hovering inches off his ankles in an awkward attempt to sit cross-legged.

The tail thumping slowed, but the whites of her amber eyes didn't show. Tentative, but not nervous. That was good. Jill gave Daisy a treat, and showing her that there was a second treat, shifted back and passed the treat to Alex.

"I'm going to sit really close to you and let her know I think you're safe," Jill said, voice low and watching Daisy's body language.

"Good plan." The rumbling words in her ear fired a trail of goosebumps down her neck. "Do you think it would help if you sat on my lap?"

"Tsk." She nudged his shoulder. "Maybe talk to her a little?"

"Like Daisy's a good girl—" her ears perked up "—and she might like to come say hi?" Alex shifted on the floor, slowly.

"Have you ever tried yoga?" she asked, eyeing the uncomfortable angle of his hips.

"Once. Too stiff."

Jill snorted. "That's like saying you're too dirty to take a shower."

"Doesn't matter. You're flexible enough for both of us."

"Alex! This is kind of like work. Rule Number Two? No flirting?"

"What? You said I should let her hear my voice." It was soothing, although she might be biased. He shot a glance at her filthy jeans. "Speaking of showers ..."

She glanced down. "Oh, I only wear these for volunteering. They're a little weird," Jill added quickly.

"Nah, you look cute," he said as he smiled gently at Daisy. "Just thinking about getting you out of them later."

"I can't take you anywhere."

"Good. Let's go back to your place after this. I have a couple of hours before my game."

The flush crept farther up her curved cheeks and the pinging under her ribs flared at his irresistible smile. "What's gotten into you?"

"I'd like to get into y—"

"Oh my god!"

"Want me to stop?"

"Absolutely not."

He gave her a satisfied nod. "I got amazing news yesterday, thanks to my brilliant, beautiful girlfriend who did in three months what me and Nick couldn't do in three years. I have two sites in the middle of nowhere ready to sign off on in a couple of weeks, so I won't have to drive half a day for thirty minutes of work. And I'm making friends with a good, good girl." The tip of Daisy's tail offered an inquisitive wag as he held the treat out for her. "So, yeah. I'm having a pretty damn good day."

Daisy's head tilted to Jill a few times—a little check to make sure everything was safe—and a few more kind words and a few minutes later Daisy had inched forward, sniffing his knuckles before delicately accepting the treat.

"I'd say something about getting you two to eat out of the palm of my hand, but ..."

"Ignore him, Daisy," Jill cooed, rubbing generous circles around Daisy's ears as she gnawed happily on the snack. "He doesn't know how to treat ladies like us."

"Now that's a sight." Travis leaned against the door frame. Jill hoped he hadn't been standing there long. "Looks like our girl likes you fine."

The dusty Volvo's engine turned over with reluctance, already hot in the morning sun. Alex winced at the distressing grind as they cranked down all the windows. So much for the good day.

Jill matched his pained expression before getting in. She had left one other recommendation off her list. That car was an old friend. He loved Anni-frid, even though he couldn't count on her anymore. Even after weeks in the shop, the car came out with more duct tape and another rattle. A new company vehicle would solve a lot of problems. Transport, write-off, reliability. She had told herself she had left it off the recommendations because it didn't really fit the profile of the process audit she had originally pitched, but she had added a slew of financial suggestions. And outside of office hours, if she'd have said that it terrified her that he could get stuck in the middle of nowhere again, in winter, with no cell service, and what if he didn't have food or water or …

She quelled the fear that lurched through her gut. Along with the annoyance that sprung up beside it.

A half day of driving for thirty minutes of work? Funny how Nick schmoozed the clients and didn't bother with the grunt work of driving two thousand kilometres a week or being away from home a third of the month. Even if he was good at it. The man could sell sand in the desert, and Alex preferred the field and lab aspects of their work. Unless they were getting paid in gold ingots—which they weren't, she'd seen a recent company bank balance—that site was a colossal waste of time for little margin.

Well, she couldn't bring it up now, and packed the thought away beside the fear and annoyance. Rule Number Three: no work talk outside of work.

Delaying the conversation had nothing to do with avoidance.

In her apartment, he kicked out of his boots and turned to her with a sly smile. "Now, about those jeans ..." he said, dropping to his knees in front of her and wrapping his hands around her waist. "Looks like you might need some help cleaning up. Just with the hard-to-reach places."

Showering together was never as fun as it sounded like it should be. Instead of suds and giggles and helping with the hard-to-reach places, one person ended up hogging the water while the other froze waiting to switch places. Nothing sexy about her lips turning blue.

"I'll be quick," she promised, unwinding his hands. "Besides, I'm bendy, remember? You're the one with the hard-to-reach spots."

He rested on his haunches and crossed his arms, mouth twisted in a half grin. Damn, that smile did it, too. So much for not using it for evil.

Everything else with Alex was better. Maybe this would be, too. She bit her lip and peeled a corner of her tee shirt up and over her head, letting it drop beside her.

"I mean, I can reach everything." She turned to give him a side profile, wiggling out of her jeans. Two steps back, hands behind her to unclasp her bra, dropped that, a leaving a trail of clothes like breadcrumbs for him to follow. His sly grin turned hungry as her fingers gently rolled her nipples, and he sucked in a breath.

"I like to take my time, start at the top and work my way down. I'm very thorough." She released her breasts and let her hands travel over her stomach, under the waist of her underwear, and opened her eyes wide. "Actually, maybe I don't need a shower. I'm already all wet."

"Jesus." He groaned and adjusted the front of his jeans. "What are you doing to me?"

"You broke the no flirting at work rule. I take following rules very seriously." She slid her hands out and stroked herself through the fabric. "Too bad. I was going to help you with your hard-to-reach spots."

He looked like he was seconds from combusting. "What if I said I'm sorry?"

"Forgiveness is important." She toyed with the elastic edges of her panties. "I think I need help taking these off. Please."

He chased her into the bathroom, giving her just enough time to grab a condom before pulling her into the shower. Steam billowed around them, water the perfect level of scalding cascading over her back. He scrubbed, firm but gentle, until every inch of her skin glowed. She could be firm but gentle, too. She ran her slicked hands down his stomach and past his erection pressed between them, feeling his balls tighten in her cupped palms.

"Do you think I'm clean enough, now?" she asked sweetly, her lips at the base of his neck. "Or did you miss any hard-to-reach spots?"

As soon as the bubbles were rinsed, he rolled on the condom, wrapped her legs around his waist, and leaned her against the tiled wall. "Hold on."

Showering together was the best idea she'd had all day.

Hair still wrapped in a towel and easing the maxi dress over her damp skin, she padded over to where he flopped haphazardly on the couch, jeans on and shirt off, head tipped back and zoned out. She curled up beside him, brushing a lock of hair that had fallen over his forehead.

Her heart swelled with the whole morning. Rachel had vibrated with excitement at her opportunity and while nothing was certain, she had a great shot at a junior analyst role. Daisy had done so well, almost returning a fetch once, and trusting in Jill enough to get close to a new person.

Her person.

He was so sweet and gentle with her girl. Didn't rush her. Just let her do what she was comfortable with. Just more of being his sexy, brilliant, sudsy self.

She was in an unfathomable amount of trouble.

"Mmm. See? Helpful," he said, eyes still closed.

"So helpful," she agreed with a shiver, and the box with her secret rattled between her ribs.

"Can I borrow your book?" He motioned his head to her library book he started while camping. "Time travelling enemy cyborg lesbians? Can't remember the last time I read fiction."

"You know you can borrow it from the library when I'm done?"

"Don't have time to get to the library."

"Let me guess … periodicals and papers only since grad school?"

He let out a muffled grunt.

"Well, I have more ideas if you want to read about something other than bioreactive organoclays before bed."

He grunted his *okay but I'm not admitting to it right now n*oise. "Don't count on it."

"How's your game going to go today with this?" She gestured at his sprawled form, loose-limbed and heavy on her couch, and tried to remember the term Marta had used weeks ago at the game. "What if you get dump tackled or something." Surely, he needed to be focused. Maybe they should wait until after he played. The way he attacked her after his games in a testosterone-fuelled passion made her think that would be a good idea anyway.

"Can't tackle me if they can't catch me," he said, then perked up as he dug out his phone. "Speaking of slow-ass punks, Dan and Marta had their baby yesterday." He smiled at the picture of the cutest little mushroom Jill had ever seen. "Olivia Daniella, eight pounds. Mom and baby are doing great." He passed the phone to Jill's outstretched hands. "Guess he'll be too busy to play for a while."

The edges of her mouth curled up as she swiped through the photos in his team's group chat. The stunned but beaming dad, tired but radiant mom, and their furious but adorable little girl. Jill had looked forward to seeing Marta again. Laughing with affectionate sarcasm at her boyfriend's lacklustre playing tactics and detailing her ultimately successful plan to pick their baby's name the first time they met. A couple of weeks later, telling Jill not to make her laugh or she'd pee herself, the almost-fully baked baby playing soccer with her bladder. Maybe she'd be at a game before the end of the season, and Jill could snuggle little Olivia, too.

He was watching her with a soft expression and the hummingbird that had taken up residence in her chest buzzed its wings.

"Do you want kids?" he blurted out.

Her hand stilled as he took the phone back from her. "Yes, one day," she said, and the hummingbird wings morphed into a drumroll. "Do you?"

"Yes," he said, giving her a hesitant smile.

Well. There's that.

That was good, right? They were looking to see where things went. Get to know each other. Find out if they wanted the same things. Higher stakes than if they both hated pineapple on pizza. The big things. And she had wanted to know, but it had felt too early to ask.

She wanted to put on her shoes and run.

—

After a quick series of texts to first confirm (1) they were staying in tonight, (2) at her place, and (3) a quick and thorough inventory of her cupboards, he arrived with grocery bags and an apology that the tortillas wouldn't be made from scratch.

"I missed you," he said, dropping the bevy of staple ingredients to add to her cupboards onto the counter and kissing her with a gentle caress on her cheek. He scrolled through his phone, landing on a channel streaming country music. "Do you like cilantro?"

No, but he was here with it already, and she wanted to be easygoing. She nodded, a flash in her chest as she squeezed him harder than usual and continued to scramble around in—maybe not a blind, but definitely myopic—frenzy.

Over the last week, the gentle swoops and hummingbird wings living at her core had all been replaced by an insistent ache, tapping from its secret box. She tried to chalk it up to her period, but that came and went with its usual lack of fanfare. Possibly it was seeing Kyle again and the lingering guilt over how she had treated him after her last visit, although he swore there was nothing to forgive. Or the needed work around her audit recommendations and diving into the venture capital proposal, but Jill was ready for that.

The ache didn't have a home. Sometimes it lodged in her stomach, leaving no room for anything else. Other times it floated up behind her lungs, knocking against her ribs for hours. Yesterday, it blocked her throat for the better part of the morning. Every time she opened her mouth and coherent words came out instead of silence had surprised her.

She had started waking up at night again. Curling into Alex's warmth on the nights he was with her. Laying still and staring at the dark ceiling on the nights he wasn't. Listening to the noises of the night, fatigue fogging her brain in the morning. When she finally had stayed in bed long enough to get up with the sun, pushing through her run in a daze, then pushing her instant oatmeal around her bowl. A few hours later, making herself choke down whatever she could stand at lunch.

The nights she spent with Alex were easier. Either he made something delicious, and their meals stretched so long as they talked into the night, she could fit food in over the course of a few hours. Or she brought takeout to the CMR office to make sure he ate on nights he worked late and brought home what she didn't eat there to pick at until bed. The nights she asked to spend alone, she worked her way through a bowl of cereal that reached unpalatable levels of sogginess in the hour it took her to eat it.

At work, she crossed the tightrope like a pro. Everything buckled down and wrapped up tight. Completed one of her files ahead of deadline. Put another on pause for the week she was away. Setting her out of office message yesterday felt like summiting Mount Everest.

A huge shock accompanied her call with Angela, when her boss casually mentioned the bonus that came with the successful grant. A sum in the low five figures—in the high four digits after tax, but *still*—would land in her bank account in the next few weeks. Jill had sat motionless at the news so long Angela asked if her video had frozen.

She hadn't told Alex. Partly because the bonus wasn't in her bank account yet, but mostly because it sat strangely in her stomach she'd made a chunk of cash off his successful grant.

The thin rope dividing her personal and professional life tied her hands a little more tightly. But even that didn't claim responsibility for the lingering ache.

Her flight to Boston departed in two days. One really, if she considered how early her flight left Monday morning

"Nothing fits," she gritted out, trying to cram a third pair of shoes and spare running clothes into her already stuffed carry-on bag. Her knees pressing her full weight onto the suitcase wasn't enough to get edges together and her fingers flew off the immoveable zipper in a fruitless tug. She tilted onto her heels with a frustrated growl and raked her fingers through her hair.

Alex's head bent over the bowl, bouncing out of time with the music as he whisked a salad dressing for the coleslaw to accompany their fish tacos.

"Come on, relax," he said with his usual ease. Just like he had several times before, but this time the tightrope that Jill had been walking snapped.

"Don't tell me how to feel!" The words sliced across the room like a machete, and he jerked up in surprise.

Oh, no. Ohnonono …

Her hands flew to her mouth, her pulse thundering in her ears.

"I'm sorry. I'm sorry," she whispered through her fingers. "I didn't mean it."

"Jill?" He dropped the whisk, his brows drawing together. "What's—"

Idiot. Now he's going to yell at you. Because you couldn't keep your stupid mouth shut.

Don't have a panic attack. Don't don't don't …

"Oh." Realization washed over his face as he dropped his head, leaning hard against the counter. "Fuck."

He moved carefully to her, sitting across from her hunched posture on the floor. "I never thought of it like that. I don't want to tell you how to feel. I'm sorry." He hesitated, drawing a breath. "What's wrong?"

This isn't a panic attack.

Jill fixed her stare on the floor. "I'm sorry. I don't know."

"It's not about … is this about your suitcase? You can check a bag—"

Then why is my heart pounding? "It's not about my bag."

His eyes hooded with concern, thumb swiping a path on her forearm, doing nothing to ease her guilt at lashing out. "Do you want to be alone tonight?"

Inhale slowly, exhale deeply. "No."

I don't know what to do.

"Will you tell me? Please don't make me guess."

This is Alex. Talk to him.

It wasn't about Alex. Well, it was. But not of him. It was of the *what next* and him. That she was moving too fast, running out of control. She knew what was happening. She had tried to tamp it down, but it was breaking free of the box she jammed it in, and she couldn't put it back.

And when it did break free, she was going to ruin it. She didn't know what to do and she was going to ruin everything when she got it wrong. And when she did, it was going to hurt. So much. And it scared her to death.

She scrubbed her hands over her face, remembering too late she had put on mascara that day and now she probably looked like a frazzled raccoon. "Aren't you freaking out? I mean, everything is so great. And you're so patient and kind and I'm …"

A mess. Not ready. The ache swelled, pressing tight against her heart and lungs, working its way up. "I'm so scared," she choked out around the rock in her throat. "How are you not scared?"

"Oh." The silence stretched as he stroked her arm. "There are a lot of things that scare me," he said, "but this is not one of them." He brushed a strand of hair behind her ear, swiping his thumb across her cheek. "When you kissed me that first time? You said your freak-out would come. It's okay if that's today."

It probably wouldn't help, but she folded against his chest anyway, Alex's pulse under her own finding a resonant frequency. It was sanctuary. A place to let it out safely. Then, before she could hold it back, the ache poured out of her in a rain of tears. Racking sobs that shook her entire body, and the harder she wept, the firmer he held her, wringing her emotion out at the source. Every doubt, every worry she held released, until she was cried out and there was no fear left inside.

It was fierce and fast as a summer storm. Her breath hitched as her tears slowed to a trickle, and to her surprise, turned to laughter. She wiped her cheeks, sniffling and smiling at the same time.

Alex looked at her in amazement. "You are," he said, "the most beautiful thing I've ever seen in my life."

Jill sniffed again, positive snot and mascara were running down her face. "Ha, thanks." She touched the streaks of tears staining his shirt. "Oh my god. I'm so sorry."

"I thought we agreed you weren't apologizing for that anymore." He stroked her hair. "You are so sweet, my Jillybean."

"I'm going to kill Sophie," she said, choking back a laugh. She let out a shaky breath and melted a little deeper into the cradle of his arms, exhausted. "Alex, I really don't like cilantro."

She knew it was coming. She just thought she'd have more time. Her racing heart hadn't calmed, beating hard against the wall of Alex's embrace. But there was no noise. No clamouring questions. Just an answer, clear and fresh as the day after the rain.

There was no closing the box now. And she was right. She wasn't ready.

TWENTY-FOUR

The alarm blerped in the darkness, and she clicked it off before rolling over. She had lots of time. In theory. Alex pulled her into a sleepy nuzzle.

"Sure you don't want me to drive you?"

"I'm sure."

It was three a.m. She only had herself to blame. The cheapest flight had her boarding at six that morning. Years of travelling with her dad had instilled in her the unassailable truth that arriving any later than three hours before a flight was a gamble. Two and a half hours early was impossibly close. Two hours was reckless. Two hours and international? God help her.

She dragged herself out of bed. "Go back to sleep."

"Mmph." His eyes were already closed again. "Text me when you land."

I deserve nine a.m. departures, she thought as she pulled on a shirt. *My sanity is worth the extra hundred and fifty dollars.*

If she had known about the bonus weeks ago and no longer needed to worry about booking a cheap flight. Now she could afford it.

Who was she kidding? As soon as the bonus hit her bank account, student loan and car payments claimed the bulk of it.

She had planned to sleep at her place, alone, the night before her excruciatingly early flight, but neither of them were willing to spend their last day before her trip apart. Alex promised her a walk through a nature reserve, but they were chased out with the arrival of the thunderstorm that had threatened to land for days. Neither of them minded, instead curling up on his couch while the tempest eased and pattered rain against the windows.

"Can I call you while you're gone? I know you're spending time with your friends, and I'm glad you get to," he had added hastily, "but a quick one? To say good night?"

There was also no way she was going a week without hearing his voice.

The lone benefit of the early flight was that she slept through most of it, and before she knew it, she was squished between her favourite people.

Kyle had picked the pub for its proximity to their hotel and its cheap appies. Jill ordered one of everything, including pineapple and olive pizza. Sophie pushed the chicken wings to the other side of the table with a grimace.

"Are we sure they aren't getting back together?" Kyle asked Sophie.

"Positive. Jill is never getting in a thousand metres of Connor again."

"You said that when she went home the summer after third year and got back together with him," he said, turning to Jill. "You were miserable when you got back."

"I'm so sorry," Jill said for the hundredth time. "I shouldn't have—"

"Stop. Enough," Kyle said. "Just, thank fucking god you finally broke up with him."

"I am a thousand percent sure they are done."

"A million percent," Jill confirmed, leaning against the cracked pleather booth.

"Okay, good," Kyle fumed. "Because I hate that guy. I hate his fucking face …"

"You never saw his face," Jill pointed out.

"Bet I'd hate it," he said, mouth twisting as if even speaking of Connor pained him, and he wrapped a rangy arm around her shoulders. "Tell me I'm wrong."

"You're not wrong," Sophie said with an evil grin, and Jill steeled herself for what Sophie had been dying to bring up. "Since we're talking about faces Ky will hate, are we going to talk about your new man?"

Well, it was going to come out eventually.

"Right." Kyle's eyes shifted from disdainful to wary. "You're seeing someone already."

Jill balked at the comment that echoed a little too closely of something her mother would say. "I didn't jump into this," she said, stung. "I don't think."

"I'm not saying that. You were single for—"

"—half a year," Sophie supplied.

"Half a year," he repeated. "Soph would go through an entire rowing team in that time."

"Wait," Sophie said. "Four-man or eight-man?"

"One of each," Kyle replied, "including the cox."

Sophie cackled. "You said cox."

"Are you guys twelve?"

"I'm not giving you a hard time," he continued. "I just don't want that little heart to break again. We lost you for so long."

Jill pressed her fingers to her eyes, trying to push the wetness back inside. God, she had missed Kyle. She wasn't going to lose her friends like that again. She wasn't going to lose herself like that again. She leaned into his hug. "Thanks."

"So?" Sophie was relentless. Jill loved it so much.

"Things are going … really well." She spun her beer slowly on the table, biting her lip to hold back her grin.

"What am I missing?" He turned to Sophie in alarm. "We don't hate him, do we?"

"Does the name Alex Campbell ring a bell?" Sophie filled in.

Jill buried her face in her beer. If she sipped it slowly, she might not have to come up for air until Sophie had drawn the outline.

"No. Should it?"

"Alex. Campbell." Sophie tried again, like saying it slower would clue him in. "Think university. First year."

His face scrunched. "Should that be familiar?"

"Um, yes?" Jill remained stationed behind her pint, and Sophie's grin widened.

A look of horror flashed on Kyle's face, and he choked on his beer. "Alex? Campbell? TA from chem Alex Campbell? That guy? He was such a dick!"

Jill squirmed in a mix of defensiveness and delight. "He's actually really sweet?"

"Am I on drugs? I'm on drugs." He sniffed his beer as if to confirm Jill hadn't slipped him something. "What the actual fuck? Do you have bad taste in men or the worst taste in men?"

Sophie was apparently done roasting Jill and got back on her side. "No, we like him," she said authoritatively, speaking for the trio. "He's such a cupcake. It's revolting. Listen, he sent me flowers for being a good friend to her."

"Oh, he did? He said he was going to." Jill's heart melted. She was changing his contact info in her phone to Cupcake as soon as she got to the hotel.

Sophie raised a brow meaningfully at Kyle, as if to say *see?*

"He failed me," he continued, ignoring the commentary. "I had to retake that class in the summer to stay in my program."

"Trust me, it's come up in conversation. I have blanket permission to extend a belated apology on his behalf."

Kyle's grimace didn't budge.

"Ky, look at her. She's glowing," Sophie said. "She's finally having orgasms she's not giving herself."

"Soph!" Jill said, then added under her breath, "But, yeah. That's pretty great, too."

"As happy as I am about your orgasms, I don't need to hear about them." Kyle's head tilted on a swivel, brows drawn together and racing for his hairline. "Is this for real? How many hours did we bitch about this guy? He made you miserable."

"Does she look miserable to you?"

Jill took that as her cue to burst into tears. "I'm sorry. I don't know why I'm doing this. I'm not a crier—"

"Oh, Jillybean," Sophie said, pulling her against her shoulder. "You are the biggest crier I know."

Kyle's frown deepened. "The only time you weren't crying if something was wrong was when you were shoving everything down." And Connor said she faked her tears to manipulate him. The irony. "What's this guy doing to you?"

"But that's the thing! Nothing's wrong." Jill sniffed and wiped at her cheek. "Like I'm scanning for red flags and I'm the one putting up the red flags and he keeps pulling them down and wrapping me up in green flags and—"

"Jilly, what if there aren't any red flags?" Sophie asked.

"Yeah," Kyle broke in. "Sometimes things don't work out for completely normal reasons."

Sophie looked at him in disbelief. "Not helpful, asshole."

"Shut up, Ky." Jill let out a tiny smile and dried the last of her tears. She shuddered a sigh and a smile spread across her features. "Alex is amazing. He's caring and smart and thoughtful and—"

"—hot as hell," Sophie offered helpfully.

Jill hitched a laugh. "He's so kind and he let me take it really slow …" She blew out a breath. Yeah, all that.

"What a dick, right?" Sophie glared at Kyle, who pursed his lips in response.

"You guys, I've never felt like this before. I'm just so—" was it this simple? "—happy."

It felt right. True.

Maybe it was that simple.

"Aw, I'm just worried. I trust you, Northrop. And Soph's met him, so ..." he trailed off, as if Sophie's seal of approval was the final sign off needed.

"Well, to be fair," Sophie said, "you should have seen our texts when Jill first found out they were going to be working together."

Kyle sprayed a mouthful of beer across the table. "You're *working* together?"

—

Jill took advantage the red light to catch her breath while Kyle bounced beside her, champing at the bit to hit his thoroughbred-like stride again. Not being a fan of sweating unless she had a naked partner involved, Sophie had opted to sleep in while Kyle showed Jill his favourite route.

"You have to speak American here," he said. "It's a thirteen miler."

"Gross, and no." Jill checked their pace. Months ago, her first runs in the thin Calgary air had been agonizing. Now at sea level again, she flew through the September morning, almost matching Kyle's usual pace for once, despite the oppressive sun. She could practically hear her dad say *it's not the heat, it's the humidity,* before laughing like he had coined the joke. Whether it was heat or humidity, she sweated so much she looked like she had stepped out of the shower.

Over the past several days, Kyle had begrudgingly let himself be convinced that Alex was no longer evil. The last of his reservations had crumbled when Alex joined a FaceTime call from his sister's place. The perma-scowl creasing Kyle's brow had released when Alex's smile broadened at Jill's introduction, his nephews crawling all over him and crowding into the frame.

"Awesome to meet you. Jill told me so much about you," all the while getting head-butted in the chin and suggesting they come to Calgary to visit, before Jill took the rest of the call in private, coming back with rosy cheeks and a goofy grin minutes later.

"I don't even like kids and that was pretty cute," Sophie had said.

"'Kay, I guess we like him," Kyle had muttered glumly.

Sophie had shaken her head and looked at them in disgust. "Why am I the only one of us who doesn't hold a grudge?"

The light turned and Kyle shot off like a race gun had fired. "So, you and Alex are getting serious?"

"Serious? Ah, maybe," she said, measuring her breath. "But we haven't really talked about the future. Directly, I mean. But sort of?" Jill's pounding heart rate was only partly to blame on the pace. "He asked me if I wanted kids."

It had been mildly terrifying. Okay, a lot terrifying.

Kyle nodded with a satisfied smile. "Good."

Good? From Kyle? What the …

"We've only been dating for two months. That's not fast?"

"He's older than you?"

"Yeah, five years."

"Probably doesn't want to get serious if you don't want the same things. Pilar asked me about marriage and kids on our second date. She's three years older than me and said, and I quote, that 'she didn't want to waste her time on some boy looking to fuck around.'"

Pilar was such a boss.

He clipped off the main road towards her hotel, breathing sounding annoyingly normal. If Jill had ever wanted to upgrade a body part, she'd swap lungs with Kyle in a heartbeat. Or his brain, since it seemed to make rational decisions.

"Didn't that freak you out?"

"Honestly? No. I knew I wanted to marry her an hour into our first date. I was glad she felt the same way I did."

"Oh, Ky. You're going to make me cry."

"Listen," he continued in his enviably oxygen-rich state, "you look really happy. And I'm not one to talk. We moved in together after four months. As long as you guys are on the same page, don't go by anyone else's timeline. More importantly," he said, grinning over at her, "you finally got fast in the last couple years. Good job, Northrop."

"Thanks," she wheezed.

Maybe she and Alex needed to have more conversations like that. About the future. If that's what she wanted …

Holy shit. It's what she wanted. Needles of excitement and nervousness spiked her solar plexus as she slogged up the four flights of stairs to her hotel room, where Sophie waited for her at the door, wrapped in a robe and a guarded expression.

"Your mom called."

Jill stared at her phone, left on the nightstand while she ran, and felt her post-run high come crashing down. It had been over a month since they had spoken. She missed mother's last two calls, both going to voicemail without her hearing the ring. Once when Jill was volunteering, out in the yard tossing the ball with Daisy. The other when Alex pinned her, face down on his bed, his chest on her shoulder blades and gasping deep into the pillow.

Jill slicked her sweat-soaked hair from her temples. Fuck it. Eat the frog.

She dialled before she could change her mind.

"Hi, Mom." She paced the short space at the foot of the bed, toeing off her shoes and setting a mental timer. Five minutes. She could do five minutes. She flicked her eyes to Sophie and put the call on speakerphone. She had support; might as well lean on it. "I'm fine. What's going on?"

"Oh, Jillian." Her mother's cloying words seeped through the phone's speakers. "Why are you always so terse with me? Can't I ask about my daughter? When are you coming home?"

She pressed her lips together, willing the throb developing behind her eyes to recede before it took hold. "I don't really have a lot of vacation time. I'm not sure."

"Well," her mother pounced, triumphant, "aren't you in Boston right now? I'm sure you can extend your layover on the way back."

Jill spun to Sophie and threw her free hand into the air. How? How did she always know? Sophie winced and pointed at her phone. Photos from the pub and city tours littered Sophie's social media. Jill hadn't posted anything in months.

Connor must have created a new account and followed Sophie again.

Shit.

"We can have a lunch date with Deborah," she continued. "Connor might even make time to see you, despite how you treated him—"

"Mom," Jill cut her off. "I don't want to see him. Ever again. You know that."

A shocked pause drew out from the phone. "Well," she said finally. "I didn't think I raised you to quit when things get hard. Relationships take work, Jillian."

"I don't want to make that work! Connor was an asshole!" Jill burst out. For years, she had danced around it. Said nothing if she could help it, and then, nothing less than the highest flattery. That the golden child of her mother's best friend was anything other than perfect. The dream her mother might have had for her was as false as the smile Jill had braved every day. No more.

"Jillian!" her mother admonished. "You've always been too high maintenance. Just because you aren't the centre of his attention every minute of the day doesn't make him an—" she clicked her tongue "—such language. Honestly."

"He—" What? What did he do? Made her feel worthless. Made her believe he was the only person who would ever care for her. Ground her down until she could barely lift her head. Sophie tracked Jill's sagging shoulders, slicing her hand across her throat in a *cut-it-short* motion. "He's not the right person for me, Mom."

"But you two are so perfect together—"

"Mom." Jill bit off her words. "We were not."

"I only want the best for you, and you always get mad at me when I try to help," she said, last words wavering wetly.

Jill sunk onto the bed, curled over the phone, and arm crossed over her torso. Sophie got on her knees into Jill's frame of view, mouthing *hang up* over and over.

You're a terrible daughter. You'll never be enough. You'll never get it right.

"I-have-to-go-I'll-call-you-later." The words left her in a rush, thumb already pressing the end call button and flopping face down onto the bed. A twist of sadness joined the guilt in her stomach.

"Your mother," Sophie said, "is a gaslighting narcissist."

Bless Sophie, for saying the things out loud that Jill felt too guilty to. "I know she loves me but—"

"That's not love, Jilly. Not healthy love."

Jill pressed the heels of her hands into her eyes. Her mother would never let it go. Months later and she still treated the New Year's Eve fiasco like Jill and Connor had a spat over how to load the dishwasher. "I don't understand. Why would she want that for me?"

Sophie curled up beside her on the bed. "I'm guessing she doesn't know you're dating Alex?"

"Are you kidding?" Jill huffed. "I don't know what would be worse. That I wasn't with Prince fucking Connor, or, god …" She swallowed. "The minute she finds out his name, she's going to google him and find out he's in her field and I can't even guess what that conversation is going to be like."

A litany of options paraded across her brain, and she shut them down.

Sophie said nothing, smoothing Jill's sweaty hair off her forehead.

"Five minutes," Jill moaned. "Five minutes and she pushes every one of my buttons."

"Our parents can push our buttons because they put them there."

Jill laughed grimly. "Well, my mother made sure I had buttons."

"You might need to not let her get close enough to push those buttons, Jillybean. Maybe you need to go no contact for a while," Sophie said, nudging Jill upright. "Have you talked to your therapist about her?"

She'd snoozed every reminder to arrange a new therapist in Calgary for months. "Not yet."

"I think you should. You've got some work to do."

TWENTY-FIVE

She'd needed every minute of her two-hour layover to clear customs at Pearson. She was the last person to board her next flight, which didn't land until eleven-thirty, which was really one-thirty Boston time. Still, even though fatigue clung heavier to her with every passing minute, she didn't sleep a second on the plane, and she still needed to wait at the baggage carousel.

But she didn't need to wait alone.

Alex stood right outside the arrival gate, and it had taken all her willpower only to run the last few steps into his arms.

"I missed you. So much," he whispered after they rocked in silence for a minute. "Did you have a good time?"

The ache in her chest pressed up into her voice box, so she nodded into his shoulder until her throat finally freed. "It was the best," she whispered. "Can you take me home?"

She had cleaned her apartment—not meticulously, but a good once-over—before she had left, so that when she got home, she could slip into clean sheets and have coffee ready to prep before bed. She left her luggage by the front door and scooped the grinds into the espresso maker for the morning while Alex cracked a few windows to let in the fresh night breeze. They dropped into the welcome embrace of her bed, tucked into the familiar feel of each other, and sleep pulled her under in seconds.

The morning sun poured through her window at the perfect angle to bounce a ray of light off her mirror and right into her eye. It was too early for street noise to come through the open window. The clean laundry she hadn't gotten around to putting away before she left waited, neatly stacked on top of the dresser she had painted a regrettable shade of orange that Rachel had dubbed "sad pumpkin." Through strangled laughter, Rachel had promised to repaint it with her. Her favourite running shorts stuck out from the bottom of the laundry pile. She knew she hadn't lost them.

And it hit her.

Her dresser. Her mirror. Her bed.

This was her life.

Her floral sheets and fake plants and cheap canvas-wrapped paintings. Her calendar filled with things she wanted to do and people she wanted to see. Her work and time and how she wanted to spend it.

In her apartment.

She had chosen everything here.

Alex's sprawled form pinned her, half-tangled, to fit them both in the double bed that had seemed like a perfectly reasonable size to buy almost six months ago, before she found a gentle giant of a boyfriend. It didn't matter if she hogged the sheets at night; he usually kicked them off at some point, anyway.

Her kind, funny, workaholic night owl. Loyal and humble. Patient and gorgeous and completely brilliant. She traced her fingers over the angle of his jaw, thumb sweeping across the ridge of his cheekbones, and teased a smile from his lips that undid her every time she saw it.

Any version of his smile was enough to undo her, and the ache pushed its way up from her chest and insisted she said its name.

"Morning," he said, his voice husky from the night. "So early."

"I love you."

The rhythm of his breath stopped, as if he wanted her words to be the only sound in the room. "Tell me I'm not dreaming," he whispered.

She felt her mouth curving up. "You're not dreaming."

"Then say it again."

"I love you." As many times as he wanted to hear it. It belonged to him, anyway. And every time she said it, she felt lighter. "I love you."

The breath he held released in a shaky sigh. "I love you, too." One large palm cradled the back of her head, the other clasping her to him, and he whispered into her hair, "I've waited to say that for so long. I love you so much."

A joy bordering on pain flooded her body, the ache turning into relief with the words floating between them instead of being pent up inside her. Known. At last.

"I couldn't wait any longer. I had to tell you." It wasn't only his smile. His words did it, too, melting her heart so that it flowed through her veins and spread heat to every cell of her body. "I'm sorry I woke you up. Do you want to go back to sleep?"

"Wake me up like that every day. Middle of the night." He rolled her onto her back and showed her exactly how much he didn't want to sleep. "Whenever you want."

She didn't try to contain the choked giggle that escaped her throat as he worked his thigh between her knees. "What if it's five in the morning?"

"I'll keep saying it," he said, not bothering to slow the trail of kisses down her shoulder. "If you had other plans today, cancel them. We're not leaving this room."

"Not even to brush our teeth?"

He collapsed face down on her neck, his shoulders shaking with laughter. He leaned over to fumble at her nightstand. "That's what you're thinking about now? I love your morning breath, too."

"Alex? Wait."

"Hmm?" His hand blindly searched the drawer, and she reached out to still it.

"I have an IUD. We're both clear." She bit her lip and continued, "We don't have to use a condom."

His eyes darkened. "Are you sure?"

Her palms travelled along the sides of his torso in response, tracing the taut contours of his ass. Over the thick muscles of his thighs, up to his heavy arm braced to hold himself up, and she guided his hands to grip her hips, and let the weight of his body press fully against her. "I want to feel all of you."

"Anything. Everything." He crushed his lips to hers and twisted onto his back, pulling her with him. "Whatever you want. It's yours."

"All I want is you."

A week apart was from him was too long. Her heart pounded in her chest as she straddled him, hands splayed against his sternum, and she glided along his cock to fit him at her entrance. The soft flesh of her hips gave under his grip, and he thrust into her with a guttural moan.

So, this was making love. Slow and tender and consuming. Long, luscious strokes uniting them. Then rocking against him, moving the pressure where she wanted it, feeling him deep inside her, nothing between them. Rolling their bodies together until she collapsed, and when he followed her moments later, revelling in the feeling of him still inside her, his hands threading through the damp tendrils at the nape of her neck.

"I love you," she said again, tracing her fingers over the steady rhythm of his heartbeat. She'd never get enough of saying it. She couldn't remember why she'd been so scared.

He was right. She was in no rush to leave this room. She had plans for the day. None of it would be done. Or maybe it would. She could do what she wanted.

There was one thing she couldn't do anymore, but that conversation could wait.

—

"Slower, and keep stirring," he said, reaching around her to steady her hand gripping the spoon.

"Like this?"

"Mm-hmm."

It probably shouldn't be exactly like this, with his teeth nibbling her neck and her leaning into him with a sigh. She let go of the spoon and closed her eyes.

No, it should be *exactly* like this.

"You're losing focus." She could feel the tease in his voice, and she tilted a grin back at him.

"Because you're distracting me again." Even as he stepped back with a last kiss, she had the sneaking suspicion he was trying to distract her on purpose, so she'd continue to rely on his culinary skills. Very crafty.

Jill's second attempt at creamy pasta primavera looked much more promising than her first, with this experiment smelling as appetizing as it looked. She felt only a little guilt she hardly wanted to eat it.

"I'm sorry it's not ice cream," she said, pushing a pea around her plate.

He repressed a smile. "I don't eat ice cream for dinner," he said. "Except when I got my tonsils out. And then Gem got mad because she couldn't have any—"

"I can't work with you anymore."

Alex stopped dead, wine glass halfway to his lips. His voice came out little more than a whisper. "Why?"

Disclosure of relationship status is required. Let HR know if anything changes. Alternative oversight is required for any potential conflict of interest. And, most importantly, Angela's final comments to her on the topic:

I trust your judgment.

"When we got together, we said we'd see where things would go," she said into her arms, hugging her legs and curling into the corner of her chair. "Things have changed. A lot."

He nodded slowly, brows drawn together.

"With the audit, I …" Jill set her shoulders down her spine. "I withheld recommendations I thought you wouldn't like. Or that Nick would think would be favouring you. He'd already—" She snapped her mouth shut and dropped her eyes instead of finishing the sentence.

"What did Nick already do?"

Shit. Of course, he'd pick up on that.

The confusion in his eyes turned wary. "Do I need to talk to him?"

"This is so much better than that mess last time," she said. "Next time we should try—"

"Jill?" Alex circled his fingers around her wrist and swiped a thumb over her palm, and her melting heart at his soft voice proved she was making the right decision.

"See? This is what I mean! You look at me like that and I'm useless."

A parade of emotions crossed his face. "Why do I think you're avoiding something?" he said, giving her a shrewd look.

Don't make me say it, she thought. *That Nick is making selfish and short-sighted decisions for your company and doesn't know as much as he thinks he does. And I'm the last person he wants to hear that from.*

"I can't be impartial anymore," she said, instead. It was still true. Just not all the truth. "Even if I thought I could, Angela would still pull me from your file. I can't blow this."

The wine glass and plate sat abandoned on the table in front of him. After a long stretch of silence, he dropped his head back and scrubbed his hands over his face. "Damn."

A dull thump of nerves shot through her stomach. With his face hidden behind his hands, she couldn't read his expression. "What are you thinking?"

"About a hundred selfish things, and none of them good enough to get you to change your mind," he said from behind his hands. "I hate it."

She didn't love it, either. She'd miss seeing him almost every day. Miss the opportunity to dig into her first venture capital proposal. She would have loved to have been there to put the recommendations in place. Well, at least the ones she had the guts to put forward. But that was the point. Stepping away was so clearly the right thing to do, it wasn't as hard as she thought it would be.

He wiped his hands down his face and held out his arms, and she slid over into his lap. "When? Will it be right away?"

"I'll talk to Angela tomorrow, and we'll need some time to transfer the file to someone else." Already a weight lifted out of her chest, and she drew breath with a new lightness.

That was it. The last of her nerves. Her struggle over her temporary position here. Her worry about moving on from Connor too fast. Her fear of working with Alex …

No more worrying about being here for a year. She would stay in Calgary. Her six-month review was at the end of the month. She could sign the permanent transfer papers then.

She still had work to do, to unpack the baggage she'd been lugging around too long. This week, when her reminder to find a new therapist pinged her again, she'd finally set an appointment. But Connor hadn't stolen into her nightmares in months. He'd creep around the edges for a while, but he didn't dominate the real estate in her brain anymore.

Her plan had gone wildly off track. Come to Calgary for a year. Get some space from everything in Toronto. Return, fresh and clear and ready to start over.

Instead, she accidentally made a life. People she wanted to spend her time with and things she wanted to do. A team she loved to work with. And, of course, she'd gone and fallen in love with Alex.

And instead of complicating things, he added one more brick to the foundation she'd laid.

They couldn't work together anymore. It was as simple as that. Now, in a week or two, she'd passed their file to Omar or one of her other colleagues. And Alex wouldn't be her client anymore. No more worry about an HR misstep or conflicts of interest or following any Rules. He'd just be her disorganized, feet-sweeping, impossible boyfriend.

She could practically feel him pouting into her hair. "This sucks," he muttered against her temple, and she tucked a smile into his chest.

"I'd have wrapped the file eventually," she said, scooting back and picking up her fork. "This is a couple of months early. And I'll make sure the handover is seamless."

She handed him his wine glass and clinked with her own. All the worries she harboured, the ones that made her deny what she felt and lose sleep at night and cloud her decisions, were just gone.

For a handful of seconds, he frowned into his glass, brows furrowed. "What do you need to tell me about Nick?"

"Nothing," she said as she casually pulled up the weather report she'd already memorized. "It's supposed to be nice tomorrow. Do you want to try going to that park again after work?"

"On the road for the next few days. I leave first thing tomorrow." He tried one more time. "How about you stay on until I'm back? We can tell Nick you're stepping back together, so you don't have to do it by yourself."

It sounded like protectiveness wrapped in a delay tactic, but she brushed it aside. "No, I can handle it. I think Angela will want to move on this quickly."

He made a noise she read as *we'll come back to this,* and she smiled that at some point she learned to decipher his grunts. She popped a shrimp into her mouth and nudged his foot under the table. Now that she had gotten her last worry off her chest, the last thing she wanted to talk about was work, and she asked the question she'd wondered all day.

"Can I ask you something?"

"Anything."

"When did you know loved me?"

"You know when," he said. "You have had my heart from the moment you first smiled at me."

Her heart squeezed between her ribs. For months, he'd kept it locked inside. When she admitted to herself what the ache in her chest was, it refused to stay quiet. "Why did you wait so long to say something?"

"I was afraid I'd scare you away if I said it too soon," he said, interlacing his fingers through hers. "I've just been waiting for you to catch up to me."

Until she was ready for him. Because he loved her, and he wanted her to feel safe.

She couldn't believe this was her life.

"I'm not scared, and I'm not going to run away."

She was right where she wanted to be.

—

Breaking into Angela's calendar was like a test run to breach Fort Knox, but Eileen loved chocolate croissants almost as much as Alex did, and that bribery was as good as any master key. Jill locked herself in her office, finger ready to click "join meeting" as soon as the fifteen-minute window Eileen found for her popped up.

Angela's face filled the screen, earbuds in and taking the call from the back of a cab. Jill gave a silent thanks that the car's movements would mask the bouncing of her leg under the desk.

"How was Boston?" Angela's ability to remember the details of almost a hundred people's vacation plans and spouse's names and a million other details was one of her many superpowers.

"It was great. I saw a friend I hadn't seen in way too long." Jill clasped her hands between her knees and launched into her spiel. "So, a couple months ago, I informed you I had entered into a social relationship with a client, and that I would disclose a status change to prevent any conflict of interest."

God, it was as awkward as the first time. Angela merely nodded.

"The client's grant application received full funding allotment a few weeks ago," Jill said, hoping the reminder of her success would soften the news. "The file is well positioned for the venture capital proposal, but I think someone with impartiality should take over from here."

Stop talking. That's all you need to say. That's all she cares about.

"I see." The corner of Angela's mouth quirked a quarter millimetre. "And this is Alex from CMR?"

Right. She hadn't told Angela which of her clients she was involved with, and her cheeks warmed. Well, the list of possibilities was short, and hopefully Angela wouldn't have thought Jill would make heart-eyes at her other current client: the married head of finance who could have been her father. Or Nick. The bizarre thought skidded off her brain.

"I, yes," she said, and crossed her legs tighter. "Alex."

Normal, casual, and super cool. Definitely not talking to my boss about my sex life.

"Oh, good." Angela looked genuinely pleased. And a bit relieved. "He and I spoke at the Stampede in July."

The trace of the panic she had felt when she spied Angela and Alex in conversation bubbled up. "Oh, did you?"

"He seems perfectly lovely."

A flood of relief washed through her. Angela wasn't mad. She was happy. Jill dropped her smile to her chest before she could hide it. "He really is."

So, the plan to avoid each other at the event didn't fool anyone. Or at least it didn't fool Angela. Well, Angela was smart, and they were apparently the least subtle people on the planet. She couldn't be surprised.

She just hoped Angela couldn't tell from the colour still flushing her cheeks how "perfect lovely" Alex had been to her before he'd left that morning, and she wrapped her thighs more tightly together over the lingering soreness.

At the end of the call, Jill snapped her laptop shut with a sigh of relief. She wished she could text Alex, but he'd be out of range until tomorrow.

One awkward conversation down, one to go.

Given his moodiness, Nick might be glad to have her out of the office. One way to find out.

The frigid CMR interior shocked her skin into a rash of goosebumps. Jill's light top would have been perfect for the usual low-twenties temperatures the office hovered at, but she sat shivering in her cardigan at her soon-to-be former desk, waiting for Nick to return after what was apparently an extended client lunch. If they had shared calendars, she would have been able to book him with confidence.

She hoped they went ahead with the recommendations. It hadn't all been bad working with him. Sure, he could be abrupt. Sometimes his jokes skated a little past inappropriate, but he had some redeeming qualities, like reading his emails and his unwavering promptness.

A cancellation notice popped up on her screen.

NickM: j, lunch going long.
another time

She repressed a groan. She wanted to have all of this done today. No matter. Since she was here, she could start pulling together the transfer file.

She proposed a new time, increased the temperature back to the CMR standard, and rolled up her sleeves. She snapped a quick selfie and thought briefly of texting it to Alex with the comment he was a bad influence on her fashion choices but remembered he wouldn't receive it until tomorrow and sent it to Sophie and Kyle instead.

Alex and Nick hadn't given her an answer on the recommendations Jill had presented, and she added it to the list to bring it up with whomever would take over. Again, the parallel stabs of guilt and regret knifed her stomach. Her colleagues were smart. She would leave Alex—no, she corrected herself; she would leave CMR—in expert hands, well positioned for the next phase. But she couldn't help but feel like she was abandoning him at the halfway point. She wanted to see it through, and honestly, it kind of sucked someone else would get to finish what she started.

Never mind not seeing him almost every day.

She pulled up the backup files for the grant. Hundreds of pages across dozens of attachments, perfectly organized. Nick had asked for a file last week, panicked it had gone missing. She had nonchalantly pulled it out of the ether in seconds because she had known exactly how to find it. She couldn't resist reminding him that he'd know where it was when they adopted naming conventions, and he scowled at her.

The financial section would be easy enough to pass on. Jill followed Blackburn standard and anyone who took on the file would be able to follow her logic, but the attachment of assumptions was a gargantuan appendix which Alex had given her directly, and with a fortifying sigh, she dove in.

She didn't have the background to understand the details, and she didn't need to, but after working with it for so long, and a genuine interest in the work of the man she loved, she flipped through the contents, fascinated.

Until it stopped making sense. Her hand stilled over the project timeline, and she flipped to the schedule.

She might not understand the details, but she did understand how time worked.

The dates were at least a year off. She pinched her brows together, opened the files side by side, and felt the blood drain from her face.

The very first time Jill met with Alex and Nick on this work, Alex had said his technology would clear a site in eighteen months. Every conversation they had confirmed it would take a year and a half. But the file in front of her—the one that they submitted to the government—said six.

The documents she submitted to the government were wrong.

The silence of the office pressed in as her ears filled with noise. Ignoring her thumping heart, she toggled the track changes to display the document's revision history and pulled up supporting data from their source documents, praying for an explanation. Something silly. An oversight.

Anything.

What used to read eighteen months now read 180 days. Everywhere in the submission. In every attachment.

With *AlexC* editing every occurrence.

Inconsistent with everything he'd ever told her and every original source document she could pull up. The patent. The initial venture capital docs. The grant submissions they attempted before they brought Jill on board.

It could still be a misunderstanding. She couldn't check with Alex. He was still out of range. Even if he was, she shouldn't go to him with this. She couldn't. This could be serious. Investigation levels of serious. Legal levels with NDAs levels of serious. Bile rose in her throat as she gripped her phone tight so she wouldn't drop it, carefully composing a text to Nick that wouldn't provoke suspicion.

Quick question. Would there
be a difference what month the
microalgae started in the year?

Would it take 18 months to
remediate a site even if it started
in the winter?

I defer to A but I think he said it would take up to 21 mos w a cold start. Why?

There might be another reason. A rationale that would explain why everything Alex had told her was exaggerated. Why he hid the change in a fundamental factor of their technology from his partner. Why the information he signed off on and she endorsed in a submission to the federal government was wrong.

But there wasn't another reason. Her thoughts careened off the inside of her skull until she admitted to herself the only possible explanation.

Alex had falsified the submission. He had committed fraud.

TWENTY-SIX

The danger of running as fast as you can, out of control, is that when someone drops a brick wall in your path, you crash at full speed. And when you've spent the last months dismantling your armour, it really, really fucking hurts.

An icicle slowly slid down the back of her neck and pierced her idiot heart. He used her. Had her build a grant submission so he could exaggerate the results. Had her sign off on it with the weight of her firm behind it. He lied. About everything. And she let herself believe it the whole time. Every false word. Every false smile. First letting herself forgive him. Then like him. Then trust him.

Fall in love with him.

She made it to the bathroom before retching up what was left of her breakfast, trying to pull oxygen through her constricted throat. God, he was fucking her because she was convenient. He told her he didn't have time for anything outside of work. Hadn't for years. And she showed up in his office, ready to snatch the first bit of affection someone dangled in front of her. She was a pathetic idiot and she had scrambled like a beggar for the scraps.

And how convenient she fell into the pattern of picking someone her mother would approve of. The one person she would have gotten off her back about getting back with Connor for.

Honestly, Jillian. You are worthless and can't do anything right.

Her knees cut painfully into the tiles, hands numb on the porcelain. A familiar overwhelming dread crushed her to the bathroom floor, and any warmth left in her body leached out of her bones. Her heart skittered against her ribs, an agonizing pressure that invaded her stomach and choked her throat. A high-pitched wheeze cut through the rushing in her ears, and the abstract realization she was hyperventilating filtered through the grey chaos crowding her head.

He swore he'd never hurt her.

He lied. It was all a lie. None of it was real.

She was a fool. A perfect, desperate fool who let herself be maneuvered like a marionette while he falsified his grant.

Oh god. The grant.

Blunt horror thronged through her chest.

I need to tell Angela. Now.

I need to tell Nick.

You are going to be fired. And you will deserve it.

The tunnel of her vision hadn't receded, but she had faked some sort of functioning for years. Her footfalls thudded through the noise in her head, and she scrambled for her phone on the desk she had worked at for months. All of it for nothing.

can we talk?

—

The Ativan Jill had taken twenty minutes ago had sliced through her panic attack and blunted any emotion she had left, and she floated in a haze down the hall she'd never walk through again. Omar's office sat directly across the corridor from hers. Once, she had successfully flown a paper airplane through their open doors and into his tea from her desk. He had told her revenge was a dish best served cold.

Now she'd never find out what he had planned in retribution.

"Girl, you look like …" He stopped, looking at her closely. "What's wrong?"

She was blessedly detached from all of this. She closed the door carefully behind her and balanced on the edge of the chair across from his desk.

"Can I ask you something?" Jill's voice came out casual. Almost matter of fact. "How do you do something that you know any way it ends, it's going to hurt?"

Omar stayed silent for a long minute. "Why are you asking me this?" he asked finally.

"Oh, I've made a terrible mistake and I'm too weak and scared to deal with it."

He took off his glasses and folded them neatly on the corner of his desk, looking at her kindly. It almost made it worse. "I haven't known you long, but I think I know who you are. You might be scared, but if you are even one percent of who I think you are, you are not weak. We both know you are not asking me what decision to make.

"I know more than anyone how hard it can be to be true to yourself. The question isn't what decision you should make. It's who do you want to be when your decision is made?"

Eileen dug out ten minutes with Angela after lunch. Jill hadn't told Omar any details, but still he had offered to sit in the meeting with her. She accepted. She didn't deserve the support, but she didn't want to tell the story twice.

"Jill, to what do I owe the pleasure of speaking to you again so soon?"

Angela couldn't have started the conversation worse if she tried.

Maybe it was best she didn't have time to prepare anything. Angela deserved the unvarnished truth and the words leaving her mouth sounded like it came from somewhere outside herself.

"I was preparing notes for the CMR file transfer after our conversation this morning, and I discovered discrepancies between their original data and the government submission. The document's editing history shows Dr. Campbell has made unsubstantiated claims about the predicted results. I believe it may have led them to receive funding under fraudulent circumstances."

Omar jerked back and Angela froze on the screen in front of them.

"When did you discover this?" Angela asked with deceptive calm.

Jill folded her hands on her lap, grateful for the medication-induced fog that buffered her from experiencing the full revulsion of this conversation. "About an hour ago."

"Wait," Omar broke the silence that threatened to suffocate her. "Alex forged results in a federal government submission?"

Her head bobbed woodenly. She had trusted him as much as she had let herself trust anyone. Ever. He had seemed so steadfast. Loyal. Passionate about his work and what it could do. He had said he had done everything he could to make this happen. She hadn't thought that would include fraud.

"You're sure?" Angela hadn't moved a millimetre.

"I checked with Nick that the predicted timeline is eighteen months. Dr. Campbell reported six."

"And why did you allow this to be submitted?" The edge that had crept into Angela's voice cut as quick as a rapier.

"Clients are responsible for endorsing the accuracy of technical files," she said mechanically. "Alex was … Dr. Campbell was quite meticulous with his data. I thought Nick had proofed it. It was only by chance that I found this."

God, that meant there could be more. She was such an idiot.

"Six months. Eighteen months. That might not be material enough for the government to pull back funding, but I don't know." Omar steepled his fingers over his mouth and blew out a slow breath. "Is there anything else to disclose?" he asked carefully.

She shrugged weakly. There wasn't anything else to tell. Angela and Omar had everything related to the file. They didn't need to know the first words out of her mouth that morning had been "I love you." That he'd held her so close that morning her toes left the floor as he kissed her goodbye, that he missed her already. That she had buried her nose against the collar of his shirt, inhaling his familiar scent to keep it with her for the next few days, already planning how to surprise him when he got back.

Surprise.

He didn't love her. He'd only said it because she had. Just another lie to keep her close while he used her. She should have known it was too good to be true.

No. She had known. She had asked herself so many times if he was real. If she was worth being treated this way. Now she had the answer.

Would he have kept up the charade until the VC proposal was complete? Or would he have been done with her when the recommendations were in place? Would the recommendations have interfered with whatever plans he had in place to commit further fraud? Was that why he hadn't wanted her to stop working with him yet? To keep her close longer so he could pull whatever maneuvers he needed? He hadn't wanted to do an audit from the start, agreed with every delay. That was probably all for show, too.

It felt like she had woken up in a different life.

"I don't think I need to tell you how serious this is," Angela said. "We need to inform the government immediately and review the rest of the file."

Yes. Inform the government. Because she had just been party to fraud. Jill nodded dully and stared at the boardroom door, mentally packing her office. She wished she'd driven that day. Now she'd have to carry a box of her things down the street to her apartment. At least it wasn't far.

"You have a choice," Angela said while pecking out a message on her phone. "You can go on administrative leave for the week, and we can discuss what you're going to do on Monday. Or, you can stay, and help clean up this mess."

Jill blinked through her haze. That was a left hook she hadn't seen coming. She'd expected raised voices, or an *I'm so disappointed in you* speech. She'd expected security to escort her to the door.

"I'm not fired?" She struggled to be sure if she had heard Angela correctly.

"People make mistakes. Sometimes they make big mistakes. It's also not the last mistake you are going to make. And you brought it forward as soon as you found it," Angela said. "Now, what do you want to do about it?"

She wanted to go home and crawl under the covers until this all passed. She wanted to wake up in Alex's arms and have this be a horrible nightmare. She wanted to rewind the last six months and never have come to Calgary in the first place.

"I want to fix this."

—

There was a small grace that a trip to CMR wasn't needed. Jill had everything saved to her laptop. She unlocked her computer and passed it to Omar, who dumped it onto the Blackburn server.

Omar's current clients were transferred to other consultants. Jill didn't know if she was relieved or not when he was pulled to supervise the review. She desperately wanted a familiar face in her corner, but the humiliation of royally botching her first—and probably only—grant, then listening to Omar's comments about what a great guy he'd thought Alex was and how he never thought he'd do something like this terrified her. To his credit, Omar didn't say a word, merely putting his head down and digging into the files.

"I wouldn't have done anything differently," he said quietly. "You did solid work."

No, she hadn't. The government accepted it because Alex exaggerated the submission. The good job she thought she had done was a lie. Jill swallowed the tears frozen behind her eyes and opened the next file. "We won't get through this today. Or tomorrow. Let's keep going."

Zahra, Blackburn's legal counsel stationed in Toronto, directed Jill to send Alex and Nick a text under the pretence to get them into the office. She had not woken up that morning thinking she would need to set up an ambush for her boyfriend.

No. Soon-to-be ex-boyfriend.

She couldn't believe this was her life.

She scrolled down to the group text with *Nick* and *Cupcake,* followed by the smiling face covered in hearts emoji, and her heart splintered as she hit send. He wouldn't get the text until tomorrow, but at least it was done. She couldn't bring herself to change the name to something vindictive, instead settling on the impersonal Alexander Campbell. He was a stranger, anyway. Might as well start to think of him as one. Either way, it didn't matter. After tomorrow, she'd delete his contact info, scrub the thread, and block him.

When she got home, she switched her phone to silent and sank into her bed, covers pulled up over her head against the light still shining through her bedroom window. His scent still lingered on the pillows and sheets, warm and piney and even with everything, smelled like home.

She tried sleeping on her couch instead, but he was here, too. Where she'd tucked up against his body, his arms around her, talking into the night.

She pulled a jacket out of the closet and curled up under it on the cold laminate floor. She hadn't got a bite of food in all day, but despite the gnawing in her stomach, the thought of eating anything revolted her.

The entire day revolted her.

After several hours, the light turned to darkness. Tears wouldn't come to release the poison that festered in her stomach and barred her throat. She rolled onto her back and stared at the ceiling with dry eyes until the sun came up.

—

Three hours into the morning's review and nothing else surfaced. Jill had kept Omar briefed on the grant from start to submission, but she still detailed every file and every attachment with minute specificity. This was as much a review of her complicity as Alex's fraud; any irregularities she hadn't disclosed could be viewed as guilt instead of an error. Every time Omar asked a clarifying question, her heart dropped through the floor.

At eleven, right when he said he should get back into cell range, her phone rang beside her, and she felt like a bomb went off in her body. Anything she said would give her away, so she tapped out a quick *sorry can't talk see you at 3* and hid her face in her hands while cursing her traitorous heart for wanting to hear his voice.

"Hey." At least Omar looked shaken up about the whole thing, too. He had met Alex. Liked him. "You did the right thing."

Since when did doing the right thing feel like betrayal?

Jill nodded, hands still pressed into her face. She still hadn't spoken to Nick. Someone must have finally gotten a hold of him. Maybe if the universe gave her a break, everything would be resolved quickly.

Right. Like legal issues so often were.

Omar looked at her with sympathetic eyes. "Let's get through this section and go for lunch. Sushi on me."

"Not hungry," she said through her hands.

"I'd bet my crooked eye teeth that you haven't eaten since yesterday. I ain't sending you home 'til you shove something down your gullet."

It sounded like something Travis would have said, and a smile almost ghosted the corners of her mouth. "Okay."

It wouldn't be true to say the three pieces of tuna sashimi, a bowl of miso, and a half picked-at order of assorted tempura—"It has vegetables, so it counts," Omar had insisted as he pushed the plate in front of her—made her feel better, but at least the light-headedness that had plagued her since yesterday was gone.

She pushed the rest of the tempura over to Omar and gripped her elbows. "What now?"

"Now, you're either going home to get some sleep, because it sure looks like you didn't get any yesterday, or hide in your office while Alex is in the building."

Her stomach and heart made a move to switch places, which likely would end up with her lunch making a reappearance. Between sitting at home and stewing in her racing thoughts or cowering at her desk and hoping she wouldn't be dragged into the meeting after all, neither option sparked joy. What she wanted was time to clear her head.

The thought of running into Alex in the hallway was too much to bear, so she closed her office door and watched the clock tick over with agonizing sluggishness. Ten minutes before the meeting start, the heavy cadence of his familiar footfalls sounding down the hall thumped hard through her chest, and she pressed her lips together to hold back the burning in her throat. If she leaned against the privacy glass, she would see his silhouette crossing the common area. Hear the muffled tenor of his voice one last time. Instead, she controlled her breathing through her constricted throat until his footsteps faded, and she crept out of her office and into the early fall afternoon.

She used to love this time of year. The back-to-school crispness of the air had always felt like the promise of a fresh start. Today, it just felt lonely. Few pedestrians dotted the pathway around her, and a dry wind rustled the leaves that were yellowing at the edges. The bench where she and Alex had ice cream the first time sat empty, the birds that had darted over the river long gone for the winter. A week ago, she had been so sure she'd stay permanently. Now the thought of following the birds out of the city sounded like a welcome escape.

She dropped onto the empty bench and pulled out her phone, ignoring the texts from Sophie and Kyle and the emails from Omar.

After how he treated her, he didn't deserve an in-person breakup, or a call. Not like she would have made it through the conversation without breaking down. Not like he'd care.

I won't say how could you,
because I guess I didn't know
you at all

Do not contact me again

She hadn't intended on landing at CMR, but with Alex and Nick sequestered at Blackburn, this was the last chance for her to grab her personal things. The grey cotton cardigan she'd left hanging over her chair for when Nick blasted the A/C. Try to open her sticky desk drawer to retrieve her favourite lip gloss. The spare flats stashed in her filing cabinet, so she wasn't toting work shoes in her bag when she walked to the office. Little things to make herself more comfortable.

What a joke.

Her runners were quiet through the front door. She was the only one of the three of them who could cross the old hardwood without making a racket. Alex had left an old copper bell on her desk he had picked up at the antique store down the street, kidding she should ring it before sneaking around the office. At least, she thought he'd been kidding.

The bell wouldn't come home with her.

She should go back to Blackburn. Omar and Angela would be expecting her. But she couldn't bear the possibility of facing Alex. What if they crossed paths in the lobby? Exiting the elevator and coming face-to-face with him as the doors slid open? She didn't know what she would do.

Angela would understand. And who knew when they would finish grilling Alex today.

Poor Nick. This was half his company. Now he had to watch it implode.

The desk drawer wouldn't budge. Didn't matter. The last time she'd swiped the lip gloss on, she'd kissed Alex on the cheek to snap a picture of the perfect pink lip marks, claiming it was obviously his colour because it looked so good on him. She would never have been able to wear it again, anyway.

She locked the office door behind her, sending Nick a text that she left the key in an envelope with the dry cleaners next door. That was it. The last ends tied up.

Nothing else kept her here.

—

The week stretched interminably.

Zahra gave strict instructions for Jill to stay out of the Blackburn office while the investigation was underway. At least that took care of her problem of avoiding Alex in the building, and she hid out in the temporary cubicle at her other client's office on the other side of town. The financial audit she'd started two months ago posed no challenge to her but was complex enough that she suggested Ashleen join her for the experience. Even as she worked across from her, she felt isolated in her grief.

The weekend was worse. She kept her eyes down while volunteering, avoiding all conversations, even Rachel. The only relief was burying her face in Daisy's neck and swallowing her sobs while the confused puppy licked Jill's cheek.

She didn't even try to get up for her run the next day, finally rising from bed when her alarm clock went off Monday morning.

And the next week was no better.

On Thursday, halfway through her third cup of coffee, a text from Omar popped up on her phone.

It wasn't Alex. I can't say anything
else. This is already too much.

Jill was packing her workstation before the notification had disappeared from her home screen, Ashleen looking up in confusion. Omar wasn't answering her texts. Neither was Angela. They must have left their phones off. Of course, they would. He'd already said he shouldn't have said anything, and Angela wouldn't allow interruptions during confidential investigations.

Fuck.

She left her car parked crookedly in the temporary parking spots in front of the Blackburn offices, not wanting to waste the time to circle the five floors into the underground parkade where her stall sat. She jammed the elevator call button repeatedly, shifting from foot to foot and wincing as several other people got on with her.

It wasn't Alex. But what did that mean? Jill bit down on her cheek until she tasted iron to stop from screaming each time the elevator discharged passengers on the way up.

Eileen looked up with surprise as Jill burst into the hall.

"Alex. Is he still here?"

"No, you just missed him."

Double fuck.

Omar still sat in the boardroom with Angela and Zahra pulled up on screen, and the three faces turned to her entrance.

"What happened?" Jill demanded.

Zahra shot Omar a fiery glare, who returned the look defiantly.

"Nick altered the submission. It wasn't Alex," Omar said.

The air rushed out of Jill's lungs. It didn't make any sense. "How? When?"

Angela looked at Zahra, who gave a resigned nod.

"Apparently the bulk of Alex's research showed it would take eighteen-months to remediate a site, but one preliminary result showed there was a possibility it could be as fast as six months," Angela said.

"The timestamps on the file edits showed Alex was on the road. He wasn't anywhere near a computer," Omar said. "Nick logged in to the system using Alex's account to send an email Alex had forgotten to send a client. While he was logged in, he modified the file."

"So, Alex didn't . . . ?"

"Nick changed the submission from what Alex said was the anticipated results to an anomaly, without Alex's knowledge," Angela confirmed. "He was counting on the government being accommodating if the results were only eighteen months after the feasibility study was complete."

"Alex would never have signed off on Nick's changes without data," Omar said. "He was furious, to put it mildly."

Blood hammered in her ears. So that was it. Alex wasn't a fraud. It was a mistake. One they could fix. They still needed to resubmit the grant. It wasn't her fault. It didn't change anything.

But it changed *everything.*

Relief flooded her, and she made for the door. She had to explain. "I need to find him."

"No. We are starting an internal investigation," Zahra said. "While it's underway, you cannot have contact of any kind with either partner of CMR."

"But—"

"And you'll need to cooperate with our team," Zahra continued.

A bucket of ice water doused her insides. "Do I need a lawyer?" she asked in a small voice.

"No, it's not like that. The investigation isn't about you."

"When can I call him?"

Zahra looked at her with diminishing patience. "When the investigation is done."

So, she wasn't in trouble. Not anymore. But she couldn't talk to Alex. He would go on thinking she didn't trust him. Hated him. Fuck, she had broken up with him. By text. Left him when everything else was falling apart around him. When he would have needed her most.

And she couldn't explain anything. And she didn't know when she could.

He'd never forgive her. Why would he?

How could you do that to him? The minute something went wrong, you assumed the worst of him. That isn't love. That isn't trust. You never deserved him.

She pressed the heels of her hands hard against her eye sockets and bit back the urge to ask if he sounded okay. Instead, she croaked out, "Can I ask what he said?"

"Just—" Omar started, but Zahra held up her hand.

"We've already said too much. If I hear any communication has happened between Ms. Northrop and CMR, even indirectly," Zahra said, looking pointedly between Jill and Omar, "I will escalate this investigation as needed to protect Blackburn's interests. Are we perfectly clear?"

The adrenaline fuelling her last hour evaporated from her bloodstream and the magnitude of the last week and a half smashed into the hollow space where her heart used to be. She stared blankly out the window, and when she opened her mouth, she took perverse pleasure in her affectless tone.

"Angela, please call me when you need me, but if it's alright with you, I think I'll take a couple of days off."

TWENTY-SEVEN

Daisy sat primly pressed against Jill's shin, posing with her cutest head tilt deployed as if she were getting her photo taken. The pair faced Travis as if they could win him over with good manners. It reminded Jill of being eleven years old and her friends asking their moms if she could *please please please sleep over and we'll clean up after ourselves and won't be loud like last time, we promise!* Parents always ended up letting her sleep over.

"She's a big girl."

"I double-checked my lease agreement and confirmed with the property management company. Each suite can have up to two animals, and no restrictions on breeds or size."

"You got a little place," Travis said, shifting his stare between Jill and Daisy.

"I live close to dog parks. And I'll come home for lunch breaks to check on her while she gets settled. She'll get lots of exercise."

"Might take her a while to unlearn old habits."

"She's young. I can teach her," Jill insisted. "She's a good girl"—Daisy's ears perked up and her tail thumped the floor—"and she's learned so much already."

"You sure you want to be doing right now?"

For months, every time she finished her volunteer shift, thinking Daisy should come home with her. The first time Daisy trusted her enough to ask for belly rubs. The time she figured out walking on the leash meant fun and exercise and not being staked in the yard alone for hours at a time. The time she cozied up to Alex while Jill scratched her ears and leaned her head on his shoulder …

She blinked rapidly and looked down at Daisy to hide her face. She'd been volunteering for almost ten years and either her parents or Connor had always forbidden her bringing an animal home. Now, on her own, she didn't need anyone else's permission.

"Yeah, I'm sure."

Travis rustled his moustache at her.

"How about this," Jill pressed, "let me foster her for a month. If it doesn't work, I'll bring her back."

So, that's how Jill, clean freak extraordinaire and renter of a shoe-box apartment, successfully negotiated signing up for a new slobbering, shedding roommate. Who followed her from room to room and spun zoomies in the living room when she was fed. Who made their elderly neighbour nervous at first, but shamelessly used her liquid amber eyes to win him over. Who was afraid of elevators, and for two weeks climbed fifteen flights of stairs before Jill figured out which toy kept her girl calm during the ride. And in the end, Travis let them make the adoption official early.

No one yelled at her for getting dog hair on the couch. It was Jill's couch, and now it was Daisy's couch, too.

—

Jill checked the clock for the fourth time, exhaled forcefully, and dialled.

"My Jillian, how are you? You just missed your mother."

"Hi, Dad. I'm okay," she said, chewing her thumbnail. She'd been practicing for days. She could do this. "Can I ask you something?"

"Of course."

"It's about Mom."

"Oh?"

Jill twisted a strand of hair around her index finger and tugged. No matter how she had rehearsed with her therapist, it sounded hard and mean. But she had lived with hard and mean her entire life, so maybe it wouldn't come out sounding any other way. "Why do we let her talk to us like that?"

"I don't know what you're talking about."

"Dad," Jill said. "You know what."

"Come on now." His placating tone swept her back to childhood. The same voice he used countless times to remind her to be a big girl, dry her tears, and did she want her mother to see her like this?

"You know how much pressure she's under," he continued. "She has a lot of responsibility. Sometimes she can be a little … anyway. She just works hard and has high expectations."

"It's not that." Jill pressed her lips together. "Nothing is ever good enough for her."

"Oh, Jillian. Your mother is …" her dad sighed. "She's a force of nature. It's easier to go along. It keeps her happy."

"But she was never happy. No matter what I did." Or what he did, but Jill left that unsaid. Her father could look at that in his own time. "I didn't know how else to live my life, and then I nearly let Connor take over the same way she had."

"Your mother is not a simple person, but you know how much she loves you. We want the best for you. Connor is …"

Jill stopped listening. He'd rather let her stay in a terrible relationship than her not check the boxes of being a perfect daughter. Or he didn't want to look too closely at his marriage. Either way, it wasn't something she could fix.

Jill forced her shoulders away from her ears. "I love you both, but I'm not going to call for a while. And if you call, I won't answer. Keeping her happy doesn't work for me anymore. I'll let you know when I figure out how I can be a part of your lives without losing mine."

Guilt pressed on the sides of her stomach, but the headache didn't come. When she leashed Daisy and stepped out into the early October morning, she walked buoyed by lightness.

—

Blackburn's investigation—which turned out to be a far less scary series of reviews—spanned four weeks.

HR and legal audited the company's fraternization policy and determined no changes were required. It had served exactly the way it was intended to. But HR mandated watching an amateurishly produced code of conduct video, just in case people needed to be reminded.

A second review tackled Blackburn's practice on the client's responsibility for signing off on accuracy of technical documents. The review team's recommendation that files over a million dollars obtain independent sign-off was accepted. Especially after a sampling of old files turned up a handful of errors that—while not enough to require widespread investigation—confirmed the need. Omar told her that more than a few consultants quietly updated their active files and pushed out project timelines to meet the new standard.

"Everybody's talking about how I screwed up," Jill said quietly, poking her ramen noodles around her bowl.

"You didn't screw up," Omar said. "People are saying you did the right thing, especially because of how hard it was. I'm proud of you. We all are."

Omar's review of her work on the CMR file wrapped within the week. In the end, he resubmitted the grant with an explanation of the discrepancies, which amounted to basically saying *sorry, feds, we made a typo lol.* The government had come back still in full support of the technology and recommitted to funding the project in full, but stipulated the submission of quarterly reports for regular updates.

"I told you it was good work," Omar had said after the confirmation email came in. "After the dates were fixed, I didn't need to change a word."

When the bonus hit her bank account two days later, she had sat numb in her office, watching the shadows move across the carpet until the sun disappeared from her window. After everything, if Nick had trusted Alex, they would have gotten everything they asked for.

Not like she was one to point fingers. If she had trusted Alex, they wouldn't be in this place, either.

The turtleneck pullover itched her neck, but she shrugged deeper into the protection of its thick wool. The sections Ashleen highlighted for her final review looked fine. Jill marked it up with a few comments, but the edits were minor, and they'd be ready to wrap this afternoon.

Which left her with room for a new file in her portfolio. Blackburn brimmed with financial experts but lacked grant writers. Angela had hinted she'd assign Jill another grant since, despite everything, her last one was so successful. Jill wasn't sure if she was kidding.

Blackburn's final review was more of an interview. After meetings with both Alex and Nick, the legal team concluded Alex had no knowledge of Nick's actions and there was no professional misconduct. Omar had shared with Jill they strongly advised reporting Nick to their governing body but gave Alex the option whether to follow through. Omar didn't know what he had decided.

That had been four days ago. They were out of the embargo. Jill and Alex were allowed to talk again.

He hadn't called.

"And that's why you should call him." Sophie's words bounced over the phone in time with her brisk footsteps. She repositioned the screen to flip off a cab while jaywalking. "What did your therapist say last week?"

Jill pulled the turtleneck over her chin against the chilly autumn gusts. The industrial park her clients were based in didn't hold much for natural beauty, and the thin midday sun did little to highlight its few charms.

She leaned on the hood of her car, scuffing her foot on the pavement. "That I tried to fix Connor after I couldn't fix my mother and I felt like a failure because I couldn't."

"Not that. The other thing."

Jill sighed. "That intimacy and vulnerability are scary for everyone, and I need to let myself feel the things or I'll keep trying to hide from them," she said, mimicking her therapist's closing comments from her latest session. She had immediately tried to deflect the conversation away, and when that happened, the insightful jerk was usually onto something.

"And do you think reaching out would be a brave and vulnerable thing to do?"

"I don't need two therapists, Soph."

"Oh, I'm not going to give you homework and a label."

"My therapist said people don't fit neatly under labels and I can't fix myself by getting a perfect score in therapy."

"I don't think that's the winning argument you think it is," Sophie said. "Also, you're deflecting."

"Maybe I do need two therapists. You're great at it."

"Stop. Deflecting."

She shouldn't have shared that revelation with her best friend. "Not deflecting."

"Why are you being so stubborn? Don't you think he'd want to hear from you?"

Yes. No. Maybe. "What if he doesn't want to talk to me?"

"I'm sure he does."

Jill scoffed. "How do you know?"

The rapid clicking of Sophie's heels and blaring car horns were the only response.

Sophie had been tight-lipped in the weeks since Jill had called her after leaving the meeting with Angela and Zahra. She had listened to Jill's convulsive sobs, then jumped on a plane to stay with her for the rest of the week. It wasn't the fun times of university, or June, or even last month in Boston, and though Jill stayed in bed for four days, Sophie gave her hugs and made sure Jill ate, showered, and rehydrated all her lost tears.

Sophie said nothing about being in touch with Alex, and Jill hadn't asked. Partly because her work forbade contact, even indirect, during the reviews. Mostly because it broke her heart to think about him not trying to get in touch with her.

She hadn't blocked him. And nothing had come through. Not a call. Not a text. Just a persistent silence sending a clear message all on its own.

If he didn't want to speak to her, at least now she could ask. She tucked her chilly fingers under her arm and pressed the phone to her ear. "How is he?" she asked in a tiny voice.

Sophie clicked her tongue. "Oh, Jillybean. How do you think?"

Alex didn't do anything he wasn't sure of. And if he wasn't reaching out, he wasn't sure of her.

So that was it. He was moving on.

Jill trudged up the stairs to the temporary cubicle she shared with Ashleen, surreptitiously wiping her nose on her sleeve. She was still at work. She wasn't going to cry. If she started again, she didn't know when she'd stop.

At the top of the stairs, her phone piped out "We Are Family" from her pocket. Kyle's ring.

She had a few more minutes before she met with Ashleen. She ducked back into the echoey stairwell and slumped against the wall. "Hey."

"You are the dumbest smart person I know."

Jill's mouth opened and closed like a fish. "I, what?"

He made a disgusted noise in his throat. "Soph just texted me. She doesn't know what else to say to you. She'll never tell either of you what the other said, but I didn't promise anyone shit. He's miserable. You're miserable. Have a conversation like fucking adults already."

She shrugged deeper into her turtleneck. "He hasn't called me—"

"You. Told. Him. To. Stay. Away. He's literally doing what you asked," he said, enunciating each word with exaggerated precision. "God, you're stubborn sometimes."

Jill ground her heel against the concrete stair. "Am not."

"You know I love you, but this is what you do. You didn't call me for months after you left Connor because you were scared I'd be mad at you, even after Soph told you to, and I'd never been happier to get a call in my life. Don't do that to him."

"What if it's too late?" she said, the tears stuck in the back of her throat rasping her words on the way out.

"You'll never find out if you don't try."

A terrifying ray of hope flared in her chest. "I don't know if I can."

"Northrop, if anyone can do the hard thing, it's you. Call him," he pleaded. "And if I'm wrong, which I'm not, worst-case scenario is he won't talk to you, and that's where you are right now. Or you don't call him, and you never talk to him again anyway. Are you willing to take that chance?"

He was right. Sophie was right. Rachel was right.

Fine. Everyone was right.

She slunk to her desk and closed her laptop with quiet click.

"Edits are done," Ashleen said. "Ready to send them in?"

"Yeah, ready. Go ahead."

Ashleen gave a crisp nod and sent the confirmation. "Thanks for bringing me on the file. I can't believe the analysis we did on this."

"Mm-hmm. Good work."

"Marco is going to be so jealous."

"Yeah."

"In fact, since I did everything on this account, you should give me your office and you can have my cubicle."

"Good idea."

"Jill!" Ashleen said. "What the hell?"

Jill looked up from her hands. "I think I need to talk to Alex."

Ashleen dropped her head back. "Ugh. Finally. Go."

Jill sat in her car chewing her thumbnail, staring at the last text she had sent Alex with a grenade ricocheting off the insides of her ribs: *Do not contact me again.* Nothing she could say would be enough. She didn't even know where to start.

This is pointless. Why would he even respond to you?

She closed her eyes and measured her breath. No more intrusive thoughts.

Even if he doesn't, I have to try.

I'm sorry

Can I see you?

She jammed her phone deep in her bag and trapped her shaking hands between her knees. No sense watching for a reply that might not come. Who knows when he'd see it. She didn't even know when he'd be on the road anymore. What if today was his new lab day? He might delete her text without reading it. Maybe he had blocked her. She wouldn't blame him if he'd blocked her. She deserved it. With him and Nick, maybe—

Her bag vibrated, and the grenade in her chest detonated.

When

Her first attempt at a reply came out so garbled autocorrect couldn't figure it out. She retyped with careful fingers.

Whenever you want

I will come to you

Then watched bubbles flicker for six agonizing seconds before

I'm at the office

I'm coming now

Fifteen minutes to drive. Five minutes to sit in her car to wrangle her shallow breathing so she didn't cause an accident when she merged onto the highway. She hadn't bothered to cover the dark circles under her eyes or put on bronzer to mask her wan complexion that morning, but it didn't matter because he would see her.

Neither the yellow wagon nor cherry pickup were parked out front. Crisp brown leaves from the tree shading the office's back windows cluttered the sidewalk. The sun peeked out from behind the hazy overcast and her feet stopped at the front door she had crossed so many times.

Should she knock? Just enter? Knock then enter? Text him? Call and ask—

Stop stalling, Northrop.

Four crisp raps and she swung open the door. The office looked like a hurricane had ripped through it. Crates and boxes stacked in precarious pyramids, binders leaning at drunken angles. A large dent in the drywall ran from floor to ceiling behind Nick's desk, which was now stacked with even more boxes. Jill's desk sat, untouched, except for the sticky drawer sitting open, her lip gloss on her keyboard.

Alex hunched on the edge of his desk, hands braced on his thighs and eyes fixed on the floor. A few days of stubble shadowed his jaw, and he looked like he had slept in his clothes. He looked terrible, and it was all her fault.

No scripts. No practice. One chance to be honest.

Here goes everything. She drew a breath and clasped her hands so tightly she thought she might dislocate her fingers.

"Hi."

He still hadn't looked at her. A muscle jumped in his cheek, as if chewing over what to say, landing on silence. He had nothing to say to her.

She couldn't blame him. She didn't deserve anything.

"Alex, I—"

"You left me." He finally looked up, and the suffering written across his features reopened every jagged tear in her chest. Heartbroken. Because of her.

She didn't try to quash the wave of guilt. "I'm so sorry. I—"

"You thought I lied. That I used you." He wiped his hand down his face. "I can't believe you thought I'd do that."

"Alex—"

"Then I thought I'd never see you again."

She wished she could sit. Wrap herself into knots to stop herself from shaking. Hold her breath until she knew the right thing to say. There was only one right thing to say.

"I panicked," she said, "and when I found it wasn't you, it was too late, and I wasn't allowed to talk to you until it was over."

He paced the room, raking his fingers through his hair. "You've had all week to find me."

She shrugged helplessly. "I was scared."

"Why were you scared?" he whispered.

"I didn't think you'd want to see me. I thought you'd hate me."

His breath left him in a rush. "I can't hate you."

That was good. He didn't hate her. That was something. The hope in her chest flamed brighter.

"I'm sorry. I'm so sorry," Jill started, twisting her fingers together. "I don't know what you want, but I love you. If you can forgive me, if you'll have me back, maybe we can start over?"

"There's no starting over."

That was it. The floor tilted underneath her as his words sunk in. The burning hope flickered out. Kyle was wrong. It hurt more than not knowing. Because now she knew. It was over.

Alex could do with her apology what he wanted. She nodded, swallowing her tears before they could fall, and tried to memorize his face before she left for the last time. Because it was over.

Her numb lips formed words that pushed past her voice box. "No, right. Of course. I'm—"

"I don't want to start over. I don't want to just pick up where we left off. I want to figure this out with you. But before we do anything, we need to talk."

A rush of relief left her so dizzy she slumped against the door frame. It wasn't over. Talking was a chance. A maybe. That was something. She swallowed, heart pounding.

"Okay, let's talk."

—

"There's a lot of hair. I haven't vacuumed today."

"I think she remembers me." Alex extended his knuckles out to Daisy to sniff, who stretched her paws and thumped her tail against the couch. His eyes crinkled at the corners and Jill's tender heart bumped in her chest.

He scratched Daisy on the chin. "You finally did it."

"She came home with me three weeks ago," she said, grabbing the stuffy toy to ease the elevator ride. "Right after I signed my permanent contract for Calgary."

Alex pulled up. "You're staying?" he asked softly.

"Yeah. I'm staying."

He tilted his head back and mouthed silent words at the ceiling. "That's great."

"Can we go for a walk?" Jill asked nervously. "I haven't really left my place much in the past month, except to go for walks with Daisy, and I—"

"We can do whatever you want."

After a few blocks to put the downtown noise behind them, the river burbled more cheerfully than it had in weeks. Alex filled her in on everything that he had been able to figure out in the last month.

When Nick made no excuses for his decision and made no effort to explain himself, Alex immediately dissolved the CMR partnership. Alex had him sign over his rights to the company, and said he wouldn't report him to their governing body for professional misconduct. After some convincing that Alex wouldn't describe, Nick complied and took his precious truck to call it square. Both sides thought they got the good end of the bargain.

Jill considered asking about the hole in the office wall behind Nick's desk, but she had a pretty good idea where that came from.

Alex had worried their clients would balk at the company's upheaval, but all they cared about was their work being done on time. Alex and Omar had plowed through Jill's recommendations, securing a field tech for the northern sites and a financial analyst to make sense of the accounting system. The tech had already consolidated hours of work off Alex's plate, and the financial analyst had worriedly brought a stack of what appeared to be Nick's personal transactions for Alex to review.

"I bet that's where the missing receipts went," Jill muttered.

"Yeah." Alex stared out over the river. "Never mind. That's in the past."

He hadn't made a move to touch her, and Jill hesitated before reaching for his hand. "I'm sorry. I know he was your friend."

"I thought he was," Alex said, "but that was not friendship."

"I'm not going to defend him."

"But?" Alex focused on their entwined hands.

"That's it. I'm not going to defend him," she said. "He was an asshole."

Alex snorted, but Jill didn't miss the sadness that darkened his features. There'd be a time to delve into all the ways Nick had been an asshole, but today was not that day.

She hadn't planned on heading there, but the red lattice of the Peace Bridge arched before them, and she steered them to the bench where she had panic-walked to meet him those months ago.

Jill gripped his hand like it might slip away. "I don't … I didn't practise anything. I don't know where to start."

"Take your time." He stroked her knuckles, slow and soothing and warm. "I'm in no rush."

Still patient with her. After everything.

"I'm seeing a therapist again. I've been trying to deal with my baggage. Figuring things out. I … I have a hard time believing I'm worth good things happening to me. My mother, Connor. I was told that I was gullible and naïve and that's why they needed to take control of everything. And when I saw the changes, I thought …"

That this gentle, honest, careful man had lied and used her. But that wasn't her. That was years of her mother and Connor crowding in and drowning out her voice.

"You never did anything to make me doubt you. You made me feel loved and safe, but I let my old patterns take over. I know I didn't deserve what happened to me, but I need to take responsibility for how I act now."

He stroked the back of her hand. "Healing doesn't happen in a straight line. I understand why you handled it that way. I hate it, but I get it. I just wish you would've talked to me after."

Four days of heartache could have been saved if she had gone to him as soon as she could. Four days of doubt and agony. She couldn't change the past, but she could take control of her future.

"I think … I feel like things are getting better. Like I'm doing better," she said. She squeezed her eyes tight, sniffed hard, and pulled her shoulders down her back. "I love you, and I promise if I get scared again, if you still love me, if you still want to be with me, I'll come to you first."

"Oh, Jill. I love you. So much. I want to be with you, and yeah," Alex said, eyes soft, "I want you to come to me."

They had a long way to go. She had a long way to go. Things to figure out. But they would talk to each other. Be gentle with each other. Learn and move forward, together. It wouldn't happen overnight, and it wouldn't be perfect, but they were worth putting in the work to heal. She was worth it.

The last of the tension that had wrapped itself around her heart for a month released, and she leaned her forehead to his. "Alex, can I tell you what I want?"

He brought his hand up to her cheek, and smiled. "Please."

"I really want to kiss you."

EPILOGUE

Eighteen months later

The tail end of the winter's snow packed hard underfoot, but the Chinook winds that had blown in overnight left the air dry and warm. Almost tee shirt weather, even in the mountains. Daisy had bounded out of the car and frolicked with pent-up energy, still spinning circles after two hours on the trail. Jill stopped to snug the laces on her hiking boots and scanned the path ahead of them.

The day couldn't be more perfect.

Alex broke his nearly half hour of silence. "It was two years ago today we met."

"We met almost ten years ago," she corrected, and dodged the incoming swat aimed for her butt.

"You know what I mean."

"I remember. Vividly."

The glowering grump from years ago had become her sweet Cupcake, her safe haven. She scrunched her nose at him and pulled him in for a light kiss, tracing her fingers at the base of his throat. They weren't hiking that fast, but his pulse jumped hard against her fingers.

She tilted her head at him. "What's up?"

"You know, you never finished what you started."

Some things would never be finished.

Slowly, Jill opened the boxes she had packed away her emotions in, with therapy helping her identify and sort the feelings she had blunted for years. She had tried talking to her parents on her mother's birthday but ended the call after her mother laid an old guilt trip on her. Then tried again at Christmas. That call lasted four minutes. At least her mother didn't try to convince her to call Connor. One day she might have a relationship with her parents again, but now, surrounded by people who loved her, the family she made here, Jill was in no rush to bring her parents back into her life until she was ready.

Patterns in her behaviour made sense, finally. Don't try to fix problems that weren't her responsibility. Stay put when vulnerability overwhelmed her. Release the fear of intimacy. It was terrifying, for a while.

And then it wasn't.

It just took time.

For a few months, Alex became even busier than he had been. Cobbling his company back together and making sense of the mess that Nick had left behind. Nick had been half right. The first rounds of test results had come back tracking to clear sites after twelve months, not the eighteen Alex had estimated. The venture capital firm Nick had been courting wasn't the only one interested, but with the cushion of the grant money, Alex pushed the decision out and focussed on research.

When her lease came up, Alex suggested they move in together instead of her renewing. Jill had enough nerves about the idea swirling in her stomach that, to Alex's quiet disappointment, she resigned her lease. But after four months, when she had more time to get used to the idea, she broke her lease and moved in.

"Now we've been together a full year," she had said, as if that had been her plan all along.

"How long do we need to be together before we can get married?" he'd asked.

She'd paused taking her books out of the moving box. "I don't know yet. I'll think about it."

Months later, when they got home from Kyle and Pilar's wedding, exhausted after the weekend event with hundreds of guests, they had collapsed on the couch without unpacking their suitcases.

"Tell me if I need to get ready for something like that when we get married," Alex groaned into her neck.

"I don't know yet," she said, smiling. "I'll think about it."

Then, at his rugby team's Christmas party, Alex had walked around with the toddling Olivia for the entire night while Marta smirked knowingly at Jill. That night as she lay awake in bed, she wondered when he was going to ask.

At Christmas in Montreal, with his family around them, laughing and singing, she wondered if it would be then.

This weekend, Jill and Alex had stolen his nephews so their moms could get out of town, and the four of them read and made blanket forts and ate too much sugar and neither of them wanted the boys to go back last night.

This morning as they sipped their coffee, with a hummingbird in her chest rather than swirling nerves, Jill had asked what he thought of her removing her IUD at her next check up, and Alex had lit up like the sunrise.

Now, they stood on a mountain top with the world spread before them in all directions.

Jill nudged his hip. "What didn't I finish?"

"I hired you to do a job," he said. "You did half of it."

"Pretty well, too."

"Amazingly well." He swallowed hard. "But you never did help with my proposal."

Oh. It's now.

Her heart skipped between her ribs, and her smile blossomed. "Yes."

"Not sure I need help with this one, but I need to know if my partner is ready." His hand disappeared into his pocket.

"Yes," she said, dancing on the spot.

"You're sure? I don't want to rush you—"

"Oh my god, Alex!" Jill screamed into the valley and launched herself at him. "Yes!"

He wrapped his arms around her and smiled into her hair. "Just making sure."

When she finally let go to give him her hand, he slid the ring on her finger, and Jill was never more sure of anything in her life.

Read on for a teaser of Cass's story, coming 2024!

Cassidy St. Claire wouldn't even be here if she'd ignored his text. She could be having a movie marathon with her best friend, wearing comfy pants and indifferent to the frizz level of her hair. Instead, she was praying her back would forgive her wearing shoes without arch support.

But ignoring him was her weakness. An Achilles heel that had been swapped for some other body part defenseless against his charms.

No, not charms. Charms were, well, charming. He had wiles.

She peeked over the top of her menu at the man positively smoldering beside her and a shiver ran over her thighs. It wasn't her fault a corner of his mouth ticked up in a way that turned any smile cheeky. Or that the man knew exactly how to dress to show off his body. Or how his faint accent rolled over her ears like auditory catnip.

Tonight, his dark eyes had cruised over every inch of her curves when he met her in the lobby of the trendy restaurant, and his brilliant grin sent a flutter straight to the silky seam of her black underwear.

"Hey, gorgeous." His whisper in her ear sent a cascade of goosebumps down her neck. Catnip. "You ready for some fun tonight?"

Fine, she had a lot of weaknesses where Nick was concerned. Including remembering that approximately half the women in a two-kilometer radius were susceptible to the same wiles she was.

He'd flirted with the coat check girl, who batted her lashes back at him. He'd left the hostess giggling like the twenty-one-year-old she probably was. Even the server, whose job it was to act interested in the hopes of a good tip, lingered at their table longer than necessary.

Cass felt like a fifth wheel on her own double date.

The couple across from her were all doe-eyed and distracted glances, fingertips trailing over each other through the night. Cass picked at the edges of her salad and glanced at her date's hands, firmly on his side of the table. Hands that had explored her entire body, but fingers that never interlaced with hers. She swallowed her envy along with a perfectly ripened tomato and stared out the huge windows letting in the last of the sunset.

"The tarte tatin looks delicious." Jill bit her lip and flicked her eyes between dessert options. "But so does the chocolate cheesecake."

"Get them both and I'll eat what you don't," Alex said, and whatever Jill whispered into his ear shook his shoulders.

Nick blinded the server with his thousand-watt smile. "What's the most delicious thing I could eat here?"

"Oh, um, everything you see would be delicious," she flustered out, then pointed at the menu and added in a low voice, "but this will melt in your mouth." She turned an awkward glance at Cass. "What would you like, miss?"

To be wrapped up in the tablecloth and defenestrated? Forty floors to the pavement below would give her enough time to rethink every one of her life choices that led to her opening his text that night. Cass folded the menu. "I'd like what she's having, please."

The gilded bathroom looked like it should have its own cover charge, and Cass stepped up to the rows of deep copper sinks. The ridiculous riot of chestnut curls she'd spent an hour trying to tame refused to behave and she adjusted a particularly willful strand into order before applying a layer of her signature Ruby Woo. Bold lipstick equalled big confidence. She needed it.

"You two are the cutest," Cass said. "I've never met Alex before, but Nick talks about him all the time. I don't know what he was so worried about."

Jill stilled and didn't meet Cass's eyes through the mirror. "Oh?"

Good one. A person with a working filter wouldn't bring up how Nick had griped about the contractor he'd hired distracting Alex from the work they had to do. The contractor who was apparently a sweetheart—and clearly not just a contractor anymore—completely smitten with his best friend, and given the celebration tonight, did exactly what he'd hired her to do. Maybe Nick didn't have the best judgement.

"I mean," Cass continued hastily as she tried to extract her foot from her mouth, "he gets a little twitchy where Alex is concerned. They've been friends a long time. But I think he warmed up to you quickly."

"Mmm." Jill washed her hands thoroughly, keeping her eyes on the shiny faucet. "So, you and Nick have been together for a while?"

Did a year of an on-again, off-again situationship count? Cass managed what she hoped was a genuine smile and shrugged a shoulder. "Something like that. We can't seem to figure each other out."

Jill's fair brows drew together. It didn't take an empath to pick out concern in the storm of emotion that crossed her face. "Well," she said finally. "I hope you figure out what's best for you."

All that time not-exactly together, it seemed more unlikely by the minute.

Jill fiddled with her lip gloss a moment and added, "That textiles exhibit you mentioned sounds fun. I'd love to tag along?"

A genuine bubble of excitement inflated Cass's chest for the first time in hours. "Absolutely, but it's only here for a few days, and it's selling out fast, and be warned I'm going to talk your ear off, and there's a whole bondage section that I need to check out for an upcoming erotic Shakespeare production I'm working on!" Cass stopped to draw breath and lowered her waving hands. "I'll send you a text?"

"I can't wait," Jill said with a choked laugh.

They left the bathroom together, her new friend floating across the restaurant to her boyfriend, and Cass to find her date for round two of their night. Dancing. Which used to be her favourite. It should be fine. He wouldn't try to merengue with her. Or maybe he would. Highly unlikely he planned to bring her to the type of place where it would be on the playlist, anyway.

Cass hitched up the corners of her mouth and stepped beside him at the restaurant's front. His eyes scanned from Alex, to Jill, and back to Alex, watching as his friend wrapped his new girlfriend in an embrace.

"I've never seen him hand over his balls so fast."

Something tilted under Cass's ribs. Is that what he called open affection? The hope of getting similar attention vanished with the last of her energy. "I think they look really happy."

Nick grunted in response and turned on the smirk that usually made Cass giggle like she'd downed a glass of Champagne. This smile was directed at the tittering attendant, who nearly prostrated herself over the counter.

Nick's a flirty guy. He's like this with everyone. Cass pretended she didn't see the attendant slip something in his pocket.

The club bounced with bodies and heat. It was the last thing she'd have chosen to do. The music pulsed, the crowd vibed, and her feet protested after a long day on set. Even with the pain killer she took before dinner, her back wouldn't forgive her tomorrow. Cass dug her thumbs into the small of her back as she waited for the bartender to pour the vodka and sodas. This was still a date Nick had asked her on, and that was something. Dinner, dancing, a chance to dress up. The hour she'd agonized in front of her closet hadn't been for nothing. The plunging neckline of her French navy blue jumpsuit earned an appreciative double-take from the bartender, and although she couldn't wear the heels she'd bought to go with it anymore, the gold Mary Janes looked gorgeous.

Not as gorgeous as the woman currently trailing her fingers up Nick's arm as he reclined against the bar. She was tall and blonde and everything Cass wasn't, and she looked ready to crawl into his pants.

The condensation from the drinks dripped over her fingers as she held her breath waiting for Nick's response. Would he gently brush her hand away? Or would he lean in and whisper in the woman's ear, like he'd done with Cass only hours ago?

Why would she wait to find out something that shouldn't be a guess?

She tipped one vodka and soda into her mouth, chased it with the second, and ordered her escape Uber without a backwards glance.

At 12:37 a.m. on a Saturday morning in the back of an Uber, Cassidy St. Claire decided she'd had enough of Nicholas Martin. For real this time.

Probably.

Acknowledgements

This might be the scariest part of writing this book, because so many people were vital to making this happen. I'm going to miss a couple of you, I'm sorry, and thank you.

To Vanessa Zoltan and the team at Hot & Bothered podcast, who had thoughtful and inspiring conversations and planted the seed for their listeners to write their own stories. I, never having written anything other than a performance report or a grocery list, thought, "Well, that's a fabulous idea for other people, but that will never be me." But now, here we are. Thank you for the inspiration.

For my beta readers Kelsey, Caroline, Carolynn, and Ashley, who gave me enthusiastic encouragement and suggestions in equal measure, all of which was timely and helpful. A special thank you to Denise, who read on planes and boats and the beach and talked to me for hours about my baby story – you are the best and I love you. Thank you!!

My editor, Vickie Vaughn, who was thorough and clever with her work. This book wouldn't be what it is without you, and I'm sorry for all the corrections I missed!

To the team at Friesen Press, thank you for doing all the heavy lifting with getting this from a file into something I get to show my mom.

Mom, that creative writing workshop you put me in back in third grade finally paid off. Thanks for believing in me.

Last but not least, my husband, the dude so nice I took his name twice. Thank you for your support, your love, your patience talking through ideas, and for helping me make this happen. Writing this book has been endlessly fun and all the more so because I get to share it with you. You're my favourite.

And thank you for reading!
If you enjoyed it, please consider rating and reviewing on Goodreads and Amazon. Readers like you help indie authors get the word out!

♡

About the Author

Ellory loves a good cinnamon roll book boyfriend, everything pink, and summer evenings on the patio with her husband and glass of wine. She lives and works in Calgary, Canada, where she spends as much time outside as possible, even if it's -30 C.

You can find her:

ellorydouglas.ca

Instagram @authorellorydouglas

TikTok @ellorydouglas

Printed in Canada